LR308

GREETING
HICKFORD
hucker

OMC

KT-479-377

Books should be returned or renewed by the
last date stamped above

Kate Thompson was born in Belfast. She came to Dublin to study French and English and had a successful career as an actress and voice-over artist before ditching the day job to write full-time. Her six previous novels have been widely translated. Kate divides her time between Dublin and the West of Ireland, is happily married and has one daughter.

For more information on Kate Thompson and her books, visit her website at www.kate-thompson.com

LIVING THE DREAM

For Cleo Dowling the dream becomes a reality. She comes into serious money and takes herself off to the pretty village of Kilrowan in the west of Ireland to write a novel. But what happens when she becomes obsessed with her sexy neighbour? Dannie Moore's love life has always been complicated, but when film director Jethro Palmer chooses Kilrowan as the location for a blockbuster movie, the effect on her life is cataclysmic. Deirdre O'Dare leaves her husband Rory behind in LA to accompany her friend, movie star Eva Lavery, to Kilrowan. When the cat's away and all that . . . And although Deirdre is writing Eva's biography, it would appear that the actress is not telling the truth, the whole truth . . .

KATE THOMPSON

LIVING THE DREAM

Complete and Unabridged

CHARNWOOD
Leicester

First published in Great Britain in 2004 by
Bantam Press, a division of
Transworld Publishers, London

First Charnwood Edition
published 2005
by arrangement with
Transworld Publishers, part of
The Random House Group Limited, London

British Library CIP Data

Thompson, Kate, 1956 –
  Living the dream.—Large print ed.—
  Charnwood library series
  1. Women novelists—Ireland—Fiction 2. Connemara
  (Ireland)—Social life and customs—Fiction
  3. Love stories 4. Large type books
  I. Title
  823.9'14 [F]

  ISBN 1–84617–087–7

Published by
F. A. Thorpe (Publishing)
Anstey, Leicestershire

Set by Words & Graphics Ltd.
Anstey, Leicestershire
Printed and bound in Great Britain by
T. J. International Ltd., Padstow, Cornwall

This book is printed on acid-free paper

To Deborah and Pat

Acknowledgements

Heartfelt thanks are due to: Susan Walsh of Dubray Books for allowing me to pick her brains; to the staff of Ballynahinch Castle Hotel for their warmth and friendliness; to the equally warm and friendly people of Roundstone whom I sorely miss. Special thanks to Penny Perrick for all the suppers in O'Dowd's and her first-rate hospitality; and to Neil and Fouz Moynihan for effecting my escape from Dublin. Thanks to my family and friends for all the support and encouragement. Thanks to fans who have checked out the website and written such lovely letters! Thanks to Gill and Simon Hess and the team for their enduring commitment, and to Declan Heeney for holding my hand and being gorgeous. Thanks to booksellers everywhere: I will sign stock for you anytime! Thanks to all in Transworld: Paul Gooney for his beautiful jacket design, Laura Sherlock for her charm and enthusiasm, Marie Gallagher for her great good humour, Beth Humphries for her vigilance, Sadie Mayne for her enviable sanguinity, and Francesca Liversidge for being the best editor a gal could ever want. Thanks to Cathy Kelly for the agony aunt phone calls, and to Marian Keyes for her extraordinary generosity in allowing me to borrow *Mimi's Remedies* from *The Other Side of the Story*, and for reading an early draft.

Thanks to real-life stars Colin Farrell, Ciarán Hinds and Bono for allowing me to feature them. Thanks to Ali Gunn, powerhouse extraordinaire, for her unswerving faith. Thanks to my husband Malcolm and my daughter Clara. I know a writer isn't allowed to get away with 'words can't express', but really, words *can't* express how much I love and appreciate you both.

Oh — and, finally, thanks to Fluffy for being — well — fluffy.

'Go confidently in the direction of your dreams!
Live the life you've imagined.'

Thoreau

Prologue

Flowers would be good. The night before, as her car had slid along the deserted main street of the village she'd clocked a florist's shop — Florabundance Two. She'd mosey down there this morning and buy a load of blooms — the floppy kind with purply petals that looked as if they'd come straight from someone's garden — delphiniums? Is that what they were called? — and hollyhocks, masses of them. Peonies would be fun in the bathroom, and maybe some little posies of 'wild' flowers for the kitchen, and for the hall table. She'd put a jug of freesias by her bed so that she'd wake up to their glorious smell in the mornings. And of course she'd have to order plants that would thrive on the deck. She'd cram every room of her house to the rafters with flowers and it would cost her a bomb, but that didn't matter to Cleo Dowling. It didn't matter a fig, and it didn't matter two hoots. It didn't matter if she splashed out as much on floral excess as Sir Elton John. Because lucky, lucky Ms Cleo Dowling had just come into serious money.

1

Cleo Dowling was a bookseller and a published poet. The poet thing had come about when she had drunkenly entered one of her poems in a poetry competition on the Internet a couple of months ago. It had been inspired by her break-up with her last boyfriend, Toe-rag Joe, and it went like this:

Murmurs of a Landscape

I hear the landscape:
I cannot see it.
I hear it in
The cry of the curlew.
I hear it in
The whisper of the wind.
I hear it in
The wash of the wave at Lissnakeelagh.
But, most vividly, I hear it in
Your voice.
I cannot see the landscape:
It lives inside my head, now.
Your voice, once plangent, vibrant,
Is silenced, lifeless, dead. How
Obscure the landscape!
My tears render me blind.
But the memory of that landscape
Murmurs mantras in my mind.

She'd typed it out in a maudlin mood after consuming a bottle and a bit of not very good Chilean Sauvignon Blanc. There had been many typos and many jabs at the 'delete' button before she'd finally made her poem 'right', and then she'd sent it whizzing off irrevocably into cyberspace. *Doh!* It was amazing what tricks the mind played when under the influence. She could sing like Dido, dance like Beyoncé and write like Andrew Motion when she was Sauvignon-blonked. The offending poem had been deleted from her computer's memory the very next day.

Cleo had completely forgotten about it until one morning a few weeks later the postman had shunted through her letterbox an envelope with a clear cellophane window on the front. The logo told her it was from Be–A–Bard.com, and beneath the cellophane was displayed *her poem* — with 'Cleo Dowling' in italics under the title.

The first words that grabbed her attention when she tore open the envelope had almost knocked her sideways. *Congratulations! After much deliberation, the judges here at Be A Bard.com have unanimously decided to include your poignant poem 'Murmurs of a Landscape' in our next collection . . .*

Oh! Someone was going to publish her poem! The rush of adrenalin had felt like champagne bubbles whooshing through her bloodstream. She, Cleo Dowling, was to be a *published author*! Oh my *God!* This was a lifelong dream come true!

Yes, Cleo, she read on, *your unique poetic*

4

talent has earned you a place alongside other equally gifted bards — chosen from among many thousands of hopeful applicants — in this beautifully presented, quality 'leather' bound volume. As she'd registered the significance of the inverted commas around the word 'leather', the bubbles began to pop. They'd continued to pop like Rice Krispies as she scanned the document, until they fizzled out completely. A limited edition entitled 'Reflections of Eternity' will be available to our discerning readers, and, as one of our featured poetic voices, you will be eligible to avail of our special discount, which means, Cleo, that you can purchase this exquisite book for only $59.95! (See our latest edition over.) Your poem has been published on our website, so be assured that evidence of your artistry is already out there in the public domain and can be read on-line by anyone in the world! Cleo had actually whimpered when she'd read those words.

The other side of the pamphlet displayed a picture of a volume with tooled gold lettering on its burgundy 'leather' cover and spine. The legend ran thus: *Poetic Pastorale: Songs by New Voices for the New Millennium.* Another photograph showed the volume displayed open. There had been at least twenty poems printed on the page, and the blurb told her that there were approximately three hundred pages in all. Cleo was no mathematical genius, but even she had been able to work out that twenty multiplied by three hundred equalled six thousand. Six thousand poems equalled a lot of aspiring poets.

And $59.95 multiplied by give or take six thousand was a *lot* of money . . .

With a sinking heart, Cleo had scrunched up the letter that made reference to her 'unique voice and creative vision', and dumped it in the bin. She'd been scammed by a vanity press. 'Murmurs of a Landscape' was an *appalling* poem, and she'd been completely mortified to think that it was out there somewhere on the Internet with her name on it. What if Toe-rag Joe should somehow find it? He'd know immediately that it was about him because the reference to Lissnakeelagh was a big giveaway. Lissnakeelagh strand was near the village of Kilrowan in the west of Ireland where Cleo's sister Margot had a holiday cottage, and the last time Cleo and Joe had been there together had been on Margot's birthday, when they'd had a big argument. Cleo had accused Joe of fancying Margot, and he'd actually had the gall to admit it.

Cleo had just spent a long weekend in Kilrowan on her own, walking by the sea and along country lanes, and dining alone in the small restaurant that adjoined the local pub. She'd surprised herself by feeling really rather thankful that Toe-rag Joe wasn't with her — he'd tended to do an awful lot of soliloquizing about his dysfunctional childhood when he'd hogged the wine bottle over dinner in the past. She had enjoyed drifting barefoot and solitary along silver beaches, picking watercress and dulse. She'd enjoyed meandering along abandoned boreens, gathering blackberries and wild flowers. She'd enjoyed wandering through woods, searching for mushrooms — then deciding against picking them in case they were poisonous. She imagined what it must be like to be a creative type — a painter or a writer who could downshift from Dublin and live on the fat of the land and the proceeds of their imagination. In fact, Cleo had relished those few days so much that she almost hadn't wanted to come back to the city.

But back she'd come — of course she had — because Cleo wasn't a boho fantasist who could drift through life without materialistic concerns, existing on dreams and hopes and prayers and watercress and wild blackberries. Cleo Dowling was, after all, a city girl — just another working girl doing the usual working girl stuff . . .

*   *   *

The phone was ringing as she swung through the door of her flat. Cleo dumped her weekend bag on the floor and grabbed the receiver before the answering machine could pick up.

'How did you get on, sweetheart?' Margot's crushed velvet voice was on the other end. 'How was Kilrowan?'

'Oh — it was brilliant! Thanks for lending me the cottage, Margot. It did me so much good.'

'I bet. It's very therapeutic to have the pleasure of your own company to yourself from time to time. Did you get much walking done?'

'Loads! Lissnakeelagh was stunning! I cycled out there yesterday and — '

'Cleo, sorry — I can't talk right now. We're

7

running late for a dinner party. I'm really just ringing to remind you that it's First Wednesday this week.'

'First Wednesdays' were what Margot had taken to calling the monthly 'salons' that she hosted on the first Wednesday evening of every month. These had started out as quite casual affairs — a kind of book group, really — but had grown in stature until they'd acquired serious social cachet. Now Margot's First Wednesdays were attended by the crème de la crème of Dublin café society: poets and playwrights, novelists and painters, broadcasters, film makers and actors (those who appeared in serious theatre or art-house films, of course. Soap opera actors were considered very déclassé).

'Oh, your First Wednesday!' Cleo said now. 'I'll be there. I've a book launch after work, but it shouldn't last too long.'

'Who's launching?'

'P. J. Munro.'

'Pick up a signed copy for me, would you, sweetheart? His stuff can be quite droll.'

'Sure.'

'See you Wednesday, then.' There came the sound of someone yelling in the distance. 'There's Felix calling me. We're going to be late — gotta dash. 'Bye, Cleo.'

Cleo smiled 'Goodbye' at her sister over the phone. Then she put the receiver down, fired her weekend bag through the bedroom door, scooped up envelopes from the hall mat, and moseyed into the kitchen. She dumped her mail on the kitchen counter and went to the fridge, considering as she reached for a bottle of white what she ought to wear on Wednesday night. She felt underdressed if she arrived in anything ordinary. Margot's friends all wore clothes from retro shops or two seasons ago Lainey Keogh (it *had* to be two seasons ago so that they could say 'This old thing?' with a surprised expression if you admired it). Cleo decided she'd dig out her velvet Ghost jacket for this First Wednesday. She'd team it with jeans, boots and that fabulous Dries van Noten scarf that Margot had let her have when she'd spring-cleaned her wardrobe recently.

Cleo had lived in Margot's shadow all her life. Margot was five years older than her — a dazzling Leo to Cleo's dreamy Pisces, a Chinese Year of the Tiger to Cleo's gentle Sheep. Cleo's childhood memories included having her eyebrows plucked by her sister, being taught (unsuccessfully) how to swish her hair and give slanty, sideways smiles, and — this was one of the more mortifying memories — Margot's valiant but unsuccessful attempt to disguise the pity in her smile when Cleo had confided in her that it was her ambition to one day write the kind of poetry penned by Seamus Heaney.

Margot was married to a wealthy gynaecologist who went by the outrageously romantic moniker of Felix d'Arcy, and she led the kind of aspirational existence that was the stuff of lifestyle magazines: indeed, her house had been featured in such magazines more than once. She had a fantastic wardrobe of boho threads, she had a devoted Weimaraner dog and a skeletal bald cat that came with a snooty pedigree (Cleo was sorely tempted to knit the cat an alpaca jumper). As well as her country cottage, she had a beautiful town house with a serene Zen garden.

Cleo actually wanted to *be* Margot, she decided now as she finished pouring wine. Some people are born cool, some achieve coolness, and some have coolness thrust upon them. Margot had been born cool, and Cleo knew that she, the perennial little sister, would — sadly — never even have coolness thrust upon her. She took a hefty slug of her wine, then set the glass down on the breakfast bar beside the pile of mail. Sitting up on a stool, she started to sift through envelopes. They were mostly ones with windows in.

God! What a pleasure it would be to get a letter from a real live person instead of a computer, with proper handwriting on the front! How glorious to get a five-page handwritten communication from a friend instead of txt msgs or e-mail, or a creamy embossed-vellum invitation to a smart party instead of a flimsy clip-art printout, or — and here her imagination took flight to the realms of highest fantasy — a love letter! A love letter from a man who used a fountain pen, not a biro; a love letter written in authoritative, slanty black script, a love letter that would make her want to take up a pen and write one straight back . . .

On slitting open the first envelope, Cleo immediately bounced back down to earth. Her heart sank as she took in how much her phone bill was going to set her back. It sank further still on scrunching up envelope number two when she saw that her subscription to the *Bookseller* magazine was due, and it sank to her socks as she registered the logo of the Be A Bard people emblazoned on envelope number three. Another invitation to buy that overpriced anthology, she guessed. Another insidious appeal to her vanity. Another cynical exercise in suckerage.

But — BARD OF ACCLAIM! she read as she extracted the A4 sheet.

'*Yes, Cleo! You read right!*' she read. '*Our judges have nominated you as an International Bard of Acclaim for the year 2004, and I am personally inviting you to your inauguration ceremony at our next Lyrical Lyceum in Boston, which is, as you know, the Cultural Capital of the United States of America.*'

She couldn't help it. She got that same *Oh-my-God!* feeling that had given her an adrenalin rush first time round. International Bard of Acclaim sounded *good!* And the invitation to the Cultural Capital of the US of A certainly lent the nomination a dash of credibility. She scanned the page, avid for more accolades. 'And that's not all, Cleo! We take real pleasure in informing you that you are in with a chance of winning our top prize of $100,000. Other cash prizes are . . . ' Wow! Sweet! More adrenalin, please, she thought. But none came. Instead, she experienced again that same feeling of fizz fizzling out that had dashed her expectations last time round.

'*Being a Bard can, of course, mean more than mere words. Being a Bard means entering into a unique marriage between lyrics and music. And since the Bards of Yesteryear sang their lyrics, at our Lyrical Lyceum we will have professional musicians interpret your words into song, so that not alone will you have an opportunity to have your words immortalized in our beautiful 'leather' bound volume, you will also have an opportunity to have them recorded for posterity on CD . . . '* blah blah blah.

Crap.

Cleo attempted to recall the words of the poem that had got her scammed, but they eluded her — apart from the bit towards the end that went:

> I cannot see the landscape:
> It lives inside my head, now.
> Your voice, once plangent, vibrant,
> Is — um — dumpty dumpty dum. How
> Obscure the landscape!
> My tears, tee tum tee tum . . .

Was *that* likely to win her the top prize of $100,000? *No*, she thought as she dumped her invitation to the Lyrical Lyceum in the pedal-bin. The chance of that woeful ode winning her anything was about as likely as the chance of Cleo Dowling having coolness thrust upon her . . .

★   ★   ★

It was Wednesday — *First* Wednesday — and Cleo was on the bus to Margot's feeling frazzled.

12

She was running late: P. J. Munro had read far too many extracts from his 'wacky' new novel at the book launch earlier. Another reason she was frazzled was because 'droll' Mr Munro had actually turned out to be surprisingly humourless and had read his material in such a boring voice that no-one was certain which were the bits they were meant to laugh at. Cleo had nominated the novel as her readers' group's Book of the Month, and she suspected her friends would be seriously pissed off with her for inflicting that little treat upon them. She'd also ordered a hundred copies for the shop, and the fact that P.J. had signed all the copies meant they couldn't be returned to the distributor.

It was at times like this that Cleo really missed her father, Jack. She would have loved to have told him about the baffled expressions on the faces of the book launch crowd, and about all the famous people who'd been there, and about the man who'd laughed in the wrong place and the woman whose mobile phone had gone off, and who had actually *picked it up and spoken into it* in the middle of P. J. Munro's editor's speech. Although her father had been dead for over five years now, Cleo still missed him so much it hurt.

She couldn't say she missed her mother, Amanda, who had gone off to Australia with an accountant just two years after Jack had died. Her mother had never had much time for her youngest daughter: she'd even used to refer to her — only half jokingly — as 'the afterthought'. Cleo had learned at an early age to say 'It's only me' every time she entered the house or picked up the phone to her mother, and had even felt quite relieved when Amanda had run off with the accountant, because it meant she could finally stop saying 'It's only me', and aim to acquire a little self-esteem.

Bing! A passenger's thumb on the bell reminded her it was her stop. Cleo got off the bus and teetered up Margot's driveway, weighed down by the books she was carrying. One of them was the Munro novel, the other an enormous tome that Margot had lent her, a tome she had promised to return ASAP. It was the new *magnum opus* by Colleen, an award-winning Irish author who had gained international acclaim for her work, and it had taken Cleo more than a week of diligent reading to wade through it. Colleen's full moniker was Colleen J. Murphy, but as her fame had grown she had come to be known simply by her Christian name. On the jacket of this, her latest novel, it was writ large:

COLLEEN
J. Murphy

The Faraway

By the award-winning author of
Völuspa

The cover showed a fuzzy, drenched-looking landscape: presumably the remote corner of Connemara where Colleen lived, just beyond the village of Kilrowan where Cleo had spent last weekend. The book that had followed the award-winning *Völuspa* had — astonishingly — received some less than ecstatic reviews, but Colleen had been excused on the grounds that she'd been recovering from nervous exhaustion when she'd written it.

Cleo reached the front door at last, hefted the carrier bag of books from her right hand to her left and tinkled the wind chimes that served as the doorbell. Then she stapled on a smile.

'Cleo! Hi!' Her sister answered the door swathed in acres of some kind of Indian fabric. The effect was startling, and it took a minute or two for Cleo to remember that kaftans were back in fashion: she'd seen a photograph of Kate Moss wearing one, so it must be true. Margot kissed her on both cheeks, then held her at arm's length. 'Hey. You look tired,' she said. 'Come in at once, and help yourself to vittles. Red or white?'

Before Cleo had time to answer, Margot was leading her down the hall in the direction of the voices that were chattering away in the dining room. 'Vittles' were how her sister modestly chose to describe the feasts she provided for her guests. This evening the long, scrubbed refectory table that had been rescued from a convent in Kilkenny boasted a mini-mountain of crudités and an assortment of home-made dips, home-made hummus with home-made granary bread, stuffed brioches, a *marmite* of home-made soup, a selection of smelly cheeses and a *tarte tatin* (also home-made, Cleo knew,

15

to Margot's secret recipe).

'How did the book launch go?' Margot passed Cleo a glass of red wine.

'Not great. He's not as droll as you might think in the flesh.' Cleo accepted the glass and handed Margot her copy of P. J. Munro's book.

'Signed?' asked Margot.

'Yup.' Cleo indicated the author's illegible signature on the flyleaf. She held up the carrier bag that still held Colleen's book. 'Here's *The Faraway*. Thanks for lending it to me.' Cleo didn't mention that she could have helped herself to a discounted copy, but hadn't been arsed.

'What did you think? She's fantastic, isn't she?'

'Yes,' lied Cleo, wishing that Margot would take the bag from her. She'd have biceps like Arnold Schwarzenegger at this rate. But Margot waved a careless hand at her and said: 'Oh — just stick it back in the sanctuary.'

'Not in the bookcase in the study?'

'No, no. You know I like to have books that really interest me ready to hand downstairs. The sanctuary's ideal.'

Margot's 'sanctuary' was her downstairs cloakroom. Cleo was just about to make some wisecrack about reading Colleen while on the crapper, but refrained. The sanctuary was nothing like your bog-standard bog — it was more of a little boudoir. In the anteroom next to the loo itself was a chaise-longue, a footstool, a butler's tray with glasses and a decanter of sherry, and a basket for Nefertiti the cat. There was a plinth supporting a fabulous fern, an elaborate gilt-framed mirror on the wall, and a Turkish rug on the floor. The joint had been featured in an interior design mag, and the journalist responsible for the piece had described it as Margot's 'sanctuary'. The name had stuck.

Cleo's arm dropped to her side again. The plastic handles of the carrier bag were beginning to gouge painfully into her fingers. 'How's *your* novel coming along?' she asked her sister. Margot had embarked on writing a novel years ago, but was having problems finding the time to finish it — unsurprisingly, given the level of her social commitments. Occasionally she would take herself off to Kilrowan on her own to 'hermit', as she called it, and devote all her time to writing.

Her sister shrugged. 'It's getting there,' she said. 'But it's tough going.'

Somebody Cleo recognized as a television presenter walked past them with his arm round someone who wasn't his wife. 'Hey, Margot!' the presenter said *en passant*. 'Wasn't that Wagner just fantastic last night?'

'*Über* fantastic, Scott!' Margot twinkled her fingers at him, then turned back to Cleo. 'So. How's work? How's life in general?'

'Pretty normal, really.' Oh, God. Her life was so *boring* compared to Margot's. Maybe she should jizz it up a bit? 'Apart from the fact that I've had some poetry published,' she said.

'Really?' said Margot. Now she'd been distracted by a passing theatre director.

Cleo tried harder. 'And I have an invite to go

17

to a writers' conference — ' (she *couldn't* call it a 'Lyrical Lyceum'!) 'in Boston.'

A kiss was blown at the theatre director, and then Margot turned back to Cleo. 'So my little sister's a published poet? I'm impressed. Who's publishing you? Gallery Books? Salmon?'

These were established Irish publishing houses who specialized in poetry.

'Er, no. I entered an online competition to be included in an anthology.'

'And you won? Congratulations! When can we expect to see you in print?'

'Oh, well. I'm not going to bother buying the book. I've seen evidence of publication on line, and that's enough for me.'

'But if they've included your poem in an anthology, surely you're entitled to a free copy?'

'No. You have to pay.'

'I don't believe you! How much?'

'Fifty-nine ninety-five.'

'*Euros?*'

'No. Dollars.'

'Fifty-nine *dollars*! So it's a Yankee scam!' said Margot. 'What an absolute scream! And what's the name of this rip-off merchant so-called 'publishing house'?'

The inverted commas could not fail to register. Oh, God. She'd have to come clean. Margot was bound to check out the site. 'Be A Bard.com,' she intoned.

'Be A Bard.com! Be A *Bard*.com! Oh, Cleo — they saw you coming!' And as Margot's laugh tinkled round the room, Cleo wished more than anything that she hadn't given in to that stupid

18

impulse to make her life sound a bit more exciting. 'Now,' said Margot, switching effortlessly into hostess mode, 'you don't mind if I leave you to get on with it, do you? I'm sorry to abandon you, beloved, but I invited a Hungarian playwright this evening, and I think he's feeling a bit out of his depth. I've been mother-henning him.'

'Oh. OK. Where's Licky?' Licky was a nickname that Felix had been landed with at school, and it had, unfortunately for Margot, stuck.

'Please don't call him that,' said Margot with a pained expression. 'You know I hate it.'

'Sorry.'

'I haven't a clue where Felix has got to. But you know mostly everyone, don't you?' continued Margot. 'Do try one of these brioches, incidentally — they're heavenly. Oh — and you might put PJ on the shelf alongside Colleen.' She dropped P. J. Munro's book into Cleo's carrier bag, then she was gone with a swirl of her kaftan, leaving Cleo feeling small, and not a little hurt. She thought her sister might have been a bit more enthusiastic about her achievement instead of dismissing it as a scam and hurtling off after a Hungarian playwright. Still, she supposed, what kudos was there in being invited to a Lyrical Lyceum of Bards when she, Margot, was beleaguered by literati? What was it to have an eighteen-line poem published when *she* had spent years at the coal face of a novel?

Hell, thought Cleo. The bottom line was that Margot's own *life* was the stuff of novels.

19

She found herself mentally composing the book-jacket blurb that would précis *The Story of Margot's Life*. It went: 'After being discovered by a top fashion photographer in the VIP lounge of a hip Dublin nightclub, stunningly beautiful Margot Dowling becomes one of Ireland's most sought-after models. On the day of her fabulous wedding to nimble-fingered gynaecologist Felix 'Licky' d'Arcy, Margot makes the cover of *Individual* magazine for the last time. She is happy to abandon the vacuous world of high fashion, deciding instead to concentrate upon writing her Novel. But will her Novel ever see the light of day? And what of her sister, lurking in the wings of the Drama that is Margot's life? Will she ever spill the beans about the time she saw Margot — '

About the time she saw Margot doing *what*? She'd never seen Margot do anything remotely ropy, never once witnessed her take a pratfall. She'd never seen her so much as pick her toenails. Margot d'Arcy was perfection personified, and she, Cleo, was a jealous, mean-minded little cow.

Feeling like getting drunk, Cleo knocked back her wine, then helped herself to another glass and a heavenly brioche before casting an eye over the surrounding glitterati. 'You know mostly everyone, don't you?' Margot had said. Well, actually, she didn't know *anyone*. She knew *of* most of the guests because so many of them were famous, but she could claim none of them as much more than a passing acquaintance. Somehow managing to juggle her brioche and glass of red, with P. J. Munro and *The Faraway* bouncing off her calf, Cleo made her way towards the hall. A scary poet with a bristly black beard gave her the once-over as she slid past him. She wondered if he'd be going to the Lyceum. Ha! Not a chance. This guy wrote lofty stuff — *real* poetry. He wasn't the kind of loser who would e-mail maudlin crap to Be A Bard.com.

The downstairs cloakroom was occupied. While she waited, she eavesdropped on a gang of well-known lipstick lesbians who were poring over a paperback book, laughing out loud as they randomly leafed through the pages.

'What made you buy it?'

'I'm writing a piece on chick-lit for next month's issue. This has been on the bestseller list for ages, and I wanted to see what all the fuss was about.'

The novel the women were perusing was familiar to Cleo. It was a mass-market paperback that had a squiggly cartoon on the front depicting a pretty girl wearing a barely there frock and silly shoes. She was contemplating an old-fashioned set of scales upon which a Schiaparelli-pink heart and a sequined handbag were counter-balanced, and from the expression on her face you could tell that she had a big decision to make. The book — by a bestselling chick-lit writer called Pixie Pirelli — had been dancing off the shelves for months now.

'Jesus! Listen to this! '*She slipped into her La Perla underwear and Jimmy Choo heels* — ' '

'Oh-my-*God*! Not Jimmy Choos *again*!'

'Or how about this? 'She strode into the meeting confident that her new Mulberry briefcase made her look the business.' Get that: it's not her who's the business — it's her bloody briefcase! Ah! Here's another brilliant bit! 'He grabbed her roughly by the wrist and pulled her into him. 'Bitch,' he hissed. She felt a surge of pure lust.' '

'As if! What self-respecting woman would want to be grabbed roughly by the wrist and called a bitch? How sexist can you get!?'

The cloakroom door finally opened, and Cleo went through. She wondered what kind of books these women would rate. It wouldn't be chick-lit or popular or romantic or commercial or crime, she knew. It would be the hippest, hottest, must-read-before-the-next-First-Wednesday kind of stuff that sold and sold and sold, but often never actually got read. Stephen Hawking's *A Brief History of Time* was a case in point.

Margot's sanctuary was full of must-read titles. Looking around, Cleo noticed the cracked spines and the dog-eared dust jackets, and the idea occurred to her that maybe Margot had never read any of them. Maybe the world was full of people who simply bought books to impress, and then distressed them before displaying them on their shelves. Cleo pictured the kind of celebrity who might appear in a highbrow Sunday supplement — posing in front of their laden bookshelves and suddenly going: 'Shite! I'd better lose the Jeffrey Archers/Stephen Kings/Pixie Pirellis before the photographer arrives! What'll I stick in instead?

Um . . . Colleen, and James Joyce and T. S. Eliot. Oh — and Stephen Hawking, of course!'

Her thoughts went back to Pixie Pirelli's silly book, and she found herself wondering what it would be like to have some drop-dead sexy man growl *'Bitch!'* at her while tearing off her La Perla underwear. It might be a pretty damn fine experience, she decided. And it might be a fine thing too to sport a Mulberry briefcase and high-heel around in Jimmy Choos. She decided she'd help herself to Pixie's book tomorrow and spend the evening escaping.

She extracted *The Faraway* from its plastic bag. Colleen glowered up at her from the back cover with dark tormented eyes, as if accusing the photographer of stealing her soul. Shadows were scooped in all the right places on her lovely face, and her sulky mouth had the appearance of an exotic crushed flower. The message was clear. *Noli me tangere!* Cleo studied the image, comparing it to the one on Pixie Pirelli's books. Pixie's jacket photograph showed her sitting at her desk, french-polished pinkies twinkling merrily over her keyboard, wearing a big Kylie Minogue smile and wifty-wafty chiffon. (Colleen had opted for a mushroom-coloured shirt in fustian, which she somehow contrived to make look sexy.)

Sliding *The Faraway* between Alain de Botton's latest philosophical treatise and Ovid's *Metamorphoses*, Cleo turned to the mirror to inspect her reflection. Her mascara was smudged, her lipstick could do with a retouch, and her hair needed brushing. Her mobile phone was still switched on, she noticed as she rummaged in her backpack for her make-up bag. Yikes! She could imagine the looks she'd get if her ring tone went off. Mobile phones were banned from Margot's soirées.

She took the phone out, turned it off, then saw before her mind's eye the insane image of Colleen's eighteenth-century heroine talking on her mobile phone in a horse-drawn carriage. Had she *really* read that? It didn't make sense! But then, she thought, as she picked the book up again and started leafing randomly through the pages, making sense wasn't what Colleen was all about. Who cared if her eighteenth-century heroine used a phone? Colleen soared alone like the literary eagle she was, and was to be congratulated for having liberated herself from such paltry constraints as historical accuracy!

Now Cleo couldn't find the bit with the phone anywhere. Maybe she had dozed off while trawling through *The Faraway* and dreamed it? But she was *certain* she'd read it — she remembered it had that new 'concierge' facility like the one on Gwyneth Paltrow's (according to *OK!* magazine).

Leaf, leaf, leaf . . . The words on the page were starting to look like they were written in a foreign language. *Cacoethes, salsuginous, syrinx, gulosity, cupreous* . . . There was even a 'pinguid' on page 408. *I'm a bookseller*, thought Cleo. *I have a degree in English and I read books for a living, and even I can't understand half of what this Colleen's on about.*

Unable to locate the passage — and beyond

caring now, anyway — she was just about to put the book back on the shelf when it fell to the floor. Cleo hunkered down, inspecting the jacket carefully to make sure there was no damage (it was a signed first edition). She was on the point of rising to her feet when she spotted a folded piece of paper that had fallen from between the pages. It was a lottery ticket she'd forgotten about, one that she'd been using as a bookmark.

She picked it up and examined it. She'd put her usual numbers down — Oh! No, she hadn't, she remembered now. Her usual numbers had been based on Toe-rag Joe's mobile phone number, and for the first time in ages she'd changed them back to her own. Knowing her luck, Toe-rag's number *would* be the one that came up this week.

Sliding the ticket into her pocket, she let herself out of the cloakroom. Through the open door of the kitchen she could hear the sound of the television, could see lovely Felix standing in the middle of the floor nursing a beer. 'Hi, Licky,' she called, feeling stupid simply because Felix was so drop-dead gorgeous he always made her feel stupid.

'Cleo! Come in and have a beer! I'm sick to the teeth of that 'delicately nuanced' Bordeaux Margot serves up.'

'I thought watching telly was *verboten* on a first Wednesday?' said Cleo, her eyes on Felix's elegant hands as he snapped the tab on a can of Bud.

'Not this evening it's not,' he said. 'I'm going

diving tomorrow and I need to check out the weather forecast.' He finished pouring and handed her the beer. 'Cheers.'

'Cheers.' Over Felix's shoulder Ann Doyle's face, topped by her trademark helmet of indestructible gold hair, was shimmering away on the telly.

'Where are you going diving?' Cleo asked her brother-in-law, but before he could answer, the phone rang.

'Off Dalkey Island,' he said, checking out the display on the phone. 'Excuse me, sweetie-pie. I'll have to take this. It's my dive buddy. Keep an eye on the forecast for me, will you?'

Obediently, Cleo moved to the breakfast bar. On the screen, Ann Doyle was still talking in her reassuring newsreader's voice. 'And the head-lines again . . . '

The headlines were exceptionally dull. EU Presidency, Bertie Ahern and the Department of the Environment, heard Cleo. Then her ears pricked up as Ann Doyle announced: 'This evening's mid-week lottery win was the highest in the history of the State. The winning numbers,' she said, 'are: 2, 3, 5, 8, 9 and 24, and the winning ticket was bought in Dublin. That brings us to the end of the news, now for the weather forecast . . . '

Cleo didn't bother with the weather forecast. Ann Doyle had just reeled off her mobile phone number.

She felt as if she was in a parallel universe, or in a film she was watching. She was definitely having some kind of out of body experience. She saw her hand on the breakfast bar reach for a pen and watched as she ticked off the numbers on her lottery form. Two. Three. Five. Eight. Nine. Twenty-four. She sucked in her breath, and felt that she didn't know how to let it out again. She'd forgotten how to breathe. When she did let it out, her breath came in a loud staccato rush. Like a somnambulist, she walked out of the kitchen in search of Margot. She found her in the crowded drawing room, laughing with a man who had to be the Hungarian playwright.

'Margot?' said Cleo, but nothing came out of her mouth. 'Margot!' she said again, realizing that this time the word had come out as a shout.

The room went silent. Margot gave her a look of concern. 'Are you all right, Cleo?' she asked. The faces of all the glitterati in Margot's drawing room had turned towards her. Cleo registered their curious expressions, feeling like an alien.

'I'm really sorry. I think I've just won the lottery,' she said.

2

'Oh, look! There's a big interview with Colleen in today's paper.' Dannie Moore folded her *Irish Times* back at the arts page and studied the photograph of Colleen that had been taken on a stretch of golden sand not far from where Dannie lived. The author was gazing out to sea, looking pensive, with a melancholy smile playing around her beautiful bee-stung mouth, and with strands of wild hair whipping around her face.

'Mm. I saw it,' said Breda Shanley as she emptied plastic bags of change into her till. 'The usual cheerful stuff. She was in earlier — bought half a dozen copies.'

' "I feel it is actually possible not to exist," ' Dannie read out loud. ' 'My self consists in my thoughts. When winter takes possession of my soul, at times of spiritual aridity, I hibernate, I cease to exist in any meaningful sense.' Janey. I see what you mean. What uplifting thoughts to start the week with.' Dannie was leaning against the counter of the local grocery shop, waiting for Breda to give her her change. ' 'The natural wretchedness of our mortal condition', blah blah de blah. Oh, shite. Reading this is going to do my head in. Did you see the one in the *Independent* last week about how inspiring celibacy could be?'

'Yeah. That was good for a laugh all right. And there was a feature on her in the *Sunday Times* yesterday. Morning, Mary, Katherine.' This to an ancient pair of twin sisters who had just come into the shop.

'Morning, Breda, Dannie. Is that that Colleen in the paper again? Sure she'll turn up in *Hello!* magazine next.'

'Indeed and she will. Whatever happened to her famous reclusiveness?'

'Arra, she's making herself more available than usual this time round because the last book didn't sell so well. Did you know there's talk of a television documentary being made about her?'

'Being made here?'

'Mm-hm. But sure aren't we used to that now? There's a television crew down every boreen in Connemara when the weather permits. By the way, Mary, the galvanized buckets came in. They're down the back there, on your left.'

'Grand, so.'

'Here you go, Dannie.' Breda handed change across the counter, then leaned her elbows on it and gave her a look of consideration. 'Don't you ever miss your old life in the telly, Dannie, and the glamour of it all?'

'Glamour? There was feck all glamorous about being a television researcher.'

'Well, 'twas surely glamorous compared to the likes of us.'

'The likes of you are worth a million times more than the stressed-out yokes I used to work with, Breda. I remember saying to a colleague that you could always find a spoon or a fork for yourself in that feckin' canteen, but you could never find a knife.'

29

'Why was that?'

'Because they were all stuck in people's backs, of course. Getting out of the rat race was the best thing I ever did.' Dannie glanced at her watch. 'Talking of moving, I'd better get me arse down to the shop. I'm running late.'

Breda looked surprised. 'You're not opening up today, are you?'

'Are you mad? I just want to get in there and get as much of the upstairs sorted as I can.'

'It's still in a mess?'

'Yeah. And I've to knock it into shape before the start of the season.'

'You'll get a nice rent for it. Remember to mention when you place your ad that it overlooks the harbour. That's worth its weight in gold. Morning, Mr Morton!'

Ancient Mr Morton had come harrumphing in for his daily fix of pipe tobacco and the *Telegraph*. It was Dannie's cue to leave. Heaving her shopping bags off the counter and yelling 'Morning!' in the direction of Mr Morton's hearing aid, Dannie waved good-bye to Breda and left the shop, heading across the road towards Florabundance Two.

Dannie and Breda had known each other all their lives. When her mother had died giving birth to Daniella, the teenaged Breda had been brought in to look after the babby and put manners on her seven brothers. Breda had always looked out for Dannie, and had kept in touch when Dannie had decamped to London and a job with a television station. And when Dannie had given up the day job and returned to Ireland to open her first flower shop — Florabundance — in Dublin, Breda had sent her a good luck card with 'Live your Dream!' written on it. She had also provided invaluable moral support when Dannie had come back to Kilrowan some years ago with a heavily pregnant belly. There had been much speculation as to who the father might be, but Breda had advised the nosier of the village idiots to mind their own business.

Today on a sublimely sunny February morning outside Breda's shop on the main street Dannie said good morning to the postman, saluted a passing farmer on his tractor, and nodded at a couple of the local publicans. Pubs wildly outnumbered shops in Kilrowan, possibly one of the most picture-postcard-perfect villages in the whole of Ireland.

Beyond the main street to the north of the village were twelve spectacular purple mountains that looked like clones of the one on the Paramount Pictures logo. To the south, a dramatic escarpment tumbled down from a blue-washed sky to meet beaches of powdery coral-coloured sand where waves lapped like kittens on some days and ravened like tigers on others. On the right-hand side of the dozy main street, fishing boats bobbed obligingly in a picturesque harbour, while on the left, terraces of nineteenth-century houses — the kind that epitomize the estate agent cliché 'oozing with character' — preened and posed prettily for the delectation of tourists. Boats and houses, mountains and seascape — all could have been

31

designed by a deity in a particularly benevolent mood, or by whoever was responsible for *The Truman Show*. Dannie sometimes felt that if she took a boat too far out to sea, she'd surely go crashing *splat!* into a sky-blue painted canvas.

This being February, all was quiet. Things were of course different in the summer months, when the place was besieged by tourists and all those denizens of Dublin 4 who bickered amongst themselves as to who had been responsible for 'discovering' this unspoilt sleepy fishing village. They descended in their hordes from June onward to open up the houses and luxury bungalows that remained empty for most of the rest of the year, and to spread their cash around. That was why it made financial sense for Dannie to open her flower shop only in that handful of summer months.

Colleen, the village's most famous resident, had been so devastated when she'd heard the flower shop was shutting for the winter that Dannie had offered to travel to Galway city on a regular basis to hand-pick the blooms that corresponded to the writer's temperament that particular week. Colleen would call her on the phone and announce that she was feeling melancholic, or sanguine, or choleric, or phlegmatic, and Dannie would know exactly which flowers to buy to suit her client's humour.

There was Colleen now, observed Dannie, as she passed the bookshop — or rather, Colleen's cardboard cut-out in the window. She paused to have a look at the display, and as she did she saw a pair of hands slide into view, busily fanning out a selection of slender volumes of poetry by one of the many local poets. Dannie stuck her head around the door of the shop to see Maureen, the proprietor, leaning obliquely into the window, trying to avoid knocking down cardboard Colleen.

'Morning, Maureen. Well! Won't Colleen be thrilled to see this?'

'She wasn't too thrilled when she dropped in earlier. She gave out yards because I'd put Pixie Pirelli's poster up next to her cut-out. She said she'd take the cut-out away if I didn't take that Pixie one out of the window and put in poetry instead.'

'No!'

'I'm tellin' ya. She said it made her feel contaminated to be in the same window as Pixie.'

'Jaysus. So literary politics can be as poisonous as any other sort?'

'Damn right. You've got to keep right up on your tippy toes to keep some authors happy. And it really would be so *not* a good idea to get up Colleen's nose. It may be a diplomatic nightmare putting up with her diva behaviour, but I have to say she's very good about signing stock for me. All these copies are signed.'

'Give us a look.' Maureen handed Dannie one of Colleen's hardback volumes. There on the title page were the words: *Doubt not your soul* in Colleen's distinctive jagged script, above her equally dramatically scribbled signature. 'It's a mad amount of euros, but I suppose I'd better buy one in case she asks me if I've read it.'

Dannie delved in her bag for her wallet. 'By the way, you *are* doing the nursery pick-up today, aren't you?'

'Yeah. And Gemma wants Paloma to come and play after lunch. Is that OK?'

'Sure. That means I'll have some quality time to myself.'

'You can spend it reading,' said Maureen, handing over the doorstop that was Colleen's book. 'I got as far as page fifteen last night.'

'How many pages are there?'

Maureen sent her a wicked smile. 'Five hundred and seventy-nine,' she said, as the till swallowed Dannie's cash. 'More moolah for Ms Colleen J. Murphy! And talking of moolahed individuals, Dannie,' she added, counting out change, 'have you heard that Oliver Dunne has bought the old Glebe House? He's converting it into an upmarket country house hotel.'

'Oh?' Dannie tried to appear casual as she tipped coins into her purse. 'So he's coming back here to live?'

'Looks like it.'

'Has he a partner on board?' she asked Maureen. Setting up a country house hotel was a very coupley thing to do, after all.

'Yes.'

Dannie felt an irrational swoosh of disappointment.

'Who?'

'His sister, Alice. She's living in the gate lodge while the big house is being done up.'

His sister! OK! 'How about Oliver?'

'He's staying on in London until he's finalized

the sale of his business. He stands to make a fair few bob from it. Travel agencies are cleaning up these days.' Maureen sent her an astute look. 'The pair of you were childhood sweethearts, weren't you?'

'Well, hardly childhood.' Dannie busied herself with the buckle on her bag. 'We went out together when we were students in Dublin.'

'Do you still keep in touch?'

'We e-mail from time to time. But I haven't heard from him in a while.'

'My memory of him is at some New Year's Eve party surrounded by a gaggle of girls. I wonder has he changed much?'

'I wouldn't know. I haven't seen him in yonks.'

That was a lie. As Dannie let herself out of the bookshop and headed down the street in the direction of Florabundance Two, she thought about the last time she'd seen Oliver Dunne, and smiled.

* * *

At around two o'clock that afternoon, Dannie decided to throw in the towel and head home for lunch. She discarded her overalls, put the lids back on paint tins and wrapped brushes in newspaper. She'd undercoated the walls of two of the rooms above the shop — the rooms she'd designated as bedrooms. She'd get round to the sitting room tomorrow, and in the meantime she must check out Bob the Builder's availability for installing a shower. And she'd have to get another land line installed, she thought, as she

35

made her way downstairs to make phone calls. She wondered how she'd cope with the responsibilities of being a landlady. What were the logistics of keeping tabs on tenants' phone and electricity and gas bills? It would be easier to install a tenant on a long-term basis, she knew, but short-term rentals were far more profitable.

Her darling shop was looking forlorn without stock. She remembered how it had looked on the day she'd first opened, crammed with flowers and with people drinking wine from plastic cups that had been raised in toasts to her future, and to the future of Florabundance Two, and, of course, to the future of her daughter Paloma, who would be starting nursery school now that Mammy had decided to go back to work.

Tapping her fingers on the scrubbed pine counter, Dannie listened to her own voice echoing around the empty space as she left a message on Bob the Builder's voice mail, phoned a department store in Galway to ask about curtains, and swore at the automaton on Eircom who kept thanking her for continuing to hold. Finally she gave up, wondering if phone companies employed human beings at all as she let herself out of the shop and headed for home.

Home was a cottage that had lain derelict for years. It belonged to her father, but had been restored by an older brother who had never had a chance to move in, and it now provided perfect accommodation for Dannie and her daughter. Home was where Paloma and Dannie spent summer evenings in the garden, and winter evenings in front of the fire. Home had roses rambling around doors and windows, and a vegetable patch where runner beans and rhubarb and curly kale grew. Home had an Aga, and smelt of toast and hyacinths.

Dannie stepped through the front door, hung her coat on the hatstand and headed towards the stairs. She wanted to shower away the grime she'd accumulated from sugar-soaping walls, and the paint that had found its way into her hair. In her bedroom she stripped off all her clothes, then moved to the wardrobe.

Some women like to fill their wardrobes with designer outfits. Others skimp on clothes so that they can indulge their handbag and shoe fetish. Dannie's thing was underwear: her cupboards were full of gorgeous lingerie. She didn't much care about the stuff she wore over it — she could dress as casually as she liked in her line of work — but underthings were different. Any time she visited town she would drop into her favourite lingerie shop and treat herself to a new robe or to lounging pyjamas or some discreetly sexy scanties, and her favourite web address of all was www.agentprovocateur.com. It didn't matter a toss that there was no man to dress up for, or that hers were the only eyes to admire the pretty things — they just made her *feel* so good! It was all to do with self-esteem. The underwear made her feel empowered in a gorgeously *womanly* way, as if she had a secret weapon. She was so particular about her underthings that she even kept them colour co-ordinated in separate drawers.

On her last trip to Galway city she had fallen

in love with a white lawn robe. It was slightly diaphanous, very simply cut in a spare empire style and subtly embroidered with elegant arum lilies, white on white. It had come with a matching shift with shoestring straps, and as far as Dannie was concerned, there was no better way of ending the day than sliding into her exquisite nightclothes after a luxurious soak in a scented bath. She didn't actually sleep in the garments — she preferred the feel of nubbly linen sheets against nakedness — but she loved to wander round her garden on a summer's evening, looking as away with the fairies as she damn well pleased in her pretty girly pyjamas or wifty-wafty nighties; and in the winter she loved to curl up by the fire with a glass of wine and a book, relishing the sensation of cashmere or satin against her skin. She had no intention of getting into the robe now — she'd save that treat for later — she just wanted to *look* at it and admire it in all its gorgeous pristine *newness*.

She riffled along hangers, bypassing exotic kimonos and slinky silk negligees, and then riffled back again. There was no sign of her latest acquisition. How weird! She'd bought it only yesterday, and had definitely hung it up before she'd gone to bed. She stood back, and as she did so she caught sight of the nightdress reflected in the mirror on the inside of the wardrobe door. It was lying stretched out on her bed.

How had it got there? She had most certainly not left it there before she'd exited the house with Paloma this morning. Had Paloma perhaps been playing a dressing-up game? Unlikely. It was difficult enough to persuade the child to get into her own clothes first thing. She turned to face back into the room, and then saw something else that made her stop dead. The drawers in the chest where she kept her more intimate lingerie were lying wide open, and she could tell even from this distance that the contents had been disturbed. Pale pinks and blues were scrambled up with reds and greens, and black was jumbled with white.

Oh, Jesus. She'd read about cases like this. She'd been visited by an intruder. A male intruder. A man had come into her room and ransacked it for sexual gratification. Her hands flew to her mouth and her eyes scanned the room. There, on her duvet, was an impression of a body. Oh God, oh God. Dannie crossed the room and grabbed her thick towelling bathrobe from the back of the bedroom door. Shrugging into it in a panic, she pulled it tightly around her and tied the sash in a double knot. She stood frozen for a moment or two, forcing herself to think. Had anything else been disturbed, had anything been taken? Worse — was he still in the house?

The guards. Call the guards. Quickly she moved to the bedside table and punched in three nines on the phone, hearing the electronic beeps sound agonizingly loud in the silent house.

'What service do you require?'

'The guards. Please be quick.'

In a barely audible voice she gave details and gently replaced the receiver. Then, senses heightened and awash with awful adrenalin, she moved back downstairs on soundless feet and cautiously poked her head around the doorways to the sitting room and study. There was no sign of disturbance in either room, nor could she see anything unusual in the hallway. The kitchen next. Nothing untoward here, either. Dannie slid along the wall, pulling a Sabatier from its sheath in the wooden knife block as she did so, then noticed with a jolt that the back door was slightly ajar. She crossed the room and very slowly pulled the door open. Stretched out on a wooden lounger on the terrace, his eyes closed against the unseasonable sunlight, was a man wearing denims and a shabby sheepskin jacket.

Dannie paused, then moved towards him with the stealth of a cat burglar. When she reached the sun lounger she raised a balletic leg and straddled him. Disoriented by the shadow that had fallen across his face, the man blinked once, twice, then looked up at her, sleepy-eyed. She dropped the knife, then undid the knot on her sash with deft fingers and slid the towelling robe down off her shoulders so that her breasts were exposed. 'You feckin' gobshite, Jethro,' she said, smiling down at him. 'You weren't supposed to get here till tomorrow.'

★ ★ ★

'You're a total perv, Mr Palmer. And the guards must think I'm some kind of deluded fantasist.' She parroted the apology she'd had to make on the phone earlier. ' 'Sorry about that. It wasn't

40

an intruder after all. No, *please* don't go to the trouble of sending a car. Sorry, SORRY, SORRY.' '

Jethro and Dannie were lying in her bed. The sheets were gratifyingly tumbled, and clothes were strewn across the room. Dannie still had paint in her hair and grime on her face, but she didn't care.

'I am not a perv. I was so disappointed not to find my flesh-and-blood woman at home that I just had to familiarize myself with her vicariously. And what better way of getting familiar with a gal than by inhaling her essence? Don't you remember — that's exactly what I did the first time we ended up in bed, that time in your apartment in Dublin.'

She remembered. It would have been difficult to forget. First he'd unstoppered her bottle of Nu and inhaled her scent. Then he'd slid her beautiful embroidered antique kimono off its padded hanger, held it in his arms and rubbed his cheek against it like a big cat. And finally he had lifted the lid on the carved Indian chest that contained her lingerie and delved both his big hands into its sandalwood interior as though he'd come across a treasure trove spilling jewels, and ransacked the silken contents. That's what he had done, here in her bedroom, today.

'Did you lie down on my bed with my robe?' she asked.

'Yes, ma'am.'

'Sicko. Did you rummage around in my underwear drawer?'

'Yes, ma'am.'

'Deviant. Did you *sniff* my underwear?'

41

'No, ma'am. I inhaled its essence.'

'Tosser.' She leaned over and kissed him.

There was a sublimely contented silence for a long moment, and then: 'Have you any new pictures?' Jethro asked.

'I do. Loads.'

'Show me.'

'I *did* e-mail them to you,' Dannie said mock-crossly. 'Why do you keep changing your address?'

'Too many people looking for me.'

'It's surprisingly easy to forget what an important person you are, Mr Palmer,' she said, sliding out from between the sheets. She opened a cupboard and drew out a box that contained all kinds of sentimental stuff pertaining to Paloma: first baby booties, a lock of her fine baby hair, her first drawing (crayon on paper — *hugely* accomplished!), and, of course, photographs. It also contained a letter that had been attached to the deeds to the small ex-grocer's shop that was now Florabundance Two, and which she had received on the day her daughter had been born. This is how it read:

Dearest Dannie

Enclosed is a gift to mark the birth of our daughter. I know you told me that you were going to devote yourself to full-time motherhood, but when Paloma has grown up a little and is going to school, you may change your mind, and if you do, I'd like to think that you might resurrect your not inconsiderable business acumen. I am

racing off to Australia to start work on a
new epic. When it's finished, I would dearly
love to spend some time with you and our
daughter in Connemara.
    With warmest wishes to you and Paloma,
Jethro

Dannie sat down on the bed, opened the box and drew out a sheaf of recent photographs of Paloma. They had been taken at a friend's fancy-dress party, and the child was wearing a halo of lily of the valley that Dannie had made for her, a pair of angel's wings, and an expression that was too good to be true.

'Wow,' said Jethro, taking the pictures from Dannie and scrutinizing them. 'She's got even prettier since the last time I saw her. How did I manage to father such a good-looking child? Ha — no need to answer that, I know. She inherited her mother's genes, thanks be to whoever's up there looking after us.' He slid an arm round Dannie's waist and dropped a kiss on her bare shoulder.

'I'd better get showered and dressed before she's delivered home,' said Dannie, trying very hard to resist the temptation to launch herself back into his arms. 'You too, Palmer. How long're you staying this time?'

'I'll stay a couple of nights if that's cool with you, but I'll have to get back on the road day after tomorrow. I've to finish recceing before the end of the week.'

'Found any locations yet?'

'Yeah. There are several possibilities. I knew I

could trust Connemara to come up with the goods. My cinematographer was totally wowed by Lissnakeelagh strand.'

'You're sorted, so?'

'Very nearly. There's just one key location we've yet to find, and I'm gonna ask you a big favour, Dannie.'

'Fire ahead.'

'We'd love to use your shop.'

'The interior?'

'No, no. Just the exterior — the interior would be too cramped for filming. We'll construct an interior set in the studio in Clare.'

'So you'd just want shots of people going in and out?'

'Sure. You'll be well compensated for any inconvenience.'

'What months are you talking about?'

'Second half of March; April and May.'

'Then there's no inconvenience, Jethro. I'm not opening again until June. I'd be happy for you to use it. Sure, if it wasn't for you, it wouldn't be mine.' Dannie kissed his mouth, resisting that temptation again, then moved into her *en suite*, leaving him admiring the photographs of his daughter. 'What's the project?' she called back to him as she turned the dial on the shower to the temperature she wanted. Hot. No — better make that cool. She needed to regain a little sang-froid.

'I'll tell you later, over chowder in O'Toole's. Can you get a sitter tonight?'

'Sure I can. But you will make pasta for Paloma before we go out?'

44

'That goes without saying. With ham, cream, Parmesan and pine nuts?'

'You remember!'

'Well, it's only been a coupla months.'

'Four.'

'Four? Jesus H. Christ. Don't make me feel guilty. I'm still gutted that I couldn't make Christmas.'

Dannie located her so-expensive-that-it-was-strictly-for-special-occasions shower gel at the back of the bathroom cabinet, and stepped into the shower. She could hear Jethro burbling on in the bedroom, but the torrents of water meant that she couldn't make out what he was saying.

Two whole days of Jethro! She was glad she didn't have to work, glad that she could dedicate all that time to him.

Theirs could best be described as an unorthodox relationship. Jethro Palmer was what a friend of hers had dubbed an *über*dude — a high-powered man of wealth and taste, a mover, a shaker, a Big Important Decision Maker. Jethro Palmer was an internationally renowned film director, who had swept Dannie right off her feet from the first moment she'd met him, and when she had become pregnant with his baby she had made the single most difficult decision of her life. She had left him.

She had left him because their lifestyles were too divergent. Jethro was a citizen of the world, not laying his hat anywhere for long, and Dannie couldn't and wouldn't become a jet-setting wife. She wanted their baby to grow up in the cradle of Connemara, a place where the pace of life was slow and measured, and where the crime rate was negligible. In Kilrowan people rarely bothered to lock their doors (hence Jethro's effortless entry into her cottage this afternoon), everybody knew everybody else, and christenings and funerals were still considered major events in the calendar.

It had cost her dearly to cut Jethro off, because Dannie was stone mad about the man. Initially she had resisted his seductive attempts to get her to change her mind — she'd thought it would be easier for her daughter to grow up without an itinerant father complicating things — but this had proved unworkable and just plain unfair on both Paloma and herself, and as time went on she had dropped her guard and relaxed her rules, and allowed him back into their lives. His visits were erratic, and his no-shows the cause of frequent tears and tantrums for both the women in his life, but people in the village now knew who Paloma's dada was, and even Dannie's father, who was a died-in-the-wool conservative, had got used to the unconventional set-up.

Two whole days of Jethro! He'd brought her a present of lingerie from Frederick's of Hollywood. She'd wear the baby-blue silk tonight, and tomorrow — when they'd treat Paloma to a trip to the beach — she'd wear the Chantilly lace under her jeans and woolly jumper.

Dannie turned off the shower to hear shrieks and excited babblings coming from beyond the bathroom door. Shrugging into her robe, she stepped into the bedroom and found father and daughter lounging riotously on her bed, surrounded by a stockade of toys and a moat of crumpled wrapping paper.

'Mammy!' yelled a beaming Paloma. 'Daddy's back! And look at all the presents he brung!' She picked up another present and tore off the gift wrap.

'Not that one,' said Jethro, deftly extricating a pair of exotic-looking handcuffs from her grasp and sending a slant-eyed smile across the room to Dannie. 'That's for your mommy.'

'What is it?' demanded Paloma.

'It's a set of handcuffs for you two to wear so that you don't get separated in the supermarket and give your mom a big fright like you did last year.'

'I won't wear it,' the child announced.

'Why not?'

'It's pink. I'm not into pink stuff.'

Jethro gave a resigned shrug. 'OK,' he said, lobbing the handcuffs across the room to Dannie. 'I can't possibly think what other use you'd have for them, ma'am, but they're all yours.'

Dannie smiled at him as she stowed the handcuffs away in her bedside locker. 'I'm sure I'll think of something,' she said.

* * *

Much later that evening, after Paloma had demolished her pasta and been tucked into bed and had an epic story read to her by her dad, Jethro and Dannie wandered down to their favourite pub for dinner. They sat at their favourite table by the open fire, and ordered their favourite wine. Unfortunately they couldn't order their favourite food because, as it was low season, lobster was off the menu, but they had chowder and baked mussels instead.

'Tell me about your film,' said Dannie. 'Is it big budget?'

'Yep. I've millions to spend.'

'Who's starring?'

'Eva Lavery, Ben Tarrant and Colin Farrell.'

'Eva Lavery? I met her just after she won her first Oscar, when I worked for the television station. She's some lady, isn't she?'

'The classiest dame in the business.'

'A bit past it, I'd have thought? She must be fifty by now.'

'She's still a sexy piece of work. Some women don't lose it. Think Helen Mirren, think Marianne Faithfull, think Charlotte Rampling. And she's perfect casting.'

'What's she playing?'

'She's playing the role of a woman who moves into a small nineteenth-century village and sets up a shop selling herbal remedies. It's based on a book by a bestselling author called Lily Wright — '

'Not *Mimi's Remedies?*'

'Yup. And the screenplay's by Deirdre O'Dare.'

'I *loved Mimi's Remedies* — I love all Lily Wright's stuff! But I've never heard of Deirdre O'Dare.'

'Nobody ever remembers the names of

scriptwriters. She wrote the script for *Halcyon Lives* — '

'Oh! I *really* loved that!'

'And she's married to Rory McDonagh.'

'*The* Rory McDonagh? The film star?'

'The very same.'

'Wow.' Dannie was silent for a moment or two, and then she burst out laughing.

'What's so funny?' asked Jethro.

'Oh, I dunno. It's just our set-up is so ridiculous, Jethro! Here's me, a bogger living in the back of beyond, listening to you talking about a 'real' life that includes film stars and bestselling authors and Oscar winners!'

'I don't know why you find it so ridiculous. Think about it. In a couple of months' time all those film stars and bestselling authors and Oscar winners will more than likely be sitting here in this restaurant swigging back pints of Guinness.'

'Janey! Life's bonkers, Jethro, isn't it?'

'Sometimes. Especially right now. *You're* driving me bonkers, Dannie.'

'Why?'

'Because I know exactly what you're wearing under that unprepossessing outfit, and it's giving me the hard-on of my life.'

'So it's time to go home?'

'It's time to go home.'

'Can we mess around with handcuffs?'

'We sure can.'

Dannie drained her wine, then leaned her elbows on the table and rested her face between cupped palms, studying him. 'D'you think of it that way, Palmer — really? Is my cottage your home?'

'Absolutely.'

'Why is that? Sure haven't you fabulous homes of your own all over the world?'

'Isn't it obvious, honey? It is to me.'

Dannie shrugged. 'Tell me.'

'It's obvious,' said Jethro, getting to his feet and holding out a hand to her, 'that your cottage is home. Because home is where the heart is.'

'Oh, Jethro. Why do you always make me cry?'

'I dunno. Because you're a sucker for sentimentality?'

'Am I?'

'You said you read *Mimi's Remedies?*'

'Yes.'

'Did you cry?'

'Of course!'

It was his turn to shrug. 'You're a *complete* sucker for sentimentality, sweetheart,' he said.

3

Deirdre O'Dare and her friend Eva Lavery were lounging on the deck of Deirdre's beach house overlooking the Pacific Ocean. They'd started the afternoon with herbal tea, and, having agreed that it was shite, had moved on to a bottle of local Californian Sauvignon Blanc. They had just packed their daughters — they had three between them — off to play under the watchful eye of Melissa the nanny on the beach below, and Deirdre's small son was snoozing in his star-spangled bedroom.

There were no men in evidence. Deirdre's husband Rory was off making a movie in New Zealand, while Eva's was back in the UK directing Jacobean drama with the National Theatre. Eva would have been with him if it hadn't been for the fact that she was doing publicity for the film she'd just finished starring in.

Deirdre had on her contemplative face. Some people look serene when they're being contemplative, but Deirdre couldn't help furrowing her brow and scrunching up her nose, which meant that she looked a bit like a hamster. As Rory could never resist reminding her.

'Hell's teeth, Eva,' she was saying. 'Once upon a time I never *dreamed* that I'd be sitting on a deck in Hollywood sipping expensive New World wine and having routine discussions about stuff like movie schedules and world-class theatre. I'm sure it's become a bit of a cliché for you — you've been famous practically all your life. But sometimes I feel like a total fraud and impostor.'

'Nonsense. The only time you were a fraud and an impostor was when you were married to Gabriel Considine.'

'That *was* a joke! But when you think about it, I'm still masquerading. I'm only here in LA because I'm married to a shit-hot film star.'

'Fiddle dee dee! You've every right to be here. You're a highly talented screenwriter, Deirdre O'Dare.'

'Well, you know where *screenwriters* come in the Hollywood hierarchy?' said Deirdre, giving Eva a sceptical look. 'What's that joke about the wannabe who was so dumb she came to LA and thought that sleeping with a screenwriter would be a good way of kick-starting her career?' She took a swig of wine and gave a shudder. 'Oh! It gives me the heebie-jeebies when I think of that casting couch stuff. I wonder would *I* ever have resorted to it if I hadn't struck lucky back in the days when I was an actress?'

'No. You wouldn't have, Deirdre. You were too guileless.'

'What do you mean? Surely it's the guileless ones who end up on the casting couch?'

'No, darling. It's the ambitious ones. If some slimeball had come on to you and tried to smooth-talk his way into your bed, you'd have found it so preposterous that you'd have laughed in his face. If, on the other hand, someone like

Sophie Burke had thought that sleeping with the enemy might give her a foothold on the career ladder, she wouldn't have hesitated.'

'I guess.'

'I'll never forget your first appearance, in that *Midsummer Night's Dream* we did together,' said Eva. 'You were very good, you know — and so incredibly pretty. Would you ever go back to acting, d'you think?'

'God, no! No offence, Eva, but I'm much happier doing what I'm doing. I get so much more job satisfaction from writing. Although I can't say I've written anything meaningful for ages, apart from erotic e-mails to Rory.'

'Sweetheart! What about *Mimi's Remedies?*'

'That doesn't count. *Mimi's Remedies* is an adaptation, and I don't get as much of a buzz out of doing adaptations. I mean I haven't written anything *original* for ages. I've loads of ideas, but production companies are fighting shy of original ideas these days. Nobody's prepared to take a gamble — they're just on the tout for remakes, or the latest bestseller to adapt. I'm restless, I guess. I'm itching to move in a different direction.'

'Why don't you write a novel?'

'Are you mad? I wouldn't have the discipline to sit down and write a novel. It's too lonely. At least with a screenplay there's loads of feedback and interaction going on, and you get to go out to lunch a lot and be sociable and bitch about other writers.'

'Do writers bitch about each other?'

'Nearly as much as actresses.'

'Wow. I'm so glad I don't go there any more now that I've resigned myself to playing old bags.'

'You're *never* an old bag!'

'I am an old bag, darling, and proud to admit it. Look!' Eva shot Deirdre a big, beaming smile. 'Look at all these wrinkles! They tell people that I've had a happy, fulfilled life. I'm so *glad* that I have happy wrinkles. Imagine having big down-turned etches around your mouth. That's living, breathing testimony to the fact that you're a miserable git and that your life's been a non-event. Happy old bags rule. We don't have to worry any more about making an entrance, or whether or not men fancy us or women envy us. After you hit a certain age nobody bothers to look any more. It's like being invisible! I love it!'

'I'd hardly call you invisible, Eva. You still make people's heads turn.'

'Pish. That's only because I'm famous. You know as well as I do, Deirdre, that in LA you're an old bag the moment you hit thirty — unless you're prepared to invest an obscene amount of money and energy in the way you look. I feel so sorry for those women who have made a career out of wearing miniature clothes, like Elizabeth Hurley and Kylie Minogue. How on earth are they going to handle it when they start to sag? And sag they will.'

'Oh!' Deirdre jumped to her feet and moved to the edge of the deck. 'Talking about miniature clothes — look! Just look at that!'

Two thong-clad Barbies were strolling along the beach below. They moved from right to left across the field of vision of a group of men old enough and sophisticated enough to know better, but inevitably, the heads moved as one, swivelling from right to left as the Barbies sashayed past, swishing their expensive hair and swaying their plastic tushes.

'They're breaking the law of gravity! Not a sag in sight.' Deirdre turned back to Eva. 'D'you know what? I caught Rory out here one day, with a pair of binoculars trained on a girl who was sunbathing. He's as sad a bastard as any of them.'

'It's a fact of life, darling. Comfort yourself with the knowledge that the older men get, the less they can do about putting thoughts into action. But it doesn't stop them looking and wishing.'

'David does it too?'

'Well, he *looks*. He knows it's not worth risking losing what he already has at home.' Eva knocked back her wine, and set the glass on the table top. 'Let's change the subject, and let's open another bottle. I feel like getting moderately pissed, and I'm starving. Any grub?'

'Mm. Come on down to the kitchen.'

Deirdre picked up the wineglasses and led the way down a stairway to another deck fronting the kitchen. It was a big room, filled with light and furnished in an eclectic style with objects old and new, childish and grown-up. A rocking chair stood next to a stainless-steel butler's sink; a comfortable-looking sofa slumped incongruously alongside a trendy Smeg fridge; a homely brown pottery teapot squatted beside a state-of-the-art espresso machine. Toys spilled out of an antique chest, and above it a massive pinboard bristled with notices as diverse as the furniture: shooting schedules, cartoons, Post-Its, children's drawings, glossy invites, school timetables and cards advertising everything from limousine services to baby-sitters.

'What do you fancy?' Deirdre asked, uncorking another bottle. 'I do a mean cheese muffin.'

'Sounds good.' Eva stretched, yawned, and headed for the sofa, settling herself into the comfortable embrace of its big cushions. In her multicoloured harem pants, layered chiffon blouse and bare feet, she had the appearance of an exotic odalisque. 'Ooh, look. A *big* saggy bit,' she said, taking hold of a couple of inches of flab that were oozing out between the scalloped hem of her blouse and the waistband of her pants. 'I suppose I should be keeping an eye on calories and not scoffing cheese muffins. I'll be in front of a camera again next month.' An expression of distaste crossed her face. 'Yeuch. That means more visits to the stinking gym. How I *hate* that place. If I wasn't in the public eye I just wouldn't bother. I'd love to laze around and get fat.'

Deirdre threw a knob of butter into a pan, fetched cheese and spring onions from the oversized fridge, and started chopping. 'I don't. Bother with the gym, that is. I went a couple of times, and gave up when I realized that it was full of exercise-obsessive types. They all went around spying on each other to see who was looking less than one million per cent perfect, and gloating when they spotted a rare candidate. They must have got loads of mileage out of me.'

'Maybe. But did it make them happy? Goodness!' said Eva, watching as Deirdre tossed grated cheese into the pan and added a few drops of Worcestershire sauce. 'This looks like a very complicated recipe. I usually just sling a muffin with a slab of cheese on under the grill. I wasn't aware you had culinary skills, Deirdre.'

'I don't. This is about the only thing I can make. Rory does fantastic scrambled eggs and stir-fries — and barbecues, of course, because all men worth their macho stuff do barbecues. I do fantastic cheese on toast and a mean French dressing, and we manage somehow.'

'I'm steeped. David's so good in the kitchen he could go on the telly. Aphrodisiac dishes are his speciality.'

'Aphrodisiacs? Ooh. So you still have a fantastic sex life?'

Eva laughed. 'I have a sex life, but the older you get the less fantastic it is. There are other benefits, though.'

'Oh? Elaborate.' Deirdre hoped she wasn't pushing things. Eva was one of the most candid individuals she knew, but there was a limit to how much you could expect people to reveal about their private lives.

'We're more . . . comfortable with each other,' continued Eva. 'There's less pressure to go through hoops, if you know what I mean. In my prime, I would have made a fantastic porn star. Now I just go with the flow.'

'And your — er — libido is . . . ?'

'Not what it was. Women peak in their thirties, you know.'

Which is where I am now, thought Deirdre bleakly. At my sexual peak with a husband on the other side of the world surrounded by bootilicious babes.

'Oh!' said Eva suddenly. 'I've just realized something!'

'What?'

'I'm talking *girl* talk! I'm not sure I've ever talked girl talk with anyone before in my life!'

'What do you mean?'

'Well, I don't really *do* intimacy. Apart from with men. I've always got on much better with men than I have with women.'

'Why's that?'

'Women were always suspicious of me. They thought I was out to seduce their husbands. Hah! As if!'

'So how come you're suddenly doing girl talk with me? Come and get it.' Deirdre slid the cheese mixture onto the muffins, and Eva unfolded herself from her odalisque pose and joined her at the breakfast bar.

'I suppose it's because I've always liked you, Deirdre O'Dare. And you're not remotely suspicious of me because you know I'm not going to try and seduce your husband. Even though Rory *is* one of the most delectable men I know.'

Yikes! Deirdre didn't mention that *she* had once made an ill-advised attempt to seduce Eva's husband, David. But maybe that didn't count: it had been ages ago, after all, before

58

they'd even been married.

'Cheers!' Eva raised her glass and bit into her muffin. 'Mm! D'you know something? This has to be the best cheese muffin I've ever tasted! And d'you know something else? I'm having an absolutely fantastic idea.'

'You are?'

'You say you're looking for a new direction in your life, yes?'

'Well, yeah. I suppose I am.'

'And I'm looking for someone to write my biography!' Eva let fall one of her theatrical pauses. She was a past master at non-sequiturs.

'Um. Your point being?'

'You can write my biography.'

Deirdre laughed. 'Eva, I'm a screenwriter, not a biographer.'

'But you're my friend! And I can talk girl talk to you! And you know virtually all there is to know about me — hell, you were even there when my long-lost son came back into my life. And you'd never do the dirty on me.'

'Well, of course I wouldn't, Eva, but don't you see — '

'It makes *perfect* sense!'

'No, no,' said Deirdre, trying to slow things down. 'It would actually make *much* more sense for you to write your own *auto*-biography.'

Eva looked blank. 'But I'd be bored out of my mind writing an autobiography! Aside from that, I haven't time. And I'm not a writer, Deirdre. You are. You *have* to do it! If you don't do it, that poisonous hack Darina Maguire will, and you know what she'll come up with.'

'Darina Maguire? Ow! Is she threatening to do you?'

'Yes. My agent rang me last week and told me to warn all my friends not to talk to her. She hasn't tried to get in touch with *you*, has she?'

Deirdre looked sanctimonious. 'She'd know better than to do that. She tried to do a stitch-up job on me and Rory once.'

'So you know how it feels. Oh, please, Deirdre! Think about it. I'd be completely upfront with you. If I had you on my case, at least Darina Maguire might get off it and I won't go down in posterity as an airheaded diva.'

'But you're off to Ireland soon to do *Mimi's Remedies* — '

'Come with me!'

'What?'

'Come with me,' urged Eva. 'Come and spend a couple of months in Connemara, and you can pick my brains all you like. I'd be glad of the diversion — you know how tedious it gets hanging around on location. You could interview me all you like in my Winnebago between takes! Anyway, you'll need to be there for script changes and stuff, won't you, since you wrote the thing?'

'No — they do all the tweaking by ISDN and e-mail now. Eva, this is an insane idea.'

'It's not! When's Rory due back?'

'In about four weeks — '

'Perfect! He can stay here and look after the kids and you can take yourself off on a little break to Ireland and keep me company.

Everyone needs time out from family occasionally. Please come, Deirdre.'

Deirdre was trying hard not to let Eva see that she was wearing her contemplative expression. 'How — how could I leave the kids?'

'You have your treasure, Melissa. And Rory's brilliant with them.'

'Yes, but that's not what I mean. I don't know if I could *bear* to leave them for any length of time. The girls could probably just about hack the separation, but my baby boy would hate me for ever. I'm his life — he worships me as if I were a goddess, Eva. It would be the ultimate betrayal of him if I left him behind.'

'Bring him with you. I used to cart Dorcas all over the world with me when she was little. Oh — do come, Deirdre! We could have such fun!'

Deirdre bit her lip. 'I — ' she began, but never got any further because she was interrupted by the love of her life.

'Mama!'

'Baby!' Deirdre slid off her stool and moved across the room to where Bruno, sleepy-eyed and tousle-haired, was standing in the doorway, clutching the Kelly Osbourne doll that was his constant companion. She swept him up and carried him across to the breakfast bar, while Eva looked on with a soppy expression. 'Oh, baby! You smell so wonderful. Look at you, all cosy and sleepy in your pyjamas. And look — Kelly is still sleepy too. Oh, I could eat you! Give me that earlobe at once!' And as Deirdre nuzzled Bruno's ear and neck, and kissed his plump cheek and inhaled glorious essence of baby boy, she knew that nothing, *nothing* on earth, could drag her away from her two-year-old son.

The two women bent their heads over the child, and did the oohing and aahing thing for several moments — Bruno basking in the attention — until a voice from the doorway made them look up.

'I hate to interrupt this orgy of babytalk, but is there any chance that you might divert a little of your attention in this direction? I have to 'fess up to feeling a tad left out,' said Rory McDonagh.

★ ★ ★

'You can tell us our story tonight,' said Aoife, cuddling into her father. It was growing dark. The O'Dare-McDonagh family were on their deck, looking so content they might just have stepped out of the pages of some lifestyle magazine. Deirdre was lying in a hammock with Bruno sprawled on top of her, twiddling her hair around his chubby fingers and gazing into her eyes. Rory was sprawled on a wooden lounger with his two girls, Aoife and Grace, snuggled one on either side of him.

'I can tell you a story right now,' said Rory. 'A true one. Are you ready to listen?'

'Yes!'

'Yes!'

'Deirdre? You too?'

'What?' Deirdre broke off crooning at Bruno and looked up at her husband. 'Oh. Yeah, sure.'

Rory took a swig of red wine, then set down

his glass. 'Once upon a time,' he began, 'there was a princess so incredibly beautiful that millions of people all over the world were in love with her. And not only was she a princess, she was a famous film star as well. And one day a big important film director came to her and said: 'If you grant me my dearest wish, which is to make a big blockbuster movie with you as its dazzling star, you will make me the happiest man in the world.' And the princess answered: 'Will you give me millions of dollars if I agree?' And the famous director said: 'But of course.' And the princess said: 'Goodie. I'll do it, so.' For she was very greedy, and even though she already had loads and loads of money — '

'Golden coins? All in a big heap in a tower?'

'Yes. Masses and masses and masses of gold doubloons and pieces of eight. And diamonds, too. And fabulous Fabergé eggs — '

'Does she wear a tiara?'

'All the time. Even when she's on the crapper.'

This piece of information elicited squeals of glee from the girls.

'But all this money hadn't made the princess happy, and despite her beauty, her face was always cross and petulant (except when she was in front of a camera), for she was very, very spoiled, and nothing made her angrier than if she didn't get her own way. And when she didn't get her own way she was a sight to behold. She would stamp her little feet in their tiny little Jimmy Choos, and she would shake her little fists until the big jewels on her wrists and fingers made people turn away because the flashes coming from them were so blinding. And people were so scared of her that they'd do anything she told them to. Except for one person.'

'Who?'

'He was a journeyman actor, who had travelled a long way across the world to appear in the film with the beautiful actress princess. Now, this actor had worked with a lot of spoiled and beautiful actresses in his career, but he had never met an actress quite as spoiled as this one. And he was tired from having travelled halfway across the world and he didn't like the way the princess spoke to him, and he didn't like the way she kept positioning herself so that the camera favoured her in all their two-shots, and he didn't like the fact that she never bothered to turn up for her reverse angles, but made a stand-in do them instead — '

'Wouldn't the actor have preferred a stand-in if she was so horrible?' asked Aoife astutely.

'Well, yes. But there is a question of respect. By sending her stand-in, the actress was very subtly dissing the actor. So one day, when they were filming a love scene together and the actress was complaining about her make-up getting smudged, the actor told her to stick her powder puff up her arse, and he walked off the set.'

Grace and Aoife applauded this and said, 'Yes! Serves her *right*!'

'Did he really tell her to stick her powder puff up her arse?' asked Deirdre, sounding equally thrilled.

'I'm afraid he did,' said Rory. 'He was very

rude to her indeed.'

'Did he use the 'f' word?' asked Aoife.

'Yes. He was a very naughty man.'

'And what happened to the princess?'

'Oh, she lived happily ever after. Princesses always do.'

'But you said that all that money *hadn't* made her happy.'

'Ah, but these kind of princesses are actually *happiest* when they're unhappy. Their very favourite hobby of all is moaning, you see, and when they've loads to moan about they are absolutely in their element. So the actor went away and the princess stayed on the other side of the world moaning and moaning and moaning to her heart's content.'

'Um. I hate to ask, but could the princess or the production company not get revenge on the actor by suing him for breach of contract?' asked Deirdre, sounding uncharacteristically careful.

'Maybe they could,' said Rory. 'But the actor doesn't care. He doesn't give a shit.'

'Language, Dad.'

'Sorry.'

'And presumably he's forfeited his fee?' continued Deirdre.

'Yup. But he doesn't give a — doesn't care about that either. No amount of doubloons or pieces of eight could compensate for having to put up with that kind of crap from a mega-diva.' He flashed Deirdre a big smile and reached for his glass. 'Now, good little girls! Bedtime! Off you go and clean your teeth and I'll be up in ten minutes.'

'Five.'

'No. Ten. I want to finish my glass of wine and have a chat with Mummy first.'

'We hate cleaning our teeth. We wish we didn't have teeth to clean,' announced Grace.

'Well, if you don't clean them twice a day, your wish could very well come true, poppet. Scoot.'

'We're scooting. But first we have to say good night to our little brother.' The two girls went over to Bruno, made hideous faces at him, then trailed off through the sliding glass doors. Deirdre heard their reedy voices receding up the stairs.

It was getting darker, and a single star had appeared in the inky blue overhead. The only sound now was the wash of waves on the shore.

'Is he asleep yet?' asked Rory.

'Very nearly. His eyes have gone all squinty.' Deirdre sipped, then raised her wineglass to her husband. 'So, darling. When will the shit hit the fan?'

'Soon enough. I've alerted the legal team. They can handle it. I'm not going to get involved.'

'She was really that bad?'

'She really was that bad.'

'Wow. So Sophie Burke has finally cast off her diva-in-training T-shirt and morphed into a fully fledged kraken.'

'You said it.'

'Did she ask after me?'

'She said something along the lines of 'How many babies has Deirdre popped out now?' '

'She said that? 'Popped'?'

'She did. I told her that in fact you were only having babies because they are the ultimate fashion accessory, and that you were putting the noses of some of the Hollywood A list seriously out of joint. I also told her that you'd written a part for her in your latest screenplay.'

'Oh yes? And which part might that be?'

'The beautiful girl whose warts and psoriasis are finally cured by Mimi.'

Deirdre laughed, and Rory smiled back at her and stretched on his lounger. 'Stop it,' she said.

'Stop what?'

'Stretching like that. You know when you do that it always makes me want to ride the arse off you.'

'Good. I'll do it again later, after the kids are in bed.' He refilled his glass, then moved across the deck to pour for Deirdre. 'How's the divine Lavery?' he asked.

'Still divine. Thanks — that's enough. I've had too much to drink already today. She wants me to write her biography.'

'Eva does?'

'Yeah. You know Eva — she was being very persuasive. But I said no.'

'What? Why?'

'Because it would involve travelling to Ireland while she's filming *Mimi's Remedies*.'

'Couldn't you do it when she gets back?'

'No. She wants it done ASAP. Darina Maguire is snooping around, apparently, intent on doing the unauthorized version, and Eva wants someone she can trust to do the authorized.'

Rory sat back down on the lounger, looking

thoughtful. 'That's some offer. I think you should do it, Deirdre.'

'What? Even if it means going to Ireland?'

'Absolutely. You've been saying yourself that you need a change of direction.'

'But what about the kids, Rory — '

'I can handle them. Piece of piss.'

There was a beat while Deirdre considered. Then: 'No,' she said decisively. 'I can't leave Bruno. He's still too young.'

'Take him with you.'

'That's what Eva said . . . '

'And she's right. The great thing about kids that age is that they've no strings. No school, no music lessons, no ballet, no tennis, no feckin' Thai Bo to practise. He's eminently portable. And you can fit in a visit to your parents in Wicklow. Give them another photo opportunity with their only grandson. Do it, Deirdre.'

'Just like that?'

'It's the only way to do anything in life. I walked off that film set 'just like that'. Life's too short to sit still for too long, sweetheart. You know that.' The pair regarded each other levelly for a moment or two, and then Rory spoke again. 'I love you, hamster features,' he said.

'Shut up! I'm thinking.' She looked away from him and started to stroke Bruno's hair.

'What are you thinking?'

'I'm thinking — where could we stay?'

'Jethro spends a lot of time in that part of the world, doesn't he?'

'Yeah. He has a mot there, and a little girl.'

'Well, maybe he could advise you about hotels.'

'I'm not sure I'd like to stay in a hotel. Too impersonal. Maybe I could rent somewhere. Would you come and visit?'

'You know I would.' Rory leant his head back against the lounger and looked up at the sky, narrowing his eyes as if contemplating some remote heavenly body. Then he smiled. 'There's one thing I'll really, really miss,' he said, 'if you do go away.'

Deirdre raised an eyebrow. 'My dazzling repartee?'

'That too.'

They smiled at each other, then Deirdre resumed her rhythmic smoothing of Bruno's hair. The child's head began to droop, and a tiny snore escaped him. Deirdre put her lips against his perfect little ear and murmured: 'Sweet dreams, baby.' Then she turned back to her husband, resisting the impulse to scrunch up her nose. 'D'you know something, Rory?' she said. 'I think I'm scared.'

'Scared? What are you scared of?'

'I dunno. Change, I think. I'm not sure I can handle it.'

'Well, you know what Lavery always says about life-changing stuff?'

'Embrace it?'

'Embrace it.'

'Daddy!' Girlish screeches came from a window above.

'It's not ten minutes yet,' he shouted back.

'Please! There's a spider!'

69

Rory sighed and swigged back his wine. 'OK. Coming,' he called. He swung his legs off the lounger, then dropped a kiss on Deirdre's forehead, and another on Bruno's. 'What's the betting that the 'spider' has miraculously disappeared by the time I get up there?' he remarked, scooping the phone from the table and letting it fall into Deirdre's lap.

'What's that for?' she asked.

'It's for you to phone Eva,' he said.

'Oh, God. Are you sure about this?' she asked, sounding helpless.

'I'm sure,' he said. 'Just do it.'

So she did.

4

'*Oh-My-God-Yay-You-Go-Girl!*'

Cleo had just broken the news of her lottery win to the staff in the bookshop where she worked. It was ten minutes after closing time, the last customer had left, and Cleo had finally been able to open the first of the dozen bottles of champagne she'd had delivered on the QT from Oddbins earlier that day. Pop! went the champagne, and there were screams and whistles and whoops and gasps, clapping of hands and big hugs and kisses, and loads and *loads* of open mouths.

Once the fuss had died down, Cleo looked at them all with tears in her eyes and said: 'It won't change my life, you know. I'm keeping the day job.'

'That's what they all say!'

'Where are you going on holiday?'

'You'll be able to buy that shearling jacket we saw in Brown Thomas!'

'And those Patrick Cox boots!'

'And those gorgeous Gucci sunglasses!'

'And a villa in Spain!'

'Or Provence!'

'Or Tuscany!'

'To Cleo!' They raised their glasses, and there was a beat before she heard someone say:

'Just remember to leave the tiara off when you come into work, won't you?'

★ ★ ★

It was this last remark that Cleo remembered most of all in the weeks to come.

Once the champagne flutes had been returned to the off-licence and hangovers and real life had kicked back in, it seemed to her as if all her colleagues were going around with 'normal' tattooed on their foreheads, and she was going around with 'freak' tattooed on hers. Their smiles seemed contrived when they spoke to her now. She would sometimes find one of them watching her with a curled lip and a 'Why *her*?' expression.

She bought the shearling jacket, but she didn't dare wear it. People raised their eyes to heaven whenever her new top-of-the-range ultra dinky picture phone rang, so she kept it switched off. More and more often her erstwhile friends would disappear off to lunch or to the pub after work without inviting her, and any time she invited herself she felt as if she were playacting very hard indeed at being 'normal'. When she did tag along, she opted for the most pedestrian item on the lunch menu because she sensed that she'd be inviting a sarky remark if she ordered anything swanky. Feeling that it might look ostentatious if she paid for more than her fair share of rounds, she was careful not to be too generous. And then she worried about looking tight. It was unworkable.

So she rang in sick one day, and never went back. She just sent in her notice via e-mail, and wondered if any of her ex-colleagues realized how miserable they'd made her. One night one of them approached her in a pub, put on a saccharine voice, and parroted what she'd said when she'd made her announcement on the last day of work she'd actually *enjoyed*. ' 'It won't change my life, you know. I'm keeping the day job.' Hey, Cleo! What the fuck got into you? I really liked you before you became Ms Moneybags.'

And Cleo hadn't bothered saying: 'Nothing got into me. *I* didn't change. But you did.'

Thankfully, her monthly book group friends had been more supportive. Once they'd got over the shock, all of them came up with brilliant ideas on how to spend the money. The usual suspects cropped up (including the villa in Tuscany), but it was her friend Martina who steered her in the right direction. Martina was of that brilliant breed of friends you rarely see, but with whom you get straight back on track any time you meet. Cleo had known her since she was six. When she phoned one day and invited herself for supper, Cleo knew that her friend had plans for her. 'You've been faffing around for long enough,' said Martina. 'I need to get you on your own and sort you out.'

'OK,' said Cleo. 'You can be my official Life Coach. The gals in my book group have been talking so much crap. One of them even suggested that I take myself off to an *über*-posh hotel on some Caribbean island where a tribe of servants look after you and you have a butler to run your bath, and you'd have to share the

73

poolside with a load of scary designer-shades-and-Rolex-wearing types. I'd *hate* that. The only thing they all seem to agree on is the villa in Tuscany.'

'That's because everyone has their own idea of what *they'd* do with your lottery money. I've fantasized about it myself.'

'Oh? What would you do with it?'

'I'd go and live in Japan, of course.' Martina was fanatical about anything to do with Japan — had been since she was at school. She spoke the language (and, even more impressively, *wrote* it) and understood the culture, but because she was an only child, her ageing parents kept her firmly in Ireland. 'Incidentally, Cleo, this villa in Tuscany thing is shite.'

'Why?'

'I'll tell you when I see you. I'm coming round now with a bottle of wine and the *Irish Times* property section.'

★   ★   ★

Twenty minutes later Cleo was sloshing wine into glasses. 'So, coach. Tell me why the villa in Tuscany idea is shite.'

'Well,' said Martina. 'All your friends are here. Why uproot yourself and move to another country where you don't even speak the lingo? The West of Ireland's easily as beautiful as Tuscany, and way more accessible. You'd want to keep a pad here in town of course, but — '

'I *have* to get out of this kip.' Cleo looked round at the minuscule sitting room of her flat, where books were stacked on every available surface like a panorama of the Manhattan skyline. 'The landlord's putting the rent up.'

Martina raised an eyebrow. 'And you can't afford it?'

'Of course I can! But I really resent being taken for a ride by that money-grabbing bastard. I want a place of my own.'

'Agreed. And I reckon your best bet would be to buy two. One here, and one in the country. The kind of place you could go for peace and quiet, and get some writing done.'

'Writing?'

'Don't you want to? You've always gone on about how you'd love to give up the day job and go off somewhere madly romantic to write. Now you can do it.'

'But I've only ever written bad poetry.'

'And now you've all the time in the world to write *good* poetry. Or a novel as big as *War and Peace*.'

Cleo looked thoughtful. 'Maybe you're right. It is the kind of scenario that most people dream about. All I ever really dreamed about was working in a bookshop or a library, surrounded by all the books I've ever wanted to read. Now I have a chance to *write* the kind of book I've always wanted to read.' Her eyes went a bit swimmy. 'Oh, I wish my dad were here!'

'What makes you say that?'

'He wanted to write more than anything, but he never had anything published. He *loved* books!'

'So you didn't lick it off the stones?'

'I guess not. Dad encouraged me to read from as soon as I started talking. I used to trundle all round the house after him with a book in my hand ordering him to 'Read the book! Read the book!' over and over again. I'll never forget him reading that bit in *Peter Pan* out loud — you know when Peter talks about dying being an adventure? Oh, God, sorry, Martina. I'm sorry. I'm going to start blubbing.'

'That's allowed.'

Cleo went over to the cupboard where she kept her kitchen towels. She tore off a wodge and blew her nose, then: 'I wish he could see me now,' she said, 'and know I'm OK. I wish he knew that I'm living my dream come true.'

'Of course he knows. He was probably personally responsible for making those lottery numbers happen. Anyway, your dream *hasn't* come true yet. Come here, now, and let's make it a reality.' Martina reached into her satchel and pulled out a copy of the *Irish Times* property supplement. Then she spread the paper out on the coffee table and put on a spoof presenter's voice. 'Well, whaddayouknow! Lucky Ms Dowling can take her pick of any des res in the country in which to write her *magnum opus*!' she said. 'Let's find somewhere with a room with a view that you can contemplate while you wait for the muse to descend.'

Cleo looked uncertain. 'What happens if it doesn't descend?'

'Well, at least you won't be starving in a garret. What takes your fancy? An apartment or a house? A penthouse or a palace? A cottage or a castle? Look — here's a mini mansion for a piddling 3.5 million.'

'Ha! I'd feel like a complete impostor living in a joint like that.'

'And I'd feel too intimidated to visit you. The staff might look down their noses at me.'

'I will never, ever hire staff. I couldn't bear the idea of someone doing my housework for me.'

'Somehow, I think I could live with that.'

Martina turned page after page of the displays of astonishing houses. There were Georgian residences and Victorian villas and converted churches. There were luxury bungalows and designer town houses and penthouse apartments. There were farmsteads and stately homes and hunting lodges. But there was nothing that fitted the bill. Some were too big, some too remote — but most of them just weren't *her*.

On the penultimate page, a headline caught Cleo's eye. 'Oh, look! It's that development in Kilrowan. It was still under construction when I was down there last.'

'The Blackthorns.' Martina made a 'yuck' face. 'Bloody awful name.'

'Maybe, but those houses were something else, Martina. I snuck onto the building site one evening and had a gander at them.' Cleo felt a flutter of excitement. The house she'd snooped around had inspired a fantasy scenario of her standing barefoot on the deck gazing out to sea as the sun set, with a glass of chilled wine in her hand. She'd be wearing something filmy and floaty, and there'd be violin music coming from somewhere. From time to time a man would emerge onto the deck through the sliding glass doors, wrap his arms around her from behind and drop a kiss on the nape of her neck. She'd heard the murmur of his voice in her ear, but she'd never seen his face. 'C'mon, Martina,' she said now. 'Let's go on line and check it out.'

One of the first things Cleo had treated herself to after her lottery win had been a replacement computer. She'd bought a brand-new svelte, very sexy little laptop and had christened it Clarabelle. She hummed a little song of praise to Clarabelle as she set her reverently on the coffee table and waited for her to boot up, admiring the while all the things about her new toy that she loved. The musical greeting, the rainforest screensaver, the purring noises she made as her clever brain cells went to work. Clarabelle was so clever, Cleo decided as Internet Explorer hove into view, that if she ever did decide to embark on writing a novel, she could very probably sit back and watch as the computer did all the work for her. She typed in the web address.

'There! The Blackthorns!' Martina was studying the screen over Cleo's shoulder. ' 'A superior development of luxury cottage-style dwellings'. As if! There's not a lot that's cottagey about these!'

In fact the only cottagey thing about the houses was the white-washed, single-storey exterior. Once inside the virtual interior you couldn't help but be madly impressed by the modernity. The 'cottages' were the last word in luxury, with under-floor heating, double glazing, high ceilings and two storeys to the rear. The sea view was to die for.

She wanted one. Oh, how she wanted one!

'I love that pale maple flooring,' said Martina. 'Very classy.'

'All that space!' Cleo was transfixed. 'The utility room looks as if it has more square metres than this sitting room. And it's self-cleaning! Oh! I've just *got* to have number 5, the Blackthorns!' She clapped a hand over her mouth suddenly and said: 'I can't believe I just said that.'

'Said what?'

' 'Oh! I've just *got* to have number 5, the Blackthorns!' ' she repeated, in a parody of her own voice.

'Why shouldn't you say it?' said Martina matter-of-factly. 'You've got the moolah, darling, and if you really want it, you should have it.'

And have it Cleo did. She went out and bought number 5, the Blackthorns the very next day.

* * *

Margot had looked a tad put out when Cleo told her that she'd bought a house in Kilrowan and was intending to go down there to write. Cleo supposed she couldn't blame her. Kilrowan was her sister's stomping ground, after all, and Margot had been the first to hit on the idea of writing a novel. They were having lunch in a restaurant Margot frequented, the kind of place Cleo would previously never have been able to afford, where the staff called her 'Madam' and unfolded her napkin for her.

'I'll have the seared tuna, Roberto, please,' Margot said to the waiter, handing him the menu and smiling flirtatiously at him before turning back to Cleo. 'Now,' she resumed. 'I'm going to have to do some straight talking, little sister. Writing isn't as easy as you might think. And Kilrowan can get very lonely in the winter months.'

'I know. But I actually really liked it when it was a ghost town. Anyway, if I get too lonely I can always come back up to Dublin once my apartment's finished.'

'What? You're buying an apartment as *well*?'

'Well, it's not finished yet. I'm buying it from a plan. It should be ready in six months.'

Margot gave her a cynical look. 'As *if*. You know how unreliable builders are. Add another year.'

'Well, at least the place in Kilrowan is ready to move into. All I've got to do is buy the furniture. Maybe you'd help me shop for it? You've got such fantastic taste, Margot.'

'Of course I'll help you. I'd love to.'

'And once I move in, maybe you could come down and introduce me to some people.'

'Darling, I hate to tell you that there'll be *no-one* there at this time of the year. During the summer it's fantastically vibrant — you know that half the population of Dublin 4 descends on the joint. But it's stone dead right now. Even I find it hard to take sometimes when I go down there to 'hermit' and write.'

'But what about all the other writers and

artists who live there? I thought Connemara was a hotbed of artistic activity. Colleen said so in an interview recently.'

'Cleo, don't you think you're jumping the gun a bit? You can't just roll up in a place like Kilrowan, announce that you're an 'artiste' and expect the creative community to welcome you in and clasp you to their bosom.'

'I don't! Of course I don't. I just thought that you might know some local people you could introduce me to.'

'I don't really know many locals. We tend to socialize with other out-of-towners when we're down there. In fact, it's rather ironic that you've bought a house in Kilrowan. We're actually thinking of decamping, and looking for somewhere new. Somewhere the weather's more clement.'

'Oh? Where are you thinking of going?'

'Tuscany,' said Margot. 'Now. What kind of furniture are you thinking of buying?'

'Well,' said Cleo, pulling a brochure from her bag, 'I got this from the estate agent. It has pictures of the house, inside and out. Take a gander and tell me what kind of a look might sit well on it.'

If Margot hadn't just had a Botox injection that morning, her brow might have managed a small, critical frown. 'Oh. The windows at the front aren't much to write home about, are they?'

'That ties in with the 'traditional Irish cottage' idea. Looking at the place from the front you'd never guess that the back has floor-to-ceiling windows. Look. That's the view from the deck. Isn't it sensational?'

'Mm.' Margot glanced at the view without comment, then opened the brochure. 'An all-white interior? Hm. A tad last century, darling. Wouldn't you consider wallpaper? It's very much back in vogue.'

'No! I want my new living space to be radiant. The light coming in off the sea will bounce off the walls, and after spending all those years in my kip, space and light are the ultimate luxury as far as I'm concerned.'

'Space, light and *tidiness*, Cleo. Less is more. This space needs to be clean and uncluttered. Your current flat is a Zen designer's worst nightmare. What's the storage like?'

'Brilliant. I'm having huge big cupboards fitted on either side of the fireplace so that I can store all my books there. And there's floor-to-ceiling storage in the lobby upstairs, and there's a walk-in wardrobe between the master bedroom and the *en suite* bathroom.'

Margot considered. 'OK. Rigorous simplicity is what I see. That means that all your furnishings must be of an uncompromisingly high standard of craftsmanship. No excess. We'll choose a very few exquisite objects. You know the golden rule?'

Cleo shook her head.

'It's this. Have nothing in your house that you do not know to be useful, or believe to be beautiful. I know just the place to take you shopping. We'll go there after lunch. Vicarious shopping! What fun!' Margot raised her glass. 'To

82

your new domicile, little sister,' she said. 'Here's to your dream house!'

* * *

They bought a couple of enormous white couches. They bought a plain oak dining table and matching chairs with very upright backs. They bought a pair of teak deck chairs that had come from a 1920s Cunard liner and a fabulous Chinese lacquered desk for Cleo to write at. They bought a couple of big abstract canvases from a gallery owned by one of Margot's artist friends, and a sculpture that Cleo didn't understand — she just loved running her hands over it. They bought a number of elaborate candelabra. They bought an antique Indonesian wooden bowl inlaid with mother-of-pearl, they bought an antique Indonesian armoire, and they bought several antique Indonesian plinths that would display her exquisite artefacts to their best advantage.

On the day Cleo Dowling finally moved into her beautiful new excess-free house in Kilrowan there was only one form of excess she craved. Flowers.

* * *

Her first morning as a bona fide householder saw Cleo re-exploring the little village of Kilrowan. She strolled all the way to the end of the village main street and back: it took her ten minutes. In Dublin it had taken her forty minutes to walk to work.

Now, as she wandered homeward past the five pubs, the bookshop, the post office, the three hotels all closed up for the winter and the craft shop with the sign in the window that read: OPEN SATURDAY AND SUNDAY, 12.00 TO 4.00, she was aware of curious eyes on her. There'd be a lot of speculation, Cleo knew, about the blow-in from Dublin with all the disposable moolah. Locals would already know all about the Jacuzzi in her bathroom and the state-of-the-art appliances in her kitchen and the ultra-hi-tech entertainment system in her sitting room. The builder who'd put the finishing touches to her house had fired questions at her like a machine-gunner to find out what she did for a living. She'd muttered something about the book trade, and about how she'd decided to take time out to write.

'The book trade?' The builder had given her a canny look. 'There's money to be made in books, so?' Cleo had attempted an ambiguous shrug. 'And what class of a book would you be thinking about writing? One of them bestsellers? Or poetry, maybe? There do be plenty of poets and artists in this neck of the woods. Sure, the place is coming down with them, so it is. D'you know that that Colleen one lives here in Kilrowan? Mad as a snake, she is. Too much time spent on her own. You mind, now, and don't be turning into a recluse. 'Tisn't good for the head.' And he'd tapped his temple twice with a meaningful forefinger.

Now, as she passed the general store she could

see through the window a handful of people congregated round the cash desk, clearly indulging in village gossip. The store in Kilrowan was manned by a friendly couple who smiled and actually *talked* to you. They stocked the *Guardian* and *Ireland's Own*, Chablis and Sunny Delight, hot-water bottles and scented candles, home-made jam and expensive dark chocolate truffles. There was more character in the doormat of that shop than there was in all the square miles of fitted carpet in all the branches of Marks and Spencer she'd ever shopped in.

She paused by the shuttered florist's shop, and squinted in through a gap.

'She's closed for the winter,' came a voice, and she turned to see the man who owned the general store emerging from his car. He came towards her and extended a hand. 'James Shanley's the name. You're welcome to Kilrowan.'

'Oh — thank you! Cleo Dowling's my name.'

'I understand you've moved into the Blackthorns.'

'Yes, I have. I moved in just yesterday.'

'It's a grand development, that.'

'Yes. It's very comfortable.' Cleo nodded towards the flower shop. 'When will it reopen?'

'June. Maybe May, when the season begins. But if it's flowers you're after, Dannie can order you some from Galway.'

'Dannie?'

'Dannie Moore. She's the florist. I'll let her know you're interested.'

'Would you? Thanks a lot. I'll need some

85

plants too. My deck looks very bare.'

'Ah, now. There's nothing worse than a bare-looking deck. Good day to you, miss.' James Shanley winked at her, then turned and ambled across the road.

Cleo felt a rush of mortification. Get *her*! Ms Swank swans into town demanding flowers and lamenting the fact that her deck looks bare! She set off up the road imagining James Shanley going into his shop where the knot of women had been congregated and telling them that the blow-in 'writer' from Dublin's pissed off because the flower shop's shut. *Oh*!

Back home (*home*!), Cleo let herself in, smiled at the restrained splendour that lay behind her new front door, then moved to the glass doors that led onto the deck and slid them open, feeling her heart swell with happiness as she surveyed her view.

Some time soon, she thought, some time very soon — maybe tomorrow — she'd start work on her novel. She'd do a little yoga on the deck if it was warm enough, then breakfast on fresh fruit before changing into the new outfit of loose trousers and matching jellaba (she'd seen pictures of Colleen wearing something similar), lighting some scented candles and settling down to work in her study. Her study! The room with a view to die for, the room that boasted a picture window through which you could contemplate Kilrowan Bay and monitor its moods, the room where she'd set up her darling Clarabelle on the lacquered surface of her scrumptious Chinese desk.

And then, in the evening, she might wander down to one of the local pubs for a bowl of chowder or a plate of Irish stew. Would she feel self-conscious dining on her own? Possibly, the first few times. She remembered how she had spent evenings dining at 'her' table in the little restaurant after the fall-out with Toe-rag Joe, and she remembered how she'd tried to look inscrutable and a little mysterious. Now, if she made an effort to strike up conversation with other diners or with the staff, maybe soon enough she'd be treated like one of the locals. Maybe she could get introduced to some of the other writers living in the area! And she could have friends down to visit, and of course Margot. She wouldn't allow herself to get lonely and run the risk of going mad as a snake like Colleen.

On her timber deck, Cleo turned her face towards the sun, stretched, and took a deep breath. Her lungs felt blasted clean by the force of the breeze coming in from the Atlantic. In Dublin she was used to breathing traffic fumes: in Kilrowan the air was so pure and uncontaminated that gulping it made you giddy.

The wind gave her goosebumps as she looked out over her garden, scanning the expanse of lawn that sloped in a gentle gradient from the foot of the deck to a low stone wall. Beyond that was the sea. This morning its mood had been benevolent — when she'd pulled up the blind in her bedroom she'd been dazzled by the spangles of sunlight dancing on the satiny surface. But now that satin was ruffled and she had a feeling that later today it'd be torn to flitters. She'd look forward to that — watching the weather wreak havoc outdoors while she sat at her double-glazed window, her bare feet toasty from the under-floor heating . . .

A movement to her left made her turn. Some animal? But no — it was just a flurry of last autumn's leaves that had got caught up in an eddy of wind in the next-door garden. Like hers, it ran down to the sea. There was no-one to be seen in the garden, but there, on a granite bench, was a hat. It was the kind of hat Clint Eastwood might have favoured in an old Western — most certainly the type of hat that could only be worn by a maverick. It was of tan cowhide, with a strap fashioned from thickly plaited leather. It wore a rugged, battle-scarred look. It had attitude.

As she stood there, the wind that had been soughing through the line of saplings that separated the two properties gusted suddenly, and the hat was blown off the bench and onto the ground. It skidded down the lawn like a low-flying UFO before another gust snatched it and whisked it up over the sea wall.

Cleo hesitated, then moved to the far end of the deck and stepped up onto the lowest rung of the railing, craning her neck to see if there was anyone beyond the boundary to whom she could call. She tried a tentative 'Hello?' but there was no response.

Well. There was nothing else for it — she'd have to fetch the hat herself. You couldn't allow something that looked so well loved, so redolent of personal history, to end up in the drink.

Quickly she descended the steps and ran down the garden on bare feet. At the bottom, she climbed onto the sea wall and scanned the shore. The hat had ended up some yards to her left, stuck on what she took to be a blackthorn bush. Cleo retrieved it with difficulty, leaning into the bush and only just managing to snag the brim with her fingers. As she carried it back up the garden, winding the strap around her fingers, she had a surprising impulse to raise it to her face and inhale the pungent smell of worn leather.

Back inside she slid her shoes on and made for the front door, swinging the hat by its strap. But something made her stop short. Setting it down on the hall table, she veered in the direction of her bathroom and ran a brush though her hair before shaking it out. Then she grabbed an atomizer and sprayed herself with a soupçon of scent. Peering in the mirror she decided that it was about time she reapplied her lip gloss, and — hey — might as well dust on a little blush and stick blue eyedrops in her eyes to give them a sparkle. Finally Cleo shimmied back down the hall, scooped up the hat and her keys and left the house.

There was no-one in next door. She rang the bell twice and used the knocker once, but no-one answered. She stood there with the hat between her hands, feeling a bit daft, and cold now, too. She wanted to go home and light a fire and chill with a book. The wind was whipping her nicely fluffed-up hair into a straggle, and she decided she was glad the owner of the hat wasn't at home after all. She set it down on the doorstep, weighing it down with a stone so that it wouldn't blow away again, and as she did, a feather alighted at her feet. Pretty thing! she thought, picking it up and inspecting it. It was a black feather with a greeny-blue sheen, sleek and glossy — from a magpie's wing, she guessed. On an impulse, she hunkered down and slipped the feather into the leather band that encircled the crown of the hat, then she straightened up and walked back into her house.

★ ★ ★

Once she'd got over the novelty of her new home and all its perks (self-cleaning rocked!), Cleo slid into a routine. She gamely tried to do yoga first thing in the morning, but she found it bored her blue. She could never get her mind to go blank and Zen like it was meant to. She was tempted to turn the radio on, but she knew that listening to the radio would be a complete cop-out. Your mind was meant to be on higher things than the morning DJ's latest prank while you were contorting yourself into the 'Plough' position or standing on one leg with your hands above your head while practising the 'Tree' and doing your breathing. The only yoga exercise she felt was appropriate when listening to the morning DJ's drivel was the 'Lion', which involved sticking your tongue out as far as it would go. She remembered having seen something in the *Bookseller* about a book called *Yoga For People Who Can't Be Bothered To Do It*, and she resolved to check it out on Amazon.

90

But she knew that it was important to get some kind of exercise. Now that she was a writer sitting on her derrière all day long she'd turn into a complete tub of lard if she wasn't careful. Especially since she spent a lot of time reading, or watching DVDs on her plasma screen, or surfing the net looking for boring websites. Maybe she should invest in an exercise bike? But that verged on the sacrilegious when the surrounding landscape was so stunning. Walking was an option — that forty-minute walk to work in Dublin had kept her weight down very effectively — but walking on your own could get lonely. So, Cleo decided to get a dog. But before she could get round to finding a dog, a dog found her.

Her name was Fluffy. She was a local backswept-haired cur who had taken to following Cleo every time she walked down the village street. Cleo had been quite touched by this love-at-first-sight behaviour until Breda in the general store informed her that Fluffy was a tart who followed everyone. She was a stray who'd decided to leave home when her master had acquired a cat, and she now lived rough. Because she had such an engaging smile, getting fed wasn't too much of a problem for Fluffy. Indeed, people dining in the local restaurant would carry out offerings of chicken, steak and even veggie-burger for Fluffy — who would eat anything. Afterwards she'd look in through the restaurant window and say thank you with eyes that were so eloquent you couldn't but succumb to the temptation to run straight back out and give her second helpings.

And when Fluffy took to visiting Cleo, resting her chin on the step that led down to the deck and shuddering with cold like Kate Winslet in *Titanic*, imploring with her beautiful eyes to be let into the double-glazed, under-floor-heated comfort of Cleo's lovely house, Cleo couldn't resist her.

When she told Margot over the phone one evening of her decision to adopt Fluffy, Margot was horrified. 'Fluffy? Not that dreadful mongrel that skitters around the village? Honestly, Cleo! Why didn't you go for something classy like a Weimaraner or a Dalmatian or something?'

'But she's got such gorgeous eyes! Her soul shines out of them.'

'Well, her eyes must be the only gorgeous thing about her. She's one of the ugliest dogs I've ever seen.'

'She's not! She's lovely and — and long.'

'She's completely out of proportion. She's got the shortest legs of any dog I've ever seen, too. And Fluffy's a serious misnomer. Bedraggledy would be more fitting.'

'She's fluffy now! I've bathed her and combed her and she looks great.' Cleo didn't mention that she had bathed Fluffy in her state-of-the-art bathroom using outrageously expensive products because they were the only ones she had. No wonder the bitch was looking so good. Posh and Becks might have envied the miracle of grooming that was Fluffy after having been treated with Philip B's Deep Conditioning Crème Rinse and Detangling Finishing Spray.

'You *combed* her! Cleo! I don't know how you could *touch* her. You'll end up with an infestation of fleas if you're not careful.'

'Anyway, I'm keeping her.'

A sigh down the phone. 'Well. That's your lookout. What are you going to call her?'

'What do you mean?'

'Well, you can't call her Fluffy. That name is *beyond* naff.'

'What would you call her if she was yours?'

'Perish the thought! But I have always rather loved the names of Finn McCoole's wolfhounds. Bran and Sceolan.'

'But Fluff's a girl. You can't call a girl Bran! She'd hate it.'

'Oh, I dunno, then. Something classical like Leda or Rhiannon, I suppose.'

Cleo tried to picture herself saying 'Sit, Leda!' or 'Come, Rhiannon!' and imagined the reproachful look that Fluffy would bestow on her. 'No,' she said with decision. 'She's definitely Fluffy.'

'I think all that sea air's getting to you,' said Margot. 'I suppose next time I come down you'll have adopted half of those suppurating, worm-eaten, one-eyed cats that haunt the village.'

'Actually, I had a great idea for those cats. I thought I might hire a photographer to do a series called 'Pirate Cats of Kilrowan'.'

'This time you really are jesting.'

'Not at all. We could manufacture the results as postcards to put tourists off coming here. Bye, Margot! I'm off to walk the dog.'

★   ★   ★

As well as walking, working became part of Cleo's routine. Every morning she sat down at Clarabelle and tootled away. She and her book group had talked a lot about what she might write. Cleo rather fancied the idea of reworking some of the ancient Irish legends she'd read as a child, and trying to produce something along the lines of myth meets Magic Realism. One of the more earnest readers had even suggested that she write *in* Irish, but she knew there was no way her leaving-cert Irish would be up to it. (*Is maith liom caca milis* — 'I like sweet cake' — was about the only thing she remembered with any degree of accuracy.)

Margot had lent her a book she swore by in which the author recommended jotting down whatever came into your head, stream-of-consciousness style, the minute you woke up every morning. This process was known as 'The Prep Pages' — a kind of mental limbering up before you got stuck into the Novel proper. You couldn't help but register the capital letters in Margot's voice every time she spoke of the Prep Pages, which was frequently. The daily ritual had evidently become more imperative to her than her morning bowel movement. Cleo had tried doing the Prep Pages, but had produced nothing more meaningful than '*Oh God horrid dream Fluffy appeared on the plasma screen and I couldn't get her out a bit like the little blond girl in Poltergeist am dreading fresh fruit for breakfast must remember to get Coco Pops from*

94

Breda's shop for a change. Um. I want to meet the Man with the Hat I want to meet the Man with the Hat I want to meet the Man with the Hat oh I give up this is grim.'

Her attempt at her Novel wasn't much better. She'd bought a load of books on Celtic myths and spirituality and she was experimenting with some ideas, but she wasn't making much progress, and — what was worse — she really wasn't *enjoying* herself very much. She'd imagined that she might play around with a style akin to Isabel Allende's, but she just wasn't getting anywhere. In fact, she had the feeling that what she had written was pretentious crap, and she was dreading Margot descending on her and demanding to see what she'd come up with.

But she persevered, because she knew that she had to do *something*. She couldn't justify an existence just hanging with Fluffy, reading and watching DVDs until the early hours of the morning, locating boring websites and moseying down to O'Toole's every other evening. She was still often the only person in the restaurant, and she'd evolved an easy camaraderie with the staff, who had filled her in on who was Who in the village. A fair number of famous names cropped up — including, of course, Colleen's — but Cleo didn't want to ask too many questions in case she looked as if she was snoopy.

The questions she wanted answered most, of course, were about the Man with the Hat. She'd seen him occasionally — at a distance, usually, behind the wheel of the Range Rover he drove. She knew it was him, because the Hat was such a distinctive shape. Sometimes she wondered if he'd kept the feather she'd tucked into the hatband, and then she'd feel a flutter of uncertainty, because it had really been a rather presumptuous thing for her to have done. Maybe he'd have thought it was a bit — well — gay!

She'd followed his Range Rover once, in her spanking new Merc convertible, and she'd promised herself that if he stopped outside the pub she would stop too and go in for a glass of Guinness. But he didn't stop, and she didn't have the nerve to follow him any further.

And then one evening she walked into O'Toole's, and there he was, sitting in her habitual place with the Hat on the table in front of him. She stopped dead. 'Oh. It's you,' she said, before she could stop herself. 'And you kept the feather!'

'Sorry?' he said, giving her an interested smile. 'What feather?' He got to his feet and drew out a chair for her, inviting her to sit with an inclination of his head. And from that moment Cleo knew she was lost.

★   ★   ★

He was a painter, he told her, originally from the small town of Westport in County Mayo. He'd graduated from NCAD in Dublin and come back to the West to live because he hated the city. He was divorced (yay! thought Cleo), but had no children. His name was Donal MacBride, but he was known as Pablo after Pablo Picasso, a nickname that had been bestowed on him in childhood on account of his Spanish looks and his predilection for messing around with paint.

'I know your work — of course I do! I saw a reproduction in one of the Sundays. I thought it was so witty. *Still Life with Pig*!'

'Thanks. More wine?'

'Mm. I suppose we may as well order another bottle!'

A meaningful pause, then: 'Thanks again for returning my hat.'

'You're welcome. I hope you don't mind the feather? It was an impulsive thing.'

'Not at all. It gives it a cocky look.'

'Ha ha. Um. We must compare houses some time. I'd love to see what you've done with yours.'

'I didn't do anything. I'm renting it. The builder told me you'd had a Jacuzzi installed?'

'Yes.'

'Cool.'

'You'd be welcome to try it out.' Aagh!

A little more desultory chat, a few more meaningful pauses and then: 'Jeepers! I didn't realize how late it was. Time flies and all that!'

'Let me help you with your coat. Steady! Mind the step. Good night, Noel, Marie.'

'Yes! Good night, Noel and Marie.'

'It's a beautiful evening.'

'Yes. Wow — just look at those stars.'

'Stunning.'

'Yes. Well. Here we are.'

'Why not come in for a Calvados?'

'Oh! I'd love that. And — um — as I said earlier, I'd love to see your house.'

★ ★ ★

The house was gorgeous. The Calvados was delicious. And the sex should have been sensational. But it didn't happen.

5

From: Jethro Palmer
To: Dannie Moore
Subject: Accommodation
Sweet thing. Can you help? Deirdre
O'Dare, our scriptwriter, is anxious to have
accommodation in the village where she can
cozy up with her small son. I took the liberty of suggesting that she approach you
about the apartment above the shop. Once I
hear back from you, I'll pass your e-mail
address on to her. Is this cool with you? In a
few weeks' time we'll be descending on you
and destroying your peace and quiet for
much of the foreseeable future. Longing to
hear your voice, longing to see you, longing
to touch you, longing to taste you, longing
to inhale your essence. Just longing. Jethro.

From: Dannie Moore
To: Jethro Palmer
Re: Accommodation
It's cool about Deirdre. Love you. Where
will you be staying, incidentally?

From: Jethro Palmer
To: Dannie Moore
Re: Accommodation
Where the heart is?

From: Dannie Moore
To: Jethro Palmer
Re: Accommodation
☺

From: Deirdre O'Dare
To: Dannie Moore
Subject: Hello!
Hello! Jethro tells me you have an apartment that I can rent. Thank you! My boy is just two — a cross between a monkey and a cherub, with edible knees. Do you know anyone who would be interested in a part-time child-minding job while I'm over there? Best wishes, Deirdre.

From: Dannie Moore
To: Deirdre O'Dare
Re: Hello!
No problem. I know at least half a dozen mother hens whose chicks (or cherubs) have flown the nest, and who would adore to look after your babby. Will you need a cot, intercom, high chair? I can let you have all of Paloma's old stuff. Cheers.

From: Deirdre O'Dare
To: Dannie Moore
Re: Hello!
Yes please! Jethro told me I'd like you the minute I met you. I like you already!

From: Cleo Dowling
To: Dannie Moore
Subject: Flowers
Dear Ms Moore,
I know your shop is closed for the winter, but I understand that you operate a local flower delivery service. Would you be interested in taking me on as a new client? I have recently moved into number 5, the Blackthorns, and my number here is 49716. I look forward to hearing from you. Yours sincerely, Cleo Dowling

Dannie made a note of the name and the number and closed down her Outlook Express.

Everyone in the village knew about the wealthy writer who had moved into number 5, the Blackthorns, but nobody had an inkling as to where her money came from. Dannie had spotted her a few times sitting on her own in the restaurant attached to the local pub, and had thought she looked lonely. A lot of the writers and artists who 'escaped' to Connemara couldn't hack the solitude and ended up fleeing, screaming, back to city life. Others ended up going slowly stir crazy. The only person who seemed to have got a handle on rural living was Pablo, the painter.

Dannie reached for the phone and punched in Cleo Dowling's number.

The ringing tone barely registered before the phone was picked up. 'Hello?!' came a voice, breathy with anticipation. Mm-hm, thought Dannie. Ms Dowling is either hoping the caller is somebody she really, really wants to hear from, or else she's simply desperate to hear the sound of another human voice.

'Ms Dowling? It's Dannie Moore here.'

'Dannie Moore?'

'Yes. You sent me an e-mail today, about supplying you with flowers?'

'Oh, yes! Thanks for getting back to me. Um. Well, are you interested?'

'Surely. I deliver customized arrangements on a weekly basis to a regular clientele. I'd be happy to include you.' Dannie chose the word 'clientele' in preference to the more accurate 'client'. She had a reputation to think of. 'What kind of look are you after?'

'I don't really know. I don't know much about flowers.'

'I'll tell you what. Why don't I come down to you there in the Blackthorns and have a look? Check out your décor? Then I'd have a better idea of the kind of thing that might suit you.'

'Oh. OK. That sounds like a good idea.'

'When's a good time?'

'This afternoon?'

'That's not great for me. I have a delivery to make.' She had to deliver Paloma to Grandpa's. He had promised to teach her how to scoop an egg up from under a hen. 'How are you fixed right now?'

'Right now is fine.'

'I'll be there in ten minutes, so.'

* * *

102

How Cleo would have loved to have been able to say: 'Right now isn't great for me, actually. I'm at a critical moment in the narrative flow of the novel I'm writing.' But it would have been a lie because there were *no* critical moments in the novel she was writing. It was just a big, flabby mess. In fact, she was delighted to have this excuse to shut down Clarabelle and talk to a human being instead. She hadn't had a decent chat to one for ages — not since the night in the restaurant with Pablo.

How gentlemanly it had been of him not to have made a move on her! He fancied her, she knew it, because the sexual tension between them had positively *shimmered*, but after the Calvados he'd looked at his watch and told her that he had an early flight to catch in the morning, to London on a business trip: some gallery there was interested in showing him. Cleo had taken her cue and said good night — he'd offered to escort her the few metres that divided their front doors! — and he'd kissed her on the cheek and told her that he'd be in touch again on his return in a week's time.

That had been precisely a week ago, which was why Cleo had leapt for the phone when Dannie had rung earlier. The next time the phone rang, she told herself, she must *not* answer with such flagrantly uncool haste.

Dannie sounded nice, she thought now as she headed towards the kitchen to put the kettle on. Maybe she should suggest meeting up for a drink later, or ask her to join her for supper in O'Toole's? Now that she'd escaped to her pastoral idyll, Cleo had to confess to feeling a bit lonely. If her writing had gone in the direction she'd wanted it to she knew she wouldn't have minded the loneliness so much. But she was beginning to suspect that writing a novel wasn't going to come as naturally to her as she hoped. It was one thing to love reading books, another thing entirely to try and *write* one.

She clicked the on switch on the kettle and wandered back into her living room, realizing suddenly that it wasn't looking as pristine as usual. Her rules about keeping all her clutter stowed away had relaxed a little since she'd moved in: there were CDs and magazines and mail — mostly junk — strewn all over the place, and she'd left last night's dishes on the coffee table. She'd stayed up late drinking some very nice Bordeaux, and had ended up dancing around the house admiring it all over again to the accompaniment of the White Stripes.

Cleo slung the CDs into the cabinet without bothering to insert them in the rack alphabetically as per her new rules. She could do that later — there wasn't time now. Dishes and the empty wine bottle were disappeared into the kitchen, scented candles were lit, and a J-cloth and Mr Sheen located just as the doorbell sounded. Abandoning Mr Sheen and covering the wineglass ring marks with a magazine, Cleo went to the door and opened it to a woman who was wearing jeans, a puffa jacket and Caterpillar boots, and who bore more than a passing resemblance to Juliette Binoche.

'Hi. I'm Dannie Moore,' said the woman,

holding out her hand.

'Cleo Dowling,' said Cleo. 'Nice to meet you. Come in.'

Dannie passed through the front door and Cleo shut it behind her.

'Nice place,' remarked Dannie. 'Very nice place.'

'Thanks. Take a seat and I'll be right back with coffee — I've just put the kettle on. Or would you prefer tea? Excuse the mess.'

'This isn't what I'd call mess. Anyway, I'm used to it. I have a four-year-old daughter to tidy up after. Coffee'd be lovely, thanks.'

In the kitchen, Cleo fiddled around with her grinder and her cafetière and her milk jug, thinking back fondly to the days when coffee-making had been simply a matter of slinging instant into a mug. When she re-emerged into the sitting room with a laden tray, Dannie Moore was wandering around, casing the joint and jotting down notes in her Filofax.

'I hope you don't mind?' she said. 'I'm not being nosy — I just want to get a feel of the place, d'you know what I mean? If I'm going to be doing your flowers on a regular basis, I want to make sure they're right for you. Have you any preferences?'

'Really, no, I haven't. Why don't you just surprise me?'

'OK. But you must be honest, now, and let me know if there's anything you're not happy with. What's that lovely smell?'

'It's a Jo Malone scented candle.'

Dannie sniffed the air again. 'Tiger Lily?'

'Yes. Well spotted!'

'That gives me something else to go on.' She scribbled in her Filofax again, then indicated the expanse of sliding glass that led out onto Cleo's deck. 'You'll be needing pots out here. Lots of them.'

'What do you recommend?'

'Well, you'll want something hardy. When the wind blows from the west the plants'll take a hell of a lashing. Next time I'm going into the garden centre in Galway I'll let you know. You could come in with me.'

'That's very kind of you.'

'Arra, not a bother.'

'Milk? Sugar?'

'Both, please. One spoon. You've a dog, I see?' Dannie had been about to sit down on the chewy rubber bone that Fluffy had left on the couch.

'Yes. I adopted her. She was living rough in the village. Sometimes I think she likes to revisit her old haunts. I haven't seen her for a couple of days.'

'It's Fluffy you're talking about, so?'

'Yes.'

'I know her well. She conned me into giving her the remains of a pheasant once, stayed the night and then abandoned me when she realized she wasn't going to get a roast dinner every day.'

'I'm feeding her that posh Cesar stuff.'

'Oh, she'll like that. She'll hang around you for a while, I've no doubt. She knows which side her bread is buttered on.'

Cleo poured coffee into her hand-painted

cups, feeling like a bad actor in an advertisement. Doing this kind of thing was a doddle for someone like Margot, who was famous for her charity fund-raising, quasi-ironic coffee mornings, but Cleo had a suspicion that playing the gracious hostess was a talent you either had or hadn't. A bit like novel writing. 'Biscuit?'

'Thanks.' Dannie took a shortbread finger from the proffered plate. 'I hear tell you're a writer?'

Oh, God! Now she felt even more of an impostor! 'Well . . . I'm trying. I'm working on a novel, but it's not easy.'

'Have you had much published?'

Cleo was about to give a derisive snort and say 'I *wish*!', but something made her change her mind. She had to have a *degree* of credibility — she didn't want the entire village thinking she was some wanky wealthy dilettante who fancied herself as an *artiste*. 'Well, yes, actually. Some poetry.'

'Wow. *Poetry*? I'm impressed.'

'Nothing very significant,' Cleo added hastily.

'Still. To be a published poet's no mean achievement. What made you decide to get into writing?'

'A love of reading. I'm a complete bibliomaniac.'

'Bibliomaniac? What's that?'

'Someone who's mad about books. I have been ever since I learned my ABC. I used to work in the book trade. That was just brilliant because I'd get loads of free titles.'

'How many would you read in a week?'

107

'Three, easily. I spend a fortune in the bookshop. If there'd been no bookshop in Kilrowan I would never even have considered moving here. I *love* that little shop. I'd buy it if I could.'

'I used to do a lot of reading, too, before Paloma was born. I don't seem to be able to find the time now, though. I bought Colleen's book there recently, but I'm finding it very tough going. I'd love something light that I could just skim through of an evening.'

'Hang on — I can lend you something ideal.' Cleo moved to one of the cupboards that housed her books, and pulled open the door. 'You'll get through this in no time at all. Let's see — P, P, P . . .'

'Janey. You've masses of books. Are they all in alphabetical order?'

'Yeah. I'm not a neat freak by nature, except when it comes to books. The first thing I asked the builders to do was to fit all these shelves, and the first thing I did when I moved in was to arrange my books alphabetically. I could lay my hands on any title within seconds. But . . . ' — Cleo ran her fingers along all the spines in the P section — 'sorry. You're out of luck. I must have lent it to someone else. Bugger. I hate it when I lend books to people and they don't return them. But you should be able to find it in the local shop, or on Amazon. Here, let me write the name down for you.'

Cleo tore a section off one of her junk mails. '*Venus in Versace* by Pixie Pirelli,' she wrote, then added the name of the publishing house and handed it to Dannie. 'Oh, and I'll tell you who else you might like. Lily Wright — she wrote a book called — '

'*Mimi's Remedies*!' said Dannie. 'Oh — I loved that. What did you think of it? I know it wasn't high art or anything, but it made me weep buckets.'

'Me too.' Cleo was delighted to have found someone that she didn't have to *pretend* with. She'd never have been able to confess to Margot that she'd enjoyed something as commercial as *Mimi's Remedies*.

'You know they're making a film of it?' said Dannie, tucking the note into her Filofax.

'*Mimi's Remedies*?'

'The very same. And they're making it here,' she added, with a kind of partisan panache.

'In Ireland?'

'Yes. Right here, in Kilrowan. Jethro Palmer, the director, decided it was an ideal location.'

'Jethro *Palmer*? He's coming to Kilrowan?'

'Yeah. And he's bringing a load of shit-hot stars with him. It's going to be a pretty stellar project.'

'Who's involved?'

'Eva Lavery is starring as Mimi. And Ben Tarrant's in it, and Colin Farrell.'

'Blimey! A major movie, being filmed here! I knew this village had its share of celebrity residents, but I never imagined there'd be an influx of film stars to contend with as well.'

'You can be in it too, if you like.'

'What? What do you mean?'

'Jethro's going to need loads of extras. The

109

whole village will have walk-on parts. Paloma says she'll have nothing to do with it unless she gets to wear a gorgeous gúna.'

'Paloma?'

'My daughter. And Jethro's.'

'Sorry. You mean Jethro Palmer?'

'Yes. He's Paloma's father. Mostly absentee, so it'll be grand having him around for a few months.'

Cleo was completely taken aback. She was dying to ask questions, but didn't know how to without looking as if she was a nosy parker. As she was casting around for a conversation opener, Dannie's phone rang. 'Excuse me,' she said, picking up. Then: 'Pablo, hi!' Cleo's ears flattened against her skull like a cat that has just been surprised by sudden birdsong. 'Oh, what a shame! No, that's fine. I'm sure I can rope somebody else in. Sean Caffrey's desperate to talk about fly-fishing. No worries. See you around.'

Dannie put her phone back in her pocket, then gave Cleo a look of consideration. 'That was Pablo MacBride — he's your next-door neighbour. He's had to cancel a talk he was due to give to our local women's group on painting. I wonder — would you be interested in giving a talk on your poetry?'

'*No!* I mean, no — I'd be crap at public speaking.'

'Ah, now, this'd hardly be classed as public. There are only about a dozen of us, and it's very casual. Every week we have a different activity, or a guest speaker comes, and we've yoga every week before the main event.'

'Yoga? I'd be into that. I tried doing it by myself, but it just felt stupid.'

'You should come, so.'

'Do we have to say 'Om'? I'd feel a bit stupid doing that, too.'

'Oms are optional.'

'Then I'd love to come. But I'll have to pass on the poetry thing, I'm afraid.'

'Shame. Maybe Colleen will oblige again now she's a new book out. Except I don't know anyone who's read the whole of it. That might pose problems when she asks for questions from the floor.' Dannie gave an incredulous smile. 'Jaysus — she must be coining it in. That *Faraway*'s been in the bestseller list for ages now. She'll be able to buy that island soon.'

'She's buying an island?'

'Yeah, she's been giving interviews about how she wants to buy an island in Clew Bay and retire there to live with her lov*air*. Ha! I'm not sure how Pablo would feel about that. He's much too sociable to be a recluse.'

'Pablo? You mean Pablo and Colleen are an item?'

'Yeah.'

'Oh.' Cleo couldn't keep the disappointment out of her voice.

Dannie slanted her an astute look. 'You've met him?'

'Yes, I — em — got talking to him in O'Toole's one night.' She knew she was blushing and suddenly anticipated with a flash of foresight the next words she was going to hear. *Steer clear of him, if you've any sense. He's a fierce womanizer . . .*

She was only half wrong. 'Steer clear of him, if you've any sense,' said Dannie. 'Colleen will go ballistic if she gets wind of any cosy tête-à-têtes going on.'

Cleo's face flamed even more. 'It was only a chat,' she said. 'I mean, there was nothing — '

But Dannie just shook her head. 'It doesn't matter how innocent it was,' she said. 'Colleen doesn't even *consider* the possibility of there being such a thing as a platonic relationship between a man and a woman. And because Pablo's such a ride she's convinced that every woman in the village fancies him. Fact of the matter is they do, but nobody would *dream* of coming on to him and running the risk of having Colleen descend in avenging harpy mode. You should have seen the treatment she meted out to a poor unfortunate German tourist who chatted him up in the pub one night last summer.'

Cleo tried not to gulp. 'What happened?'

'She narrowly avoided getting charged with GBH. She's a great one for the theatrics, is Colleen.'

'Someone told me she was doolally.'

Dannie shrugged. 'Only half doolally. She's a shrewd business head. She's big into investments.'

Cleo was surprised. She had always considered Colleen to be one of those wild bohemian types who eschewed materialism. 'Stocks and shares type stuff?' she asked.

'Mainly property. She owns two of the houses

112

in this development.'

'The Blackthorns?'

'Yep. She bought them from plan. She knew they'd bring in a huge income in holiday lets. She's renting one to Pablo.'

'So he's only here on holiday?'

'He came on holiday initially, but when he saw the light that comes in off the sea, he decided to stay. He says if you could bottle light like that you could make a fortune. And isn't he right? Look at that.' Dannie nodded in the direction of the picture window. The light bouncing off the sea made it look diamantine.

'Yes,' agreed Cleo. 'It's beautiful.'

'Just perfect for an artist.' Dannie looked at her watch. 'Janey mackers, is that the time?' she said, jumping up. 'I'd better head.'

Cleo got to her feet. 'What about money, Dannie — for the flowers? We haven't discussed that yet.'

'I'll do a costing and get back to you. Sure, won't I see you on Wednesday at the women's group? It's in the village hall. Yoga starts at seven o'clock, by the way. Bring a mat.'

'Fine.'

Cleo led the way to the front door and let Dannie out. As she turned back into her hall she resisted the temptation to open her mouth and scream like the loony in the Munch painting. Why hadn't Pablo *told* her that he was involved with someone? Why hadn't he warned her off instead of inviting her in for Calvados? He'd allowed her to make a complete arse of herself! Oh! She remembered how she'd flirted with him

— how she'd mistaken all those 'meaningful' pauses as clear indication of their sexual chemistry! She blushed now as she thought of the oblique looks she'd given him, and the smiles, and how she'd 'accidentally' brushed her arm against his as he'd helped her on with her coat in the pub, and how she'd released her piled-up hair from its comb at one stage and actually shaken it out! Oh God! But — oh, *God*! He was just so *beautiful* . . .

Stop it! Stop thinking about him, she told herself crossly. Get him out of your system at once, you silly girl, and just remember that infatuation's for tweenies, not twenty-somethings. Full of confusion, she went downstairs and dithered over the tray of coffee cups. But she couldn't concentrate on the mundane task of clearing up. Something strange was going on in her head. And then Cleo put the tray down with sudden decision, went into her study, booted up Clarabelle and opened a new file.

'Save as' the computer prompted her. Cleo thought for a minute, then: 'The Man in the Hat,' she typed. 'A short story by Cleo Dowling.'

★　★　★

As Dannie turned into the laneway that led to her house she heard someone call her name. There, parked across the road, was a nifty Alfa Romeo convertible, and inside the convertible was Oliver Dunne. He opened the car door and swung his long legs out. He'd always reminded

114

her of an aristocratic gypsy, but today the toff in him was uppermost. He was dressed in a killer suit — the sophistication of which was compromised by the fact that the tie around his neck had been pulled loose from the collar of his shirt — and his shoes were, without a doubt, hand-made. When he reached her, he bent his head and kissed her on the cheek.

'Dannie Moore. Beautiful as ever!'

'You always knew the right thing to say, Oliver, you chancer. And you look *fantastic*. What's with the posh threads?'

'I've been trying to impress the bank manager.'

She smiled up at him. 'I'd say you succeeded.' There was a pause as the unspoken thing happened between them, and then she added gently: 'Hello you. How long's it been? A year?'

'One year and four days.'

She laughed. 'Well, God bless your memory!'

'You may recall that the last time I saw you was a pretty memorable occasion, Daniella Moore. It's not every day a guy gets jilted.' He put his head on one side and narrowed his eyes at her. 'Have you still got the book of poetry I gave you?'

'Yes.'

'You remember what's inscribed on the flyleaf?'

' 'If you ever change your mind,' ' said Dannie.

'And have you?'

'Changed my mind?'

'Yes.'

115

She slanted him a rueful smile. 'No.'

'Well, damn your eyes, you gorgeous woman,' he said, taking both her hands in one of his and tracing a pattern on the palm with his index finger. 'You gorgeous, *gorgeous* woman.'

'Stop it, Oliver.'

'Why?'

'You know why. If you carry on flirting with me I'll find it hard to resist you.'

'Don't resist me, then.'

'I have to. Jethro's due in town soon.'

'Well, damn his eyes, too,' he said, with feeling.

They looked at each other, rather enjoying the moment, and then Dannie disengaged her hands from his and the moment was over.

'I hear you've bought the old Glebe House?' she said, stuffing her hands firmly in her pockets.

'That's right. I'm converting it into a country house hotel.'

'You and Alice?'

'Yes. We're aiming to make it into *The Blue Book*, and only family-run concerns are eligible.'

'How is Alice?' She didn't need to ask the question. She'd seen Oliver's sister earlier that morning in Breda's shop and had almost flinched at her politician's smile and her solicitous enquiries about her and Paloma's health. Dannie had never liked Alice. There was something — something *bogus* about her: she was quite the opposite to the engaging and expansive Oliver. She was one of those people who tried too hard to be liked, and Dannie felt guilty about not liking her, because Alice had never done anything to her to be deserving of such antipathy.

'Alice is as efficient as ever. She's up at the Glebe House now, giving the builders a hard time.'

'How long have you been back?'

'I got back last week. I would have flown over earlier, but I had to finalize the sale of the business in London. Alice has been hands on at this end.'

'So when'll the joint be ready?'

'All the major construction work's done. We just have to fit out the interior.'

'Lucky you. That's the fun bit. And where might you be living until you can move in?'

'I'm staying with Alice. She's living in the gate lodge. Tell Paloma there'll be frogs in the pond in the garden soon. She's welcome to come and see them any time. How *is* that poppet?'

'She's grand. She's turned into a real easygoing kid — not a bother on her.'

'Does she fancy a week in Disneyland, Paris? I know of some fantastic deals going.'

'I'm sure she'd love that, Oliver, thanks. But not until after her da's gone back to LA.'

'There's truth in the rumour, then?'

'What rumour?'

'That the same Mr Palmer is making a movie here in Kilrowan?'

'That's right. It'll be all go soon.' Dannie looked at her watch. 'And talking of all go, *I'd* better go. It's grand to see you again.'

He raised an eyebrow. 'Just grand?'

Laughing, she stood on tiptoe and kissed his

117

cheek. 'It's *lovely* to see you again,' she amended. Then she turned on her heel and put distance between them. She didn't even pause to wave at the door of her cottage. She shut it firmly behind her and busied herself with preparing a pasta sauce for supper.

But even keeping busy couldn't stop her thinking about Oliver. The last time they'd met had, as he'd said, been a memorable occasion. He'd had some business in the North of Ireland just over a year ago, and he'd invited her to join him for a weekend in the Culloden Hotel in Co. Down . . .

★ ★ ★

She'd just paid off the taxi, and was following the porter into the baronial splendour of the hotel lobby when she saw him. Oliver was lounging in an armchair, long legs stretched out in front of him, perusing a copy of the *Financial Times*. He was wearing a cashmere suit and what Dannie could swear was a Charvet shirt. His hair was beautifully cut; his shoes were highly polished. Women passing slid sideways looks at him, and she knew he could be hers if she wanted.

She approached, and stood waiting for him to register her presence. When he did, he let the paper fall and sat there regarding her for several moments with his head tilted on one side and a speculative expression on his face. Then he got unhurriedly to his feet, took her in his arms and kissed her first on her left cheek, then her right.

She heard his breath in her ear. 'You look so fucking beautiful,' he said. 'Are you sure you won't change your mind about single rooms?'

She took a step back and smiled. 'Single rooms is the only reason I said yes to your invite, you chancer.'

'And single rooms or not, I'm delighted you *did* say yes.'

'You always could charm for Ireland. And look at you! You look like a real *flâneur*, Oliver.'

'A *flâneur*?'

'It's a French word. Means — um — 'a fella who dresses real well'. There's never a trace of Connemara bog on *those* shoes. Hand-made?'

'In Jermyn Street.'

'And it's far from feckin' Jermyn Street *you* were reared. You're even after losing your bogtrotter's brogue.'

'And yours, I'm glad to say, Daniella Moore, is more pronounced than ever.' He raised a hand at a passing flunkey. 'Would ye ever bring us a couple of aul pints o' the black stuff, there, lad?' he said. 'Or is it champagne you're after, Dannie me bright-eyed colleen?'

Dannie laughed. 'I would *murther* a pint,' she said.

'Two pints, so.' Oliver indicated a couch, and waited until Dannie had made herself comfortable before he sat down beside her.

'How was your journey?' he asked.

'Not bad. I broke it in Dublin and stayed overnight with an old friend.'

He was assessing her openly — looking as though he was deriving *pleasure* from studying her — and she felt uncertain. It had seemed like such a mad, spontaneous thing to do when she'd had the invitation out of the blue from Oliver to join him here in County Down. She'd protested down the phone and told him to 'get away out of that!', but he'd persisted and persisted and in the end his charm offensive had worked. The one stipulation Dannie had made was that they have separate bedrooms. She hadn't slept with Oliver since her student days, and she wasn't about to embark on a fling with him now just for old times' sake.

'D'you know something?' he said. 'You're sexier than ever, Daniella Moore. When was the last time we saw each other?'

'Kilrowan. When you took me out to dinner to console me after that fecker Jethro forgot Paloma's birthday.'

'Oh. Did he make — ?'

'Let's not talk about the war.' Dannie turned her head to study her surroundings, hoping to change the subject. When she turned back, Oliver was looking at her mouth. She smiled at him.

'Sir. Madam.' The flunkey set two pints of Guinness down on the table, and Oliver signed for them. Then he raised his glass to her and said: 'To terrific memories.'

'To *really* terrific memories,' said Dannie. 'And single rooms,' she added, with meaning.

Oliver laughed, and took a swig of his pint. 'How's business?' he asked.

'Not bad. We did great during the summer. But I've decided to close in the winter months.

There's no money to be made, and it means I can be around more for the wean. She still wears the fairy princess frock you bought her, by the way.'

'I can just picture her. And how's your da?'

'Grand. Older. I felt guilty landing him with Paloma for the weekend — didn't think he'd be able for it — but he insisted. He's besotted with her. Thanks for sending him all those e-mails, by the way. He loves to hear from you, and you're very good to do it.'

'It's a reciprocal thing. I enjoy hearing from him. I've always had great respect for your da.'

'And isn't he mad about you? He says if Jethro isn't going to make a decent woman of me, you should.'

Oh! She shouldn't have said that! Change the subject, quick!

'This joint's class, isn't it?' she remarked, setting down her glass and looking around. The hotel lobby was opulent, with antique furniture and ornate plasterwork and plush carpets. Swags of heavy drapes hung round archways and window frames, chandeliers gleamed overhead, and a real fire was crackling away in a grand fireplace. Dannie stretched and squirmed a little on the seductively comfortable couch, then sighed a great big sigh of pleasure. 'Jayz, this is the life! If I were at home now I'd be running around after Paloma, or doing the laundry or the housework, or cooking for the freezer. I'm really glad you asked me here, Oliver.'

'And I'm really glad you came,' he said. 'What did you do with your bags, incidentally?'

'The porter's taken them up.'

'So you haven't seen your room yet?'

'No.'

'You've a treat in store, so.' He stood up and extended a hand to her.

'What do you mean?' she asked, allowing him to pull her to her feet.

'You're in the posh part of the hotel.'

'And you're?'

'In a standard room in the new wing.'

'Oh, Oliver! You shouldn't be giving me preferential treatment.'

'It's all in the name of research. I want to see how the two experiences compare. I'm a very hands-on travel agent.'

'Of course. I'd forgotten you were here on business.'

He led the way upstairs, then handed her a key card. 'In you go,' he said, 'and freshen up. I'll wait for you downstairs.' He watched as she swiped the card, and then he turned and left her standing on the threshold of her bedroom.

Bedroom! That was way too pedestrian a word for the suite she found herself in. It was spacious, bay-windowed and sumptuously furnished. A bed the size of a small stage was heaped with pillows, a mass of red roses had been arranged on a side table by a big, cushiony couch, and a mahogany dining table took pride of place in the centre of the floor. On the table was a cut-glass decanter of sherry with two crystal glasses, a bowl of fruit, a plate of hand-made chocolates. A dressing room with an elegant vanity unit and film-star mirrors led through to a perfectly appointed bathroom with white marble floors and walls.

Dannie wandered through the suite, opening cupboards and drawers and examining freebies. Goodie! A dotey little bag of Neutrogena products was hers for the taking, as well as the ubiquitous mending kit, notepad and shoe-cleaning sponge. Entertainment on offer included a discreet sound system, a state-of-the-art telly tucked away in an antique armoire, a selection of glossy mags — and there was a glorious view of Belfast Lough beyond the big bay windows. Finally, she picked up the *faux*-leather folder that advertised the hotel's extensive services. Tucked into a pocket in the back was a menu for in-room dining. Prawns, salmon, pâté, tournedos. Yum. Tiramisu, *mille-feuille sablé*, white chocolate tart. Even yummier. And the wine list? The wine list included Sauternes Baron Philippe, a *grand cru* Château Margaux, and Dom Perignon. 'An exceptional vintage,' she read. 'The finest champagne in the world . . . '

And Dannie tried to block out the little voice that crept into her head and told her she was a complete feckin' eejit for having stipulated single rooms when Oliver had made that phone call to her last week. After all, she had few opportunities for romance in her life, and this hotel suite was about as romantic as it got. The idea of having dinner in her room with Oliver and then making love in the oversized bed was seductive in the extreme.

It was then that she'd noticed the anthology of

love poetry on the table. She picked it up and opened it at the title page. There, in Oliver's handwriting, were inscribed the words: *If you ever change your mind . . .*

Her phone rang.

'Hey, Dannie! Darling love, where are you? I just spoke to Paloma on the phone and she says you've gone to stay with a friend in Dublin?'

'Jethro!' The sound of his voice in her ear made her feel as helpless as the heroine of a silent movie. 'Oh, Jethro, hi! Yes — I'm staying with Rosa and Michael. I decided to do a cultural weekend in the big smoke.'

Oh God. She hated the way lying made her feel.

'When are you heading back to Kilrowan?'

'Day after tomorrow.'

'Good. I'll see you then.'

'What? You're flying over?'

'Yeah. I need an injection of family life. Hearing Paloma's voice on the phone turned me into mush.'

'How long can you manage?'

'A couple of days.'

'Excellent! You're doing *all* the cooking.'

'Give me an apron and I'll do all the cleaning too.'

She laughed. 'No. I don't want you wasting energy on housework. I've other plans for you, lover.'

'Hurry home, then. See you Monday.'

'I can't wait. Love you!'

'I love you too.'

Dannie pressed 'end call' with a smile, and

stuffed her phone back in her bag. She looked around at the luxurious hotel room — at the bed with its inviting goosedown pillows, at the roses that Oliver had spent a *lot* of money on, at the decanter and glasses . . .

And she knew she'd be sleeping there on her own that night.

★　★　★

Dannie finally forced herself to stop thinking about Oliver. She put the finishing touches to the pasta sauce and sat down at her desk to think instead about what flowers to order for her new client, Cleo in the Blackthorns. Taking her Filofax out of her bag, she leafed through to the page where she'd jotted down her ideas, then came across the torn sheet of paper with the name of the book Cleo had recommended scribbled on it. She unfolded it, and was just about to put it aside when some words in bold block capitals caught her eye. **BARD OF ACCLAIM** she read. **A SPECIAL INVITATION TO A TALENTED FEW.**

What? Dannie couldn't help herself. She read on.

Dear Cleo,
We are sorry that you could not attend our last Lyceum. You may like to know that the award for next year's winning poem will be increased to $125,000, and as an International Bard of Acclaim, you are in with a real chance of winning this munificent prize.

The award ceremony will again take place in Boston, which, as you know, is the Cultural Capital of the United States of America, and after our inaugural ceremo —

Here the text broke off where Cleo had torn the paper horizontally across.

Dannie was not normally a nosy individual, nor was she in the habit of reading other people's personal stuff — but this was amazing! Why had Cleo been so self-deprecating about her poetry when she was actually an International Bard of Acclaim?

She didn't think twice before reaching for the phone.

'It's Dannie,' she said when Cleo picked up. 'Listen — you know the piece of paper that you wrote the name of that novel on? Well, I'm sorry if you think I'm a nosy bitch for reading it, but you can't be using important letters like that for scrap paper, darlin'.'

'Oh? I thought it was junk mail.'

'It's your invitation to a poets' award ceremony in Boston, Cleo.'

There was a long silence down the line before Cleo finally spoke: 'Oh. That's nothing,' she said.

'*Nothing*? Being up for a $125,000 award is *nothing*?'

'Well — oh, sorry! There's my mobile going off,' she said in a rush. 'Thanks very much for your concern, Dannie. You're very kind to have rung.'

'You're welcome, Cleo. See you soon.'

In number 5, the Blackthorns, Cleo put the phone down, then put her head in her hands. Oh, no! Soon it would be all over the village that she was an International Bard of Acclaim who was up for a major award! Should she phone Dannie back immediately and explain? But explain *what* exactly? The fact of the matter was that it was there in black and white — and the more she tried to deny it, the more convinced Dannie was likely to be that she was protesting too much. It would be better to say nothing at all.

Why hadn't she trashed the bloody letter the moment it arrived? Those feckin' Be A Bard people were nothing if not persistent. The Special Invitation to a Talented Few had been forwarded from her old Dublin address. Pah! A talented few thousand, more like.

She had been bombarded with e-mails and letters by the Be A Bard crowd. There had been requests for the necessary funds to cover costs incurred. Costs? Yes, indeed! The cost of hiring a professional musician to compose the music that would accompany her lyrics, and the cost of a singer to sing her poem at the Lyceum (she was assured that the singer's 'haunting, mellifluous voice' would give her 'wonderful' poem 'Murmurs of a Landscape' 'enhanced poignancy'. Arse. Comp*lete* arse. She wished more than ever that she'd ignored the pop-up bloody Be A Bard.com had blinged onto her computer screen all those months ago, urging her to enter their poxy competition.

The sound of the doorbell distracted her from her unmellifluous musings. The postman, most likely. She'd ordered a load of books from Amazon.com. Cleo pressed 'save' on Clarabelle, scampered to the front door and swung it open.

There, on the doorstep, stood Pablo, hat in one hand, bottle of wine in the other.

'Hi,' he said, holding out the bottle. 'I've brought you a house-warming present.'

She should tell him to piss off straight away. But then there'd be an altercation and Cleo wanted him off her doorstep ASAP before some passing village gossip might clock him and go tittle-tattling off to Colleen. 'Oh! Thanks. Come in,' she said, grabbing the wine and shutting the door behind him.

'Sorry about the other night,' he said, as he followed her downstairs to the sitting room.

'What do you mean?'

'I wasn't great company. I was hungover, and I didn't want to talk too much in case I rambled.'

'Oh. I didn't notice.' Cleo had to stop looking at him. If she didn't, she knew her mouth would open and some such words as 'You're gorgeous' would come out of it. She made an elaborate show of studying the wine label, wishing she hadn't had the flu that time Margot had had her wine appreciation evening. If she'd gone to that she might know what to say. '"Delicious served on its own as a refreshing aperitif,"' she murmured as she scanned the label, '"but don't miss the opportunity to pair it with oysters and other shellfish, and — a classic French marriage — goat's cheese'.'

'Got any?'

'Goat's cheese?'

'Oysters, preferably.'

'No oysters, I'm afraid.' She dared to look him in the face. 'But I do have goat's cheese.'

'Let's go for it then,' he said, 'and see if the marriage works.'

'Marriage? What marriage?'

'The 'classic French marriage' between Sauvignon Blanc and goat's cheese. Or are you too busy right now to be shooting the breeze with a layabout like me?'

He was irresistible. 'No. I'm not busy. Come through to the kitchen.'

The kitchen was a good idea. It gave her the chance to do things, so that she didn't have to look at him too much. She fetched wineglasses and a corkscrew, and assembled a mini picnic of bread and goat's cheese and tomatoes, while he opened the wine and poured. Sadly, the only bread she had was the rather ordinary brown wholemeal she used for toast in the morning. She wished she had a crusty baguette or nubbly granary stuff with seeds in.

Finally she sat down opposite him at the table and he raised his glass in a toast. 'Here's to new neighbours, Cleo Dowling. You're most welcome to Kilrowan.'

'Thank you.'

'You've done great things with this place.' He swigged back some wine, then gave her a narrow look. 'Although you might want to do something about the directional lighting in your upstairs rooms.'

'Why?'

'I arrived back at one o'clock this morning to a stunning display of shadow dancing going on centre stage in one of the front windows. You throw some pretty mean shapes, that's for sure.'

'What do you — Oh!' The penny dropped. Cleo's hands flew up to hide her scorching face. 'Oh, *God*! How embarrassing! You saw my shadow against the blind! Oh — you complete *bastard*! Why didn't you ring the bell and warn me?'

'I had my girlfriend with me and, for fairly obvious reasons, I didn't want to draw attention to the fact that my new next-door neighbour is someone who moves like a chick in the Bond film title sequence.'

'Oh, God!' Cleo wanted to bang her head on the table.

'There are some things in life Colleen doesn't need to know,' he continued. 'I steered her straight into the house, keeping myself neatly positioned between her and the erotic floor show.'

'I am *beyond* embarrassed.'

'I bet you are. I'm sorry. I wouldn't have brought it up if it weren't for the fact that there's a youth club every Friday in the village hall down the road. If you decided to do a repeat performance you might look out to find an audience of adolescent boys outside your window with their eyes out on stalks.'

Cleo finally removed her hands from her face.

'In that case I owe you an undying debt of gratitude. I'll get something done about the lighting right away.'

She knocked back a hefty swig of Sauvignon Blanc in an attempt to anaesthetize the zinging sense of mortification she felt. Oh, *Christ*! She remembered she'd done a load of suggestive shimmying during 'I Just Don't Know What to Do with Myself', fancying that she could cut the same kind of sexy capers as Kate Moss did in the video . . .

Ow, ow, *ow*! she thought, and 'More wine, please, Pablo,' she said, finally allowing herself to look directly into his dark chocolate eyes. And as she slid her glass towards him, Cleo Dowling felt herself sliding a little more inexorably, a little more irrevocably in love with Pablo MacBride.

★ ★ ★

They sat there for quite a long time, eating goat's cheese and getting mildly pissed. Cleo was expounding on the joys to be had from trying to find the most boring sites on the world wide web, and promised Pablo that she'd give him a guided tour some time. And as the level of the wine in the bottle dropped, the small talk they were making got more expansive. Then suddenly the bottle was finished, and Cleo had the bright idea of opening some of the Bordeaux she'd been drinking the night before.

'Mm. Bloody good wine,' said Pablo, taking a swig. 'Expensive?'

'Yeah.' She was feeling reckless now. 'But it's

cool. I can afford it. I won the lottery.'

He gave an approving smile. 'Wow. Clever girl.'

'There's nothing very clever about winning the lottery,' she said with a shrug. 'And it has its disadvantages. Half my friends went off me because they couldn't handle it.'

He gave a laugh of recognition. 'They tend to do that, don't they? I had loads of arty friends until my paintings started selling really well. Now I don't have any.'

'No friends at all?'

'Well, none of my old friends from art college. They all go around giving out yards about how facile my paintings are.'

'They're obviously just bitter and twisted with jealousy.'

'No, it's true. My paintings *are* facile.'

'What?' Cleo paused in the act of raising her glass to her lips and gave him a look of disbelief. 'How can you say that?'

'Easy. I churn them out. I could manage a canvas a day, no problem, if I could be arsed.'

'But . . . your paintings make *loads* of money, don't they?'

'Yeah.' He gave her his fantastic smile. 'It's a great big joke. For years I was struggling in a garret to create 'Art' that no-one would buy. That's the reason my wife divorced me. And then a year ago a director friend asked me to paint a semi-abstract portrait for the set of a show he was doing in the Abbey theatre, and everything changed.'

'How?'

'A society broad came up to me after the show one night and asked if I would do a portrait of her. She was a bit of a dog, so I said 'no'. But she was persistent. She asked me to name my price.'

'How much?'

'I told her 'five grand' for a joke, and she took out her chequebook and wrote me a cheque there and then. I haven't looked back since.'

'Oh! What a brilliant story! Better than winning the lottery!'

'Damn right. It's a *fantastic* way to make a living. Becoming collectable is every struggling artist's dream. People fork out stupid money for my paintings. They want to own virtually anything of mine because it gives them kudos. I hang on the walls of some of the finest houses in Dublin 4. Ha! Life's brilliant, isn't it? A blast, really.' And Pablo MacBride threw back his head and shouted with laughter.

Cleo was astonished. She'd always associated artists with *angst* and a miserable life in penury. She'd never have thought that an artist could be so down-to-earth and honest and easy to talk to, and so — well — full of *joie de vivre* as Pablo clearly was. 'You don't just do prot — portraits, do you?' she asked. Uh-oh. She was having trouble stringing her syllables together. She'd better go a bit easier on the Bordeaux.

'Nah. I do anything. I'm a complete prostitute. But portraits are a real money-spinner. People love having their portrait painted. Colleen was a bit sniffy about my stuff when we first met — too commercial for her tastes — but as soon as I offered to paint her portrait she changed her tune. It can be a pretty sexy experience, having your portrait painted. Especially in the nude.'

Cleo didn't like to think of Pablo painting Colleen's portrait. She'd put money on it being a *magnificent* nude. 'So what else do you do aside from portraits?'

'Whatever. Mermaids with sunglasses on Lissnakeelagh strand. 'Ironic' damsels dancing at the crossroads. Bathers by moonlight with pig. Lovers dining *à deux* in a pub. With an enigmatic hat on the table between them.'

They smiled at each other, and then Cleo dropped her eyes to Pablo's beautiful artist's fingers wrapped round the stem of his wineglass with paint still under the nails, and then she looked back up at his dancing dark eyes and his beautiful mobile mouth and she wanted to take his face between her hands and kiss him there and then. Instead, to her horror, she found her eyes misting over.

'What's wrong?' he asked, leaning towards her, all concern.

Oh! Leaning towards her like that only made it worse. It was so unfair that this man should have come into her life, and she wasn't allowed to have him!

'There, there, Cleo,' he said, taking her hand and stroking it. 'What's the matter?'

'Oh! Stop that.' She whisked her hand away, stood up, went to the cupboard for kitchen towel and blew her nose loudly.

'What? Why?'

'Well . . . ' she cast around wildly for the best way of putting it. 'Just imagine if your — if

Colleen could see us now. What might she think?'

Pablo looked at her as if she was raving. 'You think that Colleen might be prowling round your garden spying through the windows?'

'No — no, of course not. It's more to do with the fact that maybe *we* shouldn't see each other again in case she gets the wrong idea.'

'But how can we avoid seeing each other? We're neighbours.'

'I know. I just — I just . . . ' She found herself trailing off spectacularly.

'Oh.' He gave her a look that made her drop her eyes again. 'You mean — you think that she might think that we fancy each other?'

'Um. Yes. I do.'

She wrenched her eyes back to meet his. There was a big silence. Then Pablo got to his feet and moved across the floor to where Cleo stood with one leg wound defensively round the other. She heard him breathe out, and then he took her hands, lowered his face to hers and ran his lips along her cheek.

Cleo shut her eyes, waiting for the kiss that never came. The next thing she heard was his voice in her ear saying: 'I do fancy you. I find you *incredibly* attractive, Cleo. But I'm not going to do anything about it. Because if I do there could be a blood bath.' She stood very still, not wanting him to move away. Her cheek was electric where he'd kissed her, the shell of her ear was hot. 'Colleen cuts herself when she's jealous. It's her way of making sure I won't ever stray. She's even taken a Sabatier to her wrists on a

135

couple of occasions. It's not pretty, and I made a solemn promise to the staff in the Galway University A&E that we wouldn't be back. I would love to kiss you, Cleo Dowling, but if I do I won't be able to stop, and I'll want to do it again, and things will get very, very complicated. But I like you very much, and I hope we'll be able to stay friends.'

Cleo swallowed. 'Of course we'll be able to stay friends,' she said, extracting her hands from his and hoping her voice didn't sound as strange as it felt.

Pablo took a step backwards. 'I think I'd better go now,' he said.

She nodded, then turned away from him and looked out of the window. When she heard the front door close she moved back to the table where his hat still lay. She remembered the impulse she had had when she'd first held it between her hands, to raise it to her face and inhale the pungent smell of worn leather. She hadn't given in to that impulse then. This time she did.

6

Deirdre and Eva were lounging in the back of the limo that had picked them up at Galway airport and was now transporting them through the wild beauty of Connemara. Eva was chattering away fifteen to the dozen, while Deirdre desperately tried to take notes. A sleeping Bruno was sprawled face down across her lap, which was exceptionally convenient because it meant that she could use him as a writing desk.

'And that's the year I got cast as Juliet in the school play. Or was it the year before? Anyway, I remember that the boy who played Romeo always tried to grope me during our snogging scenes, and one day during rehearsal I just brought my knee up between his legs and gave him one in the goolies. I've used that trick since, with great effect. Once when I was doing a bed scene with Ciarán Hinds — oh. I'd better not mention his name, had I? It's very awkward all this stuff about who I can and can't mention, Deirdre.'

'Don't worry about it. It'll be my job to check out the potentially libellous stuff. You just prattle away to your heart's content.'

'OK.' Eva beamed at her. 'D'you know, this is great, chatting away about myself as much as I like. Most people have to pay a psychiatrist to listen. Or is it psychologist? I never know the difference. It's very reassuring to hear you go 'Mm' and 'Go on, Eva' all the time, as if you're really interested. It makes me feel I must have had a fascinating life.'

'You *have* had a fascinating life. I just regret not having shorthand. You're going so fast that I can't keep up. I wish you'd kept diaries that I could leaf through at my leisure.'

'Diaries? I'd never dream of keeping a diary. The potential for damage is too great.'

'To yourself?'

'Not at all, no — to other people. Just think of all the bitter women in the past who have sought revenge by publishing diaries.'

'But yours would have made such gripping reading, Eva! Remember what Gwendolen said about diaries in *The Importance of Being Earnest*?'

Eva adopted a languid drawl. ''I never travel without my diary. One should always have something sensational to read in the train.' Oh, that reminds me of the time I played Gwendolen with the RSC. What year was that? Never mind. Anyway, I was in rehearsal one day . . . '

And as the Connemara scenery unfurled like a beautiful backdrop beyond the window, Deirdre scribbled and scribbled until at last she said: 'Eva? I'm going to have to take a breather. I can't keep up, and my wrist is killing me. I'm not sure I'm even going to be able to read my own writing. Look! What's that supposed to mean?' She indicated a particularly indecipherable sentence.

'Oh. OK,' said Eva mildly. She yawned and stretched and regarded the view. 'It's like travelling through paradise,' she said. Then she added in a thoughtful voice: 'I suppose it would be a good idea if I started carrying a notebook around with me the way you do. I keep remembering incidents and then forgetting them again. If I had a notebook to hand, at least I could jot things down.'

'I've got a better idea,' said Deirdre. 'I'm going to buy you one of those dinky little tape recorders that journalists use for interviews. Then I can pause it any time I want.'

'That's certainly preferable to having to listen to me jabber away non-stop. You can fast-forward the boring bits.'

'What boring bits? There haven't been any so far. Oh — looks like we've arrived at your gaff.'

The limo had turned through a pair of wrought-iron gates and was gliding up a driveway flanked with rhododendron bushes. It pulled up outside the main door of the hotel, which was an eighteenth-century castle.

'Not bad!' said Eva gleefully. 'Yes indeed, this will do very nicely for the next few months. No — don't get out to say goodbye, Deirdre, you'll disturb Bruno. I'll see you tomorrow. Bye, darling!'

Deirdre watched as the porter carried Eva's luggage in through the massive oak door of the hotel. Today had been her first session with the actress, and she knew she was going to have her work cut out for her. The recounting of Eva's eventful half-century on the planet might make *A la Recherche du Temps Perdu* look like a pamphlet.

As the car started to move off, Bruno blinked sleepily and rolled over onto his back. 'Welcome back to the land of the living, sweetie-pie,' cooed Deirdre. 'Welcome to Connemara and our new adventure!'

★   ★   ★

A limo had pulled up outside the door of Florabundance Two, looking incongruous.

Dannie stuck her head out of the upstairs window. 'Hi,' she called down, as a woman emerged from the back of the car with a small boy in her arms. 'You must be Deirdre, am I right?'

'You're right.'

'I'll be straight down to you, so.'

Dannie threw a quick look around the flat to see if it passed muster, then rattled down the stairs to welcome her new tenant. In the shop off the corridor to her right, carpenters were constructing display shelves for her window from old oak boards, and a setdresser was unpacking a box full of antique glass bottles. Instead of FLORABUNDANCE TWO, the hand-painted sign above the shop door now read MIMI'S APOTHECARY.

'Deirdre. You're welcome. Nice to meet you at last. I'm Dannie.'

As soon as Dannie set eyes on Deirdre O'Dare, she knew she was going to like her. She

140

had the most candid eyes of anyone she'd ever met.

'Here. Let me help you with that stuff.' She indicated the bags that the driver had hauled out of the boot of the car and set down on the footpath, and between the three of them they got the luggage up the narrow stairs and into Deirdre's new home from home.

'Thanks, James,' said Deirdre, handing the driver a note and saluting him as he went back down the stairs. She turned to Dannie with a smile. 'He really is called James, you know. I'm going to have great fun every time I have to ring him and ask him to take me home. Although I won't have much call for transport here, by the look of things. This village is tiny, isn't it?'

'It is. I put an armchair and a pair of binoculars by the window so that you could survey the entire main street at your ease. You can spy on the comings and goings of all the locals and turn it into a script for a soap opera.'

Deirdre moved to the window and lifted the edge of the lace curtain. 'You're right. I've got a grandstand view. Where are the binoculars?'

'That was meant to be a joke.'

'Oh. You'll have to forgive me. I'm incredibly gullible. I tend to believe everything people tell me. Rory once told me that the reason railway tracks were so shiny was because a gang of workmen came out every morning before the trains started running and polished them with steel wool.'

'And you believed him?'

'I did.'

'Janey! You *are* gullible.'

'Ah, but Rory is extraordinarily plausible. That's why he's such a dynamite actor.' Deirdre let the curtain drop back into place. 'What pretty curtains!'

'They're antique lace. The designer found them in a junk shop in Galway and spruced them up. They're meant to be Mimi's.'

'Oh — of course. This must be her bedroom, then, from where she slings the pisspot out over John.'

'I suppose. I haven't read the script.'

'Have you read the book?'

'Yeah. Pure loved it.'

'Mama!' Clutching Kelly Osbourne, Bruno trundled towards the window and held up his arms. Deirdre obligingly swung him up onto her hip. 'This is Dannie, Bruno — shake hands. Good boy! Now, shall we explore our new home?'

Dannie had furnished the flat simply and prettily. She'd been lucky enough to purchase some superfluous pieces from the setdresser on the movie — a chintz-covered ottoman, a patchwork throw, a brass bedstead, a butler's tray — and she'd roped in one of the carpenters to do a nixer for her. He'd built wardrobes in the bedrooms and shelves in the sitting room and presses in the kitchen. She'd bought more basic items in Galway, and some framed prints to hang on the walls, along with several small watercolours of Connemara that her late mother had painted. There was a fire set in the grate, milk and butter in the fridge, bread in the cupboard, hand-milled soap in the bathroom, and flowers in a vase on a small rosewood bureau in the sitting room. The place was looking good.

Deirdre turned to Dannie with a big smile and shining eyes. 'D'you know? Since Rory and Eva talked me into doing this, I've never been convinced that it was an entirely good idea. Now I know it is.'

'I'm glad.'

Deirdre moved around the room, examining things. 'I love this little bureau,' she said, sliding a hand over its wax-polished surface. 'I'll set up my laptop there.'

'Is it a script you're working on?'

'No. A biography of Eva Lavery.'

'Aha! I'd say the same Miz Lavery has some stories to tell.'

'Damn right. Hey — cut that out, Bruno.' Bruno was chewing the flex on a reading lamp. He ignored his mother until she picked him up bodily and looked him in the eye. 'I said cut it out. Chew on this instead.' She handed him Kelly Osbourne. 'He loves Kelly Osbourne,' she said to Dannie. 'I've had to bring posters of her with me to hang on his bedroom wall. Thanks for all the baby stuff, by the way. You're a star.'

'You're welcome. I've lined up a woman from four doors down to look after him while you're working. Her phone number's written on here.' Dannie picked up a sheet of paper on which she'd written a list of useful contact numbers as well as instructions on heating, electrical appliances and rubbish disposal. 'All the electrical goods are brand new, by the way. I got a brilliant deal on the cooker, and you'll be glad to know that it's got a self-cleaning function.'

Deirdre looked apologetic. 'I'm not really into cooking,' she said. 'I'll probably just stock the freezer with ready-made crap.'

'I'll have you round some time. I love cooking. Maybe I'll do a big spread some night. Jethro suggested we invite Eva and some of the cast members to dinner.'

'Thanks. I'd love that.' Kelly Osbourne bounced off the floor and Bruno squawked. 'OK, OK, there's no damage done to poor Kelly. Here she is.' Deirdre retrieved the doll and handed her back to Bruno, whereupon Kelly's head went straight into his maw.

Dannie looked at her watch. 'I'll go now and let you get on with things. Any problems — give me a ring.'

'Thanks for everything, Dannie. Say bye, Bruno.'

But Bruno was too intent on chewing Kelly to be bothered saying goodbye, so Dannie just twinkled her fingers at him and left him and Deirdre to it.

Out on the street, a painter was undercoating her shop door with grey. She remembered from the book that Mimi's door was meant to be covered in rainbow-coloured polka dots. That might be quite fun, she thought. Maybe she'd keep it that way once the film wrapped.

A snuffling sound at her ankles made her look down. There was Fluffy, smiling up at her, looking like an advertisement for Pantene Pro V.

'Hi, Fluff,' said Dannie. 'You're looking

splendid. Cleo's done a great job on you.'

'It took two shampoos.' Cleo was strolling up the street, swinging a canvas shopping bag. 'She came home to me last night looking scruffier than ever. I put her in the Jacuzzi. She loved it.'

'Arra, I'd say she's yours for good now. Have you just come from a walk?'

'Yeah. We went for practically a marathon. I was looking for that gorgeous white pony. The last time I met him I promised him I'd bring him carrots, but he was nowhere to be seen today. I've lugged this bag for miles. I'll be eating carrots for the next fortnight.'

'Juice them.'

'Good idea. God, I'm knackered. I could murder a pint. D'you fancy one?'

'Why not? I'm free as a bird this afternoon. Paloma's gone to a friend's house to see new kittens.'

The two women strolled towards O'Toole's, Fluffy strutting fluffily at their heels, her plumey tail in the air. 'No. You can't come in, Fluff,' Cleo told her as she opened the door to the pub. 'You wait here. And don't dare go rolling in any flowerbeds and ruin all my hard work.'

The pub was empty apart from Noel the barman, who was listening to the sports results on the radio.

'I'll get these,' said Dannie. 'What'll you have?'

'A pint of Guinness, please.' Cleo took off her jacket and slung it on the banquette by the sluggishly burning fire. 'Excuse me. I must just nip to the loo.'

'Two pints, please, Noel,' said Dannie, before

145

moving to the fire. She slung on another sod of turf and poked a little life into the embers, then sat down on the banquette next to it. Someone had left a paper behind, so she picked it up and perused it while she waited for the pints to be poured, feeling sublimely contented. She was immersed in a story about Michael Jackson's nose when the door opened abruptly and Colleen made her entrance. Her mane of red hair was windswept, she was wearing her trademark crimson cloak, an ankle-length swirly skirt, sturdy walking boots and the dangliest earrings Dannie had ever seen.

'Dannie! Darling!' she rasped in the throaty brogue she'd acquired since coming to live in Connemara (she'd actually been born in Kilburn). 'How are you keeping? Arra, isn't it splendid you're looking?'

'Oh, er — hi, Colleen. And it's grand you're looking yourself!'

'I'm sorry I missed you last week. I was at a literary festival across the water. Ochone! A week away from my beloved Connemara and my heart grows heavy with pining for it.' Colleen billowed onto the banquette opposite, unhitched her cloak from the Tara brooch that kept it fastened, and shrugged the crimson wool from her shoulders. Underneath she was wearing a black cashmere V-necked jersey that clung to her breasts. A small Sile-na-gig fashioned from Connemara marble nestled between them on a silver chain, drawing the eye towards her magnificent cleavage. 'You're admiring my Sile-na-gig, I see? A present from an admirer.'

Colleen sent a meaningful smile into the middle distance. 'I have no 'fans'. Only admirers.'

'The book's doing well for you, I see,' said Dannie.

'Is it?'

'Well, it's still in the bestseller list in the *Irish Times*.'

Colleen shrugged. 'I never bother with such matters. If it makes my agent and my publishing house happy, so be it, but it is a sad fact of life that some woeful rubbish gets into that same bestseller list.' The barman hove into view with two pints of Guinness and set them down in front of Dannie. 'Ah, Noel! Another pint of Guinness if you would be so kind.'

'Are you not having your usual, Colleen?' asked Noel, who was clearly having some trouble tearing his eyes away from Colleen's Sile-na-gig.

'Indeed and I am, Noel. You may bring me a glass of red wine. The Guinness is for Pablo.'

★ ★ ★

In the loo, Cleo had suddenly been hit by inspiration for the short story she was writing. She'd started to carry a notebook with her every time she took Fluffy for a walk, an activity she'd taken to doing any time she got writer's block. Both she and Fluff were getting loads of exercise this weather. Sometimes she found that ideas came crowding thick and fast when she was walking, and she'd head back for home like Sonia O'Sullivan off the blocks. But inevitably, once she got back to Clarabelle and booted her

147

up, inspiration had vanished into the ether. She had discovered that if she told Fluffy her ideas as they meandered along boreens and beaches they stuck in her brain a bit better, but of course the simplest and most foolproof solution was to carry a pen and a notebook. She had bought one in the local store — wishing that they stocked notebooks of hand-made Nepalese paper like the ones Colleen was reputed to use — and now every idea that came her way was jotted down in scribbly biro on a Capital exercise pad. Fluffy got pissed off whenever her walk was interrupted by the muse descending, but at least now Cleo didn't feel quite so doolally wandering through the countryside lonely as a cloud, chatting animatedly to a dog.

She was still working on 'The Man in the Hat'. She had been trying like mad not to give it an upbeat ending because upbeat endings were considered so naff, but she couldn't help herself. Every time she tried to stick something profound or hiply depressing into the narrative, the story just looked really stupid, as if she'd dressed it up in clothes that were too big for it. So she'd given up trying, and now she found she was enjoying her writing much more. There had been a documentary on telly recently about *Ireland's Eye*, the weekly paper read mainly by country folk. One of the people interviewed had spoken of the pride and delight she'd felt when her first submission was published, and Cleo thought that she might send her story in when at last it was finished. But she copped herself on sharpish. The story had far too much sex in it for that to be an option.

She took the notebook and pen out of her coat pocket. Jotting down ideas while in the loo felt foolish, but she didn't want to do it in the pub in case she looked like some pretentious literary type. She hadn't forgotten that deluded Dannie still thought she was an International Bard of Merit.

Cleo crossed out a sentence that had become redundant now she'd had her most recent brainwave, and scribbled a couple more, finishing up with: 'So she buys an identical hat — but in a smaller size, and plays that very sexy Joe Cocker song about leaving your hat on!!!' She underlined the last four words to emphasize how important they were, then she stuffed the pen and notebook back in her pocket and opened the door into the pub.

Oh, God. There, sitting opposite Dannie with her back to her, was a woman with red hair that shimmered and slalomed down her back almost as far as her waist. It had to be Colleen. Cleo stood dithering in the doorway until Dannie clocked her. She knew that she must have SOS scrawled across her face, because Dannie gave her an imperceptible nod of collusion and then said smoothly to her companion: 'You may not have met Cleo Dowling?'

The redhead turned the beam of her emerald-green gaze on her, and, stapling on a smile, Cleo moved to join Dannie on the banquette. 'Cleo Dowling, this is Colleen. Cleo's just moved to the village from Dublin, Colleen.'

'You're welcome to Kilrowan! *Céad mile*

fáilte!' said Colleen with a gracious smile as Cleo sat down opposite her. Cleo noticed the glint behind the graciousness. 'What a wise move you have made, to come here to our village. Dublin has become a city of embezzlers and charlatans. It reeks of chicanery and profiteering. Thank you, Noel, very kindly.' The bartender had just set Colleen's wine in front of her. Then another pint of Guinness appeared. Oh God. Cleo could tell with appalling foresight what was coming.

'*Sláinte bradán!*' sang Colleen, raising her glass. '*Saol fada!*' And, finally, with feeling, as the door to the pub swung open: '*Bás in Éireann!*'

'Well, I hope I die in Ireland, too, my darling, but not quite yet.' Silhouetted in the doorway, Pablo swept his hat off before moving into the pub. 'A pint, please, Noel,' he instructed the barman on his way past.

'Your pint is poured. Come here to the fire and warm yourself.' Colleen turned back to her audience. 'The madman dived naked into the tide at Lissnakeelagh not half an hour ago. It's hot whiskey you should be knocking back, acushla, not the black stuff.'

'Pablo,' said Dannie, as he drew up a stool, 'this is Cleo Dowling, a newcomer to the village.' Cleo glanced at Dannie. There was something about her tone that sounded overly bright. Had she *forgotten* that she'd told her she and Pablo had already met, or was she being politic? 'You *haven't* met, have you?' Ah! The subtle stress she had put on the word 'haven't' told Cleo that Dannie was offering her a little help here.

'Pleased to meet you, Pablo.'

She registered the amused look that crept across his face. Then: 'Pleased to meet you, likewise,' he said, stretching out a hand. She grasped it, hoping she wouldn't flinch too visibly at the contact.

'So. Where in our village have you chosen to live?' Colleen was lounging back on the banquette, nursing her wineglass and studying Cleo with a casualness so casual it had to be assumed. She looked like a great cat pretending to ignore a sparrow that's just plonked down within paw's reach.

'In the — er — the Blackthorns.'

Something flickered behind Colleen's eyes, and she raised an eyebrow. 'The Blackthorns? Then you two are neighbours, for the Blackthorns is where Pablo, *a grá*, has laid his hat. And how are you finding it . . . er? Forgive me. I've forgotten your name.'

'Cleo,' supplied Cleo. 'And yes, it's lovely.' She gave an enthusiastic nod for emphasis.

'Yes. It must be, as you say, lovely to live with all modern conveniences such as there are in the Blackthorns.' Her voice dripped disparagement. 'I fear that my brawny lover will turn into a milksop, living as he does like some hothouse bloom.'

Pablo gave Colleen a cheery smile. 'Darling girl, it sure as hell beats living in a stately pile like yours where the central heating breaks down every other week.'

'Ah, but our passion keeps us warm.' She slanted him a vulpine smile and laid a hand on his thigh. 'Remember last winter when we spent

151

an entire week in bed? You immortalized that week on canvas.' Colleen trailed her hand the length of Pablo's thigh, then fixed Cleo with her Gestapo gaze again. 'And what might you do for a living, Cleo Dowling?' she asked.

Oh, God! How she'd been dreading the question. Cleo took a swig of her Guinness to buy time, then set her pint down and wiped imaginary Guinness foam from her mouth. 'I — well — I'm trying to write.'

'Really? How interesting. I, too, am a writer.'

'I know. I've read a lot of your stuff. It's terrific — astonishing! I'm a real fan of yours, Colleen. I'd be very chuffed if you'd sign a copy of *The Faraway* for me.' Maybe if she effused enough, Colleen would start talking about her own work the way most writers couldn't resist doing, and she'd be relieved of the embarrassment of having to discuss her own non-existent canon.

'A *fan* is it you are?' Colleen sounded amused. 'Aha! Perhaps one day you will become an *admirer*.' Cleo returned the smile without having a clue what the big joke was. 'And what might you be working on at the moment?' resumed Colleen inexorably.

Oh, God. 'Um — a short story,' she said.

'Indeed? And what inspired this short story of yours?'

'A . . . a hat.'

'A hat? What class of a hat?'

Cleo couldn't help it. Her eyes darted to Pablo's fedora, which was lying on the banquette beside him. Colleen followed the direction of her gaze, and Cleo blurted out: 'Oh, not that one! It was a baby's hat that I saw on the street one day. A kind of yellow woollen one, with — um — daisies on. And a bobble. It was lying in a puddle and I couldn't help wondering about the baby who had owned it and what was the story behind it — you know? Like who might have knitted it for him, and how would they feel when they realized that it was lost, and would they think that the mother had dropped the hat on purpose because she couldn't stand the sight of it? That kind of thing, you know?' Sweat had broken out underneath her arms. She hadn't improvised like that since that gorgeous Sicilian waiter had once made her late for work three days in a row.

'An intriguing conceit,' said Colleen, narrowing her eyes in interest. 'Poignant, even. Incidentally,' she added, turning to Pablo, 'I notice you've taken to sporting a feather in your hat. What prompted you to do that?'

'A passing fancy,' said Pablo, sliding his eyes in Cleo's direction. Oh God. If he'd touched her she couldn't have felt his gaze more intently. She was going to blush. She was going to blush crimsoner than Colleen's cloak. In desperation, she fixed her eyes on Dannie's, in mute appeal to her to say something to defuse the situation. She couldn't possibly know that what Dannie was going to say next would just make things much, much worse.

Dannie sent Cleo a reassuring look, then turned to Colleen with a bright smile. 'Cleo writes poetry, too, you know? She's been nominated for an international award.'

And that was when Cleo decided to spill her Guinness.

* * *

A little later, on the street, Cleo came clean with Dannie about the award. 'Listen, it's really no big deal to be an International Bard of Acclaim,' she said. 'I entered a poem in a competition run by a vanity press. It was just a crappy scam. Anyone could be an International Bard of Acclaim.'

'Oh, well,' said Dannie sanguinely, 'I think it's brilliant to have written any sort of a poem at all. Did it rhyme?'

'No. People don't publish poems that rhyme any more. They think it's much cleverer to write ones that don't rhyme.'

'They must be mad, so. I loved the poetry I read at school. All those gorgeous Shakespearian sonnets. And then we were made to study T. S. Eliot. Well! What was *he* on? All that guff about wanting to be a pair of crab claws! Janey!'

'He did manage a couple of rhymes, though. 'Go' and 'Michelangelo' being one of the more memorable ones.'

'Wow. I wonder how long it took him to dream that one up.'

Cleo put on a lofty, poetic voice. ' 'In the field the sheep all stand and baa, ruminating on Utopia.' '

'Did T. S. Eliot write that?'

'No. I just made it up.'

'There you are, you see. You *are* a poet!' Dannie turned to Cleo and laughed. 'Oh — I loved the look on Colleen's face when I told her you'd been nominated for an international award. I owe you a drink for that!'

'I don't think I'll ever go into that pub again. I'd be too scared of running into her.'

'Or Pablo, even?' Dannie gave her a sly look. 'What was all *that* about?'

Cleo tried not to look guilty. 'I honestly meant it when I said that nothing happened between us. But I have to say I really like him. He called in to me with a bottle of wine as a house-warming present, and we chatted for ages.'

'Uh-oh,' said Dannie in an ominous voice. 'D'you fancy him?'

There wasn't much point in denying it. Something told her that a denial wouldn't wash. 'Kind of,' she said.

'Well, don't say I didn't warn you. Are you coming to our next women's group, by the way?'

'Will Colleen be there?'

'Probably.'

'Then I think I'd better steer clear.'

'Oh, don't be daft, Cleo. You live here now: it's a small village and you're bound to bump into her. You can't go skulking around the place praying that you're not going to meet up with Colleen. Anyway, she only comes for the yoga, so you'll hardly even see her. She never stays for the lecture or workshop afterwards unless it's something real high-falutin'. The last time she stayed on was when some professor from Galway

155

university gave a talk on the Celtic way of living and dying.'

'What's on tomorrow?'

'How to make Easter eggs. I can't imagine Colleen staying for that.'

Cleo turned to Dannie with a smile. 'Then I'd love to come,' she said.

Excited barking from the direction of the stone pier made them turn. There was Fluffy, racing along the pier, her new barnet blowing back in the wind like Meryl Streep's in *The French Lieutenant's Woman*. She was being hotly pursued by two bully-boy Alsatians.

'Oh, no!' yelped Cleo. 'Fluffy!'

Fluff was getting dangerously near the end of the pier, and the Alastians were gaining on her. And then Fluffy did something magnificent. She put on the brakes and stopped dead, millimetres from the edge. The Alsatians went tearing past, looking like cartoon dogs when they realized what had happened, trying to claw their way back up thin air as they descended towards the briny. And the instant they hit the water with an almighty splash, Fluffy raised her chin in an attitude of victory and laughed and laughed.

★　★　★

That night Cleo phoned Margot.

'Hi!' said Margot. 'How's the great Novel coming along?'

Cleo made an ambiguous sound, which Margot instantly interpreted as a negative. 'I know. It's tough going, isn't it?' she said in a

156

sympathetic voice. 'You have to be incredibly disciplined. Are you doing your Prep Pages?'

'Mm,' said Cleo again, which sound Margot opted to interpret as positive.

'Good girl! It really helps before you start work proper, doesn't it?' she said. 'I used to absolutely *tear* through my Prep Pages, but I remember the most stupefying thing was looking at the word count of my actual Novel at the end of a day's work and realizing how infinitesimal it was. I once took an entire day to produce just twenty-six words, and I felt absolutely wrung out afterwards. How's *your* word count coming along?'

The excessive flabbiness of Cleo's novel meant that her word count was quite high. 'Fifteen thousand words,' she said. This grand total was the only thing about her work that she felt proud of because it indicated her level of commitment to her writing, but now she wasn't so sure.

'Fifteen thousand? Oh, dear me, that's *very* high, isn't it? You might want to think about redrafting at this stage, Cleo — see if you can pare things back a bit. I mean, it's not as if you're trying to write a blockbuster, is it?' Her sister's light-hearted laugh made Cleo feel even worse. 'Anyway, I'm not going to come down hard on you. I applaud your application.'

'I'm working on a short story, too.'

'Really? Interesting. Now, tell me — how are they all down there in Kilrowan? Have you run into Colleen yet?'

'Yes.'

'*Isn't* she just inspirational?'

157

Cleo knew that Margot had met Colleen once only, at a literary luncheon to raise money for charity. She also knew that Margot had forked out a small fortune for the privilege.

'And how are they all in O'Toole's?' continued Margot.

'Grand.' She didn't want to think about them in O'Toole's. At least two of the staff there had witnessed her flirting with Pablo on the fateful evening he'd invited her in for Calvados, and she was still fervently hoping that word hadn't leaked out. Quickly she changed the subject. 'Oh — I met Dannie Moore, by the way. She's lovely. She's going to do my flowers for me.'

'Oh — *Dannie*. Yes, *isn't* she lovely? I would have thought that her little shop would still be shut, though?'

'It is. She's put me on her client list.'

'Oh?' A pause, then: 'I hope you're not finding it too lonely, Cleo. It'll be another couple of months before things start to buzz in that little hamlet, and you might find yourself going out of your mind with loneliness.'

'Well, actually, the buzz has already started.'

'What do you mean?'

'Didn't you see the article in the *Irish Times* about the film they're making here?'

'No. What film?'

'They're making a film of that bestseller, *Mimi's Remedies*. Shooting's starting next week, and I'm going to be in it.'

'*You?*'

'Yeah. Jethro Palmer — Dannie's man — is directing. She says the whole village will get walk-on parts as extras.'

'Really? Next week, you say?'

'Yep.'

'Well. Maybe it's about time I came down for a break,' said Margot.

7

'We had a fantastic party that night. We played Murder in the Dark until dawn, and then we went out onto Sandymount strand with a picnic for breakfast. Champagne and bacon butties, I seem to remember, and we played cricket on the beach, still all dressed up in our evening tat.'

'Eva? Are you sure you've got the year right?'

'Absolutely. I'd just celebrated my fortieth birthday.'

Deirdre stopped the tape recorder. Eva Lavery had gone through life the way a child might go through a dressing-up box, grabbing the glittery stuff and discarding the drab. She remembered something Henry James had written — something about life being like a shop window full of desirable items. That was how Eva saw things: life was Harvey Nicks and she was a shopaholic with a limitless credit card. Deirdre wondered how any biography could do her justice.

She was tired today. Bruno had been in desperate form this morning, and she had dropped him off at the minder's house feeling guilty that she was landing someone else with her appallingly behaved son. She shouldn't have done it, but she couldn't cope with the prospect of being stuck for the rest of the day with a boy who was more like a monkey on speed than a human child.

She'd spent an hour sorting through old

newspaper and magazine cuttings this morning, before booting up her laptop and accessing Eva's file. Thank God she'd hit upon the bright idea of approaching Eva's agent about press cuttings. When she'd mentioned the subject to her, the actress had just said: 'Press cuttings? Are you mad? I've never kept a press cutting about myself in my life.'

The cuttings made fascinating reading. They traced Eva's career from when she'd left RADA and acquired her agent, right up to her last theatre role. Eva had played the gamut of greats, from Juliet through to Cleopatra. Deirdre had even come across photographs of the production of *A Midsummer Night's Dream* that she herself had appeared in when she'd first met the actress. The photograph that intrigued Deirdre most featured the entire cast together on stage — an informal shot taken during rehearsal. She spent a long time studying it. There was Eva, slanting a provocative look up at David Lawless, who had directed the production. How weird to think that they hadn't been married then! How much weirder still to realize that she, Deirdre, had been responsible for getting them together. There was Maeve Kirwan, who'd been such a friend to her. She hadn't been in touch with Maeve for ages — she should really do something about that now that she was back in Ireland. There was Sophie Burke, whose flight path from a lowly fairy in *A Midsummer Night's Dream* to mega superstar Winged Victory in LA had left a trail of burnt-out make-up artists, stylists and PAs reeling. Sophie was wearing very tight cut-offs

161

and a peevish expression. There was Rory.

Oh, *God* — there was Rory! He hadn't changed: not at all. He still had that slightly louche attitude, that careless gait, that utterly charming highwayman's smile that had casting directors falling over themselves to sign him. He'd played swashbuckling pirates and laughing cavaliers and irresistible cads, he'd played rakes and rogues and roués, he'd played cowboys and outlaws and adventurers and gamblers, he'd played profiteers and buccaneers. He'd never once been cast as a solicitor or a clergyman or a bank manager, and, Deirdre realized now, he'd never once been cast as a married man.

Last night a friend in LA had sent her a photograph of him by phone. Rory had been at some black-tie event, and the photograph had shown him looking straight down the lens at her. His dark blond hair was longer than when she'd last seen him (had it really only been a fortnight ago?), there was a joint halfway to his smiling lips and his bow tie was undone. He looked devastatingly sexy. She had rung him later, to ask him how it had gone. It had been deadly dull, he'd told her. He'd left early and come home for a swim. It was a beautiful evening there, the girls were tucked up in bed — yes, he'd kissed them for her — and he was sitting on the deck with a beer.

She'd put the phone down feeling quite feeble with homesickness, then cried a little. It hadn't been a good idea to come here after all! She missed her husband and her daughters, she missed sitting on the deck with Rory, she missed kissing her little girls good night and reading them their story, she missed the sunshine and the laughter and the sheer laid-backness of the lifestyle she lived in LA.

It was funny — when she'd first gone there, she'd thought she wouldn't be able to stick the joint. She'd certainly never imagined that she'd end up *living* there. But they'd evolved a *modus vivendi* that suited them. They didn't hang out with the major players, the megastars and the producers and the directors and the agents. They hung mostly with a contingent of expat Irish, some of whom had made it as big as she and Rory, some of whom hadn't. They didn't attend many of the glitzier social affairs; not because they weren't invited, but through choice. They were happy. Well, content, anyway.

So why had Rory chosen to go to that bash last night? Now that she thought about it, it had been dead uncharacteristic of him. If she'd been there she'd have suggested that they tear up the invite, send out for sushi and watch a video; maybe have a swim. Once upon a time they'd skinny-dipped virtually every night under the Hollywood stars, then fallen into bed and ridden each other rotten. Except she rarely swam naked any more — she was too conscious of the flabby bits she'd accrued since Bruno had been born. What had Eva called them? Saggy bits.

Sag. What a horrible, sad word that was! Why did it have such a dreary sound to it? Why did so many words ending in 'ag' have such pejorative connotations? Sag. Bag. Hag. Nag. Drag. Oh. Was she becoming a drag? Had Rory gone to that party last night because he was fed up staying in and watching videos or chilling with a beer on the deck? Was he fed up with seeing the same old faces any time they had people round, or when they went out to friends' houses for poker sessions or buffets or barbecues?

The people who'd been at the do last night had been mostly Hollywood A list, Rory had told her. But there would have been plenty of wannabes there too, gorgeous girls with pert tits and asses and glossy, glossy hair. *Young* girls. Deirdre and Rory had sworn that they would be terminally faithful to each other after they'd had a near miss when Deirdre married someone else a decade ago. The knowledge that they might not have had a second chance had given them such horrors that neither of them had entertained any notions of an extra-marital fling since their reunion. But LA was so full of stunning women that Deirdre knew Rory couldn't but be tempted. She'd *seen* girls throw themselves at him all over the place. On one occasion a nymphette had even followed him into a men's jakes to proposition him.

Deirdre looked at the photograph again, scrutinizing herself as she'd looked when she'd played Hermia opposite Rory's Lysander all those years ago. She had to admit that she'd been pretty bloody gorgeous — all coltish legs, with peach-bloom skin and eyelashes like an ad for Maybelline. No wonder he had lusted after her. She turned her attention back to where Rory stood in the photograph. He was lounging against a table, hands in his pockets, looking his usual disreputable self. Why wasn't he gazing at her with an intense air, the way David Lawless was gazing at Eva? Not only was he not gazing at her with an intense air, he wasn't even looking in her direction. He was, she noticed now, directing his best slanty-eyed look at Sophie Burke's perfect little ass.

★　★　★

'Hi!'

Cleo opened her front door to find Margot standing on the step.

'Margot! So you did decide to come down! Hey, it's great to see you! Come in. Come and inspect the joint.'

Margot kissed Cleo on both cheeks, then Cleo led the way downstairs to the sitting room and watched while Margot moved here and there, scrutinizing the place with the meticulousness of a property speculator.

'You're right about the light,' she said. 'It's fantastic. But it's very dedicated of you to go with white walls — you're going to have to repaint them every year or so. Uh-oh, there's a red wine stain on your sofa already. Naughty girl.'

'It's all right — the covers are removable. I'll give you the grand tour, will I?' Cleo was dying to show Margot the pride and joy that was her new house.

'Please.' Margot slipped off her coat, then handed Cleo a heavy, gift-wrapped something. 'Here's your house-warming present. I thought it

165

would be appropriate now that you've become a dog lover. Where is the mutt?'

'She's out playing. Thanks for this — you're very thoughtful.' Cleo started pulling at Sellotape.

'Well, I hope she's not out getting pregnant. You don't want to be landed with a litter of lookalikes.'

'Actually, I rather like the idea of Fluffy having puppies.'

'Good God, Cleo! Are you mad? If you'd gone for the pedigree option you could at least make money by selling the pups. But nobody would take the progeny of that mongrel off your hands.'

'I wish you wouldn't be so mean about her. I've become very fond of her.'

'Sorry. You know I have a thing about that animal.'

'Oh! Thanks very much!' Cleo had unwrapped her gift to find a door-stop in the shape of a dog. It had a familiar look, and then she realized that she'd seen it before. An aunt of theirs had given it to Margot for her house warming. She'd never used it. 'It's — lovely.' Cleo set it down on the coffee table and took a step back from it, as if contemplating a work of art. 'Lovely,' she said again, before moving through to the kitchen.

Margot followed her and drifted across to the cooker, which still had last night's wok perched on top of it, a dishcloth dangling from the handle. Cleo noticed now that the place was looking a bit untidy. She wished she'd been given advance warning of Margot's arrival so that she could have spruced things up a bit.

'It's state-of-the-art Neff,' supplied Cleo helpfully, desperate for her sister's approval. 'It has an ergonomic rotating handle, a single control knob and a highly effective Hydro-Clean.'

Margot laughed. 'Honestly, Cleo! You sound like the voiceover for a bad infomercial!'

'Oh. Do I? Sorry.'

From the kitchen they progressed through the dining room, then upstairs to the bedrooms. Margot's tone fluctuated between the complimentary ('*Love* the bathroom. Matki fittings? Excellent!') and the critical ('PVC windows. Ouch . . . ').

'You're not that mad about it, are you?' said a disappointed Cleo when they were back in the sitting room.

'Oh, it's splendid of its kind. But it's not really my style. You know the kind of décor I'm into.'

Margot's house in Kilrowan was a traditional Irish cottage that still looked very much as it might have done in the nineteenth century, with a half-door and a flagstoned floor and exposed oak beams and pine tables and chairs and dressers all over the place. It had wattle-and-daub panelling and limewashed walls and ceilings and a smoke-blackened cast-iron range. It was the kind of place an estate agent would describe as 'oozing with character'.

Margot moved to the window, and gazed out over the garden. 'But you do have a fantastic view,' she said, in the tone of someone bestowing the runners-up prize. 'Who's your neighbour?'

'Pablo MacBride.'

'No! That divine-looking painter? Are you serious?'

'Yep.'

'Oh, I'd love to meet him! I'd love to commission a portrait.' She moved to the window and craned her neck a bit, looking towards Pablo's house. 'Honestly, I can't understand how an artist like Pablo could live in a development like this. No offence, Cleo, but if you saw Colleen's house you'd know what I mean. Now *that's* my idea of an artist's house.'

'I didn't know you'd been inside.'

'I haven't. I'm talking about the building itself. It's that wildly romantic Gothic house on the road to Lissnakeelagh. You must have seen it.'

Cleo had indeed seen it on her walks with Fluffy. She'd often wondered who lived there because it looked like the kind of house a person might go mad in.

'So. Pablo's living next door to you.' Margot raised an eyebrow at her. 'I suppose you've been living on his doorstep, plaguing him with requests for teabags like the girl in the Barry's ad.'

'I haven't, actually. I don't drink Barry's tea.'

'Get real, Cleo. You know what I mean. He is drop-dead gorgeous. Don't tell me you haven't been tempted.'

'No, I haven't,' she lied.

'You've met him?'

'Yes. He called in with a bottle of wine as a house-warming present.'

She wished Margot had brought a bottle of wine as a house-warming present instead of that hideous doorstop. What *was* she going to do with it? She couldn't not use it in case Margot was offended. But then, Margot had never used it while it was hers, so why should *she*? It was the kind of dilemma you might see on an agony aunt's page.

'How very neighbourly of him.'

Cleo didn't like the knowing way Margot was smiling at her. 'Shall I make coffee?' she asked, jumping to her feet.

'I don't drink instant, darling. You know that.'

'There's Illy.'

'Well, that'd be acceptable. Oh — don't forget your doorstop. It's meant to stand guard at the door, according to the attached blurb.'

Cleo picked up the offending item and read the card that was attached to it. 'My name is Rufus. I guard your door for you in all weather, day and night. I am so faithful I will never leave you.' Her heart sank.

'What's that smell, incidentally?'

'A Tiger Lily scented candle. Jo Malone.'

'It's quite divine.' At least Jo Malone got the thumbs-up from Margot!

In the kitchen Cleo set Rufus by the door and started to make coffee while Margot did some more snooping. 'What's this?' she asked, taking up a flyer from a stack of mail on the counter. 'Oh, my God. Kilrowan women's group! 'Forthcoming activities include yoga, rag rug making, flower arranging, art classes and talks by experts in their field.' Well! Have you been busy with your little watercolours, my dear!' Her tone was redolent with sarcasm.

'I've only been to one so far. It was a demonstration on Easter egg making.'

Margot looked amused. 'You are *not* serious!'

'I am. I went with Dannie. I really enjoyed it.'

'It's frightfully parochial, Cleo.'

'It was great fun.' Cleo shot an oblique glance at Margot, who was still studying the flyer with a curled lip. 'And women's groups have got some street cred since Helen Mirren did *Calendar Girls*. Colleen goes. And there's a rumour that Eva Lavery's coming tonight.'

Margot's lip uncurled instantly. 'Oh?' she said, sounding excessively casual. There was silence for a moment or two while Margot continued to peruse the flyer, even though her eyes weren't moving. 'I suppose the yoga might be worth a try. Is Dannie doing the flower arranging class?'

'Yes.'

'Then that would definitely be worth going to. She's an absolute genius. Did she do the flowers in your sitting room?'

'Yes.'

'I could tell. They're glorious. Who's doing the art class?'

'Pablo.'

'Another inspired choice! Well, maybe your little women's group isn't quite so parochial as I thought. What's on tonight?'

'A talk on fly-fishing.'

'Fly-fishing? Could be interesting! I'll see you there.' Margot put the flyer down. 'What's the story about the film, incidentally? Have you discovered any hitherto dormant talents as an actress?'

'No. There haven't been any crowd scenes yet — the first one's scheduled for tomorrow. They were shooting studio stuff all last week, apart from yesterday when Eva Lavery did a scene.'

'What did that involve?'

'Slinging a bucket of pee over one of the other characters. It's a key scene in the book, remember?'

Margot made her 'Get real, Cleo' face. 'I didn't read that book. I'm surprised you did.'

Cleo wanted to stick up for Mimi and her Remedies. 'I really enjoyed it. It was a light-hearted bit of fun.'

'I find it hard to believe that an actress of the calibre of Eva Lavery would lower her standards to appear in a film like that.'

'Oh, come on, Margot. Actors can't go through life being snobby about the kind of films they do.'

'Yes they can. Look at Isabelle Huppert. Look at Tilda Swinton.'

'Yeah, but they probably earn a fraction of what Eva does.'

'Artistic integrity counts for a lot, you know. Money isn't everything, Cleo, although since winning the lottery you clearly think it is.'

'That's not true! I just think that there's more to life than arthouse films that nobody goes to see and literature with a capital L that nobody bloody reads.'

Margot sat up on one of Cleo's kitchen stools and crossed her legs, as if making a point. 'I see Colleen is still on the bestseller list. That rather disproves your theory, doesn't it?'

Cleo was feeling defeated now. 'OK. You win, Margot.' She depressed the plunger on the cafetière, and changed the subject. 'How long are you here for?' she asked. 'And is Felix with you?'

'No. He's gone off on a diving holiday to the Red Sea.'

'The Red Sea? Wouldn't you rather have gone there than here?'

'Absolutely not. He's gone off with a bunch of 'lads', for dedicated diving on a liveaboard. Anyway, we had a massive row recently.'

'Oh? What about?'

'The credit card bill started it off. He accused me of being extravagant and selfish. He said some utterly unforgivable things to me.'

Oh, God. 'Em. Like what?'

'He said I only ever thought about myself and that I had no regard for him or his family.'

'But you had them all for Christmas last year. You worked your ass off to make that a special time for them!'

Margot had had Felix's parents and sister and brother-in-law to stay for a week. She had had a drinks party with a buffet and carol singing round the piano, she had had mulled wine and home-made mince pies after midnight mass, she had staged a dinner party for twenty, and she had had the most glorious Christmas tree Cleo had ever seen, with real candles and hand-made decorations from Korea. The family had played charades and card games and backgammon, and gone for long walks, and even for a Christmas dip in the Forty Foot. Margot had taken to her bed with exhaustion after the week of festivities,

172

as had Felix's aged mother and father.

'I know! And this is the thanks I get. He said I spent too much time gallivanting with my girlfriends and going to theatre and exhibition openings and organizing my salons. He called my girlfriends harpies, and he practically accused me of being a . . . a *poseur*!'

'Oh, God!' Cleo knew that this was likely to be the worst insult Margot had ever received.

'And he said that he hadn't worked like a demon for all these years just so I could go on a spending spree and blow a fortune on designer clothes. And I said that if he'd made sure that his wife had had an ounce of sexual gratification in the past year, perhaps I wouldn't have needed to have gone shopping.'

And, Cleo speculated, that was probably the worst insult *Felix* had ever received. No wonder he'd gone off with the lads. 'So what's going to happen now?' she ventured.

'I'm staying in Kilrowan until he apologizes.'

Uh-oh, thought Cleo. After the aspersion cast on Felix's manhood, an apology could be a long time coming.

★ ★ ★

After they'd finished their coffee, Margot got up to go. She wanted to unpack and set her house to rights before the yoga class that evening. They had just climbed the stairs to the front door when the dog flap that Cleo had had installed for Fluffy burst open with a loud *thwack* and Fluff skidded through and careered down the stairs.

173

'What was *that*?' asked Margot.

'That was Fluffy,' explained Cleo. 'There are a couple of dogs in the village who are out to get her, and any time she has a close encounter with them she just heads for home and whizzes through the dog flap. They're too big to follow her.'

Sure enough, when Cleo opened the door, there were the two Alsatians that Fluffy had outwitted on the pier. 'Bugger off, you bastards!' shouted Cleo. 'And leave my poor baby alone!'

Margot gave her a 'puh-leeze' look, observed the kissing ritual, then moved away down the path. 'Oh — by the way, Cleo,' she threw over her shoulder as she got into her car. 'You might want to think about getting that doorbell chime changed. It's incredibly naff.'

Cleo was about to lob back something along the lines of: 'Jesus Christ, Margot! Leave my house alone', but she stopped herself just in time. Margot was going through relationship hell. It wasn't surprising that she was feeling all negative and brittle. So Cleo just waved brightly at her and said: 'See you at seven!'

She went downstairs and proceeded to tidy up after Fluffy, whose headlong flight had sent a kilim skew-whiff and a plant crashing to the floor from a plinth. 'Bad Fluff! Bad Fluff!' she said, wagging her finger at her doggie, who just sat there smiling so winsomely at her that Cleo couldn't be cross. 'Where have you been, anyway, you dirty stop-out? You didn't come home at all last night.' She bent down to pet her, glad to see that she was still wearing her new collar and identity tag. She'd thought that Fluff might have devised some way of getting rid of it. But there was something else new about her. Attached to the collar was a glossy, blue-black magpie's wing feather. Cleo detached it and stood there regarding it for a moment or two. Then she smiled and ran the feather along her forearm, feeling the fine hairs rise at its touch.

A couple of hours later she closed down Clarabelle. She'd got 'The Man in the Hat' into a power shower, and she was still smiling.

8

Dannie was getting ready to go out. It was women's group night, and she'd promised to bring forward her flower-arranging demonstration because Sean Caffrey, who was meant to be giving a talk on fly-fishing, couldn't make it. Of course she had no fresh flowers — she'd have to use dried, and she hated working with dried flowers. For Dannie, that was the floricultural equivalent of working with corpses. But there was great demand for dried arrangements in Kilrowan because so many houses were only ever lived in for short periods. One big house that seemed to be visited only at Christmas time by wealthy Americans boasted massive dried flower arrangements in every single one of its windows.

Dannie felt it incumbent upon her to salvage the event. Sometimes she felt like giving up on the whole idea of the women's group. Speakers were notoriously unreliable, and this wasn't the first time she'd had to step in and cover for someone at short notice. But it was an important weekly occasion in the social calendar of the village, especially in the winter months. Prescription rates for Prozac apparently soared sky high in Kilrowan out of season.

She reckoned she could do with some Prozac herself right now. She was stressed. Jethro had said he'd baby-sit, but he still wasn't home.

The phone rang. The display told her it was Jethro's mobile.

'About time,' said Dannie. 'Where are you? Haven't I to go out in ten minutes?'

'Dannie — I'm sorry. Something's come up, and I can't make it back right now. Can you organize a sitter?'

'At this late notice? I'd be feckin' lucky, you know.'

'Hot damn. Couldn't you take Paloma with you?'

'No. She'd be bored out of her mind, and she'd be disruptive. Anyway, won't it be way past her bedtime before we're finished?'

'How about asking your father?'

'Janey, Jethro — that'll be the second time I've asked him this week.'

'I'm sorry, Dannie — I really have to dash. Sorry, sorry to land you in it. I'll see you later.' And he was gone before she could say anything else.

Muttering the kind of words she never used around Paloma, she punched in the number of her usual sitter with a belligerent finger.

'You're out of luck, Dannie, I'm afraid. Emma's minding Deirdre O'Dare's wee boy this evening,' said the sitter's brother.

Dannie put the phone down, feeling even more stressed. This was not the first time Jethro had let them down. She mentally listed all the promises he'd made that he hadn't kept. She'd had to postpone a proposed family trip to Leisureland in Galway with Paloma because the shooting schedule had been changed. He'd told

Paloma that he was dying to read her her bedtime stories, but had in fact managed to do so on only two occasions since he'd been back. He'd also promised to show his daughter and her friends round the studio where the movie's interior scenes were being filmed, and hadn't yet found the time. Dannie knew that Paloma's pals were giving her stick about it.

In fact, she realized now, she herself had hardly seen anything of Jethro since he'd come to Kilrowan, even though he was living in her house. He had set up an office in the extension Dannie had had built in the event of her father becoming unable to cope on his own in the big farmhouse beyond. Several ISDN lines and all kinds of hi-tech equipment had been installed to facilitate Jethro, but sometimes Dannie felt that the stress he was under was contagious. The biggest difference between them was that while he thrived on stress, she just found it debilitating. She remembered what it had been like living with him briefly in his house on the island of Gozo, before Paloma had been born, and how unworkable it had been then. That was the disadvantage of having an *über*dude as a partner: *über*dudes were never there for you. Picking up the phone again, she speed-dialled her father's number.

'Da? I'm sorry,' she said. 'But can I ask you to do another baby-sitting session? Jethro's been delayed.'

'Isn't that same Jethro a divil?' said her father. 'I was just about to sit down and watch the match.'

'You can watch it here.'

'Ach. That means I'll miss the beginning.'

'Please, Dada?' Dannie put on her most wheedling voice. 'I'll make tea, and there's fresh barmbrack.'

'Arra, all right so,' he said ungraciously. 'I'll be there in ten minutes.'

Dannie raced upstairs to get Paloma into her pyjamas.

'I don't want Grampa to baby-sit,' complained the child. 'I want Dad. Grampa's too old to do fun stuff.'

'Ach! Cut it out, Paloma,' said, Dannie, noticing the abrupt edge that had crept into her voice. 'Amn't I under pressure now? Arms up.'

She'd almost forgotten what it was like to be pressurized. The summer months could be stressful when the shop was busy, but she had very few other worries. Dannie knew how difficult life was for most single mothers, and she often thanked her lucky stars that she'd landed on her feet with Jethro, who was generous to a fault. But she wasn't sure that this arrangement was working.

She sent Paloma off to clean her teeth while she located her yoga gear and her mat. As she passed an upstairs window she saw her father round the corner, and she noted with unease how frail he'd become. He could no longer walk without the aid of a stick, and he'd lost weight. She wondered how much longer he could continue living on his own, even though he insisted indignantly that he was in fine enough fettle. She ran downstairs and opened the door to him.

'Howrya! Aren't you the grand dada for helping me out?'

Dannie kissed him on the cheek, and he made a gruff sound to let her know that he could see beyond her blandishments. Shaking his head, he passed her by and moved slowly into the sitting room, where he dropped into an armchair. Dannie located the channel changer and handed it to him.

'That Jethro's a desperate unreliable fecker,' he said pointing the device at the television and laboriously zapping through channels.

Oh, please, Da — not now! thought Dannie.

'Why a beauty like you couldn't have landed yourself a decent, solid man with a proper job is beyond me.' Zap. 'That Oliver Dunne that you used to be sweet on is come back here to live.' Zap. 'Now, there was a catch! He's bought that old Glebe House and by all accounts he's done a fine job on it.' Zap. 'And him such a paragon, and so handsome and eligible and to be living there with his sister and no wife to look after him!'

Oh, *please* Da! 'Here, Dada — give me that yoke and I'll find the channel for you.' Dannie took the zapper from his gnarled hand and aimed it at the television. 'There, now, that's your channel! And there's tea made in the kitchen, the child's in her jim-jams, and I won't be too late.'

'Be off with you, so,' he said.

'Jethro might even be back before me. And

don't let Paloma have any sweeties. Her teeth are cleaned.' She left the house knowing full well that her father had a packet of gumdrops in his pocket, and that this last instruction would be roundly ignored.

★　★　★

The yoga class was over. Dannie was just drawing from her bag a sheaf of folders displaying photographs of her work when she heard someone say: 'Hi!' Deirdre O'Dare was at her shoulder. 'Dannie — I'd like to introduce Eva Lavery,' said Deirdre. 'Eva, this is Dannie, whose shop you're using as Mimi.'

Earlier, the village hall had gone into a spin when Eva Lavery had walked in. There were a lot more women than usual there this evening, and Dannie was not naïve enough to imagine that they'd shown up for her talk on flower arranging.

'How lovely to meet you at last!' said Eva, holding out her hand. 'I *adore* your shop — it's just perfect for Mimi. Jethro was inspired when he hit on the idea of using it.'

'Thanks. It's lovely to meet you, too. Jethro's talked a lot about you. We must have you to dinner some evening. You too, Deirdre.'

'That would be something to look forward to! I believe you're doing a flower-arranging demonstration for us this evening?' Eva rubbed her hands together as enthusiastically as the head of a hockey team before the match starts.

'I am.'

'Lucky this was my night off. There are night

181

shoots scheduled for the rest of the week.'

Great, thought Dannie, glumly. Jethro had been working so flat out that they hadn't had sex for ages. Now it looked as if the pattern was set to continue.

'Hey! Is this your work?' asked Eva, lighting on the pile of transparent plastic folders and holding one up.

'It is.'

'Well I never! This is a work of art. I'd never be able to do something like that.'

'I'm not expecting you to. These examples are just to show you that flower arranging is like the new rock 'n' roll, not some fuddy-duddy old middle-class hobby. Most people turn their noses up at the idea of going to flower-arranging classes.'

'I would have if it wasn't for you,' confessed Deirdre. 'After I divorced my first husband I swore that I'd never go to a night class in anything, ever again. I had a really hard time at an antique restoration course I was once cracked enough to embark on. It was full of women in Gucci loafers who wanted to learn fiendishly difficult stuff like repairing beading on console tables.'

'No Gucci loafer types here tonight, and no difficult stuff. I'm going to demonstrate something dead simple that everyone should be able to manage.'

'Even me?' asked Eva, handing back the photograph. 'I have dyslexic fingers, but I do love a challenge.'

'I'll try my best.' Dannie boxed the pile of

photographs neatly. She laughed suddenly. 'I love it! I love the idea of an international movie star learning flower arranging in a draughty village hall.'

'Eva's not really like a movie star, Dannie,' explained Deirdre. 'She does things that a prima donna like J-Lo wouldn't dream of doing in a thousand years. She tucked her skirt in her knickers to go paddling on Lissnakeelagh strand the other day. I got a great photograph. It's definitely going in the biography. Oh — and I got a *fantastic* photograph of Jethro on set today. I must give you a copy.'

'I'd love that. It'll remind me of what the fecker looks like. I hardly see him these days. He was supposed to be minding Paloma this evening, and then he cried off because of work.'

'Oh, that's because there was an accident,' said Eva. 'Didn't you hear? One of the crew suffered a bad electric shock and Jethro didn't want to leave until the ambulance arrived.'

'Arra, well. That's understandable, so.' Dannie looked at her watch, then picked up her photographs. 'I'd better get started. I'll talk to you later. You'll come for a pint afterwards, won't you?'

'Damn right,' said Eva.

As she moved to the top of the hall, Dannie made a mental headcount of her audience, hoping she'd brought enough materials. There was Margot d'Arcy, who she suspected had not a tither of interest in flower arranging. For her, Eva Lavery was the main event. There was Cleo Dowling, gazing into the middle distance. From the dreamy expression on her face, anyone looking at her might conjecture that she was absorbed in composing some soulful poem, but Dannie suspected she was more likely to be absorbed in a reverie about her sexy next-door neighbour. There was Colleen, swathing herself in her cloak prior to making her exit. Flower arranging might be the new rock 'n' roll, but it evidently wasn't rock 'n' roll enough for *her*.

The flame-haired diva swept in Isadora Duncan fashion towards the door. As she reached it, it opened suddenly. 'Jethro Palmer, what are you doing here?' she reproached him. 'Don't you know that on Wednesday evenings the village hall becomes a temple sacrosanct to womanhood?'

Jethro ignored her, his eyes searching the room for Dannie. When he saw her he moved straight to her, and Dannie knew before he even said it that her father was dead.

★　★　★

A heart attack, it was. The doctor was there already when she arrived back at the house, having been let in by the neighbour whom Jethro had requisitioned to hold the fort. Her father was still sitting in an armchair by the fire. The neighbour had rolled up a small towel and tucked it under his chin, so that his head did not slump forward. He looked ten years younger than when she'd seen him earlier that evening. He wore a reposeful look. He was still warm when she dropped a kiss on his forehead.

184

She sat beside him, holding his hand until the ambulance came to take away the body. The 'remains', the doctor had said, and Dannie had said back, 'No! Don't call him that! They're not the remains! He's my dada!' She gave his hand one last reassuring squeeze before taking herself off to the kitchen and leaving the ambulance men to it. Matthew and Mark were their names. She found the idea that her father should leave the house in the charge of two men with the names of apostles vaguely comforting.

In the rack on the draining board by the sink stood a plate and a mug, set upside down. Oh! He'd washed them himself. For some reason Dannie found this detail so poignant that she shed her first hot tears. Jethro poured her a large brandy and she sat down at the kitchen table to drink it. The *Irish Times* was on the table, folded over at the sports page. She opened it and scoured the television listings to see what time the match had ended. It was of the utmost importance to her that the game had been going on when her father died. It was now ten past ten. The match had ended less than half an hour ago.

'Who won?' She needed to know.

Jethro went to check it out. 'Celtic,' he said on his return. 'They scored twice in the first half.'

'Thank God. Oh, thank God.'

And then Paloma was in the doorway, rubbing sleepy eyes. 'What's the matter, Mammy?' she asked.

'Come here, my darling girl.' Dannie held her arms wide for her daughter to clamber into her embrace. 'It's a very sad thing — hard for me to

185

tell you, and hard for you to hear. Grampa just died.'

'No! No!' Paloma was inconsolable. He couldn't be dead! Between sobs, the child confessed her awful guilt. Grampa had asked her this evening when he'd tucked her into bed if she'd like him to teach her to fish, and she had told him no, that she didn't want to go fishing with him because fish were horrible and smelly, and he'd looked so sad when he kissed her good night that she'd resolved to make it up to him today by drawing a picture of his house with him standing outside it, and now he'd never have it.

'Draw it anyway,' said Dannie. 'And then we can put it in his coffin for him to take with him where he's going.'

'Heaven, Mammy! Isn't that where he's going?'

And of course Dannie had said yes, even though she knew that there was no heaven, that heaven was just an unattainable dream.

And after Paloma had gone back to bed she phoned her seven brothers, who lived in places all over the world, to tell them that they'd have to come back to Connemara for their father's funeral.

★ ★ ★

Dannie spent the days before the funeral cleaning her father's farmhouse. The most difficult part had been consigning stuff to bin bags. It had been agony to open the wardrobe door and survey the clothes that would never be

186

worn again. She had thought that the shoes would be the worst — the tartan slippers she had given him for Christmas last year, the scuffed leather boots that had taken on, through time, the shape of his feet. But in the bathroom she was gutted to find his shaving gear and, on a peg by the front door, his cap and scarf. Dannie had hunkered down on the floor with her father's scarf wound around her neck and bawled like a baby.

After she had tackled all the personal stuff she set about spring-cleaning the house, losing herself in the mundane ritual of vacuuming and dusting and scrubbing while Joe, who was the first of her brothers to arrive for the funeral, sorted out the will and concomitant legal stuff. The farm had once been prosperous, but as her father had grown older and less able, he had sold off parcels of land in order to keep it going. Joe had calculated that once it was sold and split eight ways, their inheritance would be nothing much to write home about.

She was glad that she had time to spend on her own with her brother. Gorgeous, big, dependable Joe had always been her favourite — he'd often sprung her from boarding school during her teenage years and taken her off on jaunts to Galway and Clifden. He'd taught her how to play poker, how to hold her drink, and how to roll a mean joint. The minute she'd seen his car pull up outside the farmhouse, the minute she'd launched herself into his arms and heard him call her his 'wee sis', she felt somehow safer, and she knew she was less likely to break down in uncontrollable floods again.

She was tidying the hoover away in the cupboard under the stairs when she heard him come back from the solicitor's office. She hadn't expected him home so soon: clearly the will was straightforward enough. 'I'll stick the kettle on,' she called.

'Dannie?' he said from the front door. 'We need to talk.'

She turned to him, wanting to brush away a strand of hair that was clinging to her cheek, wanting to clear the dust that had accumulated in her throat. But she did neither of those things because Joe was looking so uncharacteristically serious. 'What's the matter?' she asked.

'Let's go into the kitchen,' he said, leading the way.

'Will I make tea?'

'I'd prefer a drop of the hard stuff, myself.' Joe fetched a bottle of Bushmills and a couple of glasses from a cupboard.

Dannie sat down at the kitchen table. 'OK,' she said. 'Something really *is* up. You're after using the ominous 'We need to talk' words, and you're opting for hard liquor over tea. Tell it like it is, Joe.'

He joined her at the table and sloshed whiskey into the glasses. 'Da made his will before you came back to live in Kilrowan, Dannie.'

She went very still. Oh, God. She'd been cut out of her father's will. How horrible. How *horrible* — not because of the money, no, not at all. Dannie was appalled by the notion that she'd been such a bad daughter to her father in those

188

pre-Kilrowan days that he'd felt the need to disinherit her. 'You're going to tell me I was cut out of his will, aren't you?' she said.

'No. Proceeds from the sale of the farm are to be split eight ways.'

'So where's the glitch?'

'The cottage goes to Michael.'

'Oh. Oh, God.'

'I'm sorry, Dannie. Da left it to him because he was the one responsible for refurbishing it. D'you remember? He'd planned to use it as a holiday home before he got posted off to Bangkok.'

'Will — will Michael . . . ' She tailed off, knowing she sounded very shook. Then she screwed her courage to the sticking place and voiced the question that needed to be asked. 'Do you think he might consider selling it to me?'

'I've just been on the phone to him. He said he'd have to talk to the missus about it.'

'Oh, God. Leanne.'

'The very one.'

Dannie's heart sank. Her brother Michael did everything Leanne told him to. If Leanne gave him the go-ahead to sell the cottage to his sister, then Dannie was safe enough. But if Leanne decided to hold onto it, then she and Paloma were out on their ear. Leanne's word would be final.

Dannie sent Joe a mirthless smile. 'I'd better get ready to brown-nose, so,' she said.

★　★　★

189

Frank Moore was buried in the little graveyard by Lissnakeelagh strand, in the plot where his wife Daniella had been buried shortly after Dannie was born. The day of the funeral turned out to be one of those miracle days that you get in Connemara. A blaze of blue sky was criss-crossed with the wispy white lines of vapour trails heading westward, and Dannie thought of how, in his entire life, her father had only once set foot on a plane. He and Joe had taken a flight to London to visit her, but she'd been too stressed out to do all the London things he wanted to do — the Tower, the cruise along the Thames, the Changing of the Guard. She'd left it up to Joe to do it instead.

He had lived all his life in Kilrowan, and it had taken Dannie many years to realize that her father had always been there for her. She hadn't really known him until she'd come back here to live with Paloma. How different his life had been to the life of Paloma's father, Jethro Palmer, citizen of the world! She remembered now how it had been for her growing up in boarding school, seeing family only on holidays, and she knew now with a fierce shock of realization how important family was.

Families did birthdays and christenings and anniversaries. They celebrated Christmas and New Year and Easter together. They sat down to dinner, and ragged each other and laughed and fought and cried and comforted each other. They held wakes for their dead — and Frank's wake was a grand affair. It was held in his farmhouse, and because the day was so clement and the

190

place so crowded, the party spilled out into the garden.

Dannie had organized caterers, and the place was awash with drink. Neighbours and friends came from all over the parish, and from adjoining ones too. Her father had kept himself to himself during his lifetime, but he had been very much liked and respected. Even Colleen came, with Pablo. 'I'm sorry for your trouble,' she said to Dannie. 'Your father was a deep individual, and extremely well read. I shall miss the talks I used to have with him in the pub of an evening.'

Colleen was right — he *had* been a deep individual. Dannie had been surprised at some of the titles she'd seen on his bookshelves. They had included works by Camus, Bertrand Russell and Wittgenstein — who, she remembered now, her father claimed to have met when the philosopher had stayed one summer in nearby Rosroe many years before.

'Dannie. I'm sorry for your trouble.'

She turned to find Oliver Dunne looking down at her with a smile that contrived to be simultaneously concerned and sexy.

'Thanks, Oliver,' she said, standing on tiptoe to kiss his cheek. 'But you know, in a way it was a blessing. He was such a feisty individual that he couldn't have stuck it if his health had deteriorated much more. He wasn't able to walk without the help of a stick, towards the end.'

'I know. I called in to him last week with a bottle of Black Bush.'

'You did? Aren't you the considerate one?'

'I've told you before — I had a lot of time for your da.'

That was evidently true. Oliver was a paragon, just as Frank had told her. Jaysus! When had it ever crossed Jethro's mind to drop into her father's house for a wee dram and a chat? She was struck by the bitter irony of it. When she'd been expecting Paloma, she'd looked 'Jethro' up in a book of babies' names to find that it meant 'Excellent; without equal. A man outstanding in all his virtues.' She'd lay money on the name 'Oliver' being synonymous with sainthood.

'Funny,' said Oliver now. 'He said something to me . . . No. Maybe I shouldn't tell you.'

'Oh, go on, Oliver, please! I *need* to know stuff about my da now. Every snippet of information is precious to me now he's gone.'

'Well . . . ' Oliver appeared embarrassed now, and was having trouble meeting her eyes. 'He told me that I was the son-in-law he'd never had.'

Dannie and Oliver looked at each other, then abruptly looked away.

'Let's change the subject,' he said briskly. 'How did poor wee Paloma take her grandpa's passing?'

'Hard. Frank was the only grandpa she had.'

'Jethro's parents are dead?'

'Yes.'

There was a silly, awkward silence between them at the mention of Jethro's name.

'So,' resumed Dannie. 'How's work going on at the Glebe House?'

'We're getting there. We'll be engaging staff soon.'

'Well, good luck with it. I'm sure it'll be very successful.'

'Will you do the flowers for us?'

'I'd be glad to.'

She smiled at him, and then kept the smile fixed to her face with an effort as she saw his sister Alice making her way across the room towards her.

'Dannie. I'm so very sorry for your trouble,' said Alice with the sincerity of a chat-show host, all pained expression and 'I know just how you're feeling' eyes. She took Dannie's right hand in both of hers, and kept it imprisoned for many long moments. Alice's hands were clammy, and Dannie felt an overwhelming impulse to whip hers away and wipe it on the side of her skirt. 'But isn't it fortunate you are, all the same, that you have your beautiful daughter to console you and help you to look towards the future?' cooed Alice.

'Indeed and I am,' said Dannie, hoping that she didn't sound brusque. But Alice wasn't put off, and continued to mouth platitude after platitude.

When Dannie finally reclaimed her hand and made ready to move away, Breda Shanley descended on her and wrapped her in her arms.

'Mavourneen!' she began. 'I'm so sorry for your trouble . . . ' And as Dannie listened to the by now familiar words of comfort she realized how very, very reassuring they sounded when they were uttered with the kind of meaning with which someone like Breda invested them. She was an orphan now, she realized. An orphan who might soon have no home to call her own.

Oh, snap out of it, she told herself, and stop being so feckin' mawkish. How ridiculous to consider herself, a woman in her thirties, a homeless waif! But it was true, nonetheless — and it made her think with a rush of shock about what would become of Paloma if anything happened to her. She realized, too, that something else had been on the edge of her consciousness for a long time. She wanted, more than anything, for Paloma to have a father, full time.

★   ★   ★

It was a couple of hours later. Dannie had refilled glasses and proffered plates and listened to reminiscences about Frank and her late mother that had become increasingly maudlin as the level in the whiskey bottles dropped. She had seen Oliver leave with a stunningly beautiful girl, and had been surprised by the irrational pang of jealousy she felt. She had accepted an invitation to supper from Breda for later in the week, as well as an offer to mind Paloma any time.

Now Jethro and her brother Joe were at her shoulder.

'Did I ever tell you, Jethro,' Joe was saying now, 'that Da met Wittgenstein once?'

'He did?'

'He did indeed,' said Joe. 'Sure didn't he swear that he was responsible for Wittgenstein's most important theory on 'aspect seeing'?'

'I'll take you to Rosroe some time,' offered Dannie. 'Show you where he lived.'

Joe smiled and nodded at yet another guest who was mouthing 'Sorry for your trouble' at him from the other side of the room. Then: 'Come on,' he said suddenly. 'This is getting to me. Let's take a bottle upstairs.'

Joe helped himself to three glasses and a bottle of whiskey from the sideboard, and together he and Jethro and Dannie went upstairs and shut her father's bedroom door behind them.

The room, with its bare mattress, looked forlorn. Dannie and Joe sat on the bed while Jethro took the single bentwood chair.

'Have you spoken to Michael yet?' Joe asked her. 'About the cottage?'

'No. I haven't had time to get him on his own.'

'What are you going to keep as your memento?' Joe sloshed a reckless amount of whiskey into her glass, then Jethro's, before draining the bottle into his own.

'Memento?'

'Yeah. Your memento of Da. You'll want someting special to remind you of him.'

'That's easy.' She nodded her head at a framed painting that hung on the wall opposite the bed. It depicted a beautiful, dark-haired woman with sloe eyes, a smiling, sensual mouth, and a heavily pregnant belly. 'I'd like the painting of Mammy.'

'And you should have it. Sure aren't you the spit of her? Da would have wanted it to go to you.' Joe smiled at her. 'In a way 'tis a painting of you, too, Dannie.'

'What are you on about?'

'You're in it. You're the babby in Mammy's belly.'

'That's your mother?' Jethro had ambled across the room to have a closer look. The painting had been hung where it would be the last thing her father saw when he closed his eyes at night, and the first thing he saw when he opened them in the morning. 'It's a remarkable painting. Who did it?'

'Some young fella Da invited back to the house once for a jar,' said Joe. 'I remember it well. I was about twelve: he wasn't much older — not out of his teens. Mammy's thirtieth birthday was coming up, and Da wanted her to have something special. The bloke offered to paint Ma in return for a place to kip for a week. He was just a backpacker, but he had a mean way with a paintbrush all the same.'

'He sure did. He still does.'

'What do you mean?'

'It's a Daniel Lennox.'

'A Daniel Lennox?' Joe and Dannie's jaws dropped simultaneously. Dannie didn't know much about contemporary art, but she knew enough to recognize the name without having to think about it. Daniel Lennox was Ireland's most famous living painter. 'A Daniel *Lennox*?' she said again. 'I don't believe you!'

'I should know. I have a Lennox on the wall of my house in LA,' said Jethro. 'Besides, it says so right here, on the canvas.'

Dannie and Joe moved to stand beside him. Jethro pointed to the bottom left-hand corner of the painting where the name 'Daniel Lennox' had been written in small but clearly decipherable letters.

'I remember now,' said Joe, with a kind of awe, 'that the lad's name was Daniel. We joked about it at the time because of Ma's name being Daniella.'

There was stunned silence as they pondered the implications, and then Jethro said: 'Wouldn't your father have known how valuable it was?'

'Divil a bit,' said Dannie. 'Sure he had no interest in art. He wouldn't have been able to tell the difference between a Picasso and a Pissarro. And he was fierce scathing when he read in the paper about Tracey Emin and her unmade bed.'

They looked at each other, and then Dannie voiced the question she knew they all wanted answered. 'How much is it worth, do you think?'

Jethro shrugged. 'I couldn't hazard a guess.'

'I know who'd know,' said Joe. 'That painter fella, Colleen's squeeze. What's his name?'

'Pablo. Hang on. I'll go and get him.'

Dannie took a hefty slug of whiskey, then ran downstairs to locate Pablo. He was standing in the kitchen talking to Cleo Dowling, who was looking flushed and animated. Don't tell you I didn't warn you, Dannie thought, but didn't say.

She laid a hand on his arm. 'Pablo. Forgive me for interrupting, but I need to pick your brains. Can you come with me?'

'Sure. Talk to you later, Cleo.' Pablo disengaged himself from a visibly deflated Cleo and followed Dannie up the stairs.

In her father's bedroom Dannie indicated the

painting and said: 'What do you make of that?'

Pablo looked curious, and then he looked gobsmacked. 'Jesus,' he said. 'It's a Daniel Lennox. It's an early one, but it's definitely a Lennox. I'd know his stuff anywhere. Where the fuck did that come from?'

'It's hung there for as long as I can remember,' said Dannie.

Pablo moved closer to the painting and studied it. 'It's a beaut,' he said. 'It's a stunner.'

Dannie and Joe looked at each other, and then Joe took a deep breath and said: 'How much do you think it's worth?'

Pablo made a dubious face. 'You can never accurately predict what a painting might fetch, but at the last Sotheby's auction an early Lennox achieved a hefty sum for a living Irish artist. Of course, the instant he dies, his paintings will double in value.'

There was a loaded silence before Joe finally spoke again. 'You say it fetched a hefty sum. How much might that have been?'

'Over one hundred thousand euros,' said Pablo.

★   ★   ★

A family conference was called for the next day. It was called in something of a hurry, because six of the brothers had flights to catch. The only item on the agenda was the Daniel Lennox painting. Dannie knew that Joe wanted her to have it, regardless of the fact that it was worth a fortune. He had talked to the rest of the family about it, and had learned, unsurprisingly, that the other six siblings wanted the painting to be sold.

Oh — how Dannie yearned to have that painting! She yearned to have it with every fibre of her being. Ever since her childhood she had worshipped that image of the mother she had never known — and whose reincarnation she might be, so uncanny was the physical resemblance. She could not bear the idea that the painting might be sold, that it might end up hanging on the wall of some wealthy stranger. She told Joe that she wouldn't take part in the family conference. There was no point.

Instead she went out into the garden and headed straight to the apple tree where her father had strung up a swing for her when she was a little girl. The swing was long gone, but there was a new one in its place now, hung there for Paloma.

Dannie sat down on it. It was far too low for her to swing on, but the swaying motion was vaguely comforting. She sat there and swayed and swayed for what seemed like ages, thinking about her father and all the little things he'd done for her that she'd taken for granted. Her swing. The porridge he'd made for her and insisted she eat every morning of the Christmas holidays when she was back from boarding school, because it was good for her. The doll's house he'd built for her. He'd even cut out little bits of curtains for it, and rag rugs for the floor, but because he hadn't hemmed the edges, they'd soon got frayed and shabby-looking. She hadn't taken much interest in the doll's house, anyway. Being a tomboy in those days she'd been keener on her brothers' tree house — even though she'd rarely been allowed in.

She wanted to cry now for the doll's house with its sad little curtains and rugs. She wondered if it might be in the farmhouse attic still, and she resolved to retrieve it and refurbish it for Paloma. And the more she thought these thoughts, the more the idea that had been plaguing her for days now came into her head. A father for Paloma. A proper, stay-at-home full-time father.

She revisited each of the scenarios that were open to her, as she had done for years now. She pictured herself and Paloma living in Jethro's bachelor pad on Gozo, with Daddy flying in occasionally to visit, and she knew it wouldn't work. She pictured herself and Paloma living in LA, in a culture that was at the opposite end of the spectrum to life here in Connemara, and she knew that that wouldn't work either. And then she pictured Jethro exchanging his *überdude* status and his jet-setting lifestyle and coming here to live with her in her pretty country cottage so that he could be a hands-on, stay-at-home father, and if she hadn't felt like crying, that might actually have made her laugh out loud.

The memory came to her now of Oliver Dunne, and the dedication on the flyleaf of the book of poetry he'd left in her room in the Culloden Hotel: *If you ever change your mind.* Was he waiting for her still? Or had the beautiful girl he'd left the wake with yesterday put all

200

thoughts of her out of his mind?

'Dannie! I knew I'd find you here.' It was Joe. He stood looking down at her with serious eyes, and she knew he had something big to tell her.

'I know what you're going to say. It's bad news, isn't it?'

'It's bad news about the cottage all right. Leanne doesn't want to sell. She wants to keep it and let it as a holiday rental. But she's prepared to let you have it rent-free for a year on account of all the work you put into building the extension.'

'Big of her.' Dannie felt as if she'd been delivered a blow to the gut; and then she steeled herself to feel even more gutted. 'There's more, isn't there? Bring it on, Joe,' she said, trying to sound careless. She looked up at him, not wanting to hear the words that she knew were inevitable. *The painting's going to auction.*

'The painting's yours,' he said.

She'd misheard. 'What?'

'The painting's yours.'

What? 'What? What do you mean? How can it be mine?'

'Jethro bought it for you,' said Joe. 'He made us an offer we couldn't refuse.'

'An offer you couldn't refuse?' parroted Dannie.

'A hundred and sixty thousand.'

'What? Jesus! He can't — he *can't* have, Joe! That's insane — it's crazy, it's — '

'He did it,' said Joe. 'The painting is now officially yours.'

Dannie shook her head. 'No! No — it's not!

It's not officially mine at all! If he paid all that money for it, then the painting isn't mine, it's Jethro's!'

'He wants you to have it, Dannie. He's written cheques to all of us brothers.' Joe withdrew a cheque from his pocket and held it out to her. 'Have a look.'

Dannie took the cheque and saw, in Jethro's distinctive black scrawl, the words: *Joseph Moore. Twenty thousand euros only.* And then the signature: *J. Palmer.*

'He actually paid a hundred and sixty thousand for it?' breathed Dannie.

'Well, a hundred and forty. He didn't include your share of the value of the painting, obviously.'

Dannie looked at the signature again. *J. Palmer.*

No! J. Palmer hadn't bought the painting. He'd bought her. If she accepted his gift she would be in debt to him for the rest of her life. The signature on that cheque — on all seven of them — bound her to him more effectively than any wedding vows ever could, and she knew that Jethro was the last man on the planet she should marry.

The pain in her gut had spread, and was taking root somewhere in the region of her heart. 'Doesn't he know what he's done?' she asked Joe.

'What do you mean?'

'He's *bought* me, Joe. If I accept that painting, I might as well have 'Property of Jethro Palmer' branded on my forehead!'

'Ah, now, Dannie, be reasonable. Jethro's not the type of man to — '

But Dannie had slid off the swing and was running towards the garden gate. 'Tell him I don't want it,' she shouted over her shoulder to her brother. 'Tell him he can keep the feckin' thing. And if *he* doesn't want it, tell him to donate it to the feckin' National Gallery!' She slammed the gate behind her, and was gone.

★   ★   ★

In the cemetery that bordered Lissnakeelagh strand, Dannie laid wild flowers on her father's grave, then strode the length of the beach. She wanted the wind to blow through her brain and sweep it clear of the confused thoughts that were accumulating there. God! How fed up she was with thinking. How fed up she was with being messed around. How fed up she was with *responsibility*. For the first time in her life she wanted someone to say something like: 'Dannie, this is what you're going to do next, and I won't countenance any argument!' For the first time in her life she wanted to relinquish control to someone who would know what was best for her. For the first time in her life she wanted someone to take her by the hand and say 'This way!' And for the first time in her life Ms Verging on Homeless, Newly Orphaned Dannie Moore knew what it was like to really, really need a dada or a mammy.

A seagull screamed and she looked up, only now noticing that it was another perfect day. The stretch of golden sand was deserted apart from the flocks of busy sanderlings, the sky was washed cloudless blue from horizon to horizon, and the sea shimmered a pellucid, inviting pale green. Dannie yearned to swim. A swim would help to clear her head. At the end of the beach, in a secluded cove, she started to take off her clothes.

'Dannie!' A man's voice. She looked up to see Oliver Dunne standing high on a sand dune, silhouetted against the low-slung sun. She lifted a hand to shield her eyes from the glare, and watched as he began to make his way towards her. When he reached her he stood motionless, regarding her, then raised a hand to caress her cheek. The gesture made the tears come, and as her shoulders slumped and her hands went to her face, Oliver gathered her in his arms. He rocked her gently from side to side, and he murmured reassurance in her ear, and he stroked her hair and wiped away the tears, and it felt so *good* just to cry and cry and cry.

'Cry all you like,' Oliver said, when she apologized after several minutes of hard sobbing. 'Cry yourself a pool of tears.'

'Like Alice,' said Dannie, snuffling now.

'Alice?'

'Not your sister. Alice in Wonderland cries herself a pool of tears so big she could swim in it.'

'Is that what you were going to do just now? Go for a swim?'

'Mm-hm.'

'*Not* such a good idea, mavourneen. The

water's freezing. I've a better idea. Come with me — but put your clothes back on first. We can't have you walking down the beach in your undies, glorious as they are to behold. Arms up.'

She snuffled a bit more, but did as he told her. Oliver dropped her sweater over her head, then zipped up her jeans and held her jacket out so she could get her arms into the sleeves, and then he knelt down at her feet and tied her bootlaces for her. 'Come with me,' he said, holding out his hand.

'Where are we going?' she asked.

'It's a surprise.'

They walked in silence to the car park, where Oliver zapped the locks on his Alfa Romeo and opened the passenger door for her. As she got into the car, her phone started to ring. Jethro's number was displayed. She bit her lip, then depressed the 'off' button.

'Where are you taking me?' she asked Oliver again.

But he just tapped his nose with a forefinger. 'I told you. It's a surprise.' He opened the glove compartment and produced a soft, chocolate-coloured cashmere scarf. 'It's a magical mystery tour,' he said, leaning towards her and kissing her lightly on the lips before tying the scarf around her eyes. She felt him draw back when he finished tying the knot, and as he did so his hand brushed against her breast. Was it accidental? she wondered. Accidental or not, her nipple responded to the touch and she felt shockingly aroused.

Oliver gunned the engine, and the car took off

down the road. After some minutes it slowed, and she felt a pull to the left.

'We're going to the Glebe House?' she conjectured. 'You're going to show me around?'

'Maybe later,' he said. 'But there's something I want to do first.'

The car stopped, and he helped her out. He guided her down some steps, and she heard the sound of glass doors being slid open. Then his hand was on the small of her back, persuading her forward. She took a hesitant step, then another, and then the faint tang of chlorine hit her senses.

'You can look now,' he said, undoing the knot on the scarf and letting it fall.

'Oh!' Dannie was standing on the verge of one of the prettiest infinity pools she'd ever seen. It was underlit by myriad spotlights, and tiled in a green mosaic pattern that gave the surface of the water the appearance of flawless liquid emerald. Wooden loungers were placed at intervals around the pool, and on the end wall was a *trompe-l'oeil* mural depicting Arcadia — an Italian idyll. It was perfect.

'You wanted a swim, Ms Moore?' said Oliver. 'I invite you to baptize our pool. It was finished just this morning.' There, indeed, were the remains of workmen's tools, stashed in a far corner, half hidden by a dust sheet.

'Oh, Oliver, it's beautiful!' She felt grateful as a little girl given a gift-wrapped box. 'Am I really going to be the first to swim in it?'

'You'd be doing me an honour.'

They stood looking at each other, and then

Oliver moved towards her and took hold of the lapels of her jacket. 'Might I help you disrobe?' he asked.

Dannie parted her lips to speak, then realized that she was so muzzy with sexual desire that she couldn't articulate a single syllable. So she just nodded. Oliver stripped her bare very, very slowly, and as he did so she tried not to think of Jethro. When he finally knelt to draw off her pants, sliding them down the length of her legs and waiting for her to step out of them — one foot, two feet, like a dainty circus pony — he rose to his feet, took a step backwards and looked at her.

'May I join you?' he asked.

And Dannie lowered her eyes and felt a rush of relief as she heard herself saying: 'You may.'

9

Cleo was sashaying towards the village green with a basket of laundry on her hip, slanting provocative looks at corner boys as she went. She knew that Pablo was watching through the pub window, so she made the looks as provocative as she could, and swished her hips so that the skirts over her masses of petticoats swayed equally provocatively. Her breasts were pushed up above a tightly laced, low-cut bodice, and she knew she looked pretty damn fit. Fluffy was trotting importantly at her ankles: Cleo had washed her hair and given her a conditioning treatment the night before. She wanted Fluffy to look fantastic in this, her very first movie role.

'And — cut!'

As soon as the words were uttered, cigarette packs materialized from waistcoat pockets and Discmen emerged from gingham-covered baskets. 'Village wenches' sat themselves up on the harbour wall and hoisted their skirts to their thighs so that their waxed legs could get some sun, 'varlets' slid Ray-Bans on, and mobile text alerts went off all over the place as people reactivated their phones. Make-up made a beeline for Eva Lavery, who stood on the threshold of Mimi's shop, and the animal wrangler turned his horse round and headed back up the street to get into position for the next take.

Cleo was appearing as an extra on *Mimi's Remedies*. She'd been cast as a village wench when Dannie had opted out. She'd thought it was a bit strange that Dannie had decided against taking part in the movie, because she'd confided in Cleo that her costume with its petticoats and tightly laced corsets would be a huge turn-on for Jethro and had announced her intention of visiting him for illicit lovemaking sessions in his Winnebago during lunch breaks. Cleo hadn't seen Dannie around for a while, come to think of it. Maybe she should invite her for supper tonight.

Climbing onto the wall, Cleo hitched her skirts up like the other extras, then fished a copy of *Heat* magazine out from under the laundry in her basket. It was an unseasonably warm spring day, and the village wore a festive air. The shop fronts had been tarted up to look 'ye olde worlde', and there were troughs of bright geraniums on virtually every windowsill. The door of Dannie's flower shop was covered in rainbow-coloured polka-dots, and the window was full of blue glass bottles and phials and terracotta jars. There were fire-eaters and sword-swallowers and stilt-walkers on the street, and peddlers hawking trays of gaudy ribbons, and there was an organ-grinder with a monkey. Fluffy had got wildly excited by the monkey. Uncertain whether to attack it or flirt with it, she was now ignoring it ostentatiously, swishing her tail and making it clear who the real star of the show was.

Cleo had felt a bit stupid being an extra at

first: something told her she wasn't cut out to be an actress, but then half the village were making idiots of themselves left, right and centre, kitted out in period costume and going 'rhubarb rhubarb, rhubarb' at each other. Margot was clearly relishing every moment. For the past hour she'd been walking past the revamped flower shop, nodding her head at Eva Lavery and saying 'Good morrow, Mimi — fair weather!', take after take. The line wasn't scripted, but Margot obviously felt it was important to be 'in character'. Any time she'd been in a crowd scene so far she'd improvised 'olde worlde'-type dialogue, full of lots of 'strewths and 'sbloods. Today Margot had been given a black bombazine fan as a prop, and she was getting great mileage out of it.

There she was now across the street, sidling towards Eva Lavery the very second make-up had finished with her, intending to engage the actress in conversation. But Eva had just signalled to Jethro Palmer, and the director was on his way over to her for a private confab. Catching sight of Cleo on the wall, Margot gave up on Eva and crossed the street to join her sister. Surreptitiously Cleo stuck her copy of *Heat* back under the laundry.

'Fun, this, isn't it?' Margot opened her fan with a flourish, and swished it to and fro. 'Felix always told me I'd make a fantastic actress.'

'Have you spoken to him yet?'

'No. He's still away. But I expect I'll hear from him as soon as he gets back. Our rows never last long.' She heaved a big sigh of contentment. 'I'm so glad I came down here, Cleo. It's not every day a gal gets to feature in a movie with an international film star.'

'I wouldn't call your role a *featured* one,' Cleo pointed out. The village was currently crawling with extras, all of them being paid standard Equity rate.

'I may not be featured, but details are important. Every small detail helps to weave the fabric of the tapestry that is the movie. For instance, the reason I invest my 'Good morrow, Mimi — fair weather!' with such heartfelt warmth is because somebody watching the finished movie might think to themselves 'Aha. That woman could be the mother of a child who was cured of some fatal illness by one of Mimi's remedies.''

Cleo was taken aback by Margot's blatant volte-face. Could this be the same woman who had sneered at Mimi and her remedies and questioned the integrity of the actress playing the lead role? 'Yeah,' she rallied back. 'Or you could be a big chum of Mimi who invites her round for girly talk and sex tips over a couple of bottles of Chardonnay every other week.'

Margot looked thoughtful. 'Elderberry wine would be more of the period.'

Dear Jesus! What had happened to her sister's sense of irony?

'I've been thinking,' resumed Margot, waving her fan, 'about staying on here for a while. And since I went to that women's group, I thought it mightn't be a bad idea to contribute to the social fabric of the village by hosting my salons. On a scaled-down basis, of course.'

Cleo didn't really know what to say to this, so she just gave an ambiguous 'mm'.

'I thought I might invite Colleen. I'm dying to tell her how much I loved *The Faraway*. And Pablo. And you, of course. And Eva.'

'Eva Lavery?'

'Yes. I'm certain to get an opportunity to talk to her at some stage this afternoon. And it's my guess that she'd be glad of an opportunity to be sociable — especially with an intellectual élite. I've heard that most actors get bored blue staying in hotel rooms.'

'Mm,' said Cleo again.

Margot looked animated. 'Oh, look!' she said. 'There's Colleen coming out of O'Toole's!'

Just then came a shouted directive from across the street for the cast to resume work. Margot made a cross face at being thwarted in her social trophy-hunting. 'And please remember to turn all mobile phones *off*,' came the tired adjuration from the second assistant director.

Extras were being herded, and the make-up police were going around scrutinizing faces. Some of the crowd had taken to sneaking off between takes to enhance their bronzer and stick on false eye-lashes, and make-up was getting seriously pissed off.

'Hey, you!' one of the team shouted, jabbing an accusatory finger at Colleen. 'Wipe that lipstick off. Clinique's Red Drama wasn't around in the nineteenth century — or hadn't you heard?'

Colleen's majestic stance became even more

majestic. 'I beg your pardon! You are under the mistaken premise that I am part of your movie-making. I am not. I reside here in Kilrowan, and I have every right to walk down the main street of my village.'

'Oh, sorry,' said the make-up girl, not sounding sorry at all. 'I was bum-steered by the cloak.'

Cleo walked back up the street and automatically reassumed her 'wench' pose, balancing the laundry basket on her hip. She could see Pablo again, watching from the window of the pub, and she went weak at the look he sent her. Then the realization of how hellish it would be if Margot *did* get round to organizing her First Wednesdays hit her. She, Cleo, would have to sit and observe the kind of proprietorial behaviour that Colleen had meted out to her squeeze that time they'd run into each other in O'Toole's. No! She wouldn't be able for that. She hoped fervently that Margot's notion of hosting her salons here in Kilrowan would bite the dust.

★ ★ ★

Later that afternoon, as a scene involving Colin Farrell and Ben Tarrant was being set up, the second assistant approached Cleo and asked her to lug her basket of laundry over to Mimi's shop. She was, she was told, to spend the rest of the afternoon hanging around in the doorway, looking as though she was chatting with the proprietor.

'You mean I've to talk to Eva *Lavery?*' said Cleo.

'Yeah. It's important that we see Eva in the background of this shot for continuity purposes. So just natter away to your heart's content and ignore the camera — and don't let the fact that you're hanging with a big star faze you. You've got to act *natural*.'

'OK.' Feeling apprehensive, Cleo followed the AD to where Eva was sitting in a canvas chair outside Mimi's shop, clearly enjoying the sun on her face.

'Miz Lavery?' said the second assistant. 'I'd like to introduce you to — um — sorry. I didn't get your name?'

'Cleo Dowling.'

'Cleo Dowling. She'll be keeping you company during this scene.'

'Oh, good. I'm glad it's not that woman earlier who insisted on waving her fan at me. Extras should be banned from brandishing fans, you know. They're the biggest upstaging tools in the book. Plus,' added the actress, a mite thoughtfully, 'she was just a little *too* beautiful.'

'Oh, *shit*,' said the AD. 'That bloody dog's barking at the monkey again. Better dash.'

'Nice to meet you, Cleo,' said Eva, holding out a hand. 'Sit down on the step here beside me, why don't you? Hey! Didn't I see you at the women's group last week?'

'Yes,' said Cleo, sitting down beside the actress and sliding an apprehensive look to where the AD was in hot pursuit of Fluffy.

'That turned out to be a very sad occasion for Dannie Moore.'

'Yes, it was. There was a big turn-out, though, for her dad's funeral. That's always a comfort, isn't it, when someone dies?'

'For sure. Will there be another women's group soon?'

'Yep. There's a sign up about it in the shop. Someone's giving a talk on fly-fishing.'

'Brilliant! I must get to that.'

Cleo gave Eva a doubtful look. 'Are you — er — a keen fly-fisher?'

'Not at all. Are you mad? But my husband David is. It'll be a great wheeze to surprise him by coming out with some really knowledgeable observations next time he goes off on a fishing trip. You know, stuff like: 'The salmon must be running fleet now the mayfly's in full spate', or 'Ne'er cast a line when the elm's in decline'. That kind of thing.'

'Is that true?' asked Cleo, really just for something to say. She was a little taken aback by the film star's friendliness. 'About the mayfly and the elm?'

'Phooey, no. I made it up. But it sounds like the kind of savvy country saying that a ghillie might come out with, doesn't it? Come to think of it, Mimi comes out with a lot of that kind of stuff in this screenplay. 'Borage, thistle, dill and wort, Combine to assuage any hurt.' Must try it next time I come across some borage and wort.'

'I loved the book. It was real uplifting stuff.'

'*Mimi's Remedies*? It's a blast, isn't it? My

215

friend Deirdre O'Dare did the screenplay.'

'Deirdre O'Dare? She's taken Dannie's apartment, hasn't she? The one above the shop.'

'Yeah. She's working away up there right now, writing a biography of *moi*. I never thought anyone would be interested in *moi*, but when I heard it was on the cards that a poisonous pen type felt compelled to dish the dirt, I decided that it would be a very good thing to get a friend to dish it first.'

'Oh, I'm sure there isn't any dirt to dish, Ms Lavery!'

'Eva,' the actress corrected her. 'And there is, actually — masses. Let me tell you a lovely story about . . . '

And Eva embarked upon a scandalous tale of Hollywood bitch-craft, featuring her and another very famous film star. Halfway through the anecdote the second assistant came and took Eva's canvas chair away, and then make-up and hair and wardrobe arrived to fuss over her, and still the actress carried on regaling Cleo with fascinating gossip. This she continued to do even as the cameras rolled, and Cleo found herself getting so absorbed in Eva's stories that she completely forgot to act.

When Colin Farrell and Ben Tarrant had finished their scene, Jethro Palmer came to talk to Eva while the crew were setting up the next shot.

He gave the actress a smacking kiss, then turned to Cleo. 'Congratulations to you, too, ma'am. You're a natural.'

Cleo felt so chuffed she almost blushed.

'Thank you. But it was all down to Eva, really. She's so laid-back.'

Eva smiled, then gave Jethro a shrewd look. 'I've had a brainwave,' she said. 'I really like Cleo. Maybe she could be one of Mimi's Minxes?'

Cleo remembered that the clique of witchy girls from the book were referred to as Mimi's Minxes.

'Why not? She'd make a great Minx.' Jethro looked Cleo up and down. She couldn't help noticing that he had fantastic eyes, with irises of an unsettling shade of green flecked with amber. No wonder Dannie was besotted with him!

Cleo was just about to say Yes, please — I'd love to be a Minx, when an alarm bell went off. 'Oh! Please tell me I won't have any lines,' she said instead. Listening to Eva was one thing, but she'd cringe if she had to do any *real* acting.

'Don't worry,' said Jethro. 'We don't want Equity kicking up a stink. You'll just be required to 'rhubarb' nicely in the background.'

'What about asking Dannie as well?' suggested Eva. 'It'd be fun to have her on board as a Minx, and it might take her mind off her dad's death.'

There was a beat before Jethro answered. 'No. I've a hunch Dannie wouldn't be interested,' he said.

'Jethro! We're ready to rock.' It was the AD, looking frazzled. 'Jesus! What imbecile dreamed up the idea of hiring that fucking monkey, anyway?'

'Me,' said Eva.

'Oh. Sorry,' said the AD.

'Talk soon, film star.' Jethro dropped a kiss on Eva's cheek before turning and heading back to work.

A make-up girl approached, and Eva automatically raised her face for retouching. 'Be sure to let the AD know you're a Minx, by the way,' she told Cleo. 'You'll be on a different rate. Special extras get more euros.'

'Oh! Great.' Cleo could hardly tell her new film-star friend that she didn't need more euros because she was already a lottery millionaire who would be perfectly happy to be in the film for free. 'In that case, maybe you'd allow me to buy you a pint?'

'You're on,' said Eva. 'O'Toole's at seven? I'm meeting Deirdre then.'

'OK. See you at seven. Look forward to it!' Cleo turned away from the actress with a satisfying swirl of her skirts, feeling *beyond* chuffed that she had a rendezvous with a movie star as well as a brand-new career as a special extra.

As she strolled up the street she caught sight of Margot, who was lurking on the corner, waiting to grab her. 'What was all that about?' she asked.

Cleo gave a big smile. 'I've been promoted to special extra status,' she explained. 'I've got a part as one of Mimi's Minxes. Isn't it great?'

'Mimi's *what*?'

'Minxes. They're like her closest girlfriends.'

'Jesus!' Margot looked as if she might throw up, and Cleo couldn't work out whether Margot was more nauseated by the naffness of the

Minxes or the fact that Cleo had had such a classy upgrade. 'I suppose there'll be no stopping you now. Before you know it, you'll be Eva Lavery's NBF.'

There was no disguising the cattiness of the tone. 'Well, there's a distinct possibility of that,' Cleo replied with a bright smile. 'I'm meeting her in O'Toole's for a drink later. Want to join us?'

And off Cleo quickly swished up the main street of Kilrowan before Margot could barf on her shoes.

★ ★ ★

When Cleo went into O'Toole's just before seven Margot was there before her, sitting by the fire reading *The Faraway* and fanning herself with the prop she'd misappropriated.

'Hi,' she said. 'I've ordered you a drink. It's on its way.' She marked her place in the book and shut it. 'I'm re-reading Colleen. It's even more profound on a second reading. You uncover things you wouldn't notice first time round — the structure is extraordinarily nuanced. Thanks' — this to the barman who'd brought their drinks. Cleo couldn't help noticing the puppy-dog look Margot's smile produced. Bah! Why couldn't *she* have been a babe like her sister?

Margot laid *The Faraway* reverently next to her, then returned her attention to Cleo. 'So, tell me. What are you reading at the moment, beloved? Anything interesting?'

'*Heat* magazine,' said Cleo with blatant bravado, knowing her sister wouldn't believe her.

'Ha ha.' She didn't! 'Written anything recently?'

'Haven't had time.'

'What? Not even time for maudlin poetry?' Margot put on a 'poetic' type voice. ''I hear the landscape, I cannot see it.' Ow. Sorry. That was a bit below the belt.'

Cleo blanched. 'How did you find out about that?'

'Easy. I visited the Be a Bard website and typed in 'Cleo Dowling'. How on earth did you allow yourself to get scammed by that crowd, Cleo?'

'I was pissed.'

'Why am I not surprised? Oh well. Now I can tell my friends that my sister is an International Bard of Acclaim as well as being a millionaire. *Sláinte.*' Margot raised her glass. 'What's the word on that apartment in Dublin, incidentally? The one you were cracked enough to buy from a plan?'

Oh, God. Cleo bit her lip. She really didn't want to have to say this. 'The completion date's been put back.'

'Told you that would happen,' tinkled Margot. 'Oh! *Hi!*'

Eva Lavery and a dark-haired woman had just come through the door. Margot gave an effusive wave, and Eva sent back an uncertain smile. 'Hi,' she said to Cleo. 'This is my friend Deirdre O'Dare.'

'Sit down, sit down — let me get you a drink!'

said Margot, jumping up and giving Eva a coy smile. 'We met earlier, Eva, outside your shop. Or rather, Mimi's shop.' Then she turned to Deirdre and grabbed her by the hand. 'Lovely to meet you, Deirdre. I'm Margot d'Arcy. What'll you have?'

'A coupla white wines would be good.'

Margot beelined for the bar and Eva and Deirdre sat down opposite Cleo.

'That's my sister,' said Cleo in a low voice. 'The one who tried to upstage you with the fan.'

'Don't worry — being upstaged by extras is one of the occupational hazards,' smiled Eva. 'Deirdre, this is Cleo. She's playing one of my Minxes.'

'Hey — you'll have fun. I wish I could be a Minx.'

'Why don't you check it out with Jethro?' suggested Eva. 'I'm sure he'd love for you to feature.'

'I don't have time to mess around being a Minx. I'm up to my tonsils with *toi*, Lavery. I'm writing Eva's biography,' she told Cleo. 'I'm on some meaty stuff right now, incidentally, Eva — about Sebastian.'

'Oh! Which bit of my gorgeous son are you on?'

'The time he played Hamlet to your Gertrude.'

Eva gave Deirdre an imploring look. 'I know he behaved badly then, but do try to be nice about him, won't you?'

'Certainly I will. I always had a soft spot for Sebastian. And you'll be *delighted* to learn that

Sophie Burke has just made her first appearance.'

'Ha! You can be as evil as you like about her!'

Eva and Deirdre shared a smile. Then, as if realizing that the pair of them might look a little exclusive, Deirdre turned to Cleo. 'Do you live here in Kilrowan, Cleo?' she asked.

'Yes. I've just moved here from Dublin.'

'And what do you do for a living? When you're not being a film extra, that is.'

'Well, I — '

'Cleo's a poet. A published one.' Margot slanted Cleo a catlike look as she set two miniatures of white wine down on the table.

'Really?' they said simultaneously, then Deirdre added: 'I'm impressed.'

'Don't be,' said Cleo. 'I've only ever had one poem published by a scabby vanity press. Anyone could do it. You could submit 'Humpty Dumpty' and still be nominated as an International Bard of Acclaim. I'm one.'

'An International Bard of Acclaim? Wow.'

'I mean it. Log on tonight and enter something, and I guarantee you'll get a letter back raving about your 'unique poetic artistry'.'

'Hey. I'll do it!' said Deirdre. 'Write down the address.'

Deirdre passed Cleo a drink mat and a biro, and watched while Cleo wrote www.Be–A–Bard.com. 'Www.Be A Bard dot *con* more like,' she muttered, passing it across the table.

'Did you win stuff?'

'Not a cent. But I could have bought a faux-leather volume with my poem in. And a CD of someone warbling my lyrics. *And* a badge to sew on the breast pocket of my blazer to advise the world that I am an International Bard of Acclaim.'

'Respect!' said Eva. 'Maybe I should enter a poem too. It would look good for the blurb on my biography, don't you think? 'As well as being an award-winning actress, Eva Lavery is also an International Bard of Acclaim.''

'I'll drink to that.' Deirdre raised her glass. 'And I'll stick the poem in your biog if you like.'

'Yes! I'll do a love poem about David. What rhymes with 'sex'?'

' 'Rex'?' suggested Cleo.

'That'll do. By the way, Deirdre, he's bringing Dorcas for a visit soon. I'm expecting a call this evening to confirm.'

'Oh, you smug bitch! I heard from Rory today, and it looks like the visit he'd been planning has had to be cancelled. He's landed yet another role where he gets to swash his buckle and ride bareback.'

'More typecasting,' sighed Eva. 'How tedious.'

'You're married to Rory McDonagh, aren't you?' Cleo asked. 'I read about your wedding in *OK!*'

Deirdre made an apologetic face. 'It remains a mystery to this day how they got hold of those photographs.'

'And you're married to David Lawless, the theatre director, Eva, isn't that so?' Margot inclined a smile that was borderline obsequious. 'I thought his production of *Peer Gynt* for the RSC was fabulous.'

223

'I concurrr.' Colleen's husky brogue came from round the corner, and then the writer herself appeared, swathed in her trademark cloak. 'That *Peer Gynt* was definitive.' She smiled at the assembled company. 'Allow me to introduce myself. I am Colleen!'

Deirdre and Eva smiled back politely, clearly waiting for the surname that would never come. Then the penny dropped. 'Oh — *Colleen*!' they said in unison.

'May I join you?' Without bothering to wait for an affirmative, the writer cast off her cloak, revealing the Sile-na-gig pendant resplendent on her bosom. 'Eva Lavery. La Divina! I am a devotee of your work.'

'Thanks,' said Eva, looking nonplussed.

There was a silence while Eva and Deirdre took in the overwhelming *overwhelmingness* of Colleen, then Margot sprang into life. She leaned forward to clasp Colleen's hand. 'Colleen, I'm Margot d'Arcy. We've met before, but you may not remember. It was at a literary luncheon in the Hamilton Hotel. I'm a great admirer of your work.'

Colleen's smile became more encouraging. 'Indeed and I do remember,' she said, and Margot looked like a child who'd just been given an enormous slice of cake. 'You made some very cogent remarks about the state of modern literature.' A great big cherry had just been plonked on top of the cake. 'Ah! *The Faraway*!' Colleen's attention had been diverted to *The Faraway*, which lay on the banquette. 'And who might be reading my book?' she asked, bestowing a gracious smile around the table. Deirdre and Eva were both gazing at Colleen with their mouths slightly open. They quickly shut their mouths and smiled back.

'I am,' said Margot brightly. 'In fact, I'm reading it for the second time.' More Brownie points! Colleen now looked like a replete cat and — surrounded as she was by theatrical and literary élite — Margot looked as if she was the cat who'd got the *crème de la crème*. 'May I introduce Deirdre O'Dare?' she said, clearly delighted to effect celebrity introductions. Deirdre still looked as if she was in a mild state of shock.

'Forgive me. Should the name ring a bell?'

'No. I'm not famous.'

'That's unfair!' put in Eva. 'Why are scriptwriters always so backward about coming forward? Deirdre wrote the script for *Mimi's Remedies*, Colleen, the film that's being made here in Kilrowan. *And* she's working on a biography.'

'Ah — so you are a writer, too. Indeed, this public house is coming down with writers! You, Deirdre, a scriptwriter and biographer, you — ' a glance (a rather dismissive one) at Cleo — 'a poet. And you, Margot, let me guess.' She put her head on one side, assessing. 'A novelist!'

'Yes,' said Margot promptly.

'But you haven't had anything published,' Cleo blurted, unable to help herself. She was still smarting from the knowledge that Margot had read her crap poem on the Net, and — what was worse — quoted from it. However, the look her sister shot her made her add a hasty 'Yet!'

A phone went off — the 'polite' tone that both Deirdre and Eva favoured — and there was a little flurry of bag-rummaging. It transpired, however, that Colleen clearly favoured 'polite' mode also.

'Damn,' said Eva, dropping her little silver phone back into her bag. 'I was hoping that might be David.'

'Damn,' said Deirdre, dropping her little silver phone back into her bag. 'I was hoping that might be Rory.'

'Damn,' said Colleen, striking her forehead with the heel of her hand. 'My publicist. Go away, Leonora,' she said into the receiver of her little silver phone. 'I'll talk to you later. Yes, I promise.' And Colleen fired the phone back into her bag as if it had contaminated her. 'I despise that phone,' she announced, 'but my people insist that I carry one. I have no line in the house.'

Deirdre was astonished. 'No telephone line?'

'No. Nor do I have a television or a computer.'

'So you don't use a word-processing facility to write your novels?'

'No. I despise technology. I am proud to be a Luddite. I write all my books on hand-made paper imported — '

'From Nepal,' finished Margot.

'Brava!' Colleen looked impressed. 'How did you know?'

'I read it on your website.'

'I have a website? How extraordinary. I did not know that.'

'I don't have a television in my cottage, either,' said Margot, helpfully. 'I don't even have a dishwasher.'

'I am glad to hear it.' Colleen sent Margot a smile of approval. 'A dishwasher is a most ecologically unsound appliance.'

The barman arrived with a glass of red wine for Colleen. 'Another round, Noel, if you would be so kind,' she said, with an expansive gesture.

Eva looked at her watch. 'I shouldn't really. I've an early call tomorrow. But what the hell! It's not every day you run into an award-winning novelist and an International Bard of Acclaim in a village pub.'

'And what excitement in our small community to have such stellar personae gracing our hostelry! How is your 'movie' coming along?' asked Colleen. She pronounced the word 'movie' as if she had never heard it before.

'Fine,' said Eva. 'I'm having a blast, anyway. I get to snog Colin Farrell *and* Ben Tarrant. That's a real perk for an old bag like me.'

'I would question the use of the term 'old bag' to describe *you*, Eva,' reprimanded Colleen.

'She is too an old bag,' said Deirdre. 'Even though she's aged quite well. I know her birth date, and I'm going to unleash it on an aghast public in the biography. Be uncomfortable. Be *very* uncomfortable.'

Colleen was looking pretty uncomfortable herself, and Cleo found herself wondering how old *she* was. Older than Pablo anyway, that was for sure.

'Talking of old bags, I've thought up a brilliant

idea for saggy bits,' said Eva. 'Instead of lifting and tucking, just ask a surgeon to slit open all your saggy bits and line them with satin or velvet and then fit them with zips. That means you wouldn't need to bother with a handbag any time you go out. You could just put your keys and your credit card and your lippy in one of your bits and zip it up.'

'Nice idea!' said Cleo. 'Hey, just think — if you had loads of saggy bits you'd be a veritable walking organizer bag. People might even want to hire you to accompany them on business meetings, and boast about you. 'Here's my old bag,' they'd say. 'She has fourteen separate compartments *and* she answers my mobile phone for me.''

'There's a problem there,' said Deirdre. 'You'd have to go through the X-ray conveyor belt in airports.'

Cleo slid a look at Colleen. She looked as if she were listening to people talking in some unintelligible language. A bit rum, she thought, for someone who had dreamed up the cracked conceit of a nineteenth-century heroine talking on a mobile phone . . .

Noel deposited their drinks on the table. 'Will I put it on your tab, Colleen?' he asked.

'But of course,' she said, picking a glass of red wine off the tray and raising it high in the air: '*Sláinte!*' she said. 'Here's to your 'movie'!'

'Thanks, Colleen,' said Eva. 'Did you read the book?'

'The book? I am sorry? To which book might you be referring?'

'*Mimi's Remedies?*'

'*Mimi's Remedies?*' Colleen gave a private little smile. 'Alas, no, I have not had that pleasure.'

'It's a real life-affirming read,' said Deirdre. 'I'm going to get to meet the actual author — Lily Wright. She's coming to the wrap party. I hope she thinks I've done justice to her novel.'

'And who exactly is this 'Mimi' of the 'Remedies'?' asked Colleen.

'She's a kind of white witch,' explained Deirdre.

'Ah? I touch on witchcraft in *The Faraway*.' Colleen turned to Margot like an empress bestowing a gift. 'Perhaps, Margot, you would like me to sign your copy?'

'Oh! Thank you! But it's already signed. I picked up a signed copy on publication. I was one of the first in the queue.'

'Really? In that case, let me personalize it for you.' Colleen took a fountain pen from her hempen satchel, reached for *The Faraway* and hefted it onto the table.

'I'd say her pecs are in great shape,' Cleo heard Eva remark in an aside to Deirdre. 'I wouldn't need to bother pumping iron at all if I were signing copies of that book.'

Colleen inscribed the flyleaf with a flourish and a smile. Cleo managed to sneak a sideways look, and when she read — *To Margot. Live the Dream. Doubt Not Your Soul. Finish the Novel! XXX* — she had no doubt that this book would take pride of place on the shelf in Margot's sanctuary in Dublin for many years to come.

'Thank you, Colleen,' simpered Margot. Cleo wasn't sure she'd actually *seen* anyone simper before. It was beyond weird seeing her sister doing it.

'Haven't I seen you around the village before, Margot?' remarked Colleen, slanting her an astute look.

'You have, indeed, Colleen. I own a cottage here — An Teach Bán.'

'An Teach Bán? An Teach Bán is a charming cottage! And how long might you have been living there, at An charming Teach Bán?' Colleen articulated the Irish with panache, clearly relishing rolling the syllables round in her mouth, and Cleo had the impression that she would show off her impeccable Erse at any given opportunity.

'I bought it as a holiday home a couple of years ago, but I don't use it as much as I'd like because the drive from Dublin is so punishing. However, since I got a part in the movie I was thinking about staying on here for a while, and I was hoping to organize an evening of — ' But Margot's opportunity to issue her invite to a Wednesday salon went unseized, because:

'Christ! Who's the *ride*?' Deirdre was gazing at someone who'd just come into the pub. Her mouth had dropped open for the second time that evening.

Colleen gave her feline smile. 'That,' she said, 'is my lov*air*. That is Pablo MacBride. Pablo!' she called, stretching out an arm to him. 'A *grá*! Come to me. Come and meet La Divina Eva Lavery, and — um — ?' She gave Deirdre a

230

questioning look. 'Forgive me. I am hopeless with names.'

'I'm Deirdre O'Dare,' said Deirdre, wistfully. She was suddenly thinking about Rory.

10

'Yaaaaay!' went Paloma, and Dannie allowed herself an indulgent smile at Oliver and Paloma as they waltzed along in a Beauty and the Beast teacup and saucer. Oliver had treated them to a trip to Disneyland Paris to celebrate the fact that they were going to be a brand-new family together. She'd done the right thing, she reminded herself as they whooshed past her, laughing. She'd finally found a father for Paloma. She'd finally found someone who would do all the right Dada things with her daughter — all the things Jethro had never had time for.

Telling him hadn't been easy. In fact, she'd felt like the Terminator when she'd broken the news to him over supper in O'Toole's. It had been on the evening of the day he'd bought her the Daniel Lennox painting, the evening of the day she'd swum in Oliver's pool, the evening of the day she'd made the decision to change her life . . .

★ ★ ★

'Would this be happening if I *hadn't* bought the painting for you, Dannie?' asked Jethro. He was keeping his voice low. Since filming had started, the small restaurant was crowded every night.

'Yes. You know it would, Jethro. I've done an awful lot of thinking about this. Don't imagine for a minute that I'm just being stupid and impulsive. D'you know what our relationship's like? It's like a *geansaí* that's been unravelling for ages, and we try and try to patch it up, but we can't keep up with the unravelling and the holes just keep getting bigger and bigger. The painting was the straw that broke the camel's back. We've tried our hardest, God knows we have, but the way we've been handling this isn't good for me and it isn't good for Paloma.'

'Are you saying it's good for me?'

'Well. You're the one who gets the most out of it, aren't you? You have a loving family tucked away in a remote corner of the world who you can drop in on occasionally to say 'hi' to when you happen to be passing, and get a ride off your mot.'

Jethro winced, then recovered himself. He leaned back in his chair and resumed his lazy drawl. 'Hey, now,' he said. 'I don't think that's quite fair, Dannie. I contribute a lot financially — '

'But that's not what's important! Don't you see? Paloma needs *stability*. She needs a constant in her life, and you're not giving her that. If you'd seen the state of the child that time you promised to take her and her pals on a visit to the studio and then cried off. She was in flitters!'

'Dannie, you know why I had to let her down. I told you that the money men were breathing down my neck, and there was no way I could — '

'I know what you told me! You don't need to tell me again.' Dannie was raising her voice, and

233

people were starting to look sideways at her. She made a big effort to calm down. 'I love you, Jethro Palmer,' she whispered fiercely, leaning towards him. 'But I love my wee girl more than anything else in this world, and I'll fight like a tiger to make sure she gets the kind of emotional support she needs.'

'And you think that this Oliver Dunne dude is going to provide you with that?'

'Yes. Yes, I do. And he'll be faithful to me. Unlike you.'

He couldn't have looked more hostile if he'd snarled. 'We agreed from the beginning that both of us were free to see other people, Dannie.'

'I know. But I *haven't* been seeing other people. Jaze, Jethro!' She gave a mirthless laugh. 'How do you think I felt when I got a load of that picture of you in *Hello!* magazine with some dewy-eyed French starlet hanging on your arm? That was a real slap in the face, so it was. I felt mortified walking into Shanley's shop that week, knowing that half the village had probably seen it. And what would you have done if Paloma had spotted it?'

Now Jethro looked as if he was the one who'd been slapped in the face.

'Claudine didn't mean anything to me. She was just a — '

'A one-night stand?'

Jethro looked guarded. Then: 'Yes, ma'am,' he said.

'And that Swedish blonde at the Oscars? She was just a one-night stand too?'

'Yes, ma'am,' he repeated. 'And an exceptionally lousy lay.'

Dannie gave an unamused laugh. 'You see? What class of a relationship do we have, Jethro? What's a little girl to make of a daddy who jet-sets off all over the world and has his picture taken on a regular basis with women who aren't her mammy?'

'Other kids cope with it.'

'Oh — you mean kids like Demi Moore's or Nicole Kidman's? Yeah, maybe *they* cope. It's routine, isn't it, in those circles, to see Mammy or Daddy posing for pictures with eye-catching arm-candy? But Paloma's not an LA kid who goes to school in a chauffeur-driven limo and lives in the hothouse atmosphere of a Bel-Air mansion and has servants. Paloma's a real little girl living in the real world, and it's tough out there, Mr Palmer.'

Jethro drained his wineglass. 'You're serious about this?'

'I am.'

He set the glass down with a clunk. 'Are you going to marry him?'

'Yes.'

'And exactly when,' he curled his lip, 'do you become Dannie *Dunne*?'

It was Dannie's turn to wince. 'We haven't set a date.'

'Are you going to have his babies?'

'I — I don't know.' The question took her by surprise. She hadn't considered the possibility of having children with Oliver.

'Will Paloma call him Daddy?'

Oh, God! She hadn't thought about that either. 'No. You'll always be her daddy. She'll call Oliver by his Christian name.'

'What have you told her?'

'Nothing yet. But I'll tell her that Oliver wants to take us on holiday to Disneyland Paris to help us get over Grandpa's death. And that we'll be moving into the Glebe House when we come back because the cottage isn't really ours any more.'

'The Glebe House?'

'Yes. It's Oliver's hotel. He has his own private apartment there.'

'You've seen it?'

'Yes,' she lied. The only part of the Glebe House she'd seen had been the pool. The proposed tour had had to be deferred because Dannie wanted to get Paloma sorted and put to bed before she broke her news to Jethro.

'When do you go to Paris?'

'I don't know. Oliver's on the case now.'

Jethro regarded her gravely. 'That's a lot of new stuff for Paloma to take on board.'

'She's young enough still to see it as an adventure. And she's resilient. Janey! Hasn't she had to be, with a father like you!'

Jethro sucked in his breath, then got to his feet. 'That was an unkind cut, Ms Moore,' he said. He drew a chequebook out of his pocket, opened it, and scribbled a sum. 'I'll get dinner. You stay here, order a *digestif*. Give me an hour to pack a bag and say goodbye to Paloma. I'll send a PA for the rest of my stuff tomorrow.'

236

Dannie stiffened. 'You're moving out of the cottage?'

'Sure am.'

'Where'll you go?'

'Ballynahinch Castle. I'll book a two-bedroomed suite — that is, if it's cool for Paloma to come visit from time to time?'

'Of course it's cool, Jethro. You know I wouldn't ever stand in the way of your seeing her.'

They looked at each other for a moment or two in silence, then Jethro folded the cheque, dropped it on the table, and kissed her cheek. 'So long, Dannie,' he said. 'Good luck.'

She heard the sound of the till, and pleasantries were exchanged, and then came the sound of the restaurant door opening and closing. Dannie sat there, staring at her wineglass. Her words came back to her, the words that Jethro had described as 'unkind'. *She's resilient. Hasn't she had to be, with a father like you!* Christ. They were more than unkind — they were excoriating. She had been grossly unfair. Jethro might not be the most reliable father in the world, but he certainly wasn't a bad one, and he loved Paloma profoundly.

Dannie might have remained that way, staring at her glass and castigating herself for her insensitivity, for many more minutes if her phone hadn't alerted her to a text. Automatically she drew the phone out of her bag and opened the message. **Buked flite for 2moro eve. Tel Pal she's in 4 a treat. We're staying in da**

Cinderella Suite! Luv u. Oli. XXX.

Dannie took a gulp of wine, then unfolded the cheque that Jethro had let drop on the table. *Danniella Moore*, she read. *Twenty thousand euros only*. And then the signature: *J. Palmer*. Twenty thousand euros. Her share of the painting. Well, fuck him! she thought. Did he really think that she'd accept it? She screwed the cheque into a ball and made to throw it into the fire, then stopped herself just in time. *Some good had to come of this grotesque situation. The money would go to charity* — her father's favourite: the St Vincent de Paul.

Dannie picked up her phone again, and pressed some buttons. 'Delete message?' she read. She was just about to press 'OK' when something made her pause. Instead she scrolled down to 'Reply'. **Luv u 2**, she typed, then pressed more buttons. The image of the flying envelope appeared on the screen of her phone, and 'Message sent' was displayed.

Dannie switched the phone off, then turned in her seat and raised a hand to the waitress. 'Could I have a large brandy, please, Marie?' she said.

★　★　★

'Hi, beautiful,' Oliver said now, emerging from the giant teacup with Paloma perched on his hip. He slung an arm around Dannie and dropped a light kiss on her lips. 'Well?' he said, looking down at Jethro's daughter. 'Was that the best ride yet, or was that the best ride yet?'

'It was the best ride yet!' laughed Paloma, and

Dannie's heart went mushy with love when she saw the animated expression on her daughter's face.

When was the last time she'd seen Paloma so lit up? She remembered now. It had been the time her daddy had come back from LA unexpectedly, with presents. She recalled the way they'd looked, lounging riotously on her bed, surrounded by toys and crumpled wrapping paper, and the indulgent expression on Jethro's face as he'd watched his daughter. And then she remembered the way he'd made love to her later by candlelight, and how he'd held her afterwards, and the gorgeous clean smell of him . . . And then Dannie banished the memory from her mind and laid her head on Oliver's shoulder.

★   ★   ★

It hadn't taken long for word to get round the village that Dannie Moore had thrown Jethro Palmer over and gone and got engaged to Oliver Dunne. Breda Shanley's shop was full of the gossip. Some people tut-tutted a bit — mostly because they'd targeted Oliver as a match for their own daughters — but generally speaking people were pleased because they made such a lovely couple. Breda was glad that Dannie and Paloma's lives would acquire some sort of structure at last.

Cleo had gone to Eva Lavery's Winnebago to tell her the news, but she never got the chance. Someone had beaten her to it. Through the half-open door she caught sight of Jethro. He was sitting on the couch, his big shoulders hunched in an attitude of despair. He had his head in his hands, and Cleo suspected he'd been crying. Eva was curled up on the couch beside him, stroking his hair and crooning words of comfort, looking immeasurably sad. Cleo backed away on silent feet.

No-one was amazed when the director strolled onto the set an hour later, wearing his habitual authoritative expression. No-one in their right mind would have offered him sympathy, just as no-one voiced admiration for his stoicism. The show simply went on.

Cleo was having great fun being a Minx. It was easy. All you needed to do was remember not to act, and with Eva that was a doddle. She thought that she had never met anyone as unpretentious as the film star, or anyone who radiated more unforced *joie de vivre*. Eva seemed to grab each day, view it through rose-tinted glasses and make it special. Some days if she had time off she'd get the hotel to pack her a picnic and she'd race off to the beach, dragging Deirdre and Cleo with her. Some days she'd have cases of cold beer delivered to the set to reward cast and crew for their hard work. And on special occasions like birthdays there was always a cake and champagne. Eva was perfect casting for the convivial, sanguine Mimi. And when her husband, David Lawless, and their little girl Dorcas, arrived in Kilrowan, the atmosphere on set every day verged on the festive.

The interior set was in a studio in Clare, and

early every morning Cleo would board the bus that transported the extras, looking forward to going to work nearly as much as she had in the days when she'd worked in the book trade. In the evenings — back at number 5, the Blackthorns — she'd boot up Clarabelle and tip-tap away at the keys. She'd dumped her Novel in the recycle bin, and was concentrating instead on her short story — which wasn't turning out to be as short as she'd intended. The Man in the Hat was pretty damn fine in the sack, and Cleo was enjoying writing about his amorous exploits. She'd christened him Ricardo.

Sometimes, if Colleen was away on one of her book tours or attending some literary event, Pablo would drop in and they'd share a bottle of wine. They were enjoying each other's company more and more, especially since they'd got the sex thing (or lack of same) out of the way. Cleo visited him in his studio sometimes, and was gobsmacked by how quickly he executed his paintings. 'That one's going to a banker. That one's going to a rock star. And that one's going to Eva Lavery,' were the kind of casual remarks he came out with on an irritatingly regular basis.

'Can I have one?' asked Cleo one evening, as she opened a second bottle of wine. They were in her sitting room. At last she'd finished her short story, and she was celebrating.

'A painting? Course you can. I'll let you have one as a present,' he said.

'No! I'd have to pay you.'

'Jesus, Cleo. I don't want your money.'

'I know.' She gave him a sulky look. 'But I can't accept a free painting.'

'Can, too.'

'Won't, then! I have to pay you in kind somehow. Oh!' she clapped her hand over her mouth. 'I didn't mean that as an offer of — you know . . .'

Pablo raised an eyebrow. 'Sex?' he finished for her.

'Yes.'

It was the first time in ages that a sexual vibe had reared up between them.

Pablo looked at her, considering. Then: 'No sex,' he said.

'Absolutely not!' she enthused.

He tilted his head to one side. 'What kind of payment then?'

'I dunno.'

'*I* do.'

'Know?'

'Yes.'

'What?'

'I want to read your short story.'

'*Forget* it!'

He shrugged. 'OK, then. No painting for you, little Cleo.'

She felt completely trounced. 'Oh, come on, Pablo! You're being really unfair, you know.'

'No, I'm not. Here's the deal. I'll give you your choice of painting if you allow me to read your short story. Quid pro quo.'

'*What?* Shit, Pablo — I *can't* let you read it.'

'Why not?'

'Because it's practically pornographic!'

He gave her a fiendish smile. 'Now I *have* to read it.'

'Never!'

They were standing facing each other. Cleo's face was flaming, her breath was coming fast.

'Ah, go on, Cleo. I promise I won't read it in front of you.'

'No! *No!*' She was vacillating. 'Oh, God, Pablo! I'd be so morti — '

'You're vacillating.'

'I'm not!'

'You are.' He adopted a cajoling tone. 'I'll let you have my biggest canvas, Cleo. I'll paint whatever subject you want. I'll do a portrait — a portrait of *you*. Imagine having a portrait of yourself hanging on your wall — a portrait by one of Ireland's most collectable painters . . . '

Now it wasn't the acquisition of the painting that was giving Cleo second thoughts. It was the notion of sitting for Pablo in his studio. She found the prospect dangerously seductive.

Her short story was in a folder in her study. Without another thought — blocking the voice of reason that was raised in outrage in her head — Cleo ran into the study, grabbed the folder, then ran back to where Pablo was standing in the sitting room with the glint of triumph in his eyes. He had never looked sexier.

'Here,' she said, thrusting the folder at him. 'Now take it away.' Lunging for the window that led onto the deck, Cleo dragged it open. 'Take it away! Go go go!' she urged. 'Before I change my mind!'

He was gone.

Some forty minutes later, a tap came at the window. Feeling stiff with embarrassment, Cleo set down her wineglass and crossed the room. Pablo was standing on the deck with the folder in his hand. They looked at each other through the window for a moment or two, and then Cleo slid it open for him and backed away.

'It's about me,' he said.

'No, it's not! Don't be stupid.'

'Yes, it is,' he said. 'And it's very, very sexy. I love the way Ricardo does this.' He moved towards her and very slowly started to undo the buttons on her shirt. 'And I love the way he does this,' he said, sliding the sleeves down over her arms. 'I especially love the way he does this — ' he dropped her shirt to the floor ' — and this — ' her bra dematerialized ' — and this.' A kiss.

'Oh, God,' breathed Cleo.

'And, of course, this.' A caress.

And that was how Pablo MacBride and Cleo Dowling finally got it together.

★   ★   ★

Afterwards, Cleo clung to him and pulled the duvet over her face. 'I can't believe I allowed you to do that. And I can't believe I allowed you to read that story,' she said.

'I'm very glad you did. That story was as sexy as anything I've seen in the *Erotica Universalis* and as helpful as *Sex Tips for Girls*. Now I know exactly what floats your boat. I found the bit with the choc ices particularly enlightening, incidentally. Got any?'

'Um. I think so.'

'Good girl. Go get one.'

'*No!*'

'Why? Reckon the fantasy's better than the reality?'

'No,' she repeated in a much smaller voice. She actually found the notion wildly erotic. 'It's just — um — that it'll ruin the sheets. They're Egyptian cotton.'

Pablo crowed with laughter. 'You can take a girl out of the middle class . . . '

'Shut up. I'll get one later.'

He started to pull away the duvet. 'Hey,' he said. 'Come out from under there and let me look at you. Wow. Just look at that post-orgasmic flush. Permanent Magenta, eat your heart out.' Cleo pulled the duvet back over her face. 'I must say I found that Ricardo geezer a revelation,' she heard him muse through the goosedown that muffled her ears. 'Got any other stories I might enjoy?'

'*No!*'

'Shame. Let's start one now, while you're down there. How about this? 'Ricardo was hard again. She slid herself against him and traced the line of his ribcage with her tongue, and then she reached down with her hand . . . ' Oh! Very nice. Very nice, indeed, Ms Dowling. D'you know something, Cleo? You're even more audacious than your heroine. *Wow*. Short story, how are you?' He gave a laugh. 'I think we

245

might have the makings of a bestselling bonkbuster here.'

* * *

When Pablo and Cleo finally emerged from under the duvet, they took a shower together to wash all the ice-cream off. And after she'd been scrubbed to Pablo's exacting standards, Cleo dumped her lovely embroidered Egyptian cotton sheets in the laundry basket, slung on a kimono, then went down to the kitchen to make coffee while he dressed. It was three o'clock in the morning, she noticed. God and horror! She had to be up at half-past five to make the extras' bus on time, and she was going to look like a complete dog, not a Minx at all.

'God, you look gorgeous,' said Pablo from the kitchen door.

'No, I don't. I look wrecked.'

'That's what I mean. The best look in the world for a woman is the 'wrecked from sex' look. Whoever could bottle that would make a fortune.'

'Sit down. Have some coffee.'

'Bollocks to coffee. I'll have wine, please.'

'Pablo, it's three o'clock in the morning!'

'And there's a law about drinking wine at three o'clock in the morning? That's the beauty of my job, sweetheart. I can drink as much wine as I like any time I damn well please.'

'Well, I'll have to run on caffeine if I'm going to get through the day. There's no point in me going back to bed now.' She placed the cafetière and the wine bottle on the table and sat down opposite him.

He was leaning back in his chair, regarding her. 'Well. What the fuck do we do now?' he said.

Oh, God. Real life was about to happen. 'What do you mean?' she answered, trying to stall.

'You know exactly what I mean, Cleo Dowling. We've fancied the arses off each other since we first met, and now we've gone and done something about it, it might help to know where we go from here.'

The fly in the ointment was staring them both in the face. Its name was Colleen. Cleo wished that it would buzz off.

'She won't want me for ever,' he said.

She knew she'd have to use the 'C' word. 'Colleen?'

'Yes.' He poured coffee for her, a glass of wine for himself. 'But until then I have to be there for her. I can't allow her to find out, Cleo.'

'I know that.'

He gave her a look of perfect candour. 'She needs me. It's that simple. And I've promised to be there for her for as long as she continues to need me. I can't renege on that.'

She managed a smile. 'I think I admire you more,' she said, 'for not reneging.' There was a big silence, then: 'What makes you think she won't want you for ever?'

'She has a pattern. She's a serial — um. What's the female equivalent of a womanizer?'

'A manizer? No — a man-eater!'

'I suppose that about fits the bill.'

'Do her relationships last long?'

'She tends to jilt her lovers when she finishes the book she's working on.'

'So you're waiting to be jilted?'

'Ow. That makes me sound like a complete lap-dog, doesn't it?'

'No — you're no pup, Pablo. You're just doing what you have to do. If Colleen tries to top herself every time her nose is put out of joint then you have a real responsibility to her.' Cleo plunged her coffee, and poured. 'How . . . does she do it?'

'I told you. She slashes herself.'

'With razors?'

'Razors, knives, jagged metal — whatever she can get her hands on. She's wielded a pretty mean Sabatier on occasion since she's been with me, and I really couldn't handle a repeat performance.'

Cleo stirred milk into her coffee, contemplating. 'They're not just cries for help, are they? They say that about people who try to kill themselves unsuccessfully.'

'No. It's real enough, and it's very, very frightening. She goes wild.'

'So she doesn't — like — run a bath or do anything premeditated?'

'No. She just lashes out.'

'What makes her do it?'

'It's because she lives so intensely. Especially when she's working. She describes the writing process as akin to being in labour, and any threat to her progeny sends her into a panic. I'm like her current muse, and if I disappear the book won't get finished. And that's the single worst thing that could happen to her. She'd rather die than not be able to write.'

'It's — it's a bit mad, isn't it?'

'Yeah.' Pablo shrugged. 'But that's just the way she is. Once she's finished this book she'll move on to someone else, and start writing something new.'

Cleo found the notion quite bizarre. There was a mythological creature, she knew, who feasted on the flesh of men. That's what Colleen was like — except she didn't eat her men to beget babies, she did it to beget books.

'You're really very different, aren't you, you two?' she said now. 'I mean, she's so complicated, and you're so laid-back and un-complicated. How on earth did you get it together?'

'She picked me up. She approached me at an exhibition opening and told me straight up that she wanted to fuck me.'

'Wow.'

'She's a woman of few inhibitions.'

'Is she sexy?'

'Very.'

'Ow.'

'Don't ask questions if you think the answer might hurt, Cleo.' He picked up his glass and looked at her over the rim as he drank from it. When he put the glass down he said: 'And you must know that you are a very sexy piece of work also.'

She flushed. 'So. You'd like to go to bed with me again?' she hazarded.

'I would like to. I would like to, yes please and

249

thanks very much — especially now that you've got over any *hausfrau*-ish notions about the state of your sheets.'

'In other words, you want to have your cake and eat it.'

'And you couldn't handle that?' He made a face. 'I don't blame you. Would you rather we nipped things in the bud right now?'

'*No!* I mean — no.'

'I'm glad to hear it. So I'm afraid subterfuge is called for. Colleen doesn't come too often to my house. She despises the aesthetic. So that suits us. But I will have to continue to go to her, Cleo. You do understand that?'

She swallowed. 'Yes. I do.'

He smiled back. 'Ours won't be an ideal set-up. But then, it's not an ideal world. We just muddle through.'

'Will I come to your house?' she asked. 'Or will you come to mine?'

'I'll come to you. The alternative's too risky. And I hate to have to renege on *our* deal, but I don't think it's a good idea for me to paint your portrait.'

The disappointment she felt floored her. 'Why not?'

'Because Colleen doesn't like me painting portraits of women who aren't her. She gets suspicious. I didn't get to finish my last nude but one because she slashed the canvas in a fit of pique and threatened to slash the sitter, too.'

Cleo blanched. 'OK. No portrait. Anyway, who said anything about it being a nude one?'

'I wouldn't paint you any other way, darling,' he said, giving her a smile that made her go completely mushy. 'But I'll paint something else for you, if you like. Have a think about it while I pay a visit to the jakes.'

He got to his feet and shambled towards the kitchen door. Cleo watched him go, feeling kind of swoony and yearny. Hell. What was she *doing*? Playing sex games with Pablo would be like playing with fire in more ways than one. 'Aflame' was a very good way to describe the way he'd made her feel earlier. But when it came to Colleen, 'playing with fire' took on a very different meaning. This could be very, very dangerous indeed. Was it worth it?

No. It was way too risky. They should wait until Colleen's book was finished, and then with a bit of luck she'd set her sights on some other strapping dude. Cleo had seen Colleen slanting sexy looks at Colin Farrell any time she passed him in the village. Maybe *he* might become her next muse? She wondered what being a muse actually entailed. It crossed her mind that Pablo might feature in the *magnum opus* Colleen was currently working on, and then the words *magnum opus* brought to her mind the sheer size of Colleen's literary offerings. How long would it be before this one was finished and she was ready to relinquish Pablo? It could be months. Years . . . Oh, *God*!

Pablo was back. 'Well? Have you been thinking about what I should paint for you? 'Something with Pig'?' He slid into the chair opposite her and poured himself more wine.

251

'Yes, I have,' lied Cleo. 'Will you do Fluffy for me?'

'With pleasure.' He raised his glass to her, and leaned back in his seat, studying her. 'So. What do you reckon? Is it worth continuing this torrid affair?'

No. It's too dangerous, too dangerous, too *dangerous*, she thought. 'I don't think,' she said, 'that there's any real alternative.'

'I'll drink to that,' said Pablo, doing exactly that.

He set the glass down between them on the kitchen table. There was something incredibly final about the gesture. It was as if it marked the end of one chapter in their story, and the opening of another. They regarded each other with 'Yikes What Have We Done?' expressions, and then Pablo stood up, looking as if he was trying very hard to pretend that everything was normal. 'Shouldn't you try and snatch some shut-eye, little Cleo?'

'I wish I could, but there's no point now. Hell. 'Wrecked from sex' may look good to you, but it won't wash with the cameraman.' She drooped a bit, and closed her eyes momentarily. When she opened them again, Pablo's face was inches from hers. 'Oh! You gave me a fright!'

'Thanks a bunch. 'Wrecked from sex' evidently doesn't sit at all well on me if it produces that kind of reaction.'

'On the contrary,' she said, kissing him. 'You look lovely. And guess what? I've just thought up the first line of my next short story.'

'Oh? Run it by me.'

' 'Ricardo was wrecked from too much sex. But there were two words that didn't exist in Ricardo's vocabulary.' '

'And what might they be?' asked Pablo.

' 'Too'. And 'much',' said Cleo.

Laughing, Pablo started to peel off his shirt.

★　★　★

Deirdre O'Dare was on the extras' bus when Cleo boarded it two hours later.

'Hi!' Cleo said, plonking herself down in the seat beside her.

Deirdre looked her up and down, raised an eyebrow and smiled. 'Well, hi,' she said.

Cleo's hangover and sleep deficiency made her instantly paranoid. 'What? What's wrong?'

'Sorry, darling, but you look — well — *shagged* is the only word for it. In the nicest possible way, of course!'

Cleo suddenly saw herself with Deirdre's eyes. The buttons of her shirt were done up wrong, her eyes were slitty and her mouth was swollen, and she hadn't been able to find a brush before she left the house, so her hair was all over the place.

'Oh. Well. You're right. Is it that obvious?'

'Pretty much. You look great.'

'Like 'wrecked from sex' great?'

Deirdre laughed. ' 'Wrecked from sex' are *les mots justes.*'

'Oh, well!' Cleo hugged herself. 'I had such a *blast!*' She sent Deirdre a big smile, then: 'What are you doing on the extras' bus?' she said. 'I

253

thought a driver normally picked you up?'

'He phoned in sick. I could've stayed and worked in the flat, but there's some stuff I need to run by Eva before I can do any more on her biog. You know Colleen quite well, don't you?'

The question came from out of the blue and gave Cleo a big fright. 'Colleen?' she said. 'I don't *think* so.' Her face went Permanent Magenta again.

'Oh, sorry,' said Deirdre. 'Have I hit on a touchy subject?'

Cleo could hardly say Well yes, actually. I've just been bonking her lov*air*, so instead she said: 'Well, she's kind of a recluse. And I haven't lived long enough in the village to really get to know her. I've just bumped into her and — Pablo in the pub occasionally.'

'That Pablo is something else,' said Deirdre. 'If I wasn't a happily married woman I'd be tempted to ride the arse off . . . ' Her voice trailed away, then 'Oh,' she said. 'Sorry. Have I just put my foot in it?'

Cleo's Permanent Magenta hue looked as if it might indeed be in danger of becoming permanent.

'The reason I asked about Colleen,' resumed Deirdre, backing off hastily, 'is that she approached me with an enquiry about the possibility of a film adaptation of *The Faraway*. I haven't read it so I couldn't comment, but I said I could put her in touch with someone in LA who might be interested. Have you read it?'

'Yes. I can't see it being made into a film somehow. It's too weird.'

'Weird works sometimes. Come to think of it, *Mimi's Remedies* is pretty weird.'

'Yeah, but not as weird as *Faraway*. And Pablo tells me she's working on something even weirder right now.' *Shit!* Why had she brought up the subject of Pablo again? 'He's my next-door neighbour,' she found herself explaining in a clumsy attempt to get out of the corner she'd just painted herself into. 'Which is how I know — about Colleen's weird book, I mean. You see, I know him much better than I know Colleen.' Oh, God! 'But please don't say anything to her' (about the affair we're having, she might as well have added). 'Because she wouldn't understand.'

'I can appreciate why,' murmured Deirdre.

'Oh, 'scuse me,' Cleo said, suddenly, fishing in her bag for her phone as the text alert sounded. The message was from Pablo, though he'd signed himself 'Ricardo'. Smiling, she began composing a text message back, thumbs twinkling over the keypad.

'Hey,' said Deirdre. 'I hope you don't mind me asking, but was that from who I think it was?'

The two women looked at each other. There was no point in continuing the charade. 'Yes,' said Cleo.

'Call me an interfering bitch if you like, but my advice would be not to text back. Text messages are notorious giveaways. I know someone whose marriage was destroyed when the wife got a load of the love poetry her husband had been getting.'

'Oh. You're right.' Cleo promptly deleted the

message and stuck her phone back in her bag.

'Talking of poetry, I sent one in,' remarked Deirdre, 'to 'Be A Bard dot con'. I hope you don't mind, but I accessed yours on their site and did a spoof of it. I wanted to see if they'd notice a plagiarized version of a poem they'd already published.'

'Oh, what a brilliant idea!'

'I made it even crapper than yours.'

'You mean that was possible?'

'And I signed it 'Beulah Offenbach'. I didn't dare put Deirdre O'Dare in case anyone thinks it's truly representative of my writing ability.'

'Excellent! I can't wait to see if they fall for it.'

'Have *you* written anything recently?'

'I've been working on some short stories.'

'Any good ones?'

Cleo turned to Deirdre and smiled. 'D'you know, I wasn't sure, to begin with. But I think I've got some quite good ideas. In fact — I'm really quite excited by them.'

'Getting any feedback?'

'Yes. Plenty,' said Cleo, smiling beatifically. She was remembering the choc ice.

★   ★   ★

It was terribly dangerous. But it was fun! The grass between numbers 4 and 5, the Blackthorns became so well worn that Pablo had to start varying his route in case Colleen should chance to wander into the back garden and smell a rat.

Cleo embarked on a series of short stories featuring Ricardo, and took great glee in putting

256

in stuff like 'Ricardo arrived on the deck carrying a bottle of champagne, a box of chocolates and a packet of condoms', or 'Ricardo was wearing the T-shirt she loved that made him look so amazingly sexy — and was clearly sporting a hard-on under his faded cut-offs', or 'Ricardo was so horny that he took her the minute the door to the deck slid shut behind him . . .'

She was in love. She tried to deny it, but it was useless. Cleo suspected that she'd been in love with Pablo from the very moment she'd set eyes on his hat. The love she felt for him was like a deep, deep well. She'd tumbled head first into it and would never, ever be able to climb out, and she spent a lot of time sitting forlornly in that well, making it even deeper from the litres of tears she shed. They laughed a lot when they were together, but when Pablo spent time with Colleen, Cleo would curl up with Fluffy and cry all over her, which had the effect of ruining the poor bitch's latest hairstyle. She couldn't bear to think of Pablo in Colleen's bed, maybe doing to Colleen things he did to her, Cleo — maybe even doing some of the things *Ricardo* did . . .

Ricardo was a better lover than Casanova, or Lothario (whoever *he* was), or even Johnny Depp in her wildest dreams. Ricardo played games and teased and experimented with props like feathers and paintbrushes and curtain tie-backs, and he had clearly never heard of the term 'political correctness'. On one particularly memorable occasion he'd behaved just like the hero in the Pixie Pirelli book — the one the lipstick lesbians had been sneering at at Margot's

First Wednesday that time — and she hadn't even minded that her very expensive La Perla underwear had been torn to shreds. He even wrote her the occasional love letter, on creamy vellum paper. He used a fountain pen and black ink, and his style was italic, authoritative and slanty . . .

They were sharing a bath one day. Pablo had just come back from driving Colleen to Galway, where she was to catch the train up to Dublin for a talk in the Arts Club. Cleo hated to use the 'C' word, but she couldn't help herself. 'When you . . . visit Colleen,' she said, 'do you enjoy it?'

'I'm not going to answer that.' He regarded her gravely. 'Come on, Cleo. Wise up. We knew when we started this thing that it wasn't going to be easy, and you're just making things even more difficult on yourself.'

'I know. But sometimes I'd just love everything to be out in the open, and not to have to bother about all the clandestine stuff.'

He shrugged. 'We'll go public once she's finished the book. I promise. Even if she hasn't found herself a new toyboy by then, there's less likelihood of her inflicting damage on herself or anyone else once the newborn's arrived. Pass me the soap, darling girl.'

Cleo lobbed it across the bath. 'What's it called?'

'The book? I dunno. She doesn't give very much away about it. She doesn't usually find a title until the second draft's done.'

'How much longer d'you reckon it'll take?'

'Haven't a clue.'

258

'Christ,' Cleo grumbled. 'It feels like she's feckin' Scheherazade at this rate. Maybe it'll never be finished.'

'It has to be if she wants her money. The rest of her advance won't be forthcoming until she delivers the goods, and she's dead set on buying an island in Clew Bay. That's a real incentive for her to finish.' He chucked the soap back at her and gave her a wicked smile. 'Now let's shut up talking about Colleen, Cleo. Why don't you remind me of what Ricardo does with that power shower instead?'

'Well,' said Cleo. 'The choc ice got everywhere, so she's a very dirty little girl indeed. And once they're in the bath — '

'It's OK,' said Pablo, reaching for the shower attachment and turning it on. 'My memory's been suitably refreshed. I know what comes next.'

'Surely,' said Cleo, returning his smile, 'that needs rephrasing. Don't you mean who?'

'Of course. Silly me. Who comes next?'

'I do,' said Cleo.

11

It was eleven o'clock in the morning, and Deirdre was stranded in Galway city. She had arranged a meeting there with her agent, who was to have flown in from London, and had only just discovered that because of strike action at Galway airport all flights had been cancelled. Deirdre had taken the bus in from Kilrowan that morning instead of using the unit driver. Dannie had told her that that was a great way to see the Connemara countryside because the bus meandered from village to village and you had the additional advantage of height — and Dannie had been right. Connemara by coach was captivating. But now she had just learned that there was no bus returning until six o'clock.

Seven hours in Galway with bugger all to do! It was too early for the cinema, but there was nothing showing anyway that interested her apart from one of Rory's swashbuckling epics that she'd already seen in LA. What did women do when they had time on their hands? Have lunch with girlfriends, she supposed. And shop. But Deirdre had no girlfriends in Galway, and she hated shopping. Ladies who lunch had their hair done a lot. Maybe that's what she should do? She hadn't bothered much with her hair lately — she usually just shoved it up in a scrunchy. Yep. She'd go into that groovy hair place across the road and get some highlights, and maybe have her nails done too. That would take up a couple of hours.

She trudged into the salon and steeled herself for comments.

'Where did you last get it done? Tch, tch. The condition's not the best, is it? What products do you use? Oh — that stuff's worse than useless. It just coats your hair — it doesn't actually penetrate the shaft. The stuff in our range is excellent, you should invest in some before you leave today. Now. What about colour? Blond streaks would look great on you, give you a real lift. Take years off you, so they would. Never thought of going blond before? Hey! Go for it! And you want to have your nails done as well? No problem. Michelle will take care of that. Michelle!'

'Yeah.'

'A manicure over here, please.'

'What kind of polish were you thinking of?' asked Michelle.

'Um. French manicure?'

'French manicure's a bit footballers' wives. How about fuchsia, to match your bag?'

'Oh. OK.'

So Michelle set to work, and the colourist and stylist fetched all the arcane tools of their trade, and together they coloured and straightened and trimmed and tweaked and filed and polished, and when Deirdre had filled them in to their satisfaction about where she was going on her holidays, she finally plucked up the courage to look at herself in the mirror. 'Hey!' she said. 'Result! I look like a lady who lunches!'

Her hair felt so fantastic when she swished out of the salon, clutching a carrier bag full of straightening lotion and conditioner and volumizing shampoo and serum, that she decided that maybe she should behave like a lady who lunches and actually *have* lunch on her own, with a half-bottle of wine. And the wine gave her such Dutch courage that after lunch she decided she'd overcome her fear of shopping and give it a go.

So off she went to Brown Thomas. She bought some new underwear and she bought body lotion and scent. Then she bought a rather sexy little cardigan, a very sexy little dress and a pair of perilously sexy heels. While browsing through the make-up department she was set upon by a lady who insisted on doing a makeover on her. This time she wasn't sure about the final result when she looked in the proffered mirror. It just wasn't *her* somehow. But she bought a lipstick (fuchsia, to match her nails) because she felt obliged to buy something after all the make-up lady's hard work.

There was just an hour and a bit before her bus was due to leave, and that could be whiled away nicely in the bookshop. But she got diverted. As she made her way down Cross Street she caught sight of a sign on a chemist's door that offered Botox injections. Botox. She'd often thought about it, but wasn't sure if it was a kosher thing to do, somehow.

Hell, why not? She felt rebellious as she swung through the chemist's door. Hadn't she gone for it all guns blazing since this morning? She'd been a lady who lunched for a day, and she'd shopped till she dropped. She might as well take a final pot shot.

★ ★ ★

Getting off the bus took some doing, hampered as she was by all her carrier bags. She'd just said goodbye and thank you to the driver and was about to proceed down the main street of Kilrowan when a familiar voice made her turn.

'Fancy a pint?'

It was Rory.

Deirdre was so taken aback that she dropped all her shopping. 'What are you doing here?' she said stupidly, and then: 'Oh! What are you *doing* here!?' Abandoning the bags on the footpath, she raced towards him.

'I'm waiting for the bus that was to transport my inamorata to my waiting arms. How are you, hamster features?' He kissed her, then peered more closely at her. 'Hey. Speaking of those features — where *are* they? They seem to have been obliterated by slap. That's not like you.'

'Yeah, yeah. I know it's not really me. I had a makeover in Galway.'

'A makeover? How redundant was that? I liked you the way you were.'

'I dunno why I did it. I just had time on my hands and nothing better to do.' She stood on tiptoe so she could kiss him again, and then she said: 'So tell me, tell me — what *are* you doing here?'

'I'll tell you over that pint,' he said, gathering

263

up her carrier bags. 'Let's hit the pub.'

They hit the pub, found a quiet corner, then Rory filled her in.

'I was in London,' he said, 'to meet a VID.'

'VI — *D*?'

'Very Important Director. And since the Emerald Isle is a mere hop, skip and jump away from the big smoke, I decided to hop on a plane, skip to Kilrowan and jump the bones of my trouble and strife.'

'But all the London to Galway flights were cancelled!'

'I flew to Knock from Stansted.'

'*Stansted?*'

'A man will go through hell and high water and even negotiate Stansted airport when an opportunity for sexual gratification presents itself — especially after a period of enforced celibacy.'

'How did you know I'd be on that bus?'

'I phoned Eva.'

Their pints had arrived. Rory raised his in a toast. 'Here's to surprise reunions,' he said.

'I'll drink to that,' said Deirdre. 'You've always been very good at them.'

'Which was the best?'

'Um. The last one in LA? Or maybe the time you surprised me in Carrowcross. That was pretty special.' The memory made her smile. He'd turned up out of the blue and transported her to a fairytale castle. 'How are my girls?' she asked.

'They're good. They made cards for you.'

'Oh! Show me.'

'They're in my luggage back in Ballynahinch. I

booked us in for the night — thought you could do with a treat. Bruno's looking good, incidentally. What have you been feeding him on?'

'Lungfuls of fresh Connemara ozone. When did you see him?'

'I took him for a spin in my hire car this afternoon. We went to the beach and made sand UFOs. His vocabulary's come on since he's been here — he chattered away non-stop. I wonder where he gets that from.'

Deirdre smiled. 'I'll get someone to mind him tonight, will I? Then we can have dinner in the hotel.'

'And breakfast in bed. There's a four-poster.'

'Goodie. Will we do the tying-up thing?'

'Sure.'

Deirdre gave Rory a come-hitherish smile and swished her hair a bit.

He leaned back in his seat and studied her. 'Well,' he said. 'You certainly *have* had a makeover, O'Dare. Purply nails and all. New hair. And there's something else different about you.'

'I've lost weight?' she asked, helpfully. She'd been running on the beach nearly every day recently.

'Maybe. Yeah. I dunno. It's something about your expression. You look kinda *plastic*. Maybe it's the make-up.'

It was the Botox, Deirdre knew. Some actresses had had to give up on Botox because of the atrophying effect it had on their facial expressions. She didn't want to tell Rory that she'd had it done. She knew he wouldn't approve. But Rory was no eejit.

'You've doggone done Botox,' he said. 'Haven't you?'

She gave him a mulish look.

'What the fuck made you do that, Deirdre?'

'I'm fed up of looking like shite,' she said.

'You don't look like shite! Or rather, you didn't until now. Your lovely mobile features have gone all stiff on me. How long before it wears off?'

'A couple of months.'

'Well, at least I know that by the time you come back to LA I'll have my real wife back, not some Stepford lookalike.'

'You don't understand, Rory. It's different for men. Women don't like getting old. *I* don't like getting old.'

'You'll never grow old, Deirdre,' he said, 'because you never grew up in the first place. What fucking childish impulse told you it would be a good idea to have some strain of a bovine disease injected into your face?'

Oh! This was horrible! What should have been a glorious reunion was turning into a domestic. 'Stop it!' she said. 'Stop it, Rory. We're fighting. We haven't seen each other for weeks and we're fighting.'

'OK,' he said, after a beat. 'We'll change the subject. We'll talk about the weather instead.' He turned to the window. 'Oh, look. It's started to lash rain! Rain in Ireland! How uncommon.'

It was, as he said, lashing rain outside. 'Dammit,' said Deirdre. 'That means that all that time spent having my hair straightened will be wasted.'

'Why?'

'Because the rain makes your hair go all curly and shite.'

'Oh, good,' said Rory. 'That straight, *soignée* look doesn't suit you. Anyway, I'm looking forward to seeing your hair all tousled and gorgeous later. There's a word for that style, isn't there? What is it?'

'A shag?'

He smiled at her. 'You can always depend on a screenwriter to come up with *le mot juste*. Hell. Finish your pint ASAP, sweetheart. I want us out of here. I have a sudden burning ambition to turn crimper and rearrange your hairstyle.'

★　★　★

The next morning Deirdre's hair was well and truly shagged. She was sitting up in bed humming to herself and buttering toast while Rory talked to the VID on the phone. The sun was bouncing off the river below their window, and birdsong was blasting.

'Oh piss off, you great big boring bastard, and go stuff your job up your hole,' said Rory, pressing 'end call' and slinging his phone onto the bed.

Deirdre's jaw dropped. 'Rory! You didn't tell David Marchant to stuff his job up his hole?'

'No. Fooled you. He was off the line by then. But I really would quite like to tell him to stuff it. He wants me to play another fucking pirate.'

'You're terribly good at pirates, you know. And I love it when you tart yourself up in boots and bandannas. I'll come and visit you on location and we can have sex in your Winnebago.'

'I suppose you'll want me to keep the boots on.'

'Natch. And the eyepatch, too. Oh, look, there's Eva and David.'

Deirdre slid out of bed and into a big courtesy towelling robe before crossing the room and leaning out through the open window. Eva Lavery and David Lawless were strolling hand in hand along the riverbank. Deirdre was just about to call down to them when something made her pause. She didn't want to spoil the moment. The couple looked so content that intrusion would be indecent, somehow. She sat on the windowsill and observed instead as they crossed a bridge to a small island. They stopped halfway and leaned over the railing, looking down at the river rushing below.

'Rory?' she said. 'Do you think that we'll be like Eva and David when we're their age?'

'Still happily married? I don't see why not. Unless you decide to fuck off with some toyboy.'

'Or you decide to fuck off with some nymphette.'

'Unlikely. I ran into Finbar de Rossa with his child bride in London the other day.' Rory put on an exaggerated, Sir Laurence Olivier-type voice. ' "Rory! You're doing splendidly!' I couldn't say the same for him. He looked as if he was about to expire.'

'From a heart condition brought on by all the riding?'

'No. From terminal boredom. You forget that most nymphettes are about as intellectually stimulating as rubber dollies, sweetheart.'

'They're probably as accommodating, as well.'

'You're accommodating. Come here.'

'OK.' She slid off the windowsill and jumped onto the bed.

'Biddable, too,' he said, unknotting the sash on her robe. 'Why would I even think about riding someone else when I've a wife who picks up her cues so well?' Unfortunately, his phone got its cue wrong, and bleated at him. He checked out the display. 'Shit. I've got to take it, Deirdre. It's the Queen Bee.' The Queen Bee was Rory's agent.

Deirdre moseyed back to the window. Eva was alone on the bridge now, gazing horizonward. She was wearing something white and wafty, she'd kicked her shoes off and she looked as beautiful and as enigmatic as Greta Garbo in the closing shot of *Queen Christina*. A photo opportunity! Quickly, Deirdre grabbed Rory's camera from the back of a chair and focused in on Eva. Click, click and click again. Then Eva eased into a stretch, and made to move away. Deirdre couldn't resist it. 'Eva!' she called, and the actress raised her face to the upstairs window. When she saw Deirdre, a smile lit up her face.

Click! went the camera one more time as Eva, laughing, blew an extravagant kiss into the air.

★   ★   ★

'Join us for coffee.' It was an hour and a bit later, and Deirdre and Rory had finally shambled downstairs. Eva and David were sitting in the conservatory, a tray of coffee things on the table in front of them.

'No coffee for us, thanks,' said Rory. 'I've just asked them to send a couple of Bloody Marys from the bar. They're on their way.'

'What an excellent idea. Ask the waiter, David, when he comes, to bring two more.'

'I take it you're not working today?' said Deirdre, dropping into an armchair.

'I am a work-free zone, yes, and so allowed Bloody Marys. I damn well deserve one, too, after yesterday. I worked my ass off passing Remedies over the counter to all comers. It was the most complex scene yet. I'm surprised Jethro didn't lose the rag.'

'Jethro never loses the rag,' said Rory. 'He's a complete pro and a pleasure to work with. As are you, of course, David. What're you up to at the moment?'

'I had a production of *The Master Builder* lined up — '

'I'm sorry for your trouble,' put in Rory, making a sympathetic face.

' — but I'm having problems casting.'

'Not surprised,' interjected Rory.

'I may have to abandon it for something else.'

'If you're lucky.'

'Stop it, Rory!' said Deirdre.

'I'm trying to persuade him to stay on here,'

270

said Eva. 'I get greedy for him and my edible little Dorcas.'

'Where is Dorcas?' asked Deirdre.

'Gone off with the nanny to the beach. I wanted to take her, but I wouldn't be able for it. I'm just too damn knackered after yesterday. All I want to do is sit still and smell the coffee.'

'And take in the view,' observed Deirdre. 'I got a lovely shot of you earlier, Eva, down by the river, looking like Greta Garbo in *Queen Christina*.'

'What a compliment! You mean the end shot, when she's looking out to sea?'

'Yes.'

Eva smiled. 'Do you know how Mamoulian got that shot?'

'Mamoulian?'

'The director, Rouben Mamoulian. He told Garbo to think of nothing, to make her mind a blank and her expression a *tabula rasa*. He wanted the audience to project what they imagined she was feeling on to a blank canvas.'

'What *is* she feeling?' asked David.

'Well, she's lost her lover, she's lost her kingdom. Go figure.' To Deirdre's astonishment, Eva's eyes filled with tears. 'I'm sorry,' she said, pulling a rather grubby lace-edged handkerchief out of her bag and dabbing at her face. 'That's one of my favourite films of all time. It's so terribly sad.'

David smiled at her. 'You have your lover. You have your kingdom.'

'My point exactly,' said Eva, blowing her nose.

271

'One expression fits all.'

The waiter arrived. 'Excuse me. Your cocktails,' he said, setting two Bloody Marys down in front of Rory.

'We'll have two more, please,' said Rory, pushing his glass towards Eva. 'Take mine, honey lamb. I can wait. I didn't have as tough a day as you did yesterday.'

'Thank you, darling.' Eva raised the glass to him. 'I forget sometimes that throwing shapes can be bloody hard work.' She took a sip of her drink, and then said: 'D'you know what Garbo said when she retired?'

'What? 'I vant to be alone'?' Deirdre put on an execrable Swedish accent.

'No. She said: 'I've made enough faces.' Sometimes I feel exactly that.'

'You don't have to make any more faces, Eva,' said David, gently. 'You can get out of the game any time you like.'

'Actually, darling, I think Mimi's might be the last face I make.'

Deirdre was astonished. 'Eva! Not really? You're thinking of retiring?'

'Mm. Life's too short. I want to smell more coffee, Deirdre, take in more views. I want to have more opportunities to drink Bloody Marys, I want to lie in late. These early morning calls are starting to wreck my head.'

'But — retirement? Wouldn't you get bored to distraction after a while?'

'No. There's far too much to do! I want to be able to snuggle my girl and take her to the beach when I feel like it. I want to learn to cook — '

'Cook? *You?* Don't make me laugh,' said David.

'I do want to learn! I was thinking of taking a course in Ballymaloe. I want to be able to cook for you and for our friends, the way you do for me. I want to read all the books I've never had time to read, and see all the movies I've never had time to see. I want to bungee jump. I want to go to a desert island and skinny-dip. I want to do a course in mime.'

Three jaws dropped.

'That was a joke.'

'I have to say I'm relieved,' said David. 'You'd make an appalling mime. But why didn't you tell me all this before? If I'd known how you felt I would have encouraged you to say no to the Mimi gig. You didn't have to do it. It's not as if we need the money.'

'I did, David, have to do it — and not because of the money. I know it sounds corny, but I had to do it because it's such uplifting stuff. There's so much that's depressing and *worthy* being made these days. *Mimi's Remedies* is one of those films that will have people leaving the cinema with a smile on their faces. It's astonishingly feel-good. Think *A Wonderful Life* meets *Chocolat* meets *Babe*.'

'In that case,' said Deirdre, 'I'm beyond chuffed that you've chosen one of my scripts as your swan song.'

'Do swans sing?' said Rory. 'I've only ever heard them honk.'

Eva laughed. 'Well, I hope *Mimi's Remedies* won't turn out to be the cinematic equivalent of

273

a honk.' She tilted her head, listening, then stood up and moved to the open window. 'Listen to those birds. Why does birdsong always make me feel so happy? It's not as if they're singing because *they're* happy, after all, is it? It's all about avian territorial rights and who gets to keep the girl.' She turned back to the room and leaned against the windowsill. 'If you were a bird, Deirdre, what would you be?'

'I dunno,' said Deirdre.

'I do. You'd be a puffin.'

'A *puffin*? Why?'

'They're so terribly pretty and funny and silly on the surface, but they paddle like hell underneath. I know how hard you work.'

'I like the pretty and funny bit. Not sure about silly, though. *I* think I'm pretty prodigious. What would Rory be?'

Eva looked at Rory, considering. 'A peregrine falcon.'

'Oh, yuck, Eva! Don't give him something else to crow about. A peregrine bloody falcon!' Deirdre shot Rory a mock-scathing look.

'A bastard hawk might be more appropriate,' remarked Rory.

'A bastard hawk? Is there such a thing?'

'Yep. In the falconry hierarchy, it ranks third after the gerfalcon.'

Deirdre looked puzzled. 'How do you know stuff about falconry?'

'From that Grace O'Malley movie Eva and I did together. Remember, Eva? I had to spend hours stuck in the saddle with a falcon on my wrist. An evil-tempered bastard hawk, he was, too. No princely gerfalcon, he.'

'I'd say David's a gerfalcon, then,' said Deirdre. 'Or a golden eagle. And Dorcas is a hummingbird.'

'No, she's not,' said Eva. 'Dorcas is a dodo.'

Deirdre was taken aback. 'A dodo? Darling little Dorcas? Never! How can you possibly compare her to a dodo, Eva?'

'Because she's far too trusting. She has no street savvy whatsoever. Other kids are always taking advantage of her.'

'And what's that got to do with dodos?'

'Well, you know they were flightless?'

'Yeah.'

'That's because they felt so secure on the ground that they didn't *need* to fly. There were no predators. And then man arrives in Mauritius and all the dodos go running down to the beach to welcome him to paradise, and they promptly get massacred for their trouble, put in the pot and made extinct. I think it's one of the vilest stories about humankind ever.'

'And Dorcas is really that naïve?' asked Rory.

'She really is that naïve. I fear for her sometimes.'

There was silence for a moment. Deirdre had always suspected that Eva's eleven-year-old daughter might have a learning disability, but Eva had never brought it up and Deirdre hadn't wanted to question her about it. She knew that Astrid, Dorcas's nanny, had qualifications in teaching children with special needs, and special was just what Dorcas was. Deirdre had never met a child so full of love.

It was time to get the conversational ball rolling again. 'What kind of bird are you, d'you think, Eva?' asked Deirdre.

'Eva,' said David, 'is a phoenix — *sans* the ashes. A phoenix that burns brighter than any star in the firmament.'

Eva beamed at her husband. 'Well, thank you, darling,' she said. 'I feel like one of those special people, now, that that Beat poet wrote about. Who was it? Ginsberg?'

'No. Kerouac,' supplied Rory. Deirdre smiled to herself. Trust Rory to know his Kerouac! 'He said that the only people who matter in this world are the people who burn — like beautiful Roman candles.'

'Mummy!' The door to the conservatory burst open, and Dorcas was in the room. 'Mummy! Look what I found on the beach! A diamond ring!' The child propelled herself towards her mother, ablaze with excitement.

Dorcas was Eva in miniature, a golden gypsy. Her hair was wild, her feet bare. The skirts of her dress were wet from the sea, strands of weed were stuck to her legs, and a sprinkling of sand flew out of her hair like fairy dust as she bounced from foot to foot with excitement.

Eva took the ring from her and examined it. It was the kind of bauble you'd find in a Christmas cracker — an enormous gimcrack diamond. 'A veritable jewel,' she said. 'How fantastic! And you found it on the beach? Hey! It probably belonged to a mermaid.'

'A mermaid! You could be right. Does that mean I should throw it back in the sea?'

'Well, that's up to you, darling. I'm sure the mermaid wouldn't mind if you were to borrow it for a little. Say hello to Rory.'

'Rory!' Dorcas whirled round. Rory had got to his feet to greet her. She skeetered across the room to him and held her arms out so that he could do the picking up and swinging round thing. 'What're you doing here?'

'I came to visit you, of course, princess,' said Rory, obliging her with the swing and then dumping her, breathless, on the couch.

'Sorry for the state she's in,' said the nanny, who had followed her into the room.

'*Thank* you for the state she's in, Astrid,' said Eva. 'A mucky child is a happy child.'

David held out his hand to his daughter so that he too could admire her ring. 'Wear it to dinner tonight,' he said, 'and dazzle all our fellow diners.' He turned to Rory and Deirdre. 'Will you join us for dinner this evening?'

Deirdre gave him a miserable look. 'We can't,' she said. 'Rory's to get his ass back to the States. He's flying out of Knock this evening.'

'Knickers to Knock,' said Dorcas. 'Where's Aoife and Grace? Why aren't they with you?'

'They're Home Alone in LA,' said Rory, 'which is why I have to get back to them.'

'Home Alone? Cool!' said Dorcas, and Deirdre said: 'I trust that was one of your jests?'

'You trust right. They're wrapped up in cotton wool and watched over by Nanny Bridges and our hi-tech security system.'

'How are those gorgeous girls?' asked Eva.

'Fantastic. I spoke to them on the phone last

277

night — and look what they sent me.'

Deirdre reached into her bag and produced the cards that her daughters had made for her. Grace's card showed Deirdre and Rory wearing their finest clothes, and holding hands. Clasping their free hands were Aoife and Grace wearing crowns, and at their feet was Bruno. Grace had given Bruno monkey's ears and a tail.

Aoife's card was a map of two islands. The smaller one was marked with a green flag bearing the legend 'Ireland'. Deirdre and Bruno (wearing a pig's snout and a curly tail this time) were standing on it, waving at a bigger island where the Stars and Stripes had been carefully coloured in as a background to the likenesses of Rory, Aoife and Grace. Big splurty tears were coming out of all their eyes, and a speech bubble saying: 'We miss you, Mommy. Come home soon.' Deirdre had burst into even splurtier tears the minute she'd seen it.

She handed the cards to Eva, whose eyes misted over. 'Oh, God!' she exclaimed. She studied the drawings for several more moments, and then said, quite solemnly: 'Aren't we so, so lucky, Deirdre.'

'Lucky?'

'To belong to such fantastically happy families.'

The reverent look that Deirdre saw Eva send across the room to David spoke so eloquently of true love that it made her lower her eyes and study her nails. She and Rory had conjectured just that morning what might be the state of their marriage when they hit Eva and David's age. Now, as she picked at a chipped flake of fuchsia nail polish, Deirdre prayed that the flame of their love would still burn hot and incandescent as the love she'd seen manifest just now. The love that burned as brightly as a beautiful Roman candle.

★ ★ ★

Deirdre and Rory drove to Knock airport in his hire car. He'd told her not to bother seeing him off because she'd only blub — she always did — but Deirdre had promised him she wouldn't this time. She'd take a hackney back to Kilrowan and do all her blubbing in the back seat.

At the airport there was some problem with the computer at the check-in desk, and Rory was getting pissed off. 'You may as well go and order a drink,' he said. 'Make mine a large Bushmills.'

Glad to escape from the queue of narky-looking passengers, Deirdre scooted upstairs to the bar where she ordered a whiskey for him and a white wine for herself. She had just sat down at a table by the window when the door opened and Pablo MacBride strode up to the counter. He ordered a glass of red wine, downed half of it in one gulp, then turned to survey the room, leaning against the bar.

Deirdre reached for her phone, pretending to be intent on sending a text message. She'd never felt comfortable in the presence of devastating men — Rory being the sole exception. Well. David Lawless was an exception too, she supposed . . . and Jethro Palmer. But some of the other men she saw in the course of her daily life in Kilrowan — Colin Farrell, Ben Tarrant and Pablo MacBride, to name but three — had the killer capacity to make her proverbial knees go weak. In her peripheral vision, she saw Pablo moving across the room to her. Then: 'Hi!' he said.

'Oh, hi!' said Deirdre back, feigning surprise and feeling silly as she pressed 'send' to the non-existent recipient of her text message.

'I'll join you for a moment, if you don't mind. Colleen's having a problem at the check-in desk — the computers are down — and I thought I'd grab the opportunity to sink some liquid refreshment. Are you heading back to the States?'

'No. I'm seeing my husband off. He was here on a flying visit.'

'So you're driving back to Kilrowan once the flight's left?'

'Yes. Well, no. I'll have to take a cab.'

'Don't bother. I'll give you a lift. Give me your phone number and I'll text you when I'm ready to leave.' He slid his phone out of his pocket. 'Shoot.'

'Thanks,' she said, dictating her number. 'That's really decent of you.'

Pablo took a gulp of wine, then made a face at the glass as he set it down. 'Shite wine,' he said, settling back in his chair and giving her the benefit of a smile worthy of a film star. 'I understand your movie's going well.'

'Well, it's not over budget yet. Give it a week or two.'

'My neighbour's in it. She's a special extra. She's having a great time.'

'Cleo? Yeah, she told me she was having fun.' Deirdre took a sip of her wine. Pablo was right. It was completely disgusting, and she resolved not to drink any more of it. 'What's taking Colleen to the States? Business or pleasure?'

'Both, I suppose. She's speaking at yet another literary festival — in LA this time.'

'I must introduce her to Rory. Maybe they could get seats next to each other on the flight.' Shit! What had she just *said*? She suspected that Rory wouldn't thank her for lumbering him with the heavy-weight Colleen as a long-haul flying companion.

Pablo took another gulp of wine, made another face. 'I'd better get back to her. I told her I was visiting the jakes. She'd get cross if she knew I was abandoning her for a snifter.' He looked at the remains of the wine in his glass. 'And I wish I hadn't bothered. Château Shite, how are you? Catch you in a while, Deirdre.'

She smiled back at him, surmising that once Colleen was safely out of the way, the coast would be clear for Pablo and Cleo to make hay while the sun shone.

He was on his feet and halfway across the floor when Rory walked in.

'Oh, Pablo!' Deirdre called. 'Your phone!' She picked it up from the table and lobbed it across the room to him.

'Thanks! Catch you later.' And he was off out the door.

'Who was that?' asked Rory, sitting down

281

opposite her in the seat just vacated by Pablo.

'Pablo MacBride. He lives in the village.'

'Good-looking son-of-a-bitch,' observed Rory. 'Fancy him, do you?'

'Don't be ridiculous, Rory,' she said, going red. 'He's younger than I am.'

'Your toyboy!'

'Hardly. He's Colleen's squeeze.'

'The writer? I saw her at the check-in desk. She's a sexy broad. What does he do?'

'He's a painter.'

'Has he volunteered to paint your portrait yet?'

'Why would he?'

'Why wouldn't he? You fell for it big time when Daniel Lennox fed you that line.' Rory sent her a wicked smile. 'Although I have to say that Lennox portrait was the best money I ever spent. It's not every man is lucky enough to be able to ogle a nude portrait of his wife when she's not around to pleasure him in the flesh.'

Deirdre sent him a look of mock-hauteur. 'Well, I wouldn't sit for Pablo even if he asked me. I don't want another portrait of myself, thanks very much. Especially not a nude one.'

'I loved it when you posed for Daniel. You got so hot.'

'What do you mean?'

'You used to come back from those sessions in his studio and practically beg me for sex.'

'Nonsense. Did I?'

'Damn right. I bet you anything you like that if you weren't a happily married woman you'd have ended up in bed with him.'

Deirdre thought about it. She remembered how Madeleine Lennox had once told her how jealous she was of Daniel's sitters because she knew that they all wanted to ride her husband. 'If I'd been single I *might* have ended up in bed with Daniel,' she said now, 'because he's pretty irresistible, and because he wasn't married when I sat for him. But I'm not sure that a woman would want go to bed with any old painter just because she'd posed nude for him. I mean, take a look at the geezer up at the bar.' She directed a glance at an overweight man in a flash suit who was standing at the bar, talking self-importantly on his mobile phone.

'Your point being?'

'Well, if *he* was a painter and I was posing nude for him, there's no way I'd find the experience erotic.'

Rory laughed. 'Point taken.' He looked at his watch, then: 'I'd better make tracks,' he said, taking a pull of his whiskey.

'Wait till I get back from the loo, darling, will you? I'm bursting for a pee.'

Deirdre ran to the loo. It was a lie that she needed to pee. She'd known when Rory had said 'Better make tracks' that she was going to cry, and tearful farewells were anathema to him. She leaned against the wall and looked up at the ceiling in an effort to make the tears go back behind her eyes, and then she grabbed some loo roll and held it against her face. But there was still a lump in her throat when she went back out into the bar.

'You've a message,' said Rory, indicating her

phone. 'Sorry — I wasn't being nosy, but I accessed it because I'd asked David to text me a website address.'

'Porn, I suppose,' said Deirdre, picking up her phone. 'Why didn't you get him to text your phone, Rory?'

'It's out of juice. Queen Bee sucked it dry. Who's your ride?'

'What?'

'Your ride. It's on your phone.'

Deirdre opened her message and the words **'Ur ride awaits. Out front — 5 mins'** appeared before her eyes. Oh, God! Why did her husband have such an uncanny knack of making her feel guilty even when she wasn't? She took a swig of the disgusting wine she'd decided not to touch. She had to do *something*. 'It's from Pablo. He's giving me a lift back to Kilrowan,' she said.

'You behave yourself, O'Dare.'

'You know I will.'

She saw Rory glance at his watch, and the lump in her throat got bigger. There couldn't be much time left.

'You're going to break your promise.'

'What promise?' For an absurd moment she thought he was referring to Pablo.

'Your promise not to cry. Your eyes are going all swimmy.'

'Oh, God, Rory. I'm sorry.'

A tear blooped onto the table between them, and then the Tannoy announced his flight. 'Gotta go,' he said, knocking back the rest of his whiskey. 'Don't see me to the gate. Stay here and finish your wine.' He bent to kiss her, then he slung his bag over his shoulder and was gone.

Deirdre did as she was told, even though the wine was nasty. And the big tears that plopped into it made it taste even nastier.

12

'Dun, dun, da dun dun dun!'

Paloma was singing along to her personal stereo in the back seat of the car, wearing Mickey Mouse ears. Oliver and Dannie were driving back to Kilrowan after their Paris holiday. Dannie was glad that Paloma was listening to the headphones, because she had something of a very personal nature to discuss with Oliver.

They'd had a lovely time — until this morning. Oliver and Paloma had been exhausted at the end of every day because of all the fun stuff they'd done in Disneyland, and Dannie had been exhausted from all the shopping she'd done in the fashion capital of Europe. But this morning Alice — who had just arrived in Paris and was staying in a hotel in Saint-Germain — had phoned and arranged to meet up with Dannie for coffee. Dannie hadn't wanted to go, but she felt she ought to make an effort to get on with the woman who was to be her sister-in-law.

'You'll love what we've done with the Glebe House,' Alice had said over lattes and croissants. 'And I've picked up some gorgeous things here, as finishing touches. Any excuse to visit Paris of course, ha ha, but no-one can rival the French for those all-important little details. I'm having quantities of stuff shipped over. You might want to choose some items for your own apartment

— please feel free to have first pick, Dannie. I'm definitely going to keep some things for my own use. I picked up a couple of dotey little antique carriage clocks — I'm mad into clocks, so I am. And I got a gorgeous runner for the hallway of my apartment.'

'Apartment?' Dannie's coffee cup hadn't made it to her mouth. 'I thought you were staying in the gate lodge, Alice?'

'Oh, no — that was just temporary, until the apartments were completed in the big house. And once we do up the gate lodge it'll make a grand romantic retreat for honeymooners, or couples who want that little bit of extra privacy. They can cater for themselves there, or stroll up to the Glebe House for a full Irish breakfast if they prefer. We've high hopes of making it into next year's *Blue Book*.'

'So you're going to be living in the big house, Alice?'

'Oh, yes. I'll need to be on stand-by for guests, 24/7. And won't it be grand for you to have a resident babysitter for Paloma? And any other babies you may happen to have?' A meaningful smile.

Dannie hadn't been able to take in much more of the conversation. Her mind had gone into freefall.

'But I thought you knew that?' Oliver was saying to her now. Paloma had turned up the volume on her Discman, and the tinny beat was starting to give Dannie a headache. 'Alice was only staying in the gate lodge until her apartment in the main house was finished. If the work's gone according to schedule she'll be able to move in some time this week.'

'Da dun!' went Paloma in the back of the car.

'So you're telling me that Alice is going to be living in the Glebe House? With us?'

'Yes. But don't worry, the apartments are completely separate, in the west wing. The west wing! Doesn't that sound grand? I'm going to love being a country squire.'

Dannie felt a flash of pure panic. She took a couple of deep breaths to try and calm herself, and then said: 'Oliver. All this was news to me until this morning.' He turned to her, about to say something, but she pre-empted him. 'I don't want to talk about it now. I'll need to do some serious thinking — but we're going to have to sit down and have a long chat about things when we get home.'

'OK,' said Oliver equably. 'When we get home, then.'

Home. Home? Where *was* home? Where was her home to be from now on? The prospect of moving into the Glebe House with Alice was unthinkable. How could Oliver ever have imagined she'd countenance such a notion? Oh, God. The enormity of what she'd done was overwhelming. What *had* she done?

'Dun dun da dun dun,' went Paloma in time to her music.

And then Dannie remembered with an agonizing wrench where home was. Home was where the heart was. Where *was* it now, her home — her heart? Oh, God. The panic started to mount again. *What had she —*

'Da Dunne.'

* * *

'Look. I'm certain you'll change your mind when you see the joint.'

It was dark, apart from the candles Dannie had lit, and the flickering glow of the outdoor heater. Paloma was in bed, and Dannie and Oliver were sitting in the garden of her cottage, sharing a bottle of wine.

'Alice has done a beautiful job on both apartments,' he continued. 'She's even offered to let us have the one with the sea view. We could go there now — '

'I can't leave Paloma.'

'Tomorrow, then.'

'Yeah.'

Dannie was feeling dog tired. They'd been travelling since lunchtime, and she couldn't think straight. She wanted more than anything to be left alone in the comfort of the beloved cottage that was no longer hers.

'We'll have our own bathroom, of course,' he explained.

'Jesus, Oliver! I should hope so!'

'The kitchen's shared, but that makes sense. We can all eat together.'

She wanted to cry. How could he not understand that there was no way she could share a kitchen with another woman!

'Who'll do the cooking?'

'Well — that'd be your job, wouldn't it? Sure,

you may as well cook for four as for three. One extra mouth to feed will be no bother to a domestic goddess like you, darling. Alice will have all her time taken up with the running of the hotel, of course, especially in the high season.'

'And what about me in the high season? I have a business to run too, you know!'

'Oh.' He gave her a slightly put-out look. 'I kind of assumed you'd sell the business. We don't need the income, after all, and we might want to think about starting a family of our own soon.'

Dannie looked even more dismayed. 'Look,' said Oliver, misinterpreting. 'If you really don't want to cook we'll manage somehow. But you've always said that you enjoy cooking.'

'I *do* enjoy cooking, but I want to cook for my family, not . . . ' she couldn't bring herself to say it.

'Not for my sister,' he finished for her. He gave her a grave look. 'Alice *is* family now, Dannie. Or she will be, once we get married.'

A silence fell. It was so eloquent it was excruciating. Then: 'You've changed your mind, haven't you?' he said. 'About us getting married.'

'I . . . Oh, God, Oliver. I don't know.'

Another silence fell, then: 'Listen,' he said gently. 'I love you, Dannie, and I want more than anything for you to be my wife, and to have babies with you. But we don't have to rush into anything. We've all the time in the world to see how things pan out. Why don't we just play it by ear for a while?'

'How do you mean?'

'Well, why don't you divide your time between here and the Glebe House? I can't stay here in the cottage with you for obvious reasons. A hotel's a hands-on business, and I'll have to be there and available night and day, at least until we're up and running. But you and Paloma could come and stay any time you like — maybe during the week when things aren't so hectic in the hotel. See how we all get on, as in a kind of trial marriage. Then, if we do decide to go for it, we could move into the gate lodge. Alice had earmarked it as a romantic retreat for guests, but I'm sure she'll understand if you'd rather live at a bit of a remove from the hotel. The refurbishment should take about six months, and by that time we'll have sussed whether things are going to work out between us or not.'

Dannie nodded. She'd already told Paloma that Oliver was going to become a kind of second daddy to her, and she could hardly turn around now and tell her that he wasn't. She'd showed her daughter the beautiful Victorian rose-cut diamond ring that Oliver had bought for her, and explained that that was what men bought for women when they loved them so much they wanted to marry them. And Paloma was so fired up by the notion that she was going to be living in a house with a swimming pool, and that she was to be allowed to have a dog at last, and a daddy who would be around to do all the daddy-type stuff that her friends' daddies did. Dannie remembered how well the two of them had got on in Paris. Oliver had taken Paloma on rides that were way too sissy for him, he'd bought her presents, he'd picked her up and carried her piggy back whenever she complained of being tired. She couldn't bear the idea of snatching that new happiness away from her daughter after such a short time.

She bit her lip, considering. 'This is really sweet of you, Oliver. And you're absolutely right — marriage isn't something that should be rushed into. I suppose we've been a bit giddy about the whole thing.'

'I've loved you for ever, so I'm beyond feeling giddy. But I'm a very patient man, Dannie, and I can wait a while longer. I'll woo you, Ms Moore, and I'll win you, too. See if I don't.'

She smiled at him. 'You already swept me off my feet when you proposed to me in your swimming pool. I'm a sucker for romance.'

Dannie leaned towards him and kissed him lightly. Oliver pulled her against him to prolong the kiss, but just then the church clock began to chime midnight.

'Hell,' he said, relinquishing her. 'I'd love to take you to bed right now, darling, but it's late and I've a load of work to catch up on. Will you come tomorrow to the Glebe House? Have a dekko at the apartment?'

'Of course I will.'

'She's done a great job, Alice has. Made a really comfortable living space for us. I think you'll be impressed.'

If Alice's taste in clothes was anything to go by, Dannie wasn't so sure. But she managed a smile. 'I'll call round in the morning,' she said, 'after I've packed Paloma off to the nursery.'

She was glad that Alice wasn't there when she called at the Glebe House for the guided tour the following day. She tried to keep her expression neutral as Oliver showed her around, but it was difficult. How could he have thought for a minute that she could be happy living here!

Alice's taste erred towards opulence. Oliver told Dannie that his sister had looked to the Culloden Hotel — where they'd spent that weekend a year or so ago — for inspiration. But the Culloden had got it *right*. Here in the Glebe House things just looked overcrowded. There was a lot of mahogany furniture, a lot of Regency stripes, a lot of swagged *toile de jouy*.

Alice had furnished Oliver's apartment before he'd announced his intention of marrying Dannie, and she'd obviously had a bachelor look in mind. Brass and leather featured prominently, and all black goods were stowed away in reproduction armoires to give the joint a 'country gent' feel. There was even a cocktail cabinet. Dannie felt that her heart couldn't plummet any further.

Oliver had been a bit economical with the truth when he'd said that the kitchen would be the only room they'd have to share with his sister. The adjoining dining room would clearly be communal too. She pictured herself sitting opposite Alice at the long mahogany table on the leather-upholstered chairs making the kind of small talk they'd made in that café in Paris, and she felt sick.

They had their own sitting room and, of course, bedroom with king-sized bed and — Dannie was appalled to see — floor-to-ceiling mirrored sliderobes, but when Oliver finished the grand tour with a 'Well, what do you think?', there was one glaring omission staring Dannie in the face. She couldn't believe that he hadn't mentioned it.

'Where's Paloma supposed to sleep?' she asked.

'Don't worry, I've thought about that. We're going to sacrifice one of the guest rooms for her.'

'What do you mean — sacrifice one of the guest rooms?'

'One of the rooms in the main wing of the house will have to be redecorated — made more child-friendly. Alice has already looked into it — she was even sussed enough to realize there'd need to be an intercom since she'll be down the corridor from us. I'd never have thought of that. Just shows that I've a load of parenting skills to learn.'

'Down the corridor. How far down the corridor?'

'Not far. Don't *worry*, Mammy!' He ruffled her hair. 'By the way, I thought you and Paloma and I could take a trip into Galway this week and choose furniture and wallpaper and stuff. Make it into a proper little girl's room.'

'Hang on, Oliver. You're saying that Paloma won't be sleeping in the apartment with us.'

'Well, not strictly speaking. Why don't you come and have a look now, to set your mind at rest? Just let me go and get the key. It's in Alice's bureau.'

Oliver turned and left the room, leaving Dannie stone-cold with horror. She couldn't stay here. The hideous furnishings were pressing in on her like sarcophagi. Opulence clogged the air and she felt as if she might suffocate. She had to get out.

She ran out of the apartment and down the main staircase. As she pulled open the heavy front door of the Glebe House she heard Oliver's voice echoing down the stairs, plangent with incomprehension.

'Dannie? Dannie! Where are you going?'

She didn't answer. When she hit her car, her phone was ringing. Oliver's number was displayed. She switched the phone off, turned on the ignition and took off down the drive. Some current affairs stuff was being broadcast on the car radio, but she was oblivious to it. At the bottom of the drive she indicated right, and waited for a tractor to pass. She wanted to go to Lissnakeelagh strand, to the hiding place she'd discovered as a child, the place no-one knew about except her and Paloma. And Jethro.

She'd taken Jethro there because she had no secrets from him. They'd skinny-dipped there, and then they'd made love listening to the lapping of the waves. Afterwards he told her that she was sexier than Deborah Kerr in *From Here to Eternity*, and she'd laughed and told him to 'get away out of that'. The memory made her lean her forehead against the steering wheel and ask herself again the question she'd been asking since their return from Paris yesterday — *What had she done?*

She'd made a mistake. It was that simple. She'd sacrificed the love of her life for Oliver Dunne, a man she realized now she didn't really know. *Why* had she done it?

The answer came from the voice that was impinging on her consciousness from the radio. 'Stability in a child's life is of paramount importance,' the voice was saying. Well, *she* knew that! 'All the experts are agreed that when they reach a certain age children from two-parent families out-perform those whose family circumstances are prone to fluctuation or disruption, and that these children are generally happier and more confident than — '

Dannie reached for the 'off' button. She didn't want to hear any more: she just needed to do some very hard thinking. Think, Dannie! *Think!*

On analysis, the only conclusion she could arrive at was that she'd messed up bigtime. Was there any course she could take to make things better? Oh, God, oh, God — think *harder!*

OK. She may have messed up her own life, but she was an adult, after all, and responsible for any mistakes she might make. Her overriding concern now was how badly she might mess up Paloma's life. How badly would she bruise her daughter's psyche when she went to her and told her that actually, no, they weren't going to be moving into the Glebe House after all, and Oliver wouldn't be picking her up from school and taking her riding and doing all those things with her that he'd promised to do . . .

A loud caw distracted her, and she saw a single magpie flap out of the chestnut tree that grew in the garden of the gate lodge. *The gate lodge.* She remembered what Oliver had said about it last night, and she studied it now from a new perspective. It was a pretty house, with miniature turrets and a castellated roof. It could be made into a real homey home. Oliver hadn't been too far off the mark when he'd called Dannie a domestic goddess — she'd always had a talent for transforming her surroundings. The flat she'd once owned in Dublin had been turned into a sultana's boudoir, and the Kilrowan cottage that now belonged to her brother and the awful Leanne was worthy of a feature in *Country Interiors* magazine. She could do a lot with the gate lodge.

She considered. Why not do as Oliver suggested? Why not move into the Glebe House only for as long as it took for renovation to be completed on the gate lodge? If she threw herself into the restoration project the joint could be ready in fewer than six months, she knew it could. She'd worked her ass off getting the flat above the shop into shape for Deirdre O'Dare to move into, and she had real motivation for making the gate lodge habitable. And as soon as it was, she and Oliver and Paloma could move out of the suffocating apartment in Glebe House and into their new home.

She felt better now she had a plan. She could just about bear to live under the same roof as Alice if there was an escape route, and that's exactly what her gate lodge project would be. She'd inspect the place later today, and have a chat with the builders who'd been responsible for the refurbishment of the big house. She'd get herself a hard hat and she'd be there before them in the mornings, and she'd work hands-on with them till the job was done. And once her home was ready to move into, maybe the thin film of ice that she'd felt accumulating around her heart since her dada died would start to thaw.

Dannie released the handbrake, turned the car round and switched the radio back on. The child-rearing expert had shut up, and Annie Lennox's 'Sisters are Doin' it for Themselves' was playing. It gave her spirits a lift. She could do this. She could make a going concern of her new life. Jesus — she'd have to! Dannie had always been a fighter, and she was spoiling for a fight now. She headed back up the driveway feeling a lot more buoyant than when she'd driven down it.

★ ★ ★

Dannie packed clothes and toys for Paloma, but few other possessions. She'd leave everything in the cottage until her new home was ready, and then she'd move wholesale, and relinquish the cottage to her sister-in-law. She had decided that it would be too disruptive for Paloma if she did as Oliver had suggested and divided her time between the Glebe House and the cottage — it would be disruptive enough once Paloma was spending weekends in Ballynahinch Castle with her real father — so Dannie had made the decision to live exclusively with Oliver in their apartment. She had thought she might cry when she turned off gas and electricity and locked the door of her old home behind her, but she hardened her heart. Dannie had always known when it was time to move on.

Paloma's room in the Glebe House might be temporary accommodation, but Alice had made sure that it was as child-friendly as possible. She'd set up the two-way intercom so that Dannie could monitor her daughter at night, and she'd bought a chest for Paloma's toys, and a doll's house and a television. Dannie didn't like the idea of Paloma having a television in her room, but, she reasoned, it gave her even more of an incentive to get the gate lodge sorted and her family into it ASAP.

The lodge was bigger than Dannie had imagined from the outside, with three bedrooms and a bathroom upstairs, and a sitting room, dining room, study and kitchen downstairs. Oliver told her she could turn the study into her own private retreat, since he planned on using a room in the main house as an office. Once they'd moved out of their apartment it was to be converted into a de-luxe suite for residents, and the kitchen and dining room they were currently sharing with Alice would revert to her.

Dannie couldn't wait. She felt like an unreal person when she put food on the table in front of Oliver's sister in that horrible dining room with its Mr Sheened table. She couldn't bear to listen to Alice as she enthused about Dannie's cooking, asking for recipes and going 'Mm mm mm!' as she ate. Sometimes Alice would come and watch television in their sitting room instead of going to her own room, and Dannie felt like screaming at the running commentaries she'd deliver as they watched soap operas, or the 'insightful' advice she'd offer politicians on the news, or her awful high-pitched snicker during comedy programmes. The only thing that kept Dannie sane was the prospect of flying the coop and feathering her own nest in the house at the bottom of the driveway.

Her instinct about Oliver had been right. He was proving to be a fantastic father to Paloma. He read her bedtime stories, he took her riding, and he was teaching her to play tennis on the court at the back of the house. However, his flair in the paternal department didn't arouse any dormant feelings of broodiness in Dannie. She continued to take her contraceptive pills religiously, and Oliver just shrugged when he saw them and said: 'We'll wait until you're well and ready, Dannie.'

Sex with Oliver was good, and sex with Oliver was nightly. Dannie remembered how she'd been pissed off with Jethro when he'd been too tired and overworked to make love, and she tried very hard indeed to block out the times when he *hadn't* been too tired. But those memories were too precious and too vivid to block effectively. The most disturbing thing for her was that it was always Jethro's face she saw in her mind's eye every time she came.

★ ★ ★

She was reversing her car into a parking space outside Breda Shanley's shop one afternoon, not long after she'd moved into the Glebe House. Dannie was finding it a little weird living two miles outside the village. In the past she'd been able to nip out to Breda's any time she ran out of milk or if she wanted a newspaper or a chat. She could duck into O'Toole's if she fancied a bowl of chowder or a pint. Now she had to take the car in. Two miles wasn't a long way to drive, but somehow the physical action of getting into a car made a big psychological difference.

'There's Daddy!' squealed Paloma from the back of the car, and for a crazy moment Dannie wondered who she meant.

She switched off the ignition and turned her head to see Jethro. He was having a confab on the street with Eva Lavery, pointing down towards the pier where arc lights were being set up and cameras were being hefted onto shoulders and key grips were doing whatever the hell it was key grips did. It had been nearly a week since Dannie had last been in the village, and she'd almost forgotten that a movie was being made there.

She watched as Jethro described something in the air with his big hands. The actress nodded in understanding, then gave him her best flirtatious look and made some remark that caused him to throw back his head and laugh. Dannie felt an awful, awful stab of jealousy. Oh, God! How sick of her! She should be glad that Jethro was getting on with his life, staying happy and flirting with

301

women. She should be glad for him . . .

Paloma was out of the car already, running towards her dada and holding onto her Mickey Mouse ears. She'd taken to wearing them all the time, even in bed. Dannie busied herself with her seat belt and a little bag-rummaging business before getting out of the driver's seat and setting off after her daughter. Jethro had swung her up into his arms, and was listening to her excited jabber with an indulgent smile.

'Well,' she heard him say as she drew abreast of them, 'I bet Mickey Mouse really misses you, too.'

'Yes, he does! He cried when I told him I was leaving!'

'Hi,' said Dannie, with studied nonchalance.

'Ma'am.' He inclined his head.

'Hello, Dannie,' said Eva. 'Excuse me, Jethro, for a minute, will you? I need to check something in my script.' And the actress moved off, discretion personified.

Jethro lowered Paloma to the ground. 'I take it you had a good holiday?'

'It was good, yes. How've you been?'

'Busy.'

'Keeping to schedule?'

'Only by working flat out. You'll have your shop back soon.'

'Oh?' Oh, God. 'You're wrapping?'

'All the location stuff's done. We've only interiors left.'

'You're still staying in Ballynahinch?'

'Yes, ma'am. Maybe you'd like to come visit tomorrow, Paloma? I'm taking the day off.'

'Yeah yeah yeah!' said Paloma. 'Can we go riding?'

'Sure.'

'D'you know there's a kind of horse called after me, Dad? It's called a Palomina?'

Jethro smiled at her mispronunciation. 'A Palomina is a fine animal, toots. I'm not surprised they named it after you.'

'Will I leave her up to you in the morning?' asked Dannie, in her politest tone of enquiry.

'No. I've a better idea. Why don't you come out to Ballynahinch this evening when we're done here and stay over?' Of course the invitation wasn't addressed to her. It was addressed to their daughter. 'Well, sweetpea? What do you think? You can stay in my trailer and draw or something until we wrap for the day. And I'll buy you an ice-cream, and — um — what other stuff do you like? A comic book, maybe?'

'Yay! Can I, Mam?'

'Of course you can, pet lamb.'

'Polar!' went Paloma. 'I'd better get him.' She scudded back to the car. Polar was Paloma's teddybear. She never went anywhere without him, and any time Dannie was asked the question about 'The Only Item You're Allowed to Fetch from a Burning Building', the answer was always 'Polar'.

She steeled herself to look at Jethro. 'When would it suit for me to pick her up tomorrow?'

'Around seven o'clock?'

'Fine.'

Oh God. This was grim. They were talking in

that awful stilted way divorced people talked in films. Well, wise up, girl! she told herself. This is the way we'll be talking from now on and for ever.

'You're going to have to buy a toothbrush for Paloma,' she said. 'And what are you going to do about jimjams?'

'I'll let her have one of my T-shirts.' Oh! He'd done that for her once, when she'd visited him in a hotel and had spilled coffee on her nightdress. She'd loved the fact that his T-shirt had been way too big for her, and that it had smelt of him.

Now she gave him an overly bright smile as Paloma danced back to where they stood, swinging Polar by the paw. 'Fine. OK, then. Well, I'd better go. Have fun.' She forgot to add an exclamation mark to the 'Have fun'.

'See you tomorrow.'

'Bye, Mam!' Paloma dismissed her with a wave, then turned back to her father. 'Can we watch a DVD tonight, Dad?' she said, clinging onto his arm.

'Sure can, toots. I can let you have a sneak preview of — ' He bent and whispered into her ear, and whatever he said produced a shriek from Paloma.

'But that's not due out for ages! How come you've got it?'

'Because,' he said, 'I am what's known as a man of some influence.'

'A man of some influence! That is so cool! My dada's a man of some influence!'

Dannie turned and walked back up the street. She should have gone straight into Breda's to get the ingredients she needed for supper this evening. Instead, she went into the pub. She needed a drink to steady her nerves.

* * *

After supper, Alice — thankfully! — said good night and went off to her own quarters.

'C'mere, Dannie, you sexy thing,' said Oliver, moving to the bedroom door and holding it open for her. 'I've been feeling horny all evening watching you make like Nigella Lawson.'

He slapped her flank as she passed by into the room, unbuttoning her shirt as she went. Then he shut the door, made a lunge for her and pushed her onto the bed.

Kneeling down behind her, Oliver undid the clasp of her bra and pulled the straps down over her shoulders. Then he started kissing the nape of her neck, fondling her breasts and looking at her all the time in the mirror. 'Look how beautiful you are,' he said. 'Go on, have a look.' She tried to demur, tried to turn away, but he just laughed. 'There's no shame,' he said, 'in looking at something so beautiful. Doesn't it make you want to touch yourself? Go on.' He pulled down the zip on her jeans, and guided her hand under the band of her panties. 'Go on,' he urged, rubbing himself into the small of her back. 'I'll help you. Good girl. That's lovely. Oh, *God*, yes — that's lovely!'

And on he went, encouraging, murmuring inducements in her ear, seducing her with his voice and his caresses. And Dannie remembered

305

a time when Jethro had done something similar in his house in Gozo, when he'd taken her from behind in front of the mirror in his bathroom, and suddenly she was moaning and crying out as she surrendered to the rush of her orgasm.

Oliver came then, quickly. They lay back on the bed in post-orgasmic languor for several moments and then Oliver got up and stretched. 'What time is it?' he asked.

Dannie glanced at the carriage clock that had been a present from Alice. 'Ten to nine.'

'Damn. I'm supposed to meet Bob in O'Toole's at nine. He wants cash for that plumbing job.' Zipping himself up, he picked up his jacket from the back of a chair. 'How dare you be so feckin' distracting, Dannie.'

'Personally speaking, I think you got your priorities right.' Dannie slid out of her clothes and into her robe.

'D'you want to come with me?'

'No. I'm feeling antisocial.'

'Shame. I'd like to show off my gorgeous, sexy new fiancée.' Oliver gave her a lecherous look, then blew her a kiss and left the room.

Dannie wandered into the kitchen to pour herself a glass of wine. She didn't know what to do with herself next. There was nothing on telly, she knew. She'd finished the book she'd been reading, and had loved it so much that she didn't want to start another one that might disappoint. Maybe she should ring Oliver and ask him to pick up a DVD in the village? Nah, there was no point — he'd forgotten his phone. It was there, lying on the kitchen table.

The idea of the DVD made her think of Jethro, and she wondered what was the advance copy of the DVD he'd promised Paloma. She pictured them now in his suite in Ballynahinch Castle, watching telly and ordering room service. Just the thought of Paloma made her feel homesick for her little girl, and she moseyed on bare feet towards her daughter's bedroom to fetch a vest or some other item of the child's clothing that she could cuddle and keep on her pillow overnight.

She opened Paloma's door and turned on the light. What she saw when she flicked the switch made her yelp with fright. There, sitting on a club chair by the window, was Alice.

The other woman appeared to have got just as much of a fright as Dannie: she jumped to her feet and made a sound in her throat. The two of them stood there looking at each other for a moment, then Alice said, 'Em. I suppose you're wondering what I'm doing in here.'

'Yes. I am.'

'Well, I just came in to see if there was anything more that needed doing to the child's room.'

'But you were sitting there in the dark!'

'I was thinking, Dannie, how lucky you are to have a little girl. Especially such a dotey one as Paloma is. And then the sunset caught my attention just as I was about to leave the room, and I got lost in the view. Look there, beyond the hill.'

Dannie didn't want to move to the window. She didn't want to move any nearer to this woman than necessary. Instead she took a step to her left and leaned sideways a little, the better to see out of the window. There, indeed, were the remnants of a magnificent sunset scrawled across the horizon.

But there was something not quite right about this. Dannie was deeply disturbed by the notion of Oliver's sister sitting in the dark in her daughter's bedroom, like some big bloated spider. She stood in silence, willing the woman to leave the room.

It worked. Alice mumbled something inarticulate before sidling past Dannie and out through the door.

Dannie sat down on Paloma's bed and stared at the floor, feeling numb. The woman had every right, she supposed, to come into Paloma's bedroom. This was her house, after all. But it just didn't feel *good*.

Oh, God. How stuffy the room was! How long had Alice *been* there? Dannie got to her feet with an effort, and moved to the window to open it. She took a couple of breaths of ozone-rich air, then crossed to the door and switched off the light. But before she could step into the corridor, a sound from the speaker on the intercom made her turn. It was the tinny chime of the carriage clock in her bedroom striking nine.

In the darkness of the room, the light on the two-way intercom glowed like a bloodshot eye.

13

Cleo loved it when Colleen went off on her literary tours. She felt as if Pablo belonged to her exclusively then. They never entered each other's houses by the front door in case they were seen, but the decks at the back were relatively private, and they ran in and out on a daily basis like kids asking pals if they were coming out to play. There had been a near disaster today when Margot had visited Cleo. Pablo had rolled up on the deck stark naked, but luckily Margot's back had been to the window and Pablo had just given Cleo a glum look and shuffled back unnoticed to number 4, the Blackthorns.

'What's the story with Felix?' Cleo asked Margot, pouring the green tea her sister had brought her. 'He's been back in Dublin for a while now, hasn't he? Shouldn't you think about going back home now that you've no more work on the film?'

Oops. She shouldn't have said that. She knew that Margot was miffed that she was no longer required to be a film star on *Mimi's Remedies*. As one of Mimi's Minxes, Cleo was still called occasionally to work in the studio, but now that all the exterior shots of Kilrowan were in the can, very few of the villagers were used as extras any more.

'I'm in no hurry to go home,' Margot said, cool as you like. 'I'm perfectly happy here for the foreseeable future. I'm having an affair.'

'*What?*'

'I'm having an affair.'

Cleo was virtually struck dumb. Excuse me? Was this her sister with the perfect marriage speaking? 'Oh my God, Margot. Who with?'

'I'm not at liberty to disclose the identity of my lover.' Margot gave her an arch look, then curled her legs under her on the couch. 'But I know you're bound to be curious. I dare say you'll want to know how it happened?'

Cleo wasn't sure she did really, but Margot was clearly only too happy to oblige because she careered on without waiting for any response. 'When he came back from holiday, Felix told me quite bluntly on the phone that he'd had a fling with some bimbo he'd met in Egypt, so I retaliated by telling him that I was having an affair with someone here in Kilrowan. It wasn't true at the time — although there *was* an incredibly intense sexual vibe between us — but it's true now.'

'You mean, you deliberately went out and had a fling just to get back at Felix?'

'Who said anything about a fling? This is for real, Cleo. I'm leaving Felix and moving in with my lover.'

Now Cleo *was* struck dumb. She could think of absolutely nothing to say except: 'Cor.'

'I'm forging a brand-new life for myself,' went on Margot. 'Unfortunately, as my lover is quite well known, we'll have to keep our relationship under wraps for a while. There's also a prior — rather volatile — relationship that will have to be sorted before we make our affair public.'

'You mean he's married?'

'Let's just say there's the potential for problems. But they're not insurmountable. Our passion is strong enough to overcome any obstacles.' A little private smile, a little sip of wine. 'Hah! Felix used to boast all the time about his sexual prowess, claiming that because he was a gynaecologist he knew exactly how women were designed. I phoned him last night and gained enormous pleasure from telling him that actually he hadn't a clue. Sex with . . . my lover is stratospheric. Do you want to know what we got up to last night?'

'I'm not sure I do, actually.'

Margot shot her sister a pitying look. 'Don't be so uptight, Cleo,' she said, shaking back her hair and stretching her arms out along the back of the couch. Cleo got the impression that she was trying to look like the personification of sensuality. 'You can be a terrible prude, you know. Sex is something to be celebrated.'

She wondered what Margot would say if she told her that actually she was having a beyond torrid affair with a ride who had just turned up stark naked on her deck sporting an enormous hard-on. She felt sorry for poor Pablo, who was probably at this very moment leafing through the pages of the *Erotica Universalis* or some similar work of erotic art, searching for images by Matisse or Picasso that would vicariously satisfy his lust for her.

'Sex with a soulmate is more about making

311

love with the mind than the body,' continued Margot. 'Fleshly considerations are transcended.'

God. Her sister really could talk a load of guff sometimes. More to do with the mind than the body, my arse. She thought of the fun she had during her sex games with Pablo and said: 'But is it *fun?*'

Margot looked at her as if she hailed from the planet Zog. 'Fun? What's sex got to do with 'fun', Cleo? 'Fun' is for comic books. You should try reading Henry Miller. Try reading Anaïs Nin.'

And you should try reading some of my short stories, Cleo wanted to say, but didn't. Instead: 'I've read Anaïs Nin,' she said, pettishly.

Margot ignored her. 'We lay in bed last night, reading the poetry of Catullus out loud to each other,' she said, giving a delicious little shiver. 'My lover combed my hair and then painted my face — and my body ... My God — the sensations produced by a wet sable-haired brush!'

What? Hey! That was a trick of Ricardo's! What was going on here?

'And afterwards we took a bath together and played around with the shower attachment,' Margot was purring now. She'd picked up the feather that had detached itself from Fluffy's collar and regarded it with a smile. 'Feathers make fantastic sex toys, too, you know. I lost count of the number of times I came.'

Feathers! Not feathers as well! Holy schomoly! Was Margot having an affair with Pablo? Was her secret lover a serial womanizer? Was he stringing her along, delighted with himself that he'd hooked a couple of sisters?

'And this morning we breakfasted on honey and — '

Cleo didn't want to hear any more details. In fact, she wanted her sister out of there now. She needed to do the confrontational thing with Ricardo/Pablo.

'Oh, shit!' she said, jumping to her feet. 'I'm going to have to chase you, Margot. I completely forgot that I had something dead urgent to do today.'

'Urgent?'

'I've — um — to take Fluffy to the vet and have her wormed.'

'Ew!' said Margot, jumping to her feet and brushing off any dog hairs that might have accumulated on her skirt. 'Worms aren't catching, are they?'

'No.' Cleo wanted her sister out of there ASAP. 'But fleas are. She has those too.'

With a clatter of kitten heels, Margot was gone.

As soon as Cleo heard the front door shut, she made a beeline for Pablo's deck and marched straight into his studio without bothering to knock. He was lounging on a stack of cushions on his divan, wearing a sarong, eating a sandwich and watching a video of *Sex Tips for Girls* that they'd recorded for future enlightenment. He looked like a spoilt pasha.

'Wow. Look at that,' he said. 'I didn't know they manufactured vibrators that are nearly as big as me. Has Margot gone?'

313

'Yes.' Cleo moved to the television and turned it off.

'Hey,' said Pablo through a mouthful of sandwich. 'They were just about to try that one out. I wanted to see how they got on.'

Cleo stood directly in his line of vision and assumed her best confrontational stance, feet apart, arms akimbo. 'Are you having an affair with her?'

'What? Having an affair with who?'

'With my sister.'

He gave her an incredulous look. 'Are you mad?'

'My sister just told me that she's having an affair with a man who sounds just like you.'

'Elaborate.'

'She told me that he's in the public eye, and that he's in a volatile relationship.'

'Wow. He sure does sound like a veritable clone. The similarities are astonishing.' He held up a finger. 'One — yeah, I'm in a volatile relationship. Two — I'm in the public eye.' He held up a second finger, then added a third. 'And three, I'm having an affair. But it's *you* I'm having the affair with, jealous boots, not your sister. I couldn't possibly have an affair with your sister.'

'Why not?'

'Because she has no sense of humour.'

'Neither has Colleen.'

'*Touché.* But Colleen is a fantastic ride, and I'm not sure I could say the same for your sister — *if* I ever bothered to find out, which I haven't.'

'What makes you say that?'

314

'She has that look about her, Cleo, that posey look. She'd be one of those women who, once you get them into bed, start behaving as if they're in some French arthouse film — all self-consciously 'sensual', if you know what I mean.'

That was the very impression Cleo herself had got earlier, when Margot had shaken back her hair and stretched herself on the couch.

She was curious now. 'Are there women like that?'

'God, yeah. There should be a law against exposing women to arthouse sex. They fake their orgasms so badly.' Cleo couldn't imagine anyone who went to bed with Pablo having to fake an orgasm. 'Now. Does that satisfy you that I am definitely not riding your sister?'

'I . . . guess.' She gave an unconvincing nod, then narrowed her eyes at him. 'There was something else, though.'

'Tell.'

'She mentioned that she'd taken a bath with this man, and that he'd done the thing with the shower — you know? The thing Ricardo — sorry, I mean *you* — do so well. *And* he painted her body with a sable-haired brush, and I'm almost certain that he played the honey and the feather trick on her as well, because Margot — '

Pablo laughed, then stretched out a hand to grab hers. 'Sweetheart, don't you know that there are no new ideas on the face of the planet?' Cleo allowed herself to be pulled down onto the cushions. 'Maybe those tricks are just *zeitgeisty*

315

stuff. Maybe they were on *Sex Tips for Girls*. Maybe they're even featured in an arthouse flick. Mm. Nice. Very nice. Do that little wriggle again.'

Cleo complied.

'Inspirational! I happen to be working on a Nude with Pig at the moment,' he said, undoing the buttons on the front of her dress. 'And I have a sudden overwhelming urge to have a good look at your breasts to remind me of how beautifully luminescent soft white girly flesh can be.' He unhooked her bra with deft fingers. 'Now. Let me just peel off this little polka-dotted confection — very pretty, incidentally — and study your flesh tones. Ooh. Your nipples have gone all pointy, darling. Why is that, I wonder? Don't tell me you're becoming sexually aroused. Are you?'

And that's how Cleo and Pablo ended up breaking the rules they'd made about only ever having sex in number 5, the Blackthorns, and having sex in number 4 instead.

* * *

'Why do you have a television in your studio?' asked Cleo, about an hour later.

'So I can watch MTV while I paint.'

'MTV?'

'Yeah. Some of those pop princesses can be pretty inspiring.'

'You mean, you find pop more inspiring than something classical like Beethoven or Mozart or Carl Orff?'

He gave her a 'get orff' look. 'It's not the music I find inspiring, darling. It's the bootyliciousness of the princesses.'

She remembered how she'd imagined him leafing through the *Erotica Universalis* earlier for — em — inspiration. How could she have got him so wrong? Pablo MacBride clearly had no real interest in culture at all! 'God. You're a complete savage, aren't you!'

'Yup. But I actually paint better when I'm horny.'

'Really? Do all artists paint better when they're horny?'

'I dunno. It's not the kind of question that's bandied around at exhibition openings.'

She wriggled against him again. 'Do you paint in the nude?'

'Not quite. But I like to hang loose, so I wear a sarong.'

'Jesus! You *are* an unashamedly horny bastard, aren't you?' She gave him a look of reluctant admiration. 'But then, you really are very sexy, Pablo MacBride.'

'Well — you know what Colleen says?'

Cleo hated hearing anything about Colleen, but she was curious. 'What does she say?'

'All sex is art, all art is sex.'

The sound of the doorbell ringing came from upstairs.

'Colleen!' yelped Cleo, grabbing her dress and darting for the deck.

'Don't be daft,' said Pablo, winding the length of batiked cotton around his waist and knotting the ends. 'Colleen never bothers with the bell.

She has a key. Anyway, she's not due back from her tour yet. Die, motherfucker!' he added, swatting a passing fruit fly with the fringe of his sarong before heading for the stairs. He paused halfway up to smile down at her. 'Have you,' he asked, 'got used yet to having to go upstairs to answer the front door in your house? I still feel weird doing it.' He turned back and carried on up, looking completely unconcerned.

How could he keep his cool at such a moment? marvelled Cleo. She had shrugged into her frock and was now shimmying into her knicks and fumbling with buttons. She fully expected to hear Colleen's dramatic baritone float down the stairs, and was poised to take flight from the deck, but the next voice she heard was Deirdre O'Dare's, saying: 'This is to say thank you for the lift back from the airport.'

'No reward necessary,' came Pablo's response. 'It was a pleasure getting to know you. Come in and have a drink.'

'I'm not disturbing you, am I?'

'Not at all. I already have company. My neighbour called in to borrow a cup of sugar.'

'Hi!' said Cleo when Deirdre appeared on the stairs. She had adopted her best nonchalant stance, but she could tell she wasn't fooling Deirdre.

'Oh hi, Cleo,' said Deirdre with an amused smile. 'I just called round with a bottle of wine for Pablo. By the way, Pablo, Rory sat next to Colleen on the LA flight. She, er — introduced herself.' She didn't add that Rory had told her that Colleen had issued an upfront invitation to

318

visit her in her hotel room once they landed, which offer he had politely declined.

'Make yourself comfortable, Deirdre,' said Pablo, ambling in the direction of the kitchen with the wine bottle, 'and I'll get glasses.'

Deirdre and Cleo stood looking at each other for a moment or two in silence until they were sure Pablo was out of earshot, and then Deirdre smiled. 'Well. I could do with a girly chat,' she said, lowering the pitch of her voice. 'Fancy meeting up for a drink some time soon? Why don't you drop by after yoga this evening?'

'I'd love that,' said Cleo. She shot a look towards the kitchen door. 'I could do with some good girl talk, too.'

'He's a really kosher bloke,' said Deirdre, nodding in the same direction. 'We had a great chat on the way back from Knock airport. I was in flitters because I'd had to say goodbye to Rory, and Pablo really cheered me up. It's funny, because I was a bit in awe of him initially.'

'In awe? Of *Pablo*?'

'Yeah. I've always been in awe of great-looking men. And then I find out that most of them are pussycats.'

'Pablo's that, all right. Oh, God, Deirdre — I'm so *smitten*!'

'I'm not surprised.' She raised an eyebrow. 'I couldn't help sneaking a look at the bulge beneath the sarong. Is the sex swoon-inducing?'

'Beyond swoon-inducing,' said Cleo with feeling.

The sound of a cork popping came from the kitchen, and the two women adopted a studiedly careless air — Cleo pretending to study the canvas that was propped on Pablo's easel, Deirdre sending an imaginary text message on her phone — as Pablo came back into the room with the wine bottle and three glasses on a tray.

'What were you witchy women whispering about?' he asked, then answered his own question. 'Girl stuff, natch. Hey, look, it's sunny out. Let's go sit on the deck.' He slid into French waiter mode, balancing the tray above his head, and started moving towards the open window. '*Venez avec moi, mes jolies dames, et* let's — um — *buver du vin en plein air.*' Then he froze. 'Fuck,' he said.

Cleo and Deirdre followed the direction of his gaze. Beyond the sea wall a figure was striding along, crimson cloak billowing in the wind. Colleen paused at the gate that opened into Pablo's garden, and laid a hand on the latch.

'Oh, fuck. She's not going to like this,' said Pablo. 'She's *especially* not going to like the fact that I'm entertaining two very fit chicks, wearing nothing but my sarong.'

Thrusting her phone into his free hand, Deirdre swung into action. 'Turn that off!' she commanded. She grabbed the tray from him and moved quickly towards the kitchen door. Blind with panic, Cleo followed her. 'Keep her on the deck if you can,' instructed Deirdre over her shoulder to Pablo. 'And try even harder to keep her out of the kitchen. We're going to have to hide in here.'

'Oh my God oh my God. Surely we could make it to the stairs?' gibbered Cleo, dithering on the threshold of the kitchen and sending a desperate look at the only escape route available to them, which shone like a beacon on the far side of the studio.

'No.' Deirdre set the tray down on the kitchen table, grabbed Cleo by the hand and dragged her into the room. 'There's no way we can make it without being seen from the garden. If Colleen sees a flurry of activity, can you imagine? It'll only arouse her suspicions bigtime. Just keep calm, Cleo. If she does happen to come into the kitchen we tell her the truth. That I'd brought Pablo a bottle of wine to thank him for driving me from the airport.'

'It'll be cool,' said Pablo in a low voice from the studio. 'Deirdre's right, Cleo. I'll make some excuse to get rid of her ASAP.'

In the kitchen, Cleo ran to the back door and tugged frantically at the handle. It was locked and there was no key in the keyhole. She looked round anxiously, hoping that there might be a cupboard or something to hide in. Of course there wasn't, she knew that. The room had been built to the same spec as hers.

'Look. Sit down,' said Deirdre in a low voice, indicating the table. 'I'm going to pour us some wine, and if the worst comes to the worst and she comes in here, just act natural. She can hardly jump to the conclusion that she's stumbled across some kinky threesome.'

Oh yes she can, thought Cleo, remembering that the video box on top of the television bore the legend *Sex Tips for Girls* writ large in her curliest capitals. She took the glass proffered by

Deirdre and swigged back some Dutch courage.

There came the sound of greetings from the deck, and Cleo went so tense that if someone had pushed her she'd have fallen to the floor like a cardboard cut-out. It got worse. The murmurs were becoming louder. Pablo had evidently failed in his attempt to prevent Colleen from entering the house, and her voice was coming audibly from the studio now.

'I am footsore,' she was saying. 'And heartsore. That's what has brought me back to my beloved Kilrowan sooner than anticipated.'

'How long have you been back?' Cleo was amazed that Pablo could contrive to sound so casual.

'Three days. Maybe four. In my soul-searching, in my quest for truth, I have lost count of the hours. I have retired at dawn and risen at twilight. I have slept in the sun, and walked with my cats by dead of night.' There came the sound of a mobile phone. Cleo looked at Deirdre with eyes bigger than Habitat saucers. Oh *God*! Had Pablo forgotten to turn Deirdre's phone off? The phone rang and rang, and Cleo went stiffer and stiffer with awful apprehension until finally: 'Leonora!' they heard. 'What is it? Arra, cannot you let me be? I signed twelve thousand copies, I spoke to twelve thousand dolts who all asked the same questions, I scintillated on chat shows and read extracts of *The Faraway* until I was hoarse. Is it any wonder I drew the line at appearing on *The David Letterman Show*?' There was a pause, presumably to allow Leonora to beg. Then: 'No,

Leonora. My talent is God-given. To have appeared on *The David Letterman Show* would not just have been akin to sacrilege — it would have been an act of prostitution. Let me be. I have dreams to live, and tales to tell. I bid you *slán*.'

'They wanted you to go on *David Letterman?*' Pablo asked.

'Yes. Oh — how I despise LA, Pablo. How I despise that plastic society. And how I *despise* my mobile phone!' There came the thwump sound of an object being hurled against cushions, then the rhythmic sound of restless footsteps as Colleen — presumably — paced the room. Every time the footsteps went past the kitchen door, the two women sitting at the table exchanged looks and nearly forgot to breathe.

Finally, the footsteps came to a halt. 'Ah — let me lie here, Pablo, and rest awhile.' Colleen's voice was low, throaty, seductive. 'My love, *a grá* — my soul has been in torment.'

Cleo and Deirdre exchanged horrified looks. Oh, God. It was clear that Colleen had plonked herself down on the divan in the studio. Would Pablo find *any* way of shifting her now? Worse — would Colleen extend an invitation to him to join her for a lovemaking session on the very cushions upon which he and Cleo had disported themselves earlier? She couldn't sit in his kitchen and listen to *that*. And — oh, God! Cleo clamped her hand over her mouth and gazed at Deirdre with even wider worried eyes. Oh God, oh horror — would Colleen find the bra that Cleo had discarded earlier — the one she'd

323

forgotten in her panic to put back on when Pablo had gone to answer the door?

Deirdre tried to pucker her Botoxed forehead at Cleo in a 'what's wrong?' kind of frown.

'My bra,' mouthed Cleo, doing a 'my bra' mime, and pointing towards the door.

'Out there?' Deirdre mouthed back, and Cleo nodded just as the portentous words: 'Pablo? To whom does this belong?' thundered round the studio.

A vision appeared in Cleo's mind's eye with perfect clarity, a vision of a resplendent Colleen reclining on the divan, holding aloft Cleo's pretty rosebud trimmed, pink polka-dotted bra. There was a profound silence, and then, for the second time within five minutes, Deirdre O'Dare sprang into action.

★   ★   ★

Deirdre thought fast. Registering Cleo's Bambi-caught-in-the-headlights expression, she took charge. She pulled her dress over her head, unhooked her bra, kicked off her sandals, then grabbed a sheet from the overflowing laundry basket on the floor and wound it round herself. She was going to have to draw upon her erstwhile acting skills bigtime, she thought as she sent a gobsmacked Cleo a brief nod of reassurance.

'Pablo? Have you, in my absence, been entertaining a woman?'

It was her cue. Deirdre took a deep breath, picked up her wineglass and strolled out through

324

the kitchen door into the studio.

'Oh, hi, Colleen!' she said, feigning surprise. 'Welcome home! Rory was singing your praises on the phone the other evening. When did you get back?'

Colleen had been reclining against cushions on the divan. When she saw Deirdre, she drew herself up like an empress. 'What,' she asked, 'are you doing here?'

'I'm sitting for Pablo,' said Deirdre, 'didn't Rory tell you? He's commissioned a portrait of me. In — um — the nude. I have to say I'm a little apprehensive. That's why I had to go get myself a glass of wine first. Dutch courage.' She raised her glass at Colleen, mustering all her confidence. '*Sláinte*,' she said.

Pablo rose to the occasion with panache. 'I didn't want to tell you about the commission, darling, because I know you're leery of me doing nudes of other women. But when Rory rang, he made me an offer I couldn't refuse.'

'When has money ever been a consideration for you?' hissed Colleen. She looked like a cat whose fur has been stroked the wrong way.

'Pretty much since I started earning some. But it's not the money so much as the kudos. You know it'll look good on my CV. Whaddayaknow! A shit-hot movie star to add to the list of luminaries who collect my paintings!'

Colleen narrowed cat's eyes at him. It was clear that she wasn't convinced.

Pablo returned her look with a cynical shrug, and raised an eyebrow. 'Hey, Colleen,' he said in a placatory tone. 'You know there's no way that

I'd make a move on Deirdre. It's widely known that Rory McDonagh and Deirdre O'Dare have one of the happiest marriages in Hollywood. They're famously faithful to each other.'

Deirdre saw Colleen's expression flicker, and she knew she was thinking back to the proposition she'd made to Rory on the flight to LA, the invitation to accompany her to her hotel room. The one that he had graciously — fortuitously — declined.

The ensuing silence was weighty with meaning as Colleen deliberated. Deirdre was casting around for something else to throw into the melting pot, when Colleen's phone went off again. 'Ay!' cried the diva, holding her hands to her ears. 'How I am persecuted!' She proceeded to throw cushions onto the floor in an effort to locate the offending object, finally grabbing it and pressing 'end call' with a peremptory thumb.

'Well,' she said, rising majestically to her feet and fixing Deirdre with a Medusa stare. 'In that case I'd better let you get on with your . . . sitting. But, Pablo, a grá. Hear this.' She made a gesture of warning. The little silver phone in her hand gleamed like a gun. 'We need to talk. I'll call you.' With a swirl of her cloak, she moved to the window, descended the deck and glided down Pablo's garden towards the sea, red sails in the sunset.

'Wow.' Deirdre managed a shaky smile. 'I deserve an Oscar for that,' she said. 'Or at the very least, a refill of wine. Yoo-hoo! You can come out now, Cleo.'

Cleo's face, when she peered round the

kitchen door, was putty-coloured.

'Thank you. Oh, thank you, Deirdre,' she said in the smallest voice in the world. 'You are, quite simply, the stuff of legend.'

'Bring on the wine, Cleo.'

Cleo's head disappeared back round the door, and when she emerged she was carrying the tray. The glasses on it were making a clinking noise. 'See how much I'm still shaking?' she said, setting the tray down on the table and handing round glasses.

Pablo took his and raised it to Deirdre. 'That was some class act,' he said, looking her up and down speculatively. 'And I must say, the prospect of painting you in the nude is a distinctly appealing one.'

'You're not painting me in the nude, Pablo MacBride. I'm not having my flabby bits immortalized on canvas.'

'What flabby bits? I think you're in great nick. And now you've gone and told Colleen that Rory's commissioned your portrait, don't you think it would be only wise to supply the evidence? She'll get even more deadly suspicious if no painting materializes.'

'I am *not* posing nude, Monsieur MacBride.'

Cleo had a sudden brainwave. 'I know! Do my body and stick on Deirdre's head!'

'Get real! That's a preposterous idea, sweetie-pie.'

'No, it's not. I think it's a great idea. It's actually in an erotic short story by Anaïs Nin called 'The Maja'.'

'Elaborate.'

'It's about an artist who paints his naked wife while she's asleep, then alters her face so's no-one can recognize her. Oh, go on Pablo! You promised me a portrait of myself, remember? This is a way of keeping that promise. I'd *love* to pose nude for you.'

' "The Maja"?' Pablo looked contemplative. 'Did you know that Goya painted two Majas — one naked and one clothed, to spare her modesty?'

Cleo gave him a mock-coy look. 'Will you paint clothes on me to spare my modesty?'

'What modesty?'

Deirdre smiled at them. The pair were clearly completely cracked about each other. She was reminded of herself and Rory, when they'd been in their first flush. Oh, what the hell — it wasn't every woman who had the opportunity of having her portrait painted by her lover. Cleo and Pablo deserved something special. 'I'll let you have a head and shoulders photograph to copy,' she said, 'but sitting for you will be Cleo's job.'

'Yay!' said Cleo. 'Where'll I sit for you? In number 4, the Blackthorns or in number 5?'

'Where do you think, you bimbo? You're not setting foot in my gaff again after what happened today.'

Deirdre moved to the table and sloshed more wine into her glass. 'It's a lovely thing, Cleo, to have your portrait painted — especially when you're still young and unselfconscious. I have a gorgeous nude portrait of myself hanging over our bed in LA.'

'Who painted it?' asked Pablo.

'Daniel Lennox.'

'Lennox? Wow. I'm impressed.'

'He did it years ago in France, when I was still young and beautiful.'

'You're still young and beautiful,' said Pablo gallantly, as he crossed the floor in the direction of the divan to pick up a cell phone that was ringing in 'polite' mode. 'Leonora, again,' he said, checking out the display. 'I'll let it ring out. I don't want her moaning on to me about Colleen and her non-bloody-appearance on *The David Letterman Show*.'

'Hang on, Pablo,' said Deirdre. 'That's Colleen's phone?'

'Yeah.'

'But she took her phone with her!'

'Shit,' said Pablo. 'That must have been yours, then. I dumped it under a cushion after you handed it to me.'

'What? Why?'

'How else could I get rid of it?' He spread his hands in a gesture of helplessness. 'No pockets.'

'Didn't you turn it off?'

'That phone is a triumph of design over function. What is it with those girly phones? You'd need fingers smaller than Barbie's to do anything on them.'

'But how could Colleen have made such a stupid mistake?' said Deirdre. 'They're different makes.'

'You think she'd notice a detail like that? She's a complete technophobe. All phones look the same to her.'

'Bummer!'

'Give her a ring now and ask her to bring it to yoga tonight,' suggested Cleo.

'Good idea.' Deirdre took the phone from Pablo and punched in her own number. 'It's engaged,' she said.

'Maybe you should try texting her,' said Pablo. 'I'd love to know how she'd handle 'Uv da rong fone'. She'd probably think some alien was trying to contact her.'

Deirdre laughed, then reached for her bag. 'I'd better make tracks. I'm getting withdrawal symptoms.'

'Withdrawal symptoms?'

'I need a baby boy fix. I'll see you later, Cleo.'

'Later?'

'Girls' night in the village hall. Followed by girls' night in my gaff.'

'Girls' night!' said Pablo. 'Hey! Maybe you should bring along that video of *Sex Tips for Girls*, Cleo.'

Cleo gave him an 'as if' look. 'Jesus! Men are so pathetic. Do you really think that us girls are so sad that we sit around talking about sex all the time, like SJP and her pals?'

'What do you talk about then?'

'Art and literature, of course.'

'All the more reason to watch *Sex Tips for Girls*, then. I'm sure they could give you a few intriguing ideas for a new short story.'

Deirdre didn't ask.

14

Dannie was really looking forward to the women's group tonight. She had asked Eva Lavery to give a talk after the yoga session on her career as a movie star, and she knew there'd be a big turnout. Eva had been a bit dubious about giving a talk; she hated public speaking, she'd told Dannie, because she had no character to hide behind. But Dannie had reassured her that all she needed to do was answer questions from the floor. 'What if there *are* no questions?' Eva had protested. 'There'll be loads,' had been Dannie's response. 'People will be falling over themselves with curiosity about you, Eva.' Eva had looked sceptical. 'I dunno about that,' she'd said. 'I bet they'd much rather have Colin Farrell.'

Going to the women's group was also a way for Dannie to get out of the stultifying confines of the Glebe House. The atmosphere there had become worse than ever since the evening she had found Alice in Paloma's bedroom. The idea that she'd been sitting there in the dark, listening to the sounds of Dannie and Oliver making love over the intercom, filled Dannie to overflowing with disgust. She actively avoided being in her sister-in-law's company now, taking herself off to bed early or disappearing down to the gate lodge to see how the refurbishment was coming along. She was counting down the weeks. She couldn't *wait* to move in there.

As anticipated, the village hall was packed. Deirdre O'Dare had turned up with Cleo Dowling, and Cleo's sister Margot had managed to insinuate herself into a seat beside Colleen. Dannie had heard from Breda Shanley earlier that Margot was thinking of taking up permanent residence in Kilrowan, and that she was planning on hosting a monthly salon for all the local artists. No wonder she was brown-nosing Colleen.

For once the diva hadn't made her usual ostentatious exit after the yoga session finished. Word was out that she was hoping that someone would acquire the movie rights to *The Faraway*, and that Eva Lavery was her casting choice of preference for the female lead. It would hardly be the most tactful move on Colleen's part if she swirled out of the village hall before Eva was due to speak.

The actress had arrived earlier in one of the film unit's transport Mercs. Dannie had spotted Jethro in the back before the car took off again, but he hadn't seen her. The stolen glimpse had made her heart turn over — which was a funny feeling, since she'd almost forgotten that she had a heart. The Sunday Paloma had spent with Jethro, Dannie's heart had been wrenched inside out when she'd rolled up to Ballynahinch Castle to take her daughter home. Father and daughter had had a fantastic day at the local stables, but all the activity had taken its toll on Paloma, and left her tired and fractious. She hadn't wanted to leave her dada, and had cried all the way back to the Glebe House. To make matters infinitely worse, she'd told Dannie that she thought her 'auntie' Alice was creepy.

Eva was winding up, now, signing autographs for fans. She'd spoken a blinder, filling her audience in on her days as a rock chick, on her subsequent stellar career as an actress, and on her perfect marriage to David Lawless. She'd been asked questions ranging from 'Do you feel, Eva, as if someone has stolen a portion of your soul when you finish filming?' (from Colleen); to 'What's it like to snog Colin Farrell?' (from a gaggle of teenage girls new to the group). The answer to the first question had been 'No', the answer to the second 'Orgasmic.'

'Hi.' Deirdre O'Dare was at Dannie's shoulder. 'Fancy joining us for a glass of wine? Cleo and Eva and I are going to hit my gaff. Or rather — your gaff.'

'It's officially yours while you're living there. And I'd murder a glass of wine,' said Dannie, glad for an excuse to delay going home. 'How's the child care been working out for you, by the way?'

'Great. That sitter you recommended is a total star. You don't use Emma any more, do you?'

'Haven't needed to since I moved into the Glebe House. Oliver and Alice are there to mind Paloma.'

'Who's Alice?'

'My future sister-in-law.'

'Lucky you to have an obliging sister-in-law!'

'Yeah,' said Dannie, without conviction.

Message alerts had started going off in the hall

as phones were switched back on.

Deirdre's ears pricked up. 'Oh, that reminds me — I'd better get my phone back,' she said. 'Colleen nicked it earlier today.'

'*Colleen* nicked your phone?'

'Inadvertently. See you shortly, Dannie.'

Dannie accessed her own phone to find a rather sweet text message from Oliver. She pressed 'home' — still finding it a strange thing to do — and heard the phone ringing in the apartment. She prayed that Alice wouldn't pick up.

'Hi, Dannie me darling!' Thank God it was Oliver.

'Hi, you!'

'How was the evening?'

'Gas. Very entertaining. Listen. I'm going off to sink some wine with the girls. Is that OK?'

'Go for it, Dannie. You haven't been sociable for a while. Hell, I could do with a drink myself, now you mention it. I badly need a stiff one after interviewing prospective staff all day.'

'Why don't you drive in?' As soon as the words were out of her mouth, she regretted them. She didn't like the thought of Paloma there on her own with Alice.

'Erm. I think not. You don't want your boyfriend ruining your girly evening, do you?'

She smiled. 'I suppose not.'

'But I want you to promise me one thing, Dannie. If you find yourself over the limit, give me a ring and I'll come in and collect you. I know you girls when you get the corkscrews out.'

'What about *you* being over the limit? You're

after saying you were going to have a stiff drink?'

'I'll limit myself to the one. You go ahead and enjoy your evening. If I haven't heard from you by midnight I'll know you've overdone it, and I'll be expecting your call.'

'Thanks, darling. But you mustn't wait up.'

'I'll go to bed if I feel like it. But I honestly won't mind if you decide to phone at two o'clock in the morning. I'd rather that than you fooling yourself into thinking you can handle the car after a feed of booze. Promise?'

'Promise. You're a dote. And talking of dotes, is Paloma asleep?'

'Ages ago. No worries. Enjoy yourself, sweetheart.'

Dannie blew a kiss down the receiver to her fiancé (her fiancé! It still felt weird to call him that), then put the phone back in her bag and moved across the room to where Deirdre and Cleo were talking to Colleen and Margot. Dannie didn't feel up to Colleen tonight — she hoped that Deirdre hadn't included her in the invitation. She needn't have worried. When Deirdre extended a polite invitation to the writer to join them, Colleen announced that it was her intention to go for a swim by moonlight. Dannie hadn't noticed any moon tonight, but she was sure that a minor consideration like that wouldn't put Colleen off.

'What about you, Margot? Would you like to join us?' asked Deirdre.

'No, thank you,' said Margot, 'I have a liaison with my — Novel.' Dannie couldn't help noticing the sideways look that Margot shot at her sister. Something furtive was going on here! Ah, but then, Dannie reminded herself, furtive things went on in all families. Hers included. She'd witnessed Margot flirting with Pablo MacBride through the window of O'Toole's earlier that evening. Maybe her dangerous liaison was really with him?

Colleen had swathed herself in her cloak, preparing to make her exit. 'Be sure to thank La Divina Lavery from me,' she told Dannie, 'for a most edifying evening. It was a pleasure to hear another artist talk so eloquently on the act of artistic creation. Incidentally, Deirdre,' she slung over her shoulder, 'Rory telephoned. I told him I'd be returning your phone to you later. He said it was nothing urgent.'

'Oh. He must have been surprised when you answered!' said Deirdre.

'Not when I explained that I had appropriated your phone erroneously.'

'Any message?'

'No message,' said Colleen, peremptorily. What was going on *here*? wondered Dannie. Another weird vibe! Thank God Colleen and Margot had both turned down Deirdre's invitation to socialize if they were going to behave in a way that was guaranteed to give people tense, nervous headaches. All Dannie was intent upon tonight was having a bit of fun and drinking a lot of wine. She'd take Oliver up on that offer of a lift home later, she decided, and leave her car in the village tonight.

★ ★ ★

336

'Sorry about the mess.' Deirdre's babysitter Emma was dumping a load of Bruno's toys into a chest and sweeping the coffee table clear of empty Diet Coke cans and takeaway cartons. 'He's only just gone to bed.'

Dannie hadn't been in the flat above the shop since Deirdre had moved in. She looked around curiously, noticing the idiosyncratic touches her tenant had added to make the place her own. A sweet pair of flowery slingbacks strutted their stuff on a shelf, a Lainey Keogh coat was displayed like an old master on a wall, a Japanese parasol hung from the ceiling, and a peacock feather fan took pride of place on the mantelpiece.

'Oh, God,' said Deirdre, handing a clutch of euros to her sitter. 'Sorry about that. Was he a handful?'

'Divil a bit. We were having so much fun, we just lost sight of the time.'

'That's good to hear. Thanks, Emma.'

Emma let herself out with a jocular 'Don't drink too much!' and Deirdre turned to her guests. 'Make yourselves comfortable,' she said. 'And phooey to red or white. We're having champagne.'

'Are we celebrating something?' asked Eva.

'Yeah. Life.' Deirdre ducked into the kitchen and emerged with champagne and wineglasses. 'Sorry I can't run to flutes,' she said.

'That's my fault, as the landlord,' said Dannie. 'How was I to know when I was kitting this place out as a holiday let that champagne flutes might be considered a basic household item?'

Pop! went the champagne, and Deirdre started pouring.

'Deirdre?' asked Cleo. 'Why do you have shoes on your shelf and a coat hanging on your wall?'

'Because they're works of art, really, and I love looking at them. It's a trick I learned from you, Eva. Remember that time a film company put you up in a dancer's flat while he was off on tour? And it was so hideous you sat down on the hall floor and cried?'

'I'll *never* forget that kip,' said Eva with a shudder. 'The *pièce de résistance* was a cut-glass punchbowl on the dining table that had matching cups all hooked around the edge. The prospect of spending four months there was so appalling that I flung my only ever diva strop and told them to find me somewhere else within a week. Which they did.'

'But you know what she did to keep herself sane for that week?' Deirdre told Dannie and Cleo. 'She unpacked all her shoes and placed them strategically all over the flat, in places where she'd come across them and think, 'Oh — maybe life's not so bad after all, if there are shoes like these to be had!' I remember there were shoes on the cistern in the loo, and on all the windowsills, and on the Welcome mat in the hall. And there was nothing in your fridge except champagne, M&Ms and your favourite Manolos.'

'So, Deirdre!' Dannie invested her voice with mock indignation. 'If you're into displaying shoes to cheer yourself up, does that mean that *this* flat is as kippish as the dancer's was?'

338

'No, no — not at all!' protested Deirdre. 'I love it here. It's just that any time I spend time away from home now, I always bring some of my favourite things with me, as a kind of comfort.'

'It's not a bad idea,' said Dannie, thinking of the horrible apartment she was currently incarcerated in. 'But I'm not sure about the parasol, or the fan.'

'Why?'

'Didn't you know? An open umbrella indoors is inviting bad luck. And peacock feathers are the eye of the devil.' Dannie laughed at herself. 'Amn't I the dab hand at country lore?'

'Oh, well,' said Deirdre, unconcernedly handing round champagne. 'Here's bad cess to bad luck, and here's to the good life — and to getting arseholed.'

★ ★ ★

It was some time later. Bruno had woken from his slumber and was now being passed round the circle of adoring females. He was clearly — as was his due as a baby boy — enjoying the attention being lavished on him. Each time he ended up in Deirdre's lap he put his hand over her mouth if she tried to speak to anyone who wasn't him.

'I'd better call my driver,' said Eva, yawning and accepting more champagne. 'Put him on stand-by for — say — one o'clock?'

'I take it you haven't an early call in the morning?' asked Deirdre.

'No early call. Not even a wake-up from my

rise-and-shiny daughter. David's taken her off to Alton Towers for frolics.' Eva upended her bag to access her phone, and a mass of junk spilled out.

'Wow, Eva. You could fill a landfill site with that,' observed Dannie.

'I know. It's shameful, isn't it? D'you know, I can't think why someone hasn't set up a roaring business in bag-clearing for people like me. After all, they do it for people's wardrobes and houses.'

'I wish they'd do it for computers,' said Deirdre. 'I never bother deleting e-mail. I've got stuff that goes back to practically before Bruno was born.'

Eva started absently going through the detritus that had come out of her bag. 'What's this? A receipt from Saks for a handbag. That's funny. I have no recollection of ever having bought a handbag in Saks. Oh! A poem written by Dorcas. Sweet! Listen: 'I love my mummy. I came out of her tummy. She is yummy and she's plummy.' And this is . . . what? The breakfast menu from the Four Seasons Hotel in Beverly Hills.' She ran her eyes over it. 'It's *insane*, you know. Who dreams these things up? 'Smoked Salmon Eggs Benedict on Toasted Brioche with Spinach and Caviare'. 'Blueberry and Orange Scented Buttermilk Pancakes, Pure Vermont Amber Maple Syrup'. 'Huevos Rancheros with Sunnyside Up Eggs, Quesadilla of Chorizo, Black Beans and Jack Cheese'.'

'Oh, yuck. Think I'm going to be sick,' said Cleo. 'What are the prices like?'

'A mere thirty-something dollars for bacon

and eggs,' said Eva. 'I remember that was Jethro's favourite. I'd feel so jealous sitting in the dining room with him while he breakfasted like a king and I had to make do with non-fat yoghurt and carrot juice just so's I could squeeze into my Oscar outfit. David used to have steel-cut Irish oatmeal.'

'What's that?'

'We hadn't a clue. He only ordered it because it seemed a patriotic thing to do.'

Eva carried on examining items from the little mound of souvenirs on the floor, exclaiming over long-lost postcards and puzzling over the provenance of the more exotic of the banknotes and stamps that she found ('Was I *ever* in Cancún?'). Deirdre and Cleo continued to coo over Bruno and laugh at Eva's more outrageous discoveries, but Dannie wasn't listening any more. Their voices were coming as if from a long distance away, and Dannie knew that it wasn't just the champagne that was producing this vaguely out-of-body effect on her. It had been the mention of Jethro tucking into breakfast in the Four Seasons Hotel.

They'd done that once too, except it hadn't been the Four Seasons Hotel in Beverly Hills — it had been the one in Dublin, and it hadn't been in the dining room, it had been in bed. And of course, of *course* they'd made love afterwards, and the love-making had been so mind-blowing that Jethro had cancelled all his business meetings and spent the rest of the day in bed with her. Dannie felt tired now. Drained of fizz, like flat champagne. The evening had lost its lustre, and it was time to go . . . home.

'Look at the time!' she said, checking out her watch. It actually wasn't that late — barely midnight, but she would have to be on the ball tomorrow to get down to the gate lodge before the builders arrived. 'I'm off!'

'How are you getting home?' asked Deirdre. 'You can't drive after all that champagne.'

'I'll get my driver to take you, if you like,' offered Eva.

'No worries,' said Dannie. 'Oliver said he'd come and collect me. I'll give him a bell. If I start walking he can meet me halfway.'

She got up, kissed Deirdre, and said 'thanks for a lovely evening'. Then, while Cleo and Eva were engrossed in some photograph that Eva had found amongst all her rubbish, she let herself quietly out of the flat and onto the main street of the village.

It was deserted — apart from Fluffy, who immediately came skedaddling over to greet her. 'Howrya, Fluff,' said Dannie. 'I've a feeling your mistress won't be home for a while yet. She's having a girly night with some friends. But you can keep me company, if you like.' Together they set out along the main street. It was a mild evening. There were stars out but, as Dannie had observed earlier, no moon for Colleen to swim by. 'Have you a man in your life, Fluffy?' Dannie asked the dog, looking at her speculatively. 'Or maybe it's more than one man you have, like me? That's when life starts to get complicated, don't you agree, Fluff? You try and do what's best, but sometimes you mess up.' As they passed by her cottage, Dannie sent a yearning look at its benighted windows and overgrown hedge. 'I lived there once upon a time,' she told Fluffy, 'in that fairytale cottage with a handsome prince. But now I live in a mansion with a wicked witch. Well, maybe not a wicked witch. A kind of troll, I suppose . . .'

And the further Dannie walked with the dog, the more she warmed to her subject. Fluffy was better than a shrink, she decided. In fact, spilling the beans to her small friend was so therapeutic that after a mile or so she decided she wouldn't bother phoning Oliver and that she'd walk the rest of the way instead. Finally she stopped at the main gates of the Glebe House and ordered Fluffy to go home, feeling a bit guilty that she'd dragged the poor creature all this way. The fact that a fat cloud had now obscured the stars and was starting to drop rain made her feel guiltier still. Poor Fluff's hairdo would be ruined.

Dannie made her way up the drive and let herself in through the front door. There was still a strong smell of paint in the lobby, and all the furniture was shrouded in dust sheets. Most of the furnishings that Alice had chosen for the hotel were genuine Victorian — unlike the repro stuff in the apartment. Dannie passionately hated the Victorian look; something about it always spoke to her of prudishness and suppressed sexuality. But Alice loved it. She had bid a lot of money at auction for a grandfather clock to put in the lobby, claiming that guests would find its tick comforting. It was standing sentinel at the foot of the stairs ticking away now, its white-draped frame giving it the appearance of a ghoul. Dannie didn't find the sound comforting at all — to her the tick always sounded like a rebuke — and tonight the bastard clock was ticking her off for staying out after midnight. Tch, tch, tch — you bold girl, bold girl, bold, bold, bold girl!

Upstairs in the apartment the sitting room was empty. Oliver must have gone to bed. He'd more than likely have fallen asleep waiting for her to phone. She hoped so. She didn't feel like talking to him, didn't feel like being falsely genial about her girly night — and she most certainly did not feel like having sex.

Dannie went to the kitchen to get a glass of iced water, then checked on Paloma, who was sleeping soundly, still wearing her Mickey Mouse ears. Dannie set down her glass, slipped the ears off and laid them on the bedside table. She was just about to leave the room when she realized that there was no light displayed on the intercom. Quashing the sense of irritation she felt — reminding herself that Oliver wasn't used to the minutiae of fatherhood and couldn't be expected to remember stuff like switching on intercoms — she flicked the 'on' switch and left the room.

Halfway down the corridor she remembered she'd left her glass on the bedside table. She turned back — and was glad she had, because a second glance at the display on the intercom told her it was on two-way mode. As she stooped to pick up the glass she became aware that a

344

murmured conversation was coming over the speaker.

'Why don't you try phoning her to see if the coast's clear?' It was Alice's voice. 'She's obviously there for the duration, Oliver, or she'd have rung by now.'

There was a pause, then Oliver said: 'OK, I'll phone her, but if she wants me to pick her up, Alice, I'm going. No two ways about it.'

Dannie's phone was in her pocket. She didn't want it going off and waking Paloma. Her thumb moved to the 'off' button.

'It's gone straight to voice mail,' said Oliver, after several moments. Then: 'Hi, darling,' she heard him say. 'It's after midnight, so I suppose you girls are largeing it. I'm going to get some shut-eye, but don't hesitate to phone when you want to come home. I won't be grumpy, I promise. Love you!'

There was another pause, then: 'Is that true?' Alice said.

'Is what true?'

'That last bit, about loving her?'

'You know it is. I've loved her since we were kids.'

'You've loved me since we were kids.'

'I know. But that's a different kind of love. And you can't give me babies, Alice.'

'Oh, Oliver!' there was a susurration coming from the room now, a strange kind of rustling sound. 'Make love to me now? Please? Just one last time?'

Dannie went stiff with a horror that threatened to floor her, but seeing Paloma stir in her sleep

345

made her lunge for the intercom to turn it off. She stood frozen in the centre of the room for several moments. Incest? Could it be possible? Were Oliver and his sister making out in her room? No. She'd misheard. It was too grotesque for words, too grotesque to be true, too grotesque for her to even contemplate . . . But — oh! — the image of Alice sitting in the dark listening to her brother making love to her, Dannie, flashed across her mind's eye with such clarity that some cautionary little voice in her head told her she *had* to check this out for herself.

She moved through the door of Paloma's room and down the corridor to the apartment. Once inside, she slipped off her shoes and crossed the landing to the bedroom on silent feet. The door was ajar, but not enough to allow her to see what was going on in there. She could hear, though. There was movement from somewhere deep inside the room, and then she heard Oliver give a groan low in his throat. It was the kind of groan he gave when making love. Oh God! Another groan came, and another. 'We'll have to be quick, Alice.' He was breathing fast and hard now. 'It's far too dangerous. This *has* to be the last time.'

Alice was panting too, a bitch on heat. 'I love it when it's dangerous. It's always been dangerous. Oh, God, you're so beautiful,' she cried out. 'Oh, God, look at us — how beautiful we are together, Oliver! Oh God, oh *God*!'

More groans from him, a protracted sigh from her, then: 'Oh, God, yes! Jesus! *Alice*!'

346

Dannie's hands went to her face, and as they did, the front of her T-shirt was drenched with icy water from the glass she'd forgotten she was still holding. She barely registered the cold shock. Real life was unravelling — she was a leading player in the worst nightmare she'd ever had. She stood there frozen, immobilized, until Alice's low post-coital laugh spurred her into action. Then she took a single step forward and pushed open the door.

They were sprawled, clothing awry, limbs obscenely entwined on the king-size bed, gazing at each other with glazed eyes.

As Dannie raised her hand, they turned to her. She was only half aware of their appalled expressions because her focus was on the reverse image reflected in the wardrobe doors on the far side of the room. Feeling strangely, preternaturally calm she took aim — then pitched her water glass with surprising force at the mirror image of her affianced and his sister. And as shards of glass fragmented onto the floor Dannie turned and walked from the apartment, knowing that she would never go back.

★ ★ ★

Paloma was fretful at being woken. 'Mammy, no!' she whimpered. 'Paloma's sleepy.'

'Come on, come, come, good babba.' Dannie wrapped her daughter tightly in her duvet and hefted her in her arms.

'No!' said Paloma, as Dannie started towards the door, 'No Polar!'

'Look — Polar's coming too.' She moved back to the child's bed, grabbed Polar by the paw, then made for the corridor and ran its length.

Her bare feet made no sound on the great staircase that led to the gloomy lobby of the Glebe House — all she could hear was the ticking of the grandfather clock and then, like an ominous punctuation mark, a single *dong* as one o'clock rang out. Dannie yanked at the iron handle on the massive oak door, and then she was on the step, leaning against the jamb and gulping for air. But she couldn't stop; she had to go on. Leaving the front door lying wide open behind her, she fled down the drive, clutching her precious bundle.

'Rain, Mammy!' protested Paloma. 'Polar'll get all wet.'

'Here!' Dannie thrust the bear into her daughter's needy hands. 'Cosy him under the duvet.'

The garden was illuminated sporadically by solar-powered lamps that came on automatically in the evenings. Dannie ran down the driveway like a character in a computer game, hearing the rhythmic pounding of her bare feet on the tarmac. Occasionally she was aware that she had trodden on some object — a pebble, a piece of metal — but she didn't falter, didn't flinch, didn't even register the pain she knew she should be feeling. The thud, thud, thud of her feet just went on and on, until something made her stumble.

'Dannie! Dannie!' she heard.

Oliver was calling from the steps. She threw a

look over her shoulder. The lobby of the house was lit up now, and his shape was silhouetted against the rectangle of light that was the open front door. Adrenalin flared, and she increased her pace. It was raining harder now, and Paloma was whimpering in her arms, straining to look around. 'Where are we going, Mammy?' came her plaintive voice. 'Where are you taking me?'

'I'll tell you when we get there, sweetheart. Hush, now.'

Where *was* she going? Dannie wondered. She paused momentarily when she hit the road, unsure which direction to take. She was breathing hard, and her eyes were wet with rain. Not tears. She had never shed a tear for Oliver Dunne in her life, and she knew she never would. Tears were precious commodities, and Oliver was not worth wasting them on, any more than she — no-brain Dannie Moore — was. She had been monumentally stupid. She had ruined her own life and possibly Paloma's, and she did not deserve a crumb of self-pity; not even one single tear. She wrapped Paloma tighter in the duvet, wiped the rain from her little face, then turned left, towards the village.

She couldn't go to her cottage. If Oliver came looking for her that's the first place he'd go. Could she go to Breda, seek refuge there? Breda had been her surrogate mother, after all, and tonight Dannie needed mothering like never before. But tempting as it was, she knew that confiding in Breda was out of the question. Kilrowan was a small community, news travelled fast. And she didn't think she could handle the speculation that would be rife following the breakup of an engagement that had lasted less than a month.

But the village beckoned still because her car was there. She didn't care that she was over the limit — she'd drive to some remote place where she and Paloma could spend the rest of the night in the car.

There came the sound of a motor somewhere on the road. Dannie hadn't thought the adrenalin that was driving her could have risen any higher, but now she felt it soar inside her, like rocket fuel. Oliver? Could Oliver be in pursuit of her?

The only thing she could do was hide. There was a ditch on the other side of the road. Dannie veered towards it so sharply that the weight of the child in her arms shifted, and she stumbled and pitched forward. In an effort to protect Paloma, she twisted to her right and landed heavily on her hip, with her left leg bent under her. Paloma was crying now, struggling to escape from the straitjacket of her duvet. Dannie could hear the engine of the car rounding a bend in the road. She managed to get to her knees to face the oncoming headlights and then lifted a hand in warning, hearing her own voice scream 'No!'

Her senses were assaulted by blinding white light, the sound of screaming brakes and the fierce smell of rubber burning against asphalt as the car swerved and skidded past them, coming to rest some thirty feet further down the road.

A silence seemed to go on for ever before the car doors opened and two figures emerged, one of them carrying a torch. They moved towards Dannie, seeming to drift like ghosts, and Dannie wondered if indeed she herself was dead. She looked down at Paloma, who was clearly in shock — face ashen, lips white, eyes wide. When she put out a hand to touch the child's face, a thin mewling sound came from her.

Dannie started to mutter the mantra chanted by all mothers when awful stuff happens. 'It's all right, sweetheart. We're all right. Everything's going to be all right.' She stroked her daughter's hair rhythmically, automatically — 'It's all *right*, it's *OK*, it's all *right*' — then looked up as she heard the footsteps approaching. A man dropped to his knees beside her, followed by a woman.

'Sweet Jesus, Dannie!' said the woman, sucking in her breath with shock. 'Whatever's happened to you?'

It was Eva Lavery.

★   ★   ★

It felt surreal in the extreme to be sitting in the back of an S-class Merc, *en route* to a posh hotel, soaking wet and with bare feet. The smooth motion of the car combined with the subdued rhythm of the windscreen wipers had had a soporific effect on Paloma: the child was slumped across the back seat with her head on Dannie's lap, eyes closed, lips slightly apart. Her face was still pale with shock.

'You'll be needing a doctor,' the driver was saying. 'The hotel can organize one for you.'

'I don't want to be disturbing a doctor at this

hour of the night,' said Dannie. 'I'm sure an ice pack'll do for my ankle till the morning.' Her left ankle had taken a knock and was badly swollen.

'It's not your ankle you need to be worried about,' came the reply. 'Post-traumatic stress will kick in before too long, mark my words. Jaysus. I could be doing with some tranks meself. You're lucky 'twas a professional driver you met on the road. Had it been anyone else — maybe someone with a few jars on them — I hate to think what state yis'd be in now.'

'*James*.' Dannie saw Eva turn to the driver and furrow her brow. The single word was enough to stop his dissertation on worst-case scenarios.

The car was turning through the gates of Ballynahinch Castle. 'Eva, are you *sure* about this?' asked Dannie. It was the third time since getting into the car that she had asked the question. The actress had offered to put Dannie and Paloma up in her suite in the hotel. Her spare room was free for the next few days while David and Dorcas dallied in Alton Towers.

'Absolutely.' Eva had asked Dannie no further questions since the one she'd asked her on the road: *Whatever's happened to you?* Dannie had been in too much shock to answer, but she knew she would have to volunteer some class of an explanation as to why she'd been running barefoot along the road at one o'clock in the morning, carrying her small daughter through pelting rain.

The car glided up to the front door of the hotel, and James applied the handbrake. Paloma woke. She sat up, looking around her with a

352

dazed expression. 'It's Daddy's castle,' she said, and at last the expected tears came. 'I want my daddy!' she yowled, with surprising energy.

'Baba, it's very late at night,' said Dannie. 'Your daddy'll be asleep.'

'*I want my daddy!*'

For once Dannie was at a loss as to what to do. She got out of the car and helped the child out of the back passenger seat, sh-ing and there-thereing ineffectually. Paloma was bawling her lungs out, verging on the hysterical now.

'I know what to do,' said Eva, with decision. James was holding the heavy front door of the hotel open for her. She passed through and went straight up to reception, where the night porter was filling in a crossword. 'Could you put me through to Mr Palmer's room, please, Martin?' she asked.

'Certainly,' said Martin, picking up the phone.

'No!' Dannie hissed in a whisper to Eva. 'I don't want to see him!'

'You don't have to,' said Eva, evenly. 'But Paloma does. It's only fair, Dannie. Now.' She hunkered down to Paloma's level and took the child gently by the shoulders. 'Shh, shh, sweetheart. Your daddy'll be here in a minute.'

Feeling more surreal than ever, Dannie watched as Eva took the receiver from Martin and spoke into it. 'Jethro. Sorry to disturb you at this late hour, but can you come down to the lobby? It's urgent. I'll explain when you get here. Thanks.' She put the phone down, then said: 'Martin, show Ms Moore to my suite, please, and run her a bath. And then could you organize sandwiches and — ' she turned to Dannie and raised a eyebrow in enquiry ' — brandy?' Dannie nodded gratefully ' — brandy to be brought up. And an ice pack. And I'd like a doctor to call in the morning. I think tomorrow's time enough, Dannie, don't you? Or would you rather see him now?'

'The morning's fine,' said Dannie, automatically. Her voice sounded very strange to her own ears. 'I may not even need — '

'A precaution, if nothing else,' said Eva, standing firm. 'Now, let Martin show you up and run you a bath. I'll be up presently. And take it easy on that foot.'

Dannie gave Paloma a big hug and a kiss, and left her sitting in the lobby on Eva's lap. She felt guilty abandoning her beloved daughter, but there was no way she could allow Jethro to see her like this, no way she could stand up to his interrogation. She followed the night porter upstairs and along corridors until they came to Eva's suite. It was beautifully appointed, but the surroundings barely impinged on Dannie's consciousness. She sat down stiffly on a couch. From the bathroom came the sound of flowing taps. She didn't even have money to tip the night porter! Her bag was in the sitting room in that grim apartment in the Glebe House.

It didn't matter. She wouldn't think just yet about how she'd get it — or any of her other possessions — back. As far as she was concerned she had snatched her two most valuable possessions from the maw of hell tonight: her daughter and her daughter's beloved teddy bear.

She returned the night porter's 'Good night,' then moved into the bathroom and stripped off her clothes. T-shirt, jeans, bra, knicks. All the clothes she had, all soaking wet — and her jeans were covered in mud. She'd have to ask Eva if she could borrow something to wear tomorrow. Tomorrow! Oh God, oh God! She didn't want to think about tomorrow. She stepped into the bath, lay back, then slid under the water.

It helped a bit. By the time Dannie had had a perfunctory bath, wrapped herself in a towelling robe and unsnarled her hair with one of the complimentary combs, the suite's rightful tenant had arrived along with room service. The night porter laid out plates, cutlery and glasses, then withdrew, murmuring thanks for all the euros Eva bestowed upon him.

'So,' said the actress, pouring brandies, 'you'll be glad to know that Paloma's a lot happier now. She stopped crying the minute Jethro lifted her up and gave her a daddy-bear hug.'

'I am glad,' said Dannie. She sat down on the couch, rested her ice-packed foot on the coffee table in front of her, and took a sip of brandy. And for the first time since she'd heard the opening words of the nightmare that had unravelled her entire life — *Why don't you try phoning her to see if the coast's clear?* — she felt safe. Oliver would not find her here. 'What did you tell Jethro, Eva?'

Eva curled herself into the armchair opposite and regarded Dannie with her candid blue eyes. 'I told him a great fat fib,' she said. 'I told him that Paloma had been staying overnight at

Deirdre's because you hadn't been able to get a sitter, and that she'd had an awful nightmare and woken up from it needing her daddy. And that I had volunteered to bring her to him here.'

'Does he know *I'm* here?'

'I didn't mention it. Paloma may, but because she's very confused he'll attribute anything she tells him to her nightmare — and hopefully just humour her.'

'Thank you, Eva. I'd really rather he doesn't know.'

'Fair enough.' There was a silence, and then Eva said: 'Do you want to tell me what happened?'

No. No-one could ever know. Dannie was just about to form the words 'No. I don't, thanks all the same,' when she found herself saying exactly the opposite: 'Yes, thank you. I would like to tell you.' And before she could stop herself, she was confiding in Eva the whole story.

Then tears were streaming down her face, and Eva's arms were around her. Dannie sobbed for some minutes, and then she was being guided into the adjoining room and her legs were being levered up onto the bed between cool linen sheets. After she'd been persuaded back against soft, soft goosedown pillows, Eva dried her tears with a tissue and turned off the bedside light. And then a kiss was being dropped on her forehead and Eva was whispering 'Sleep tight' from the doorway, and for some reason Dannie felt that she had a mother at last — that somehow her mother was visiting her in the shape of Eva Lavery — and the next thing she knew . . .

Light was filtering through the curtains, and she was waking up in a four-poster bed to the smell of freshly brewed coffee.

15

It was Grace's birthday. As soon as it was feasible time-wise, Deirdre picked up the phone to LA. The nanny, Melissa, answered.

'Hi, Deirdre! The birthday girl's not here, I'm afraid.'

'Oh. Bummer. Where is she?'

'She was at a slumber party last night. Aoife, too.'

'Well, in that case I'll talk to Rory.'

'Rory? Rory's not here. Didn't he phone you?'

'No.'

'He's taken off to the desert.'

'What? When?'

'Yesterday.'

'*Yesterday?* The day before Grace's *birthday?*'

'Yeah. I must say I thought the timing was a bit dodgy, too.'

'Well, *fuck* him!' Deirdre was fuming. Rory occasionally took off to the Mojave Desert on his motorbike to commune with nature. Normally she didn't resent this time spent apart from the family — he came home from the expeditions feeling so regenerated that the benefits had a knock-on effect on their domestic life — but to choose to disappear just before Grace's birthday was downright selfish. 'Has anything been organized? A party or anything?'

'Yeah — there's a gang of kids coming here. I've entertainers lined up, and caterers, and they're going to have a ball.'

'I hope so. God, I feel like shit. Poor sweet Grace, not having either of her parents at her birthday party.'

'I'm not sure you'd want to be here, actually.'

'What makes you say that?'

'There's a clown coming.'

'Ew!' Deirdre had an aversion to clowns that bordered on the pathological. 'Look, Melissa, tell Grace to phone as soon as she can. I trust Rory got her something gorgeous?'

'Sure. Loads of fairy princess stuff.'

'At least he got that right. Well, bye, honeybun. Have a great day.'

'I will. That clown is pretty damn fit.'

'Oh, stop, Melissa. Too much information!'

Deirdre put down the phone yearning to be able to pick it straight up again and read Rory the riot act, but since Rory didn't carry a phone when he went to the desert there was no point in yearning. The desert thing was something he did when a new movie was imminent, maintaining that taking time out from Tinseltown helped him get his head together before shooting started. His agent *hated* it when he disappeared on these safaris, and Deirdre was frequently on the receiving end of frantic phone calls demanding *when* exactly he was coming back, and bemoaning the fact that he'd show up looking woefully unkempt and with a most un-Hollywood attitude. She adored these reunions. Rory would turn up boasting golden stubble and sun-bleached hair, tanned from head to foot (with *no* white bits!), and after five or six days on his own in the desert he'd be raring to go.

But to go AWOL on Grace's birthday was unforgivable! Unable to pick up the phone to him, she rang Eva instead.

'That bastard's gone and fucked off into the desert on Grace's birthday!' she ranted. 'My daughter's celebrating her birthday without either of her parents there to help her blow out her birthday candles.'

'You need a shoulder to cry on,' said Eva. 'Leave Bruno at the minder's and I'll send my driver for you.'

When she put the phone down, Deirdre felt guilty. What had she to complain about, really? She was a privileged person. She was married to a man who so seldom gave her cause for grief that she erupted like Mount Etna on the rare occasion he transgressed. She was being offered tea and sympathy by one of the most generous women in the world. She could offload her son onto a minder, and be transported a couple of miles up the road in an S-class Merc. How many women in the world needed a shoulder to cry on more than she did? Millions. *Millions.*

Sometimes this realization filled her with self-loathing. Sometimes it made her thank her lucky stars, or whoever was up there keeping an eye out for her. And sometimes she wondered if whoever was up there was laughing his or her ass off at the idea of Deirdre O'Dare sailing merrily along on the river of her life, unaware of the fact that Niagara Falls might be just around the next bend. This was the thought that shook her most.

360

When she arrived at Ballynahinch, Eva was sitting in the conservatory reading a Moomintroll book. She got to her feet when she saw Deirdre, and came out to join her in the garden. 'Let's take a walk,' she said. 'It's a beautiful day.'

It *was* a beautiful day. Funny — Deirdre hadn't even noticed that until now. 'Yes. Let's,' she said.

They headed down the driveway and took a left along a track that bordered the river. Their feet on the packed earth made a satisfying thudding sound. Birdsong was rampant, the river was in spate. Eva threw her head back and looked up at the big, big, blue, blue sky, and then she turned to Deirdre and smiled. 'I know it's a terrible cliché, but this really is one of those days that makes you feel glad to be alive, isn't it?'

'Mm.' Now Deirdre felt even worse. How dare she gripe about anything on a day like this? 'What time have you to be on set?' she asked.

'I don't. The grips or gaffers or some such have gone on strike. I'm twiddling my thumbs until things have been sorted.' She slid a pair of sunglasses on. 'So,' she said. 'Tell me all your worries.'

Deirdre filled Eva in on Rory's desert débâcle.

'There, there,' said Eva mildly, when she'd finished. 'No worries. Grace won't even notice the absence of parents, what with all the excitement. Kids that age are incredibly resilient, you know.'

Deirdre wasn't convinced. 'Maybe. But honestly, Eva, if I'd known he was going to play Runaway Dad I'd never have left LA. I'm sick with myself that I did.'

'Be reasonable. He didn't know this film was going to happen before you decided to come to Ireland.' Eva plucked a stem of wild garlic and rolled it between her fingers.

'He could have turned it down.'

'What? Just because his domestic arrangements changed? Don't be daft, darling. It's not in an actor's nature to turn down work. Mmm.' She passed Deirdre the garlic flower. 'Smell that.'

Deirdre sniffed and gave a perfunctory 'Mm' before continuing. 'Don't you think he might have relaxed the rules and dispensed with his bloody desert palaver for once?'

Eva stopped and regarded Deirdre with an unusually serious expression. 'Listen,' she said. 'One of the reasons you came to Ireland was because you needed head space. Just as Rory needs his. Doesn't he always go into nomad mode before the start of a shoot? It's his ritual. Why should he change his *modus operandi* just because you're not around? I think you're over-reacting a little.'

Oh! Deirdre hated being told she was over-reacting, especially by someone as worldly wise as Eva Lavery. She decided to make an effort to be sanguine. 'OK. I'll merely be in a huff with him when he finally deigns to get in touch, rather than in a stonking fury. But he might have had the cop-on to phone me himself and tell me about it rather than assigning poor Melissa the messenger role. I used the 'f' word to her, and she's surprisingly easily shocked, for a Californian.' They walked a while in silence, then: 'Any news?' asked Deirdre.

There was a fractional pause before Eva answered. 'No news.'

'Last night was fun, wasn't it? Isn't my landlady a honeybun?'

'Dannie? Yes, she is. And so's Cleo. She's got a cracking sense of humour.'

'Can I let you in on a secret?' Deirdre was usually quite good at keeping secrets and rarely divulged them to anyone, but she knew that Eva was a safe bet. The actress never, ever broke faith with anyone. 'She's having a scene with that painter, Pablo. D'you remember — the one we met in the pub that day?'

'Colleen's squeeze?' Eva looked a little taken aback.

'The very one.'

'Uh-oh. She'd want to watch out. I know Colleen fancies herself as a liberal-minded boho type, but I can't see her being so liberal-minded that she'd smile on any attempt to annex her lov*air*.' Here Eva mimicked Colleen's rolling brogue.

'You'd be right. But *she's* no saint, either. She propositioned Rory on the plane to LA.'

'Really?'

'Mm. Quite blatantly, too.'

'What did Rory do?'

'Oh, you know Rory and his 'roguish charm'. He thanked her for the generous offer, but talked his way out of it.'

'She probably fancies him more than ever now. Talking about roguish charm, that Pablo of hers has got it in spades.'

'They're very sweet together.'

'Pablo and Colleen?' Eva sounded surprised.

'No. Pablo and Cleo. The *really* sweet thing is that he's secretly painting a portrait of her.'

'What do you mean, 'secretly'?'

'Well. I happened to drop by one day and . . . '

Deirdre outlined the ruse she and Cleo had dreamed up to wangle a portrait out of Pablo.

'Ingenious!' said Eva, when she'd finished. 'How very romantic! And how very, very dangerous.'

'I think Cleo kinda likes the danger. An element of danger in a relationship can be exciting sometimes.'

'I am *so* over that,' said Eva, with feeling. 'Being happily married is as good as it gets.'

'Damn right,' said Deirdre. 'We're very lucky, Eva, aren't we?'

'You've said that before,' said Eva. 'But it's a sentiment that bears repetition, and one well worth drinking to.' She gave Deirdre a kiss on the cheek. 'Let's stroll back to the hotel and have a jar, sweetie-pie.'

★ ★ ★

Eva's 'jar' was, unsurprisingly, a glass of champagne. Deirdre opted to sink a pint of Guinness.

'How's the biography coming along?' asked Eva. They were sitting by the big fireplace in the lobby of the hotel with a plate of sandwiches in front of them.

'Fine. I've finished the first draft.'

'Can I read it?'

'No, you cannot. It's not in good enough nick yet. I had an idea for the jacket, by the way.'

'Oh? A photograph of me looking wildly glam?'

'No. The one I took of you on the bridge here. Remember? When I caught you looking like Garbo in *Queen Christina*.'

'Oh, yeah. Garbo *is* a good look.' Eva took a thoughtful sip of champagne. 'So. When do you think it'll be on the shelves, this *magnum opus*?'

'Depends on who's publishing. I suppose it could be ready by this time next year. I'll ask my agent to run it by some of the bigger publishing houses soon, once I've polished up the first three chapters. She might even get us an auction. That'd be great for publicity.'

Eva looked dubious. 'People won't be *that* interested, surely?'

'Don't underestimate yourself, Eva,' Deirdre scolded her. 'You're a big star. And remember *Mimi's Remedies* will be out this time next year. There could be massive interest.'

'This time next year?' said Eva. 'You're absolutely right. There *will* be massive interest. Sales will go through the roof. Good.'

'You'll be able to pay off all your debts. Maybe even manage to exchange the cardboard box for a second-hand caravan!'

Eva gave an abstracted smile at Deirdre's little joke. Money, after all, was hardly a consideration for the actress. This book was being written to set the record straight before someone else could warp it, not as a cynical exercise in coining it.

365

A car pulled up outside the window, and Deirdre saw Dorcas's nanny get out with Dannie Moore's little girl. 'Hey, there's Astrid. Didn't she go to Alton Towers with David and Dorcas?'

'No. David told her it was time she took a break.'

'So what's she doing minding Paloma?'

'I asked her to do it while Jethro's at work. Paloma's staying here in the hotel for a few days, with her daddy. She's been pining for him, apparently.'

Paloma came dashing through the door of the hotel, waving a teddy bear dressed in a pair of red dungarees with 'Happy Days' emblazoned in yellow on the bib. 'Look what Astrid bought for Polar! And she got me new stuff too because I had only pyjamas. I went into the shop in Galway in my pyjamas and welly boots that the hotel lent me. It was *so* cool! And Polar and me are sleeping in a big four-post again tonight!'

'Cool!' said Eva and Deirdre together, and the child danced away towards the stairs, pursued by a carrier-bag-laden Astrid.

Deirdre turned a perplexed face towards Eva. 'What on *earth's* Paloma on about, going shopping in her pyjamas?'

Jethro's car had just pulled up outside. 'Listen!' Eva shot Deirdre a 'careful!' look and lowered her voice. 'There's been a row,' she said, speaking quickly. 'Dannie walked out on Oliver last night, and took Paloma with her. I picked them up on the road and brought them here.'

'Jesus!' Deirdre's eyes went wide with shock.

'That must have been some row. Where's Dannie now?'

'In the spare room of my suite, resting. Jethro doesn't know she's here, and Paloma thinks her mother's gone home to the Glebe House. She's in a bad way. Now, *shh*!'

The door to the lobby had just opened. Jethro walked in, and smiled when he saw them. 'Ladies of leisure — but not for long. You're back to work tomorrow, film star.'

'That dispute's been settled, then?' asked Eva.

'Yeah. Diplomatic wizardry saw to that.'

'Yours, I take it?'

'I had something to do with it. May I join you?'

Eva gave him a flirtatious smile. 'That would be our pleasure,' she said.

It was astonishing how the actress could switch from 'urgent' to 'chilled' mode with no apparent effort, observed Deirdre. No wonder she had a clutch of Oscars under her belt.

Jethro sat down, crossed one long denim-clad leg over the other, then signalled to a passing barman. 'Bourbon, please,' he said. 'A large one. It's been a bitch of a day,' he added, turning back to Deirdre and Eva. 'But we're nearly there. Just a coupla weeks and we're wrapped.'

'Where's the party going to be?'

'I thought the community hall in the village would be good. We'll have it prettied up *Mimi* style, and invite everyone who contributed.'

'Everyone? In other words, the entire village. That's going to be some kick-ass party,' said Deirdre.

367

'Sure will,' agreed Jethro. 'There'll be people flying in from all over. The author's coming — '

'Lily Wright?' said Eva with great excitement. 'Oh, what fun! I'm dying to meet her.'

'And a load of Hollywood hotshots have invited themselves. Speaking of which, Deirdre, will Rory get over?'

Deirdre did some mental calculations. 'He might manage a flying visit. He's starting work on a new project soon.'

'Let me guess. 'Buccaneers of the Bahamas'?'

'Or 'Frigates of French Polynesia'. Or some such.'

'He's good at that swashbuckling stuff.'

'Don't I know it.' Deirdre allowed herself a private smile. Despite her annoyance with Rory over his desert caper, she couldn't wait to get back to LA, couldn't wait to see him, couldn't wait to experience again the effect he had on her. He was, after all, her drug.

★   ★   ★

Several days later, Deirdre swished out through the polka-dotted door of Mimi's shop on a mission to the village store to buy the most special bottle of *premier cru* Bordeaux they had in stock. She was wearing the flirty little number she'd bought in Brown Thomas on the day she'd masqueraded as a lady who lunches, teamed with sexy, strappy heels. It was Jethro's birthday, and he was celebrating it over dinner in Ballynahinch Castle with a hand-picked selection of friends. Deirdre had bought him an old-fashioned windy-up toy glider with polystyrene wings, and she thought she ought to offset the silliness of the gift by including something with a little more gravitas. She knew that particular Bordeaux had to be OK, because it came from one of Rory's favourite châteaux.

Dannie's car was still parked on the main street of the village where she'd left it on the girly night that had turned out so tragically for her. Deirdre wondered if Jethro had invited her to his birthday dinner. Probably not. Relations between the couple were reputedly strained since Dannie had ditched him for Oliver. Where might Dannie be now? Deirdre asked herself. Was she still in hiding in Eva's suite? Or was she once again ensconced in her pretty cottage? How fast it had all happened! Deirdre shuddered to think that a life could unravel so irrevocably in such a short space of time.

'Hey! Where are you off to in your satin and tat?' Pablo was lounging against the harbour wall, looking effortlessly sexy.

'Jethro Palmer's having a birthday dinner in Ballynahinch Castle.'

'Posh!'

'Yup. Très posh. What are *you* up to, corner boy?'

'I am taking my ease, madam. Why don't you join me and shoot some breeze?'

'I'd be glad to. I've half an hour to go before my driver comes for me.' Deirdre effected a little hopping motion that was intended to lift her onto the wall beside him, but couldn't manage it in her heels.

'Here,' said Pablo, gallantly offering her a helping hand. 'Allow me.'

'Thanks.' As she swivelled into a sitting position beside him, she noticed that her skirt had ridden up a little. Surreptitiously, she tugged at the hem, and Pablo's eyes went straight to her legs.

'Leave it alone! I'm admiring the view.' He smiled at the look of mock indignation Deirdre gave him, and she couldn't help smiling back. It was impossible not to smile at Pablo. 'A driver, eh?' he said speculatively. 'Now there *is* posh.'

'Well, he's not my driver. He's Eva's.'

'Do all LA luminaries have drivers?'

'A-list actors do, and Eva's as A as it gets.'

'How's the biog coming on?' he asked.

'It's getting there,' she said. 'I've done all my research and I've finished a first draft.'

'You'll be heading back to LA, soon, so?'

She shook her head. 'No. I'm going to hang on here until the movie wraps. The wrap party'll be a kind of full stop — if you know what I mean — because it looks like it'll be a high point in the narrative of Eva's life story so far.'

'How's that?'

'*Mimi's Remedies* is set to be her last ever movie.'

'You're not serious?'

''Fraid so. She's decided she's going to retire once *Mimi*'s in the can. There are too many other things she wants to do with her life.'

Pablo shrugged. 'That makes sense. 'Get out while the going's good' is generally a pretty reliable maxim.'

'Oh, look, isn't she dotey!' said Deirdre. She pointed to Fluffy, who hove into view on the main street, squired by two very handsome retrievers. The smug bitch was looking resplendent today, sporting Hello Kitty hair accessories and Schiaparelli-pink toenails. Cleo had evidently given her a pedicure.

'Bad dog, Fluff,' Pablo rebuked her. 'Have you no shame? Look at you flirting away, all done up like a dog's dinner. Go back home to Cleo at once.' But Fluffy just shot Pablo a superior look, and sashayed on regardless.

'How's the portrait coming along?' asked Deirdre.

'It's looking pretty good. Thanks for the mugshot, by the way.'

'You're welcome.' Deirdre had put a photograph of herself through Pablo's letterbox. It wasn't a particularly flattering photograph — she'd had her hamster face on — but that hardly mattered since Cleo's face was the one that would be grafted onto the painting once it had undergone Colleen's scrutiny. She gave him a disingenuous look. 'Incidentally, which part of 'me' are you working on at the minute? The face or the body?'

'Curiously enough, the body's my chief concern,' he said. 'But I've sketched in a face that bears an uncanny resemblance to yours. I think you'll be impressed.'

'I'm sure I will be. I'm dying to see it when it's unveiled.'

There was a pause as they regarded each other sombrely, then Deirdre slanted him a wicked

371

smile and suddenly they were laughing out loud at their innuendo-heavy banter. What fun it was to flirt when there was no danger of things getting meaningful! thought Deirdre. No wonder Fluffy was looking so pleased with herself as she paraded with her beaux down the main street of Kilrowan like some flash French tart!

But things were getting serious with Fluff now, she saw, as another dog tried to muscle in on the *ménage à trois*. A flurry of barking erupted, and Fluffy looked poised for flight. She was too late. The stranger in town had wrestled her to the ground, and her sparkly pink toes were waving wildly in the air.

'The ignominy!' said Pablo, launching himself off the wall. 'I'd better rescue her. Enjoy your dinner, Deirdre.'

She remained sitting on the wall for a while, admiring the sangfroid with which Pablo handled the dogfight. When he finally succeeded in sorting it out, Fluffy strutted after him down the street, looking like a damsel whose champion has just won the tournament.

Deirdre was just about to slide down off the wall when something caught her eye. A motorbike was parked outside Breda Shanley's shop, and a gaggle of giggling girls had materialized on the other side of the street. Ben Tarrant must have got himself *another* new bike. He was an inveterate collector, and set all the female hearts in the village aflutter every time he posed for photographs astride his Harley or Kawasaki or whatever. There he was now, clad in a fringed suede jacket — a bit like the one Rory wore on *his* motorbike, she noticed — with his windswept blond hair straggling out from under his helmet. He was lounging against his bike, and although his visor was down she sensed that he was looking directly at her. And something about his demeanour — something *predatory* — gave her the distinct impression that he'd been watching her for some time.

What was going on? Did Ben Tarrant fancy her? Impossible, she told herself. Ben had only recently got married and he couldn't yet have the hots for anyone other than his beautiful young wife. Feeling vaguely uncomfortable, she was about to twinkle her fingers at Ben when he raised his hands to his helmet and doffed it. Deirdre nearly fell backwards off the sea wall. It wasn't Ben Tarrant under the helmet. It was Rory.

She froze in an attitude of stupid, fish-faced astonishment and watched as her husband strolled down the street towards her, swinging his helmet by the strap.

'Surprised?' he said, when he drew level with her. 'You shouldn't be. I've got so good at pulling this stunt that it's become rather commonplace, don't you think? Maybe I should stop surprising you, Deirdre.'

She found her voice. 'But I love surprises!' she said. And then she wound her arms around his neck and kissed him. He didn't respond. After a moment or two, she cut loose and gave him a winsome look of enquiry.

Winsome didn't work either. There was

something new, something profoundly disturbing, about the way he was looking at her. And then she noticed something else disturbing about his appearance. Normally when he came back from his desert ritual he radiated rude good health. But Rory looked rough. His hair was more wrecked than a Rasta's, he had an unwashed appearance, and there was a fierce smell of drink off him.

Completely unsettled, Deirdre suddenly felt compelled to make small talk. 'Um. So — so how was your desert retreat, darling?' she asked.

'I didn't go to the desert.'

'But Melissa said — '

'Forget what Melissa said. I didn't go to the desert. I went on a bender.' Deirdre reassumed her expression of fish-faced astonishment. 'Surprised again, Deirdre? Were you surprised when I didn't return your tender kiss just now? You see, I can't read surprise in your expression. That Botox stuff sure does do exactly what it says on the tin. You know that clever actresses have stopped using it, don't you? But you're even cleverer. It's a handy mask for you to hide behind when you're dissembling, Deirdre, isn't it?'

'What? What are you talking about?'

Rory reached out a hand and rubbed her bottom lip with his thumb. It wasn't an affectionate gesture, nor was it remotely erotic. It was brusque. He looked at the vermilion stain on his thumb, and then he looked back at her. 'You've taken to wearing a lot of slap,' he said. His eyes meandered down to her cleavage, and then to her legs, where the hem of her dress was still ruched over her thighs. 'Sexy get-up. Quite the little libertine. Is he a boob man? Or is his preference for legs? Or, more accurately, for what's *between* those lissom legs.' Rory made an obscene gesture with his middle finger.

'Jesus Christ, Rory — what are you on about?'

'Come on, my little dimwit. Pay me the courtesy of acknowledging that while I may be a cuckold, I am not also a thick.'

'What . . . what do you mean . . . cuckold?' A clenching sensation started somewhere in the region of her gut.

Rory gave her that smile again. That smile that was so scary she'd have infinitely preferred a black look. 'I understand your boyfriend wields a pretty mean paintbrush. Is that what made you change your mind about sitting for your portrait?'

'But — but I'm not!'

'Oh? Why, in that case, should Colleen feel compelled to tell me a big fat fucking fib?'

'Colleen?'

'I spoke to her on your phone. She told me she'd mistaken it for her own when she picked it up that day in Pablo's studio. The day you first sat for him. In your pelt.'

'Oh!' The clenching feeling relaxed: she felt flooded with relief. 'Oh — *that*!' She laughed now, but the tension that had wound her tight as a spring made the laugh sound forced. 'That was so *funny*!'

'Forgive me if I appear a tad challenged in the humour department,' said Rory. 'Perhaps you might share the joke with me?'

'It sounds terribly complicated, Rory, but this is what happened. You see, Pablo has this clandestine thing going on with this girl Cleo, and they'd been making out one day when I arrived at his house with a bottle of wine for him. And Cleo had left her bra in his studio, and Colleen arrived, so we — Cleo and I — hid in the kitchen. But Colleen found the bra, so I pretended that I was sitting for a nude portrait that you'd commissioned.'

Rory looked at her in silence for a long time, and then he clapped his hands together in a slow round of mock applause. 'Brava,' he said. '*Bravissima*! My genius wife has come up with yet another splendid scenario for a Hollywood bonkbuster. Or should it be a French farce? It's certainly preposterous enough for both genres.'

'But it's true! I know it *sounds* insane, but that's the way it happened.'

Rory looked at her with scepticism writ plain on his face. Then he reached out and ran the palm of his hand down the side of her cheek. The hand curved around her jaw and an index finger lifted her chin. 'Do you beg him for sex?' he said. 'The way you used to come to me, gagging for it after a session with Daniel Lennox? Do you perform a striptease for him, or do you just tear your clothes off so that you can get down and dirty as fast as possible? Your story is as far-fetched, my darling,' he said — and there was a frightening glint in his eye — 'as something out of Alice in fucking Wonderland. Or should I make that 'Deirdre

O'Dare in Cloud Cuckoo Land'?'

Deirdre realized now that Rory was quite drunk. In other circumstances she would have bridled, told him to mind his mouth, but something told her that that was the wrong tack to take. She flailed around for a way out of the mess. 'Look. I'll phone Pablo, if you don't believe me. He'll corroborate.'

'I'm sure he will. It would be in his interest to, wouldn't it?'

Deirdre took her phone out of her bag, then realized that of course she had no number for Pablo. She vacillated, aware that Rory might mistake her hesitation as guilt. Oh, God! Oh, *God!* This wasn't happening! This *couldn't* be happening to her. 'Believe me.' Deirdre's voice came on a breath so tiny it was barely audible. 'Please believe me, Rory.'

They were staring at each other now, eyes locked, as if trying to read one another's souls. Deirdre's soul was there on her face, exposed, vulnerable, defenceless — willing him to believe from its very depths. And maybe he was convinced, because something behind his terminally cynical expression flickered into life momentarily, and then:

'Deirdre!' came a voice like a rasp from the door of O'Toole's pub. 'How is the portrait shaping up?' Colleen sailed towards them, listing a little. She had evidently consumed a great deal of wine. 'And Rory McDonagh! Nice to see you again.' She directed a flirtatious nod at him, before returning her attention to Deirdre, running an eye over her form, assessing. 'I saw the rough sketches. The likeness is a fair one, although I see Pablo has — er — how shall I put it? — *enhanced* your embonpoint.' She drew herself up to her full, regal height, and then: 'It *flatters* you, Deirdre,' she hissed. With her customary flourish, Colleen turned and swirled up the street like the Red Queen. Alice in Wonderland's arch-enemy.

When Deirdre looked at Rory, the life she'd seen flicker there had been extinguished. He didn't say anything. He didn't need to. His expression was eloquent, and it told her more clearly than words could that his love for her was dead.

'Rory,' she said, as he turned away. 'Rory.'

She didn't follow him as he moved back to where his hired bike was parked. She stood frozen like an ice sculpture, hugging herself, one leg wrapped around the other, and watched dry-eyed as he slung a leg across the machine and gunned the engine into life. And then Rory McDonagh rode down the main street of the pretty little village of Kilrowan, and out of Deirdre's life.

16

Cleo was lying starkers on her couch while Pablo concentrated on flesh tones. These same flesh tones had had the disastrous effect of completely distracting him from the job earlier. There'd been two false starts to today's sitting.

'If we keep riding each other at this rate the bloody thing will never be finished,' he grumbled.

'I don't want it to be finished. I'm loving it too much. I think this painting should be like Penelope's tapestry.'

'Who's Penelope?'

'Penelope who was married to Odysseus in the Greek myths. She worked on a tapestry all day, then picked out all the stitches at night.'

'So you're telling me this Penelope was the ultimate loser. What made her pull a silly stunt like that?'

'Because she'd promised to marry one of her many suitors once the tapestry was finished, and she didn't want to. She was waiting for Odysseus to come back to her.'

'I infer from that that you're going to start erasing all my brush-strokes just so's we can have a ride every day?'

'Something like that.'

'Stop smiling like an eejit. I thought you wanted to look mysterious and languid in this painting.'

'It doesn't really matter what my face looks like, does it, since it doesn't feature? I could be squinting and sticking my tongue out and wearing a red nose.'

'Good idea. Maybe I should put a red nose on Deirdre to lend the portrait one of my trademark 'quirky' touches. Colleen would love that.'

Cleo smiled again. 'What inspires those 'quirky' touches you're so famous for?'

'A love of lucre. They're the reason I'm collectable. In some art college right now I can guarantee you that some poor schmuck is writing a dissertation on the significance of the pig in *Bathers by Moonlight with Pig*.'

'And what *is* its significance?'

'It has none. I knew I'd never sell a boring painting called 'Bathers by Moonlight'. So I stuck a pig in and whaddayaknow — it was snapped up. People are suckers. Jesus, Cleo — I remember you told me the first time we met that *Still Life with Pig* was witty!'

'Isn't it?'

'Don't ask *me*! The broadsheets seemed to think so. But I did think my portrait of the former Taoiseach was quite witty. The big baloobah actually asked me to put a pig in. Thought it would give him street cred.'

'And did you?'

'I did. With pleasure.'

'So the portrait's called 'Taoiseach with Pig'.'

'Well, he calls it that. I just call it 'Pig with Pig'.'

'Oh, Pablo! What made me fall in love with someone so irreverent?'

There was a pause. Pablo looked at her, and then he put down his brush. 'Are you?' he asked.

'Am I what?'

'In love.'

There was another, longer pause. 'Yes.'

'In that case, if I asked you to marry me, would you say yes?'

'Yes.'

'The millionaire lottery winner marrying the penniless painter?'

'I'd hardly call you penniless.'

'You forget that I had a long career in a garret before I started to sell. I have had truly mountainous debts to dispatch. I don't even own my own house, Cleo.'

'I don't mind. I have more than enough moolah for both of us. And your paintings are still going to fly.'

'What happens if I get fed up doing cynical 'quirky' stuff? What happens if I get fed up being a media whore?'

'Go back to doing the stuff you used to love. And tell all the oh-so-happening people who want portraits by you to piss off.'

'That's the most motivational thing you've said yet.'

They laughed, then looked at each other with desperate eyes.

'What about Colleen?' they said simultaneously.

'We could run away,' said Cleo. 'We could buy a camper van and run away to Europe. Tuscany or somewhere. I heard they do fantastic camper vans that have — '

'I'll tell her,' said Pablo.

'When?'

'When I come back from London.'

'You're going to London?'

'Tomorrow. Some loved-up gallery wants to do a beauty parade for me.'

'What do you mean, a beauty parade?'

'They want to represent me in the UK, so they're strutting their stuff for me bigtime. Champagne, lunch somewhere posh, blah blah blah.'

'When will you be back?'

'Day after tomorrow.'

'And you'll tell her then?'

'I will.'

'Oh, God.' Cleo bit her lip. 'This has all happened very fast.'

'I know. I couldn't believe it when I heard my own voice asking you to marry me.'

'Do you want to take back the offer? I won't hold you to it if you do.'

There was an ominous silence, and then Pablo said: 'No. I don't think so.'

'OK. Well, er. When do you think we should do it?'

'You're going to need time to organize things if you want a big wedding with hats and stuff.'

'Are you mad? No! I don't want that.'

'Thank God for small mercies. Shall we do the barefoot thing on a beach somewhere?'

'Yes!'

'Well, that's settled that, then.'

And Pablo and Cleo smiled at each other a bit

foolishly, and then he picked up his paintbrush and went back to work.

★   ★   ★

'*Ricardo reached for his paintbrush, and dipped it — not into the paint, as she'd expected — but into the pot of Nutella that she'd smeared on their baguettes earlier.*'

It was the following afternoon, Pablo was gone, and Cleo was working on a new short story. She had quite a collection of them now. Sometimes she allowed herself to fantasize about sending them off to a publisher under a pseudonym, and getting a letter of acceptance back. And then she thought — no! The prospect of someone finding out the true identity of the author was too horrifying. She could imagine word getting round the trade, and all her old colleagues in the bookshop turning pages and pointing out bits to each other and sniggering, and then she remembered those lipstick lesbians who'd sneered at Pixie Pirelli's book all those months ago at Margot's First Wednesday, and she knew she wouldn't be able for it. The story she was working on today was yet another one about a painter who did extraordinary things with his paintbrush.

'*He moved towards where she lay naked on the divan and —* '

Ding dong! Bummer. She'd just got to a particularly intriguing plot point. She'd have to make up some excuse to get rid of her unwelcome visitor.

It was Margot. 'You've still got that naff doorbell,' was the first thing she said. The second thing was: 'Is that dog here?'

'No. She's out with her boyfriend.'

'In that case, I'll come in,' said Margot, handing over a bottle of wine and slipping out of her coat. 'Pour some of that for me, will you, Cleo?'

Cleo automatically did as she was told. What a schmuck she was! she thought as she cut the foil and wielded the corkscrew. What was it about bossy Margot that turned her into a sheep? *Margot had a little lamb*, she thought. *A lamb whose name was Cleo. A dozy little Piscean to Margot's fiery Leo.* Well! That was a masterpiece worthy of Be A Bard dot con!

Margot's nostrils narrowed as she sniffed the air. 'Jo Malone grapefruit?' she asked.

'Yup. How's — um — ' Oh. Cleo wasn't sure who she should ask after — Felix, or Margot's lover.

Margot helped her out. 'My lover?' She threw back her hair before setting herself down on Cleo's couch and tucking her elegant feet beneath her. 'My lover is pure euphoria. My lover is the real thing.' There was a pause while Margot gazed dreamily at the view beyond the picture window. The sound of the cork popping shook her out of her reverie, and she turned back to Cleo. 'I will admit that I did think initially that my *affaire* might have been a classic rebound thing, you know — a way of getting back at Felix.'

'Well, having a sexual relationship with another man when you're married to a gynaecologist is about as insulting as it gets, I would have thought. Cheers.' Cleo handed her sister a wineglass.

Margot gave a tinkling laugh and raised an amused eyebrow. 'Who said anything about a relationship with a *man*?'

Cleo clocked the meaningful emphasis and promptly choked on her wine.

Margot's smile became even more meaningful. 'You see, Cleo, retaliation by having an affair with another man would have been merely childish. But retaliation by having an affair with another woman is so much more! It's a glorious affirmation of the supremacy of the female sex — the very pinnacle of vengeance.' Margot was warming to her subject. 'I told you that Felix used to claim that he knew exactly how women were designed. How *could* he know? He doesn't have a clitoris. And since I've been having rampant sex with someone who does, I now know how to pleasure a woman ten times better than Felix with his so-called 'expert' knowledge.'

Cleo wasn't sure what to say. 'Oh, God, Margot. So you actually 'do' it?'

'Sex with another woman is, I will have you know, a revelation,' said Margot, stretching languorously.

'But isn't she all kind of squishy and — erm — *moist*? I love nice lean men with all their muscly hard bits.'

'Don't you find Anaïs Nin erotic? Her descriptions of female sexuality are peerless. Apart from Colleen's, of course.'

'I suppose. One of those Nins actually gave me a great idea for a story of my own.' Cleo smiled as she thought of the canvas that was still touch-dry. Pablo had finished all her bits late yesterday. All he had to do now was paint on Deirdre's face.

'Try reading them again from a new perspective. Those stories are a celebration of womanliness. My lover is soft, white, plump, yielding, voluptuous . . . '

Cleo felt like putting her hands over her ears and humming loudly.

'You should see Colleen's new work,' continued Margot. 'It's remarkably erotic. I have some of it by heart.' She cleared her throat in an affected, actressy way, and Cleo's heart sank as she realized she was going to be treated to a sample rendition. ' "She lay back, laughing with her feral, pointed teeth',' said Margot, in Colleen's accent. She was a remarkably good mimic, Cleo noticed. ' "The animal odour of her affected me like the smell of civet. I had to possess her . . . " '

Margot paused for effect, then took a sip of her wine, looking at Cleo over the rim. The look was mock-guarded; there was a kind of private amusement there. She put the glass down, but continued to smile at her sister with her feral, pointed teeth . . .

The penny dropped with a thunderous clunk. 'Oh. My. God. It's Colleen, isn't it?' said Cleo. 'You're having it off with Colleen.'

'Oops. I've let the cat out of the bag, haven't I? Although I will say that it's a tad vulgar to describe what we have going on between us as 'having it off'.'

Cleo got the distinct impression that Margot's cat had actually been let out of the bag quite intentionally. Margot had always been a star fucker, and now that she was actually fucking a star, she wanted her sister to know all about it.

'Well,' said Cleo. 'All I can say is 'Oo-er'. The tabloids are going to have a field day when they find out about this.'

'Tabloids, schmabloids. Colleen's not ashamed of her sexuality — of the fact that she's fallen under the spell of another woman.' Another enigmatic smile, another sip of wine. 'She's writing about me, now. She calls me her muse. That was me, in the extract I quoted from the book she's working on at the moment, incidentally. The one with the feral, pointed teeth,' she added unnecessarily.

Cleo asked the question she'd been wanting to ask since Margot's cat had escaped from the bag and gone on the rampage. 'What about Pablo?' she said.

Her sister adopted the kind of concerned expression favoured by Oprah Winfrey. 'That's going to be a problem. Colleen says he'll be devastated. Especially since she's betrayed him with a member of her own sex. Men find that really hard to take. I had first-hand evidence of that, of course, when I told Felix that I'd left him for a woman. She's asked me to move in with her, by the way.'

'*Colleen* has?' Margot gave her a 'doh!' look, and Cleo felt stiff with stupidity. 'And will you?'

'As her muse, Cleo, I think it would be irresponsible not to.'

If she hadn't been feeling so surreal, Cleo would have sniggered. 'And how do you think people in the village will react when they find out you're lezzers — I mean, lesbians?'

Margot gave a little smile of hauteur. 'We prefer to call ourselves Sapphics,' she said. 'And people can think what they like. As for Pablo, personally I thought a threesome would be interesting, before she makes the final break with him.'

Cleo choked on her wine again.

'I suggested it to Colleen,' continued Margot, 'but after some consideration, she came to the conclusion that it mightn't be such a good idea. It might cause him even more emotional damage when he comes to learn that she's chosen me — a woman — above him, a mere man.'

'Oh, I agree with Colleen,' said Cleo with feeling. 'I think a threesome is a totally *ferocious* idea, Margot.'

'God! You are *so* out of touch with your sexuality, Cleo. You are *so* fucking uptight.' Margot's laugh rang out brittle as crystal, and suddenly Cleo wanted to smash it to bits.

She set down her glass with such force that wine swilled all over the table and Margot stopped laughing. 'I'll tell you why I think it's a dreadful idea, Margot. It's because *I* am fucking Pablo. I'm having the most astonishing sex of my life with him. In fact, he fucked me three times yesterday, right where you're sitting.' She saw Margot flinch and shift a bit on the couch. 'We are riding each other rotten, he's painting a portrait of me in the nude, and we're getting married on a tropical beach. So I think describing me as 'uptight' is a little off the mark, don't you? I actually think I'm quite a radical dame. Nearly — though not quite, of course, because I could never aspire so high — but *nearly* as radical as you, Margot.' She wasn't quite so childish as to add a 'So there!', although she felt like it.

It was Margot's turn to choke on her wine, and when she did, Cleo felt a surge of triumph. She'd done the impossible. She'd bested her sister. 'Little' Cleo Dowling had finally stood up to be counted.

But she had to hand it to Margot. She regained her composure with remarkable éclat. 'Well, well, well. I wonder what Colleen will have to say about that?'

'Pablo's going to tell her tomorrow.'

'He won't need to now, will he?'

'What do you mean?'

'Because *I* am going to tell her now. I'm going to tell her that my little bitch on heat of a sister has been having it off with her erstwhile lover.'

'What? Why? You wouldn't, Margot!'

'Damn right I would.'

'But . . . *why?*'

'Because,' Margot said, rising to her feet with effortless elegance, 'you need taking down a peg or three, Cleo. Who do think you are? You with your vulgar lottery millions, swanning down to Kilrowan and posing as a writer in your swanky house! A published poet, my arse! You're a laughing stock, Cleo, that's what you are. You with your 'Best Friend' Eva Lavery and your egregious name-dropping of fucking Ben Tarrant and Colin Farrell and Deirdre O'Dare all over the place as if they were your intimates. You with your 'special extra' status!' Margot put on a simpery voice. ''I'm ready for my close-up, Mr Palmer!' And now you're trying to steal Colleen's thunder by annexing her lover. You've always been a little notice-box, Cleo. You've always been desperate for attention. Daddy's little pet, with your nose in your books and your BA in English and your award-winning essays! I suppose if he were still alive you'd be bouncing around puffed up with pride going: 'Hey, Daddy — I've been promoted! Hey, Daddy — I've been published! Hey, Daddy — I've won the lottery!' Well, you've succeeded in attracting a lot of attention to yourself. You're right in the spotlight now, Cleo! How good does it feel?'

And Margot picked up her coat with a flourish worthy of Colleen at her most theatrical and left her little sister standing all on her own in her beautiful house with hot tears pricking her eyes.

★　★　★

About an hour later, her phone rang. It was Pablo. 'What the fuck's going on?' he said. 'Colleen's just been on the phone to me ranting and raving about you.'

'Oh, Pablo, I'm sorry, I — '

'Not as sorry as you're going to be, sweetheart, if you don't get your ass out of there pronto. Colleen's on her way down to you now to give you a piece of her mind.'

'Oh, *shit*!'

'Get out of there, Cleo.'

'But where'll I go?'

'Book yourself into a hotel.'

'Are you serious?'

'I am abso*lutely* serious. Colleen is beside herself with rage. I don't want to wind you up, sweetheart, but you are in danger. Just grab your bag and go. Phone me when you reach somewhere safe.'

'But — '

'*Go*, Cleo!'

She went. She drove straight to Ballynahinch Castle and booked in for the night, and then she rang Pablo from her room to tell him where she was.

'Good girl,' he said. 'Stay there until I get back. With a bit of luck, Colleen'll be well Xanaxed by then, and she'll be easier to handle. We'll just have to ride out the storm, baby.'

'I feel awful, Pablo. It's all my fault!'

'How in hell's name did she find out?'

Feeling very small, Cleo told him. There was a long pause on the other end of the phone, then came Pablo's robust laugh. 'No shit! Colleen's been doing the bold thing with your sister! Well, shiver my timbers and knock my dick into a cocked hat!'

'Aren't you upset?'

'Upset? Are you mad? I think it's hilarious. I just wish she'd told me straight up. We could have avoided all that hugger-muggering and I

391

could have painted half a dozen nude portraits of you by now, and inspired at least half a dozen raunchy short stories.'

A piece of the jigsaw that had been annoying Cleo for ages slipped into place. 'Oh!' she said. 'I've just realized something.'

'What?'

'*That's* how Margot learned those tricks.'

'What are you on about?'

'Remember she told me her lover did things to her with paintbrushes and feathers and other stuff from my stories? Colleen must have learned them from *you*.'

'Well, more accurately, from *Ricardo*. You're the one who made up that stuff, baby.'

'*Oh!*' She was outraged. 'You complete *bastard*! You learned all these sex games from me, and then you go and try them out on Colleen!'

'Be reasonable. You *knew* I couldn't not sleep with Colleen, Cleo. Otherwise she'd have known something was up.'

'Yes — but to do Ricardo stuff on her wasn't fair. Ricardo's mine!'

'The paintbrush thing was the only one I tried out on her, honest.'

He sounded contrite, but she wasn't convinced. 'Honest? Not the choc-ice thing? Or the thing where I pretend to be asleep?'

'Promise. Honest injun. Are you mollified?'

'Nearly.'

'It was *much* more fun doing it on you, Cleo.'

'Really?'

'Really.'

'OK. I forgive you for the paintbrush, then. Crikey! I can't believe she went and tried that trick on Margot.'

'This just gets funnier and funnier,' said Pablo. 'But it's given me a really good idea. Why don't you write a story about Ricardo and a couple of lesbians?'

'Two words spring to mind, darling,' she said with hauteur. ''Fuck' and 'Off'. However, you'll be interested to know that Margot actually suggested a *ménage à trois* to Colleen.'

'A *ménage à trois*? Between me and Colleen and your sister?'

'Yep.'

'That's a ferocious idea.'

'That's what I said.'

'But you do know men have a thing about sisters, Cleo? I'd actually much prefer a *ménage à trois* with you and Margot.'

She stuck her tongue out at the phone. 'Your little jest fails to amuse, Pablo. What time shall I see you tomorrow?'

'My flight gets into Galway at 3.30. I'll drop by the hotel on my way. And then . . . ' The pause he let drop was weighty with menace.

'And then?'

'We take cover and watch the shit hit the fan, sweetie-pie.'

★   ★   ★

Cleo didn't much like being in a hotel room on her own, especially one as gorgeous as this one, with a beautiful four-poster bed that was crying out for two people to snuggle up in it. She took a shower and got into a bathrobe and surfed channels, hoping for something to distract her from her morbid thoughts of Colleen, but there was nothing to escape into — reality was rampant on telly this evening. Then she remembered that Eva — her New Best Friend! — was staying in the hotel.

Reception put her through.

'Well, hello, darling! What brings you here?' said Eva.

'Um.' Cleo hadn't thought up an excuse. 'I'll tell you when I see you. Will I come to your suite?'

There was a hesitation. 'No. I'll come to yours.'

'Oh. As long as you don't mind slumming it. I'm in a 'superior' room, not a suite.'

'I'll pretend not to notice.'

'I'll order the wine.'

Five minutes later, Eva was at the door. 'Well,' she said, stepping into the room, 'this *is* superior. What makes you treat yourself to a night in Ballynahinch? Is a significant other imminent, by any chance?'

'No.' Cleo felt really silly now. She could dream up absolutely no explanation for the fact that she was staying all by herself in a posh hotel a mere fifteen minutes' drive from her own home. 'I'm actually trying to avoid someone.'

'Perfectly understandable. Sartre was absolutely right. Hell *is* other people.' Eva moved to the window. 'You've a river view, too. Heavenly, isn't it?'

Cleo had been too abstracted to even notice the view. 'Mm. Will you have a glass of wine, Eva?' she asked.

'Of course. I'd love one.'

Cleo poured and handed Eva a glass, feeling a little less unsettled. This had been a *good* idea! 'Is David still away?' she asked.

'Yes. He's coming back for the wrap party, though. Are you coming?'

'Am I invited?'

'Absolutely! You're a Minx, after all — a VIP.'

Cleo smiled. She wondered what Margot would say if she could see her now, sitting in a superior room quaffing chilled Bordeaux with her movie star New Best Friend and being invited to a stellar wrap party as a VIP. Then the dagger words that Margot had stabbed her with earlier that day came back to her, and she bit her lip.

What power sisters had to hurt! Sisters knew each other's Achilles' heels, knew where to aim for maximum impact. That stuff about her father had been accurate and devastatingly hurtful. Cleo had always known that her daddy had been proud of her. Margot had been a Mummy's girl, but Cleo had been Daddy's from day one. It was Daddy to whom she'd bring her homework notebook with the gold star, Daddy who she'd look for and wave to in the audience at the school concert, Daddy she'd call for when she had nightmares or when she was sick. And when Daddy had died, there'd been no-one to whom she could show off the good stuff in her life, no-one to be proud of her achievements. Her mother had been more interested in her new husband, and it seemed that Margot had ceased to be interested at all since Cleo won the lottery and got herself her own life.

'What's wrong, Cleo?' Eva had moved to the couch, and was sitting there watching her.

'I was just thinking — it's silly really, it's actually really, really silly — but . . . I've no-one to be proud of me.' And for some stupid, stupid reason all the tension that had been tamped down inside her for the past few hours welled up and Cleo started to cry.

Eva moved towards her and said 'there there', and she was so very good at it that Cleo cried even more. And when she finally stopped crying, she said: 'You know something, Eva. You do 'there there' better than anyone I know.'

'Thank you. That's the nicest compliment I've ever had,' said Eva. 'Do you want to talk about it?'

Oh God, yes — of course she did! Cleo talked and talked and talked. She told Eva about the horrible stuff Margot had said, and about the friends in Dublin who weren't friends any more because she'd won the lottery. She told her how bereft she'd been since her father died — that awful, awful feeling of being abandoned by the person who loved you most, that aching loneliness that sometimes made her weep at night in bed on her own when Pablo was off with Colleen . . . And then she stopped, and looked at Eva with huge, guilty eyes. 'Oh. I shouldn't have said that,' she said.

'Said what?' said an unfazed Eva. 'I didn't hear a thing.'

But it was out now, and Cleo *wanted* to talk. So she told Eva all about Pablo and the silly short stories and the portrait and Colleen and Margot, and by the time she got to the Margot bit, it all seemed so ludicrous that she was actually laughing out loud. 'Oh, dear, Eva, I'm so sorry. How many times did I say 'I' during the course of that monologue? Probably as many times as Madonna in her *American Life* album. D'you know, one day when I was bored on the film set I played that CD on my Discman and counted the number of times she used the personal pronoun. The number of Is, mys and mes came to nearly five hundred.'

'Well, you're allowed to use the 'I' word a lot when you're upset,' said Eva. 'But it's inexcusable for Madonna. What's she got to moan about?'

'I suppose she doesn't have a dog like Fluffy.'

Eva laughed, then gave Cleo the benefit of her wise gaze. 'You *do* have someone to be proud of you, you know, Cleo. You have Pablo. You don't have to be embarrassed at showing *him* your gift.'

'My gift?'

'Your propensity for happiness.' Eva picked up her bag and started to rummage through the contents. 'It's the greatest gift there is, and I've evidence to prove it.' She handed Cleo a snapshot. 'I took this the day you and Deirdre and I went skinny-dipping on Lissnakeelagh.'

397

Cleo took the photograph. It pictured her and Deirdre running barefoot along Lissnakeelagh strand, laughing back to camera, happiness personified.

'Keep it,' said Eva, 'as testimony to your happiness. Live your dream to the hilt, Cleo. Enjoy your lottery millions. Take pleasure in your lovely house. Relish your writing.'

'*Writing?* Most people would call it scribbling!'

'The begrudgers call it scribbling. Just as they call acting 'mugging'. Submit a story to the *Erotic Review* and see how those begrudgers react if it's published.'

'What's the *Erotic Review?*'

'It's a monthly magazine that publishes erotic stories and drawings. Classy stuff — not smut. I've been reading it for years. They send it to 'Mr E. Lavery' because they assume that only men subscribe, but I love it. I read it out loud to David and it drives him wild. Lucky Pablo to be marrying a broad who writes raunch!'

Well, thought Cleo. Anaïs Nin, eat your heart out!

Just then Cleo's mobile rang. The caller display told her it was Pablo. 'Do you mind if I take this, Eva?' said Cleo.

'If it's who I think it is by your radiant expression, I should be extremely cross if you didn't,' said Eva.

Cleo smiled and put the phone to her ear. 'Hi, honey,' she said. 'What's up?'

'I've got some really bad news, Cleo, I'm afraid.' Pablo's tone was urgent. 'You're going to have to brace yourself. I've just had a call from Breda Shanley.'

'Breda Shanley?'

'You know — from the village shop. She didn't know how to contact you, so she rang me as your neighbour and possible key holder.'

'Key holder? What are you on about?'

'She wanted to know if I had a phone number for you. You've got to get back there right away.'

'Why?'

'It's on fire.'

'What?'

'Your house is on fire, Cleo,' said Pablo.

★ ★ ★

Of course Cleo's paranoid imagination had painted a picture of a crazed Colleen dousing number 5, the Blackthorns, with petrol and setting it alight, but the forensics people told her that there was a much more mundane explanation for the fire. A scented candle had been left burning on a carved Indonesian plinth and it had been knocked over, probably by Fluffy charging in through the dog flap. It had landed, spilling wax, at the foot of Cleo's lovely wifty-wafty muslin curtains. ('Told you you should have had them fire-proofed,' Margot had said on the phone when she'd rung to sympathize. 'And didn't you look at the instructions? You should never leave candles unattended.' Although Cleo had had to admit that that was the only narky thing she'd said. After that she'd been comparatively sympathetic and made some quite good 'there there' noises when Cleo had cried. But, Cleo remembered, *nobody* did 'there there' like Eva Lavery.)

Fluffy had gone AWOL. No dog's body had been retrieved from the burnt-out Blackthorn, but nothing could convince Cleo that Fluffy hadn't perished in the fire, and she was distraught. She didn't care about her Turkish carpets or her Indonesian furniture or her stupid Neff appliances that she hardly ever used. They were all insured and could be replaced. But nothing could replace gorgeous Fluff, who had, after all, been the first friend she'd made on arriving in Kilrowan.

The bitch showed up some days later while Cleo and Pablo were mooching miserably around number 5, inspecting the damage. She didn't even have the grace to look guilty: she just sashayed up, smiling her infectious smile, and said 'Hi!'

'Fluff!' cried Cleo, picking her up and hugging her. 'You bold, bold, darling dog for staying away for so long!'

'Darling dog? I'd have thought she might have deserved a bit of a ticking-off for committing arson,' remarked Pablo.

'No. That wasn't her fault. It was mine for running out of the joint in a panic and leaving that candle burning. Of all the dumb-ass things to do!'

'Then it's *my* fault really for getting you so wound up about Colleen that night,' said Pablo. It seemed that Colleen had not been so hell bent on vengeance as Pablo had thought, because there'd been no visitation. Perhaps she realized that it would be inappropriate to lay into Cleo when she'd just lost her house and most of her possessions. 'I got a letter from her today that you ought to know about,' he added, when Cleo had finished her love-in with Fluffy.

'Oh? Was it a poison-pen one?'

'No. But it's not good news. She's told me to vacate number 4.'

Cleo looked glum. 'Well, we knew that might be on the cards. When?'

'She's given me a month's notice.'

Trying to look on the bright side, Cleo did some calculations. 'There's always my flat in Dublin,' she suggested. 'It won't be ready for a few more months, but we could rent somewhere until it is.'

'D'you know something? I think I've got a better idea,' said Pablo, taking her by the hand. 'Come with me.'

He led her into the garden of number 4, and up onto the deck and through the sliding doors into his studio, and then he booted up his laptop. The image that took shape on the screen was that of a camper van.

'This is meaningful,' said Cleo.

'It's a camper van.'

'I know it's a camper van.'

'It's just that I remembered what you said, that time you sat for me when I asked you to marry me. You said something about running away in a camper van.'

'Was I serious?'

'I dunno, but it seemed like a pretty smart

idea so I thought I'd log onto a site and have a look.'

''A symbol of freedom, independence and luxury',' read Cleo. 'Wow! I like the sound of that! 'Designed to meet the demands of our customers' every whim.' Even better!'

Together they perused the image of the camper van, admiring all its gleaming features.

'Look,' said Pablo, scrolling down. ''The facilities include toaster, oven, coffee-maker.' And you can have up to a seven-foot four-inch bed!'

'Blinging!' said Cleo. 'Hey, what's a power sofa?'

Pablo scrolled down some more. 'Something to do with 'no fuss' bedmaking.'

'Sounds like my kind of bedmaking. Oh, look, a stand-up shower! I wonder is it state-of-the-art power?' she said, sliding him a provocative look. 'And you can have three bathrooms! In a *camper van?*'

'No, sweetheart. That's three bathroom *layouts.*'

'Let's have a look at the Advanced Brochure request,' said Cleo, with mounting excitement. 'Let's see — blah blah blah. 'Does simple and comfortable driving, parking and camp set-up appeal to you?''

'Yes,' said Pablo. ''Will pets be travelling with you?''

'Damn *right!*' said Cleo. ''Will you need to use the van as an office?' Um, no — but *you* might want to use it as a studio. I'm sure that can be arranged — the light looks pretty cracking with that skylight-looking yoke. OK! Let's fill in the form.'

And as Pablo MacBride and Cleo Dowling filled in the Camper Van Advanced Brochure Request Form, Fluffy strolled into the kitchen and ate all the Parma ham and profiteroles that they'd bought for lunch.

17

Deirdre wasn't functioning. She barely ate and she barely slept. She hadn't taken a shower since the evening Rory had walked out on her. Every day she dropped Bruno off at the child-minder's, and every day she went back to the flat above Mimi's shop and crawled back under the duvet. Sometimes she drank to numb the pain. Sometimes she stuck her nails into her flesh because physical pain was more endurable than this mental anguish. She wished she had Xanax. She wished she had morphine. Sometimes she wished she were dead. Life without Rory was not a life. Life without Rory was a vortex. When she woke in the night and reality came crashing through the defensive web that her dreams had spun, the pain she felt was so intense it was terrifying. She'd curl herself up into a foetal position and whimper and keen. Sometimes she stifled a yowl. If Bruno hadn't been in the room next door, she wouldn't have bothered about the stifling.

When she picked her son up from the minder's house she tried to act normal, but sometimes she couldn't hold things together, even around her beautiful boy, and she'd cry and cry and cry. And Bruno would look scared and bewildered, because he'd never seen his mother cry before. He'd cling to her and beg her to stop, and then he'd start crying too. And as much as she yearned to, she knew she couldn't go home to her other babies just yet, because she couldn't inflict her deranged behaviour on them. She needed time on her own to find some perspective on where she was going now in her life, because she was in a maelstrom. She'd read an interview with Nicole Kidman in a magazine once, about how terrifying her split with Tom Cruise had been for her, and the actress's words came back to haunt her: *When I love, I love so much it's dangerous . . .*

Her flat became a place that was somewhere between a prison and a retreat for her. The child-minder's house was just a few doors down the road, so she only had to leave her flat for a few minutes each day. If she saw anyone she knew on the street she'd duck into a doorway so that she didn't have to say anything. It cost her enough in self-discipline even to greet the child-minder with a 'Good morning'.

In the flat, she didn't answer the doorbell and she didn't answer the phone. She erased any messages that weren't from Rory. In other words, she erased *all* her messages, because Rory did not call once. She expected that the next communication from him would be via a solicitor, and then her world would fragment irrevocably.

She had phoned Melissa for information about him, but Melissa didn't really have any. Rory hadn't returned to LA after his flying visit to Ireland, she told Deirdre, he'd flown to French Polynesia to start filming his newest pirate epic. Melissa also told her that it was impossible to connect to the mobile phone network there, and that any time Rory phoned home to speak to the girls it was from his hotel. Deirdre tried his mobile number without success, and any time she tried phoning the hotel she was asked her name, then told by a smooth French accent that Mr McDonagh was not available. She suspected that he'd left instructions at reception that her calls were not to be taken. So she gave up.

On one exceptionally wretched morning Bruno started to kick up a scene on the way to the child-minder's, crying and pleading with her not to leave him. But she had no choice. She *needed* space to herself to grieve: it was tough enough trying to act upbeat around her baby son in the evenings — she simply didn't have the energy to do it all day as well. She was trying unsuccessfully to disengage Bruno's clingy fingers from hers so that she could ring the doorbell when she heard a car horn from behind her, and her name being called. She glanced over her shoulder. Oh, God. It was Eva.

Eva got out of the passenger seat of her transport Merc and crossed the road to Deirdre. 'You're still sick?' she said. Deirdre nodded. Then she dropped to her hunkers on the footpath and doubled over in anguish. Eva knelt down beside her. 'Do you need a doctor?' she asked. Deirdre shook her head. 'Come, sweetheart. Stand up.' Eva took Deirdre in her arms and helped her to her feet, then she picked Bruno up and cradled him. 'Come with me to the shop, cuddly bunny,' she said, 'and we'll buy a present for Mummy to cheer her up, and something for you as well. What would you like? An ice-cream?'

Bruno nodded through his sniffles.

'OK. Deirdre — you go on up to the flat, and we'll be back in two shakes of a lamb's tail.'

Deirdre managed to do as she was told. She climbed the stairs to the flat and sat down on the couch to wait for Eva. Something was happening. This was better. Eva would help. She'd know what to do.

Five minutes later, Eva was back with a happier-looking Bruno. He had ice-cream all over his face, and an invitation from Cleo Dowling to go to the beach with her and Fluffy to make sand castles.

'Isn't he the lucky boy!' said Eva. 'We bumped into Cleo in the shop, and when I told her that Bruno was having a day off from the child-minder's she asked him if he fancied a day on the beach.' Deirdre intuited that the invitation had been effected with more than a little diplomatic wizardry from Eva. 'Does he have your permission to go?'

Stapling on a wan smile, Deirdre said: 'Of course. Have fun, baby.'

She blew her son a kiss as Eva disappeared through the door of the flat with him, then slumped back against cushions, feeling drained. She was all cried out. She lay inert, numb, until she heard Eva's returning step on the stair, and then she made an effort to sit up straight and look a bit more together.

'Don't worry. He was quite happy to go off with Cleo,' Eva told her as she entered the room.

'But I sensed somehow that the child-minder was a bad idea.'

Deirdre nodded.

'I asked him what he thought Mummy would like to cheer her up, and the astute child said 'champagne'. However, I also picked up a bottle of vodka and the makings of a Bloody Mary just in case champagne's inappropriate.' Eva delved into a carrier bag and took out a bottle of fizz and a bottle of Smirnoff. 'Which would you prefer?' she asked.

'A Bloody Mary. Please.'

'Coming up.'

Eva went off into the kitchen, and Deirdre could hear the sounds of ice tinkling and liquid splooshing, and then her friend was back, bearing two Bloody Marys so laced with Worcester Sauce they looked almost black. Deirdre took a gulp of hers, and felt it warm her stomach. 'Thanks, Eva,' she said.

'I knew something was wrong. Your voice was weird when you rang to say you couldn't make Jethro's birthday dinner. I would have come sooner, but I've been working my ass off.' Eva sat down beside Deirdre on the couch. 'You haven't been sick, have you? You've been in the horrors.'

Deirdre nodded. 'Rory's left me,' she said.

* * *

Two Bloody Marys later, Eva got to her feet. 'I'm going back to the hotel,' she said, 'and I'm going to write to him.'

Deirdre looked dubious. Eva was the most

positive person on the face of the planet, but even she would find it difficult to cut through the tough carapace of scepticism that Rory had constructed around himself. 'You'll never convince him that it was all a tragic misunderstanding,' she said. 'You know what a cynic Rory is.'

'I'll convince him,' said Eva. 'I give you my solemn promise that I'll convince him.'

Deirdre looked long and levelly at Eva. There was something about the actress's expression that verged on the beatific. 'Are you an angel, Eva Lavery?' she asked.

Eva gave a throaty laugh. 'No. I'm a white witch,' she said.

'Just like Mimi. Talk about typecasting!' Then Deirdre slumped again. 'There's no point in sending him an e-mail,' she said. 'He won't get it. He can never be arsed accessing mail when he's away from home.'

Eva shook her head. 'I'm not going to e-mail him,' she said. 'I'm going to write a proper letter and send it Fed Ex.'

'Why?'

'Somebody once told me that if you send something private on e-mail, you might as well write it on a big billboard for all the world to see. This is for Rory's eyes only.' She leaned forward to embrace Deirdre, then made for the door. '*Courage, ma petite*,' she said on the threshold. 'Hang in there. And let me know as soon as he gets in touch.'

'You really think this will work?' asked Deirdre.

'I don't think it, darling,' said Eva, giving her a jaunty salute. 'I *know* that this will work.'

★ ★ ★

Dannie had spent nearly a week in Eva's suite, trying to make sense of things. She'd put her engagement ring in an envelope and posted it to Oliver along with a note asking that he send her possessions and those of Paloma to the cottage.

She'd moved back in. After spending so long in Eva's spare room, she felt she couldn't inconvenience the actress any more. 'You're not inconveniencing me!' Eva had protested when Dannie told her she was leaving. 'That bedroom's lying empty — someone might as well use it.'

But Dannie had insisted that it was time for her to get her ruined life back on track. Anyway, David and Eva's daughter Dorcas were due back soon, and she'd have to leave once they arrived.

The afternoon before she moved out, she had gone to Eva's bedroom to leave a thank-you note on her pillow. Not realizing that the actress had returned earlier than usual that day, she opened the door to see her sitting at her desk, writing a letter. She was just about to apologize for the intrusion when something made her stop short. Eva was crying as she wrote. Dannie had backed out of the room and shut the door quietly.

It had been such a weird incident that she wondered when she looked back on it if she hadn't dreamed it. To see Eva Lavery crying was a shocking thing — a bit like seeing the most popular girl in school crying. You just never imagine that someone who seems to have it all might possibly have problems too.

Dannie felt like shit when she thought about that now, back in her cottage. Eva had been so good to her. She'd lent her clothes and poohed-poohed Dannie when she apologized for having no means of footing the bill for her meals and accommodation. She'd listened imperturbably to Dannie's tearful narrative of the events of that awful night and she'd listened to her concerns and worries about Paloma and the future. All in all, Eva had been so amazingly supportive of her that Dannie felt she should have offered some support in return. But the actress's demeanour when Dannie had come across her crying had told her that whatever grief Eva was suffering was of an intensely private nature. She hadn't wanted to interfere.

On top of everything else, Dannie had missed Paloma like mad — it had been the longest time in her life that she had spent apart from her daughter. It had felt very weird indeed to spend all that time in Ballynahinch Castle, knowing that Paloma was staying on the next floor with Jethro. She hadn't left Eva's suite in case she ran into either of them — except to take walks in the woods around the hotel, knowing it was unlikely she would run into Jethro there. He'd be doing too much moving and shaking to take time out for leisurely strolls. She had had all her meals delivered to the room, and she'd done a lot of thinking.

It seemed to her now that it would be

impossible for her to stay on in Kilrowan. It had nothing to do with the gossip and rumour-mongering that would inevitably get going once word was out that the happy couple had split so soon after their engagement. It was to do with the fact that she never wanted to see either Oliver or Alice again in her life. She knew that if she did, she would be filled with such venom and rage and disgust that she would do something awful — she would grind broken glass into Oliver's face, or seize Alice by the hair and gouge her nails into her eyes.

It wasn't just the betrayal — it was the fact that they had tarnished her very existence. She felt as if someone had taken a filthy rag and rubbed it over every aspect of her life. She felt grubby. Kilrowan felt grubby. The cottage which had once been a cherished home felt grubby. She itched to spring-clean.

Oliver had had the stuff that she'd left behind in the Glebe House delivered to the cottage in boxes, but she hadn't wanted to go near them because of the contamination that clung to them. She'd just asked the delivery man to dump them unopened in the garden shed. The accompanying letter from Oliver had gone in the bin. She supposed it contained some kind of explanation, some kind of apology. But she didn't want to know what childhood dysfunction drove him to take his sister to bed, she didn't want his excuses, she didn't want more grubbiness in her life. She'd barely been able to touch the letter, knowing that his hand had made contact with the paper, that his tongue had licked the envelope — *oh*! The notion made her want to be physically sick.

Sometimes the image of Oliver coupling with Alice on the bed in which he'd had sex with her (Dannie couldn't call it 'making love') came unbidden into her mind, and she felt giddy with nausea. The idea that Paloma might have woken, might have wandered into the apartment and witnessed the act, was too horrific for words.

All her thinking had led Dannie to only one conclusion: she was going to have to leave Kilrowan and search for a home somewhere else in the world. The idea that she'd been driven out by Oliver Dunne and his sister made her hate them even more. She had never guessed that she could hate with such passion. But Eva had told her not to look at it that way, to look upon it instead as an adventure, to embrace the change. 'I don't believe in endings,' she'd said when Dannie had said goodbye to her the previous day. 'I only believe in beginnings. And beginnings happen when you vent bad energy.'

So Dannie vented the bad energy by throwing herself into housework the minute she moved back to the cottage, vacuuming and scrubbing and polishing. She wondered what her sister-in-law would do with the joint when she claimed possession. She knew that Leanne's taste veered towards the fussy, and she visualized the airy simplicity she loved being compromised with cheesy ornaments and chintzy furnishings. She also wondered about where she, Dannie, would fetch up next. She supposed the world was her oyster now that she no longer had family to

413

keep her in Kilrowan.

Where in the world . . . There'd been a television quiz show called that once. Where in the world would she go with her small daughter? Not a city. After London and Dublin she'd learned that village life with its unhurried pace suited her. Maybe somewhere sunny? That was the downside about village life in Ireland — in the winter months you were practically a prisoner in your own home. And then she remembered a village that Deirdre O'Dare had told her about, in the Languedoc in the South of France where she and Rory had a holiday home. It was idyllic, according to Deirdre. A place where the living was easy, laid-back and languorous. Dannie pictured herself and Paloma sitting at a table on some sleepy French *terrasse*, shooting the breeze with the locals before heading back to their new home with baguettes tucked under their arms, and the image was so appealing that she picked up the phone to Deirdre to ask her all about it. But Dannie only got the answering machine, and Deirdre did not return her call.

★　★　★

The Fed-Exed letter would take four working days to reach French Polynesia, Eva told her. Today was Wednesday. Rory would not receive the letter until next Tuesday at the earliest.

Deirdre breathed, slept little and ate virtually nothing for those six days. On Tuesday she spent most of the day hunkered by the phone, cheek

414

on her knees, arms wrapped round her shins, rocking herself to and fro. The phone did not ring. At midnight Deirdre picked it up to call Eva, regretting it the minute she heard the voice on the other end. Eva sounded very dopey: she had clearly been fast asleep.

'Oh, Eva, I'm so sorry! You're probably on call at the crack of dawn tomorrow, aren't you, and I've gone and woken you up?'

'No worries, Deirdre. Any word from Rory?'

'No.'

'Well — remember that French Polynesia's in a different time zone.'

'Ahead or behind us?'

'Haven't a clue. Never could work that one out,' mumbled Eva. ''Night, darling. And don't worry. It'll work.'

'Good night, Eva.'

Deirdre put the phone down, ripped out the jack, and raced to her laptop with it. Now that she had something to do she suddenly felt energized. She logged on, and had just typed 'French Polynesia' into Google when a roar from Bruno's bedroom made her jump to her feet.

'Bad dream go way!' Bruno was wailing as she tumbled through the bedroom door. 'Go way! Mama, make dream go way!'

Deirdre got under the covers at once, and took her boy in her arms and soothed him and stroked him and sang him songs until the bad dream receded and Bruno was finally asleep again with Kelly Osbourne clutched in his plump fist.

And that was how she ended up spending the

night in Bruno's bed, sleeping fitfully, yearning for the phone to ring, while, back in the sitting room, the Google search engine purred away, perusing all things pertinent to French Polynesia.

* * *

She woke very late the next day to the sound of the doorbell. Deirdre knew instantly who it was because the 'dada dada da' rhythm of the bell was the way he always announced his arrival.

Bruno knew it too. 'Daddy!' he cried, as Deirdre swung him up in her arms from the bed. She took the stairs at a lick, Bruno clinging to her with his arms around her neck and his legs wrapped round her waist, and pulled open the front door of Mimi's shop to find Rory standing there.

They stood looking at each other for a long, long moment, before Rory spoke: 'I can't stop surprising you,' he said. 'And I can't stop loving you, either.' And then he moved towards her and folded her in his arms.

'Bruno sandwich!' chirped Bruno, who was still attached to Deirdre like a limpet.

'Bruno sandwich,' echoed Rory, and Deirdre, who had thought she was all cried out, started crying again. Rory took limpet Bruno from her and reached out a hand to brush tears from her face.

'Mommy cries all the time,' said Bruno.

Rory looked at Deirdre over Bruno's head. 'All the time?' he asked her in a very grave voice.

416

She nodded. 'All the time,' she said, reaching up and pressing his hand against her cheek.

'I'm sorry,' he said. 'Do you forgive me?'

'Of course I do. I'm a fool for the love of you.'

'I'm sorry,' he said again. 'I nearly blew us right out of the water.'

'You'll pay for it.'

'Damn right. I already have, some. A very macho film crew witnessed me blubbing one day, and that's about as humiliating as it gets.' Rory's expression changed and he gave her a wicked smile. 'I've done something else that'll make you cry even more,' he said.

'Oh, God, no. I've no tears left. What have you done this time?'

Rory took a step to one side and looked down the laneway that ran adjacent to Mimi's shop. 'You can come out now,' he said, and then Aoife and Grace appeared from around the corner, jumping up and down with excitement and shouting 'SURPRISE!'

And of course the tears Deirdre thought she didn't have left sprang straight to her eyes and blinded her as she hunkered down and opened her arms to embrace her precious, precious daughters in a circle of perfect love.

★ ★ ★

The flat was chaotic. Grace and Bruno were poking each other to see who would give way and cry first, and Aoife was playing a computer game that made frequent and very loud exploding noises. Bruno had ransacked Rory's rucksack to find the present that had been bought in the airport (Kelly Osbourne with a new hairstyle), and Rory's stuff was strewn all over the joint. They'd had takeaway fish and chips for supper, and there were empty cartons and unwashed glasses on every surface. But Deirdre didn't care. They were *familia intacta* again, and the world was a fine and dandy place to be — not the arid wasteland it had been just yesterday.

Rory and Deirdre were lying in each other's arms on the couch. 'Should we book into Ballynahinch?' asked Rory. 'There isn't room for five people here.'

'I kinda like it here. It's cosy — like camping. There's a sofabed in Bruno's room that Aoife can sleep on, and I can improvise a bed out of cushions for Grace. How long are you here for?'

'I'll stay until *Mimi*'s wrapped and you're ready to come home.'

'It should be wrapped tomorrow. The party's on Friday. What about *your* film, incidentally? Hasn't shooting started on that?'

'Yeah. But they haven't started principal photography yet. I asked if my stunt double could cover the long shots.' Most shit-hot A-list actors claimed to do their own stunts, but Rory had no truck with that kind of macho posturing. 'Who's going to take care of my family if some pyrotechnic wizard fucks up?' he'd been quoted as saying.

'How on earth, beloved,' asked Deirdre now, 'did you get here so fast?'

'By bumsucking. I owe David Marchant bigtime. As well as tweaking the schedule, he lent me his jet.'

'You flew here in a private jet?'

'Damn right. As did the girls and Melissa. I told her to hire a Lear in LA.'

'Where is she?'

'She's doing what all good Americans do and tracking down her Irish ancestors in Kerry.'

'And she hired a Lear to get here? How much did *that* cost?'

'I'm not telling you. Anyway, damn the expense. Some family reunions are worth paying through the nose for.'

'Jesus, Rory! You moved heaven and earth to get your ass over here! What made you do it?'

'I'll tell you later.'

There came a squawk from Bruno. Rory got to his feet and assumed the role of circus ringmaster, while Deirdre contemplated the chaos from the couch. 'Hey, you two — Bruno, Grace — cut it out! It's time you were in bed,' Rory warned them.

'No, it's not,' said Grace.

'Yes, it is. You're jet-lagged and knackered.' He turned to Aoife. 'OK, Killer Queen. Finish up there. If you're in bed in ten minutes you get a longish story. If you're in bed in fifteen minutes you get a shorter story, and if you're in bed in twenty minutes you get no story at all. Now. What's it to be?'

'But — '

'But me no buts,' said Grace, in a perfect imitation of her mother's voice. She snatched

419

Kelly Osbourne from Bruno who hollered 'Kelly! Kelly Kelly Kelly!'

Rory put on his he-who-must-be-obeyed voice. 'Give him back his doll, Grace, and stop winding him up.'

Fifteen minutes later the girls were in bed, and Bruno had been bathed and changed. Deirdre was lying back on the couch with her baby in her arms, humming to him as he manipulated Kelly Osbourne's arms and poked the doll's nose and cheeks the way he'd poked Grace earlier. Deirdre could hear the murmur of Rory's voice from the other room as he read the girls their story, and again she marvelled at how capricious life could be. Which of the gods up there had petitioned Zeus on her behalf? she wondered. Aphrodite, undoubtedly. Unless, of course, Eva Lavery really *was* a white witch who could work magic . . .

Rory emerged from the girls' room, shut the door gently behind him and regarded his wife. He looked tired, and most uncharacteristically serious.

'How did this happen?' asked Deirdre, smiling at him. 'What spell did Eva cast on you to effect this spectacular reunion?'

Rory put a hand up and ran it over his head. There was something disturbing about the gesture. 'Deirdre,' he said. 'I had a letter from her.'

'I know,' she said. 'She told me she was going to write to you.'

'It's not good news,' he said.

Deirdre felt a sudden flash of fear. 'You mean

'. . . you're not — you're *not* going to come back to me?'

'I'll come back to you all right — if you'll have me after that Pablo débâcle,' he said. 'I mean it's not good news about Eva.'

Another volt of fear shot through her. 'What do you mean?' she asked.

Rory moved to his rucksack, took an envelope from one of the pockets and handed it to her. 'Read this,' he said, adding: 'Is there any strong liquor in the house?'

'There's vodka in the kitchen.'

'I'll fix us shots.'

Deirdre looked at the envelope she held in her hands. It bore the logo of Ballynahinch Castle and was addressed to Rory in Eva's distinctive italic hand, in violet ink. Deirdre's fingers were shaky as she drew three pages from the envelope. Each was covered in writing so dense and untidy that the elegant script on the envelope could have been written by a different person.

'Dear Rory,' she read.

You must believe Deirdre. What she told you is true, beyond a shadow of a doubt. There has been no affair between Deirdre and Pablo. Your wife has not been unfaithful to you. You know me well, and you know that I respect my friends' privacy and would never interfere in anyone's business unless I thought it absolutely necessary. In this instance it is not just necessary, it is imperative. I cannot allow the marriage between two of my most beloved friends to founder and die.

I am going to tell you something that you will find upsetting, Rory, so be brave. I am dying. I have terminal cancer, and I will not live another six months. The only other people in the world who know this are my specialists. I have asked them to be completely honest with me, and have been told that any treatment could be messy and humiliating, and may only prolong the agony, so I've told them I don't want it. The pain is manageable — I have painkillers that kick in fast when I need them to, so that's good.

I'm sorry for burdening you with this, Rory, but you will understand now that it is essential that you go straight to Deirdre and put things right. I will not be happy or at peace until I know things are OK between you, and (here's the blackmail bit!) you *do* want my final days to be happy, don't you?! So don't be sorry — be glad, because some good must come of this.

Please let me know ASAP when you and Deirdre have sorted things out — I'll be on tenterhooks until I hear from you.

I love you both so much.

Eva. XXX

Deirdre looked up. Through a blur of tears she saw Rory. He was leaning against the jamb of the kitchen door with two glasses in his hand. Without a word he moved to her, set the glasses down on the coffee table, and kissed her on the forehead. He took a dozy Bruno from her and settled him on the couch beside her, and then he pressed a shot glass into her hand. 'Down it in one,' he said.

★ ★ ★

The next day Deirdre picked up the phone to her baby-sitter and asked her if she'd do her a big favour and take the kids to the beach. When they'd been packed off, she picked up the phone again and dialled Eva's number. The PA answered. 'Hi, Deirdre! Eva's on set, but she's just about to wrap. Get ready to party!'

Deirdre had lost all sense of time. 'Tonight?' she asked.

'No. Tomorrow.'

'Is Eva heading back to the hotel once she's wrapped?'

'Yes.'

'Can you pass on an urgent message to her from me?'

'Sure. What is it?'

''He's here',' articulated Deirdre.

'What? That's the message? Just 'He's here'?'

'Yes. She'll understand.'

'OK. See you tomorrow!'

Deirdre put the phone down and turned to Rory. 'She's on her way back to the hotel,' she said. 'Let's go.'

They drove to Ballynahinch Castle in Rory's hire car, but they didn't go inside. They just sat on a bench in the garden, holding hands, waiting for Eva to arrive.

As soon as Deirdre saw the black Merc roll up the drive she rose to her feet and raised a hand, but Eva didn't see her. Deirdre watched as the actress stepped out of the car, and when she saw her face contort with pain, she couldn't bear it. She ran to Eva and wrapped her arms around her, and as she did she heard her murmur: 'No tears. You mustn't show your distress.'

Eva disengaged herself from Deirdre's embrace, and, aware that the eyes of a number of tourists in the car park were on her, she adapted an ostentatiously casual demeanour. 'Come up to my suite, why don't you?' she said, touching Deirdre lightly on the arm and moving towards the door of the hotel. When she saw Rory approaching, her face became luminous, as if lit up from within. 'You always were my favourite leading man,' she said in a low voice. 'I can't bear to think that I'll never get a chance to snog you now.'

'Yes, you will,' said Rory gallantly. He swept her into an embrace and kissed her long and hard, and the tourists all applauded.

When he finally relinquished her, Eva's knees buckled suddenly and she clutched at Rory's arm for support. 'Wow! You can certainly make a gal swoon, Rory McDonagh! I'm quite weak at the knees after that!' She smiled at her little joke, but her face was grey. Deirdre somehow managed a smile back. 'I'm sorry about this. I stupidly left my painkillers behind today. Let's go up straight away. Incidentally — I ordered champagne as soon as I got your message, Deirdre.'

They walked into the hotel with Eva leaning heavily on Rory's arm, and made their way to her suite.

Once inside, the actress made straight for the bathroom, and emerged shaking a pill from a pillbox into her hand. 'Pop the champagne, Rory,' she commanded.

Within seconds, Rory was pouring fizz into flutes and handing them round.

'To you,' said Eva, raising her glass. 'To the reunited happy couple.'

'No. To *you*,' said Deirdre.

'Yeah, all right. To me, too, then. I think I deserve it, don't you?' She sat down on the couch and swallowed her pill with a swig of champagne. 'You're not meant to drink on these,' she said. 'But fuck it. The movie's wrapped and I can do as I damn well please now.' She shot Deirdre a look of reproval. 'Please don't look so tragic, Deirdre. It's only going to make things worse. If I've managed to spend the past few months working harder than a Butlin's redcoat to appear upbeat, then I think you might make an effort too.'

'Sorry, Eva.' Deirdre took a gulp of champagne.

There was a pause, and then: 'How long have you known?' asked Rory.

'Seven or eight months.'

'So you knew when you agreed to do *Mimi's Remedies*?' Deirdre was astonished.

'Yup. That's what made me decide to do the

movie. As you know, I don't normally have much truck with sentimentality, but I decided that if I had to sing a swan song, it might as well be something full of *joie de vivre*. Could you imagine if I'd gone out on a note of Bergmanesque *angst*? Think how David and my darling Dorcas would feel!'

'Didn't the insurance people cop on from the medical?'

'No. My cancer is called the silent killer. It's ovarian. It was discovered during a routine visit to my gynaecologist. If I'd been arsed to go sooner I might have been in with a chance, but it was already well advanced when I saw him.'

'Has it been tough, holding it together?' asked Rory.

'Of course it has, darling. Mimi has been the performance of a lifetime.'

'You're a heroine,' said Rory. 'A complete star turn.' Another pause, then: 'What will you do now?' he asked.

Eva turned her head to look out of the window. 'I don't know,' she said. 'The pain is getting less bearable. It seems to have peaked in the past week. But I'm drawing the line at treatment. I don't want Dorcas or David to watch me suffer in a hospital. I can't allow their last memories of me to be that way.'

Deirdre searched for a light — any glimmer of hope — at the end of the dark, dark tunnel Eva was travelling down. 'Are you *sure* about the treatment? Might it not help if you looked for a second opinion — '

'Darling, I've had a second opinion — of

course I have. Both specialists say that hospitalization is inevitable if I opt for treatment. And since I *hate* hospitals with a vengeance, I'm not going to die in one.'

'What about alternative medicine?'

'I've investigated that too, but I have to say I'm not convinced by the alternative thing. A bit too *Mimi's Remedies* for me. And don't even *suggest* astral healing.' She smiled at them, and then her smile faded. 'I've found myself thinking about David a lot, of course, and of Dorcas, and how devastated they'll be.'

'You haven't said anything about this to David?' asked Rory.

Eva shook her head. 'Not a dicky bird.'

'When will you tell him?'

'I don't know. I don't know a lot of things. This dying game's uncharted territory.' Eva picked up a cushion, wrapped her arms around it and held it against her, then threw it to the floor with a distasteful expression. 'Oh! I'd forgotten that only bad actresses ever do that comforting stunt with the cushion.' Another smile. 'I'm glad to talk to somebody about all this, though, at last. It's been fantastically lonely.'

'Would you have 'fessed up if the Pablo débâcle hadn't happened?' asked Rory.

'No. But I knew that 'fessing up was the only way of making sure you two got back together. It had to be done. I suppose the Pablo débâcle was a kind of divine providence.'

Divine providence . . . A thought occurred to Deirdre. 'Is *this* the reason you approached me about the biography, Eva? Because you knew

427

you . . . ' she almost couldn't get the words out. There was a lump in her throat the size of a golf ball — bigger — but she knew she had to make a huge effort to be as brave as her friend: 'Because you knew you were dying?'

'Bright girl,' answered Eva smartly. 'I don't mean to sound terminally cynical, but the dying thing'll be a real coup for the book. That, and the fact that *Mimi's Remedies* will be out at the same time. You stand to make loads of money, and so does my estate.'

'But I don't *want* to make loads of money out of your death.'

Eva's smile was full of sympathy. 'I know you don't, darling, but *I* do. I want to leave behind a great big stash of cash for David and Dorcas. I suspect that David will be so devastated by all this that he won't be able to work again — for a while, at any rate — and I need to ensure that my loved ones have enough to live on.'

'There's always life insurance,' pointed out Deirdre.

'That's not enough,' said Eva matter-of-factly. 'Dorcas will need a trust fund. She's not going to get through life without a *lot* of help financially.'

Oh, God. She'd just have to go for it. 'OK,' said Deirdre, with feeling. 'I will do my darndest to make sure that this book becomes a bestseller. I am determined to make — '

'I *have* thought about suicide,' said Eva, interrupting. The word hung in the air like a stalactite, or a sword.

'*Eva!*' said Deirdre, and Rory put his head in his hands.

'Obviously that would solve a lot of problems — and I would love to die with some dignity, if such a thing is possible. Oh, God. I'm sorry — I'm upsetting you both. I'll stop.'

'No, Eva,' said Rory, taking his head from his hands, and moving to sit beside her on the couch. 'Keep talking. We want to hear anything you have to say — don't we, Deirdre?' He shot her a look, and she nodded.

'Thanks. I'm most grateful to you both. It's a great relief to talk.' Eva's smile was looking more strained, Deirdre noticed. 'However. To die by my own hand is not an option because no whiff of suicide must ever get to the wet-nosed gutter press. No matter how dignified my exit, the scandal sheets would distort it, and I don't want my death to be scandalous because that will make life hell on earth for David and Dorcas.'

Hell on earth, Deirdre thought, was what Eva was going through now. She was living a nightmare. This was deathbed stuff.

Eva's voice was going a bit wobbly. 'Look after David, won't you, you two? Help him through. Oh!' A little laugh. 'Sorry — I sound like Melanie in *Gone with the Wind*.'

'Except you're a better actress than Olivia de Havilland,' observed Rory.

'Thank you. She was an awful milksop in that, wasn't she? You know — I'd love for David to marry again after he's gone through the whole grieving process. Some gorgeous young thing like our nanny, Astrid. Dorcas *adores* her — she'd be ideal marriage material!'

Oh, God. This was awful. Eva contemplating

David's future after her own death had made the whole thing seem much more real, and Deirdre knew she was going to cry. Quickly she got to her feet. 'Sorry. I need to go to the loo,' she said.

In Eva's *en suite* she cried — *again*. So many tears! The world really *was* a vale of them; then she wrung out a wodge of loo paper in cold water and applied it to her swollen eyes. When she went back into Eva's sitting room, the actress was lying on the couch with her head in Rory's lap, and Rory was stroking her hair.

Eva sent her an apologetic smile. 'Sorry, darling. I just wanted to borrow your gorgeous great hunk of comforting manhood until my own gets here.'

Deirdre adopted her best light tone, trying to sound conversational. 'When's he due?'

'Any time now. He and Dorcas are flying in for the wrap party. Dorcas is wildly excited. I've got her a new gúna to wear, and . . . '

It was harrowing listening to Eva talking about Dorcas and her new party dress when the actress was preparing for death. Deirdre had to change the subject. She looked at Eva with desperate eyes and cast around for something to say that might help. And all she could come up with was: 'Well! This is a pretty pickle!'

'It is indeed!' said Eva with a laugh. 'It's a fine kettle of fish, a grand can of worms and a big bag of cats to boot.' 'Polite' mode purred from her handbag. Eva lifted herself off Rory's lap with a visible effort and fished out her phone. Her expression when she registered the display verged on the incandescent.

'David!' she said into the receiver. 'Where are you? Fantastic! Come up at once!' Ending the call, she turned to Deirdre and Rory. 'I'm going to have to chase you,' she said. 'My beloveds are downstairs.' Eva made to stand up, and then something awful happened. She crumpled in on herself and landed back on the couch, sagging and looking ashen.

'Eva!' said Deirdre. 'Let me get a doctor!'

'*No!*' She uttered the word so fiercely it emerged as a snarl. 'No doctor. Just give me my pills, please.'

The pillbox was on the coffee table. Deirdre shook one onto the palm of her hand and gave it to Eva, who swigged it back with champagne. She held out her hand again. 'Give me another one,' she said, then, on seeing Deirdre hesitate: 'Give me *another* one, Deirdre,' she repeated.

Deirdre obliged.

'Now put them back in my bag, and hand me the mirror that's in there.'

Again Deirdre obliged, handing Eva a little vanity mirror.

The actress inspected her face and tidied her hair, and then she tucked her feet under her on the couch and rearranged the folds of her dress. She looked up at Rory and gave him a big smile. 'I'm ready for my close-up, Mr de Mille!' she said.

'And you look bloody gorgeous, Ms Lavery,' replied Rory. He took her hand and lifted it to his lips.

Eva raised a flirtatious eyebrow at him before giving an autocratic little wave of her hand. 'Now

431

— *shoo*, you two!' she said. 'And don't worry! Be happy!'

Once outside the room, Rory took Deirdre in his arms and they held each other tightly until they heard the chattering sound of Dorcas's voice on the stairs. Then, turning, they ran in the opposite direction, hand in tear-wet hand.

18

Dannie was scrubbing the surround of the fireplace with great force when there came the sound of a car horn from outside the cottage. She went to the window and looked out. Parked outside the garden gate was a nifty little red Corvette, and Paloma was waving from the passenger seat like a member of the royal family.

Dannie ran to the door and down the path. Jethro was getting out of the driver's seat, and her heart did something stupid. She tried to make her welcoming smile merely friendly, but it was compromised by the blush she felt starting to rise.

'Howrya, Jethro!' she managed, and then 'Howrya, Paloma! Welcome home, honeybun. What has you riding in such style?'

'Dad got a fun car to drive me round. We thought a show-fur was too grand for places like the seaside.'

Dannie had seen the Corvette parked outside the hotel on occasion, but hadn't made the connection with Jethro.

'Are we going back to living in the cottage, Ma?' asked Paloma now, getting out of the car.

'For the meantime, lovie.'

'And Oliver too?'

'Ah, maybe not.' Oh, sweet Jesus, Mary and Joseph. She hadn't expected to have to deal with the issue of Oliver so soon. She'd have to stall.

'Go on in there, now, to the house. There's chocolate cake in the fridge.'

'Chocolate cake!' Paloma scooted to the front door, then turned round. 'Coming, Da?'

'No, sweetheart. I have a lunch date. Blow me a kiss, then go get your cake.'

Left alone with Jethro, Dannie's face went redder. 'Thanks for looking after her,' she said.

'It was my pleasure. I had Eva's nanny, Astrid, to help out. She's a star.'

Dannie felt a flash of jealousy. She had seen Astrid on a couple of occasions. She was young and blond and golden of skin, and she had a fantastically infectious laugh. Eva had told her that Dorcas was mad about her. 'So,' she said, changing the subject, 'what made you hire a nifty red Corvette?'

'I did it for Paloma. I felt guilty that I wasn't able to spend as much time with her as I wanted, so any time I could we took off for the beach with the soft top down. More fun for her than a stuffy chauffeur-driven Merc.'

'It's a beaut. It reminds me of — '

They looked at each other. They both knew what the car reminded her of. It was as sexy a motor as the little soft-topped Karmann Ghia that Jethro had presented her with once upon a time in another life.

'Feel free to take a spin,' he said. 'She's a dream to drive.'

Dannie shook her head. 'Thanks, but I'd better get back to the wean.'

There was a pause, then Jethro said: 'My having Paloma to stay wasn't just about her

434

missing me, was it?'

Another pause, then Dannie shook her head. 'No. You're right. I had . . . issues to sort. I needed some head space.'

'Issues — to do with Oliver?'

'Yes.'

'It hasn't worked out for you, Dannie?'

'No, Jethro. It hasn't.'

His eyes went to her ringless left hand, and just then Astrid waltzed round the corner. 'Got them!' she said, brandishing choc ices.

'How I *luff* Irish ice-cream!'

Oh, God, thought Dannie. This honey-skinned beach babe even had a sexy Swedish accent. Could life get any *worse*?

'Astrid,' said Jethro, 'this is Dannie. Dannie, Astrid.'

'Hi!' Astrid juggled ice-creams and wiped her right hand on the seat of her shorts before extending it to Dannie. 'It's so great to meet you at last. I've had such fun looking after Paloma all week — haven't we, Jethro? I'd have been very bored if it hadn't been for her. Thank you for lending her to me.'

'You're welcome,' said Dannie. 'I hope she was well behaved.'

'She was just-right behaved, but not too *well* behaved. Kids who are too well behaved have less fun, in my experience — my darling Dorcas being a case in point. Sometimes she can be a real brat!' Astrid gave Dannie the benefit of her great smile, and then she turned to Jethro. 'Can I drive back to the hotel? I am so *dying* to have a go of that car.'

'Sure,' said Jethro. 'But let's leave it until after lunch. We're going to O'Toole's for crab claws, Dannie,' he told her. 'D'you want to join us?'

Dannie could think of no more extreme torture than being sat across a table from these two *rides*, watching them gnawing on crab claws and sucking the juice from their fingers. 'No, thanks,' she said, with a smile that a ghoul might have found frightening. 'I'd better get back to Paloma. There's probably chocolate cake all over the kitchen floor by now.'

'Oh,' said Astrid. 'She's having chocolate cake? She won't want this, then.' She held the spare choc ice aloft. 'I know, Dannie. You can have it!'

The ice-cream was in Dannie's hand before she could demur. 'Thanks,' she said.

'By the way,' Jethro said over his shoulder as he held the car door open for Astrid, 'the wrap party's tonight. You're very welcome to come.'

'Thanks,' said Dannie again. 'But I don't want to go out on Paloma's first night back in the cottage.'

And then, with a flurry of 'Byes' and 'See you arounds', the happy couple got into the little red Corvette and drove off, leaving Dannie standing holding her choc ice and looking like someone who'd just been handed the booby prize.

* * *

In O'Tooles, the McDonagh-O'Dares were sitting at a long table having chowder and chips when they saw Eva Lavery walk past the window in the direction of the transport Merc that was parked on the other side of the road. Deirdre rapped on the glass, and Eva waved at them, and mouthed 'Hi!' The next moment she was coming though the door. She was wearing jeans and a T-shirt, and Deirdre noticed for the first time that she'd lost a fair amount of weight.

'Hi, pals,' said Eva, sitting down at their table next to where Deirdre sat with Bruno on her lap. 'Go on — give me a go of Bruno, Deirdre. I have a craving to grab handfuls of plump baby flesh. Look at you, gorgeous!' she crooned as Deirdre handed him over. 'How many hearts are you going to break in your lifetime?'

Bruno looked aghast. 'None!' he said. 'Bruno good boy!'

'What can I get you to drink, Eva?' asked Rory, getting to his feet.

'A glass of Guinness would be lovely, thanks.' Eva settled Bruno in her lap and starting squeezing his chubby bits with gentle fingers.

'How are you feeling today, Eva?' Deirdre tried very hard not to invest the words with too much meaning, but it was difficult.

'I'm fine, darling.' She leaned down and reached into her bag, then held up her pillbox and shook it. 'These little mojos are *the* business.'

'And how are David and Dorcas?'

'Great form. They're taking it easy back at the hotel. Alton Towers did for David. He says he's never been so scared in his life. Dorcas had a blast, of course. Ooh, baby — let me nibble your little earlobe! Let me poke your chubby cheek! Let me inhale your glorious *babyness*!' And Eva

437

leaned over Bruno and breathed in with relish.

'I wouldn't do that if I were you, Eva,' warned Aoife. 'Sometimes Bruno pongs worse than a stink bomb. I always spray him with Mom's perfume before I go near him.'

'Not today, he doesn't pong. He smells just the way a baby should. Don't you, Broonie Woonie Croonie? 'To *market*, to *market* — to buy a fine horse!'' And Eva ruggled and bounced Bruno until he laughed out loud.

'What brings you into Kilrowan, Eva?' asked Deirdre, admiring the way Eva was handling her son. Bruno didn't allow many people to 'ruggle' him.

'I wanted to buy thank-you presents for the cast and crew — but of course I haven't been able to get everything I want. The bookshop's closed due to a bereavement, so I can't buy up all the signed copies of *The Faraway* for people. Joke,' she added, as she saw Deirdre's alarmed expression. 'But I did want to get a load of those beautiful hand-made maps of Connemara as souvenirs. Filming here has been one of the most joyous shoots of my life. I'm going to have to dash into Galway this afternoon to get them. Why do I always leave everything till the last moment?'

'Because you've got so much going on in your life that you can't manage to stuff everything in,' said Deirdre. In spite of her thinness, Eva was looking more robust than she had yesterday. Her painkillers must have kicked in bigtime: she seemed so vibrant that it was impossible to think that she had so little time left. Not even six

438

months of life lay ahead of her. Deirdre couldn't allow herself to dwell on it. She'd only start blubbing again if she did. 'Are you all set for the party tonight?' she asked, noticing abstractedly that she'd got pretty adept at changing the subject recently. Well, it was one way of coping with the awfulness of real life, she thought: keeping it at bay with the adroitness of a parrying swordsman.

'Damn right I'm set,' said Eva, looking hungrily at Grace's plate. 'Can I have one of your chips, Grace?'

'Yeah, but they have ketchup on. Do you mind?'

'Not at all. I love ketchup.' Eva leaned across the table and helped herself to a handful of fat chips. As she did so, something outside the window distracted her. 'Holy schomoly! Look at the flash car Palmer's just pulled up in! What a beaut! What is it, d'you know?' She directed the question at Rory, who'd just come back with her Guinness.

'It's a Corvette,' he said. 'I saw Jethro in it earlier. He picked it up in some fancy car-hire place in Galway to ferry Paloma around.'

'A red Corvette! Just fancy. Like in my very favourite Prince song of all time. How sexy is that!'

The door to the pub opened and Jethro walked in with Astrid, who pretended to be scared when she saw Eva. 'Sorry, boss,' she said. 'I was just taking Paloma back to Dannie. I'll be back on Dorcas duty straight after lunch.'

'Take your time,' said Eva. 'Dorcas is fine. I

439

told her that if she wanted to stay up for the party tonight she'd have to take a nap in the afternoon, because she's jaded after Alton Towers. David'll have tucked her up in bed by now.' She indicated to the waitress to set two more places at the table. 'Join us,' she told Jethro and Astrid.

'A nap?' said Deirdre. 'A nap sounds like a bloody good idea, Eva. I'll make those girls take one this afternoon as well, otherwise they'll be pure crotchety by midnight and ruin the party for me. I have absolutely no intention of playing Cinderella this evening.'

Jethro sat down in the chair next to Eva. 'I *love* your car,' she told him. 'You have the best taste in cars of any man I know.'

He shrugged. 'It's a bit girly for me,' he replied. 'I really hired it for Paloma. Do you want a go in it? You can drive us back to Ballynahinch after lunch if you like, if you don't mind a squeeze. It's strictly a two-seater. Astrid and Paloma were sardined in the passenger seat this morning on the way to the beach.'

'Oh, but *yes*! I'd love a go.'

'Boo hoo,' said Astrid. 'You said you'd allow *me* to drive back.'

'Cat fight over a Corvette!' said Rory. 'Go, you girls!'

'How about this?' said Eva. 'Let Astrid drive back to the hotel, and I'll take the car on into Galway. I've shopping to do there — as long, of course, as that's OK with you, Jethro?'

'Sure,' he said equably. 'I might come in with you. I could use a massage. But I'll share the

440

Merc with you and David tonight, Eva, if you don't mind. I'm planning on getting mildly trashed and I'll want to be driven home.'

'Perfect. Quid pro quo,' said Eva, gazing out the window at the covetable convertible. 'Oh, I love the idea of driving barefoot through Connemara with the sun on my face and the wind in my hair. Pity I've no Isadora Duncan-ish scarf to trail after me.'

'You can have mine,' said Deirdre, unwinding a swirl of rainbow-coloured silk chiffon from around her neck and draping it over Eva's shoulders. 'This is great for driving in convertibles.'

'When did you last drive in a convertible?' asked Rory.

'Well, the back of your motorbike's nearly as good,' she amended.

'Do you really drive barefoot, Eva?' asked Jethro.

'Eva's driven barefoot for as long as I've known her,' said Deirdre, remembering how she'd come across the actress barefoot in a Spar shop once, not long after she'd first met her. How far away that time seemed!

'Do your feet smell, Eva?' asked Grace.

'Grace! Mind your manners,' said Rory.

'Well, if I didn't *wash* them they'd smell,' said Eva. 'I dunno what they smell like right now.'

'Worse than Bruno, d'you think?'

Eva laughed. 'Maybe not worse than Bruno after he's done a poo.'

'Well, that's the grossest smell in the world.' Grace and Aoife had finished their chips. 'Can we go to the shop and get ice-creams?' asked Aoife.

'You can have ice-cream here,' Deirdre told them.

'But ice cream's more fun on a stick!'

'Oh, go on, then.' Deirdre fished in her bag for her purse, but Eva pre-empted her.

'Here,' she said, handing Aoife a fifty-euro note. 'Buy the dearest ice-creams in the shop and keep the change.'

'Eva! You spoil them!' said Deirdre, as the girls gabbled their thanks and then shot off to the shop.

'Allow me to spoil them a little,' said Eva. 'There's not enough spoiling going on in the world. I'm going to spend the rest of my life spoiling people rotten. The ones who matter, that is. I gave David a first-rate massage this morning — ' a lustful groan escaped Rory, and Deirdre shot him a look of mock-reproval ' — and when Dorcas wakes up from her nap she'll find her new party frock hanging at the foot of her bed. Come to think of it, I'd better remind David to put it there. It's the kind of detail men tend to forget.'

Eva took her phone from her bag, and her pillbox, and Deirdre looked the other way while Eva surreptitiously popped one of her 'mojos'. Through the window she could see a long-suffering James reading the sports pages in the driver's seat of Eva's transport Merc.

'While you're at it, you should let your driver off the hook, Eva,' she said, nodding towards the car. 'I'm sure James has better things to do than hang around Kilrowan all afternoon.'

'You're absolutely right, darling,' said Eva. 'How thoughtless of me. Oh — look! Here's another tape for you.' She took an envelope out of her bag and passed it to Deirdre. 'Remember you asked me if I had any anecdotes to do with filming the remake of *All About Eve*? There's some great stuff on this about Sophie Burke, but you may not be able to use it. It could be libellous. Excuse me.' And Eva went outside to dismiss her driver and call her husband.

Deirdre watched the actress through the window as she spoke to David. She paced the footpath as she spoke, but her pace had a spring in it. Occasionally she'd throw back her head and laugh. The rainbow-coloured chiffon scarf drifted around her as she moved, giving her the appearance of having gossamer wings.

'Look,' said Rory. 'She's Titania.'

'Who's Titania? asked Astrid.

Jethro looked appalled. 'Where were you educated?' he said. 'Don't you know your Shakespeare?'

'Never read him in my life,' said Astrid cheerfully.

'Then let me enlighten you. Titania,' said Jethro, 'was the Queen of the fairies.'

'Queen of the fairies? No,' said Astrid, scrutinizing Eva through the window. 'My boss is not a wiffy-waffy fairy. She's an angel.'

Deirdre smiled as she watched Eva. Only she knew who Eva Lavery really was, she thought, as she watched the actress turn and smile back at her through the pub window. Eva Lavery was someone who made good things happen. Eva Lavery was a white witch. Eva Lavery *was* Mimi of the Remedies.

★ ★ ★

An hour later they were ready to go. The party settled the bill and headed for their respective cars. Deirdre called to Aoife and Grace, who were watching fish being gutted on the pier with manifest fascination. Eva gave a sleeping Bruno over to Deirdre, and kissed her on the cheek. 'By the way,' she said. 'Can I keep this scarf? It's highly desirable.'

'Of course you can,' said Deirdre. 'The colour's better on you than it is on me, anyway.'

Then Aoife and Grace came running up to Eva to say thank you to her for the ice-creams, and Deirdre overheard Aoife whispering: 'Don't tell Mom and Dad, but we bought a farting machine in the shop. It's the best thing we've ever bought. We're going to play great tricks on people at the party tonight!'

'Thanks for the warning,' replied Eva in a low voice. 'In that case I'll know not to sit down *anywhere* tonight!'

There was a kerfuffle as Fluffy appeared and the girls admired her hair accessories, and then Rory approached Eva and kissed her on both cheeks. 'I'd love another snog,' he said, 'but somehow I don't think it's appropriate in front of the kids. Catch you later, Lavery.'

'Eva! Come on,' shouted Jethro from the passenger seat of the Corvette. 'We gotta make

444

tracks if you're to get in and out of Galway before this evening.'

'Listen!' Eva's face lit up. 'He's playing 'Little Red Corvette' on the sound system. How perfect can you get!'

She turned and ran across the road to where Astrid was gunning the engine, and climbed nimbly onto Jethro's lap. Astrid put the car into gear and took off down the main street of the village with a '*Whee!*'

Eva laughed, and turned to wave goodbye to Deirdre and Rory, silk chiffon flying in the breeze, hair a golden pennant. And then the car rounded a bend in the road and was gone.

★ ★ ★

Later that afternoon Dannie and Paloma were in Breda Shanley's shop, buying fish fingers for supper. The food in the hotel had been good, Paloma had told her mum, but it had been a bit too posh for her. Tonight she wanted fish fingers and oven chips, and could they watch one of the new DVDs Daddy had given her?

Paloma's wish was Dannie's command.

'Hey. Long time, no see. How are things?' Breda asked Dannie as she came through the door.

Dannie could tell that the question was loaded. Word must be out that she was back living in her cottage. It was time to play the 'Go Fetch' game with Paloma, so as to keep her out of earshot. 'Paloma,' she said. 'Go fetch me a carton of milk, a box of whatever cereal you fancy, and the drinking chocolate I like. The Green and Black's one.' The child scooted off obligingly.

'Well?' Breda raised an eyebrow.

Dannie knew there was no point in beating about the bush where Breda was concerned. Her friend was too shrewd to be fobbed off with fibs. She went for it. 'You might as well know that things aren't good, Breda. I've left Oliver. I won't be going back to him, and I won't go into details.'

Breda nodded. 'That's fair enough. And I won't pry.'

Dannie swallowed. Thinking about Oliver made her throat go dry and her heart rate accelerate in a most unpleasant way. 'Have you seen him?' she asked.

'A couple of times, in the car. He hasn't been into the shop. Neither has Alice. The hotel has opened, though.' Breda looked to left and right, then lowered her voice. 'Word has it it's turned into a money pit, and it's not doing as well as — '

Dannie didn't want to hear anything more about the Dunnes. 'I'm putting the shop on the market, Breda,' she blurted.

Breda looked stunned. 'Jesus, Mary and Joseph, Dannie! Why?'

'I've got to get out of this village. Maybe even get out of this country.'

'But — this is your *home*!'

Dannie shook her head. 'Not any more. Not since Da died and Michael and Leanne got the cottage. Hey! Good girl,' she said to Paloma, who had come back with the requested items. 'Now go fetch me a pack of loo roll, the yoghurts you like and the washing-up liquid with the baby fairy on it.' She turned back to Breda. 'I've done it before,' she resumed, when Paloma had disappeared. 'I did it when I left Kilrowan for London, I did it when I left London for Dublin, and I did it when I came back here to start over with Paloma. I can do it again.'

'But *where* will you go?'

'I don't know. I suppose the world's my oyster. Paloma's at an age where it would be easy enough for her to settle anywhere. She could pick up a new language like *that*.' Dannie snapped her fingers.

'Yeah.' Breda looked sceptical. 'But could *you*?'

'My French isn't bad. I did an exchange one summer years ago. It'll be rusty now, of course, but I wouldn't rule France out. I hear the Languedoc's beautiful.' Dannie was talking off the top of her head. She still had no idea where in the world she wanted to go. All she knew with any certainty was that the magic of Connemara was tarnished, that it would never polish up for her, and that it was time to move on.

'Would LA be an option, maybe?'

Breda was clearly trying to figure out if a reunion with Jethro was on the cards. 'No. Absolutely not,' Dannie told her. 'Jethro and I are ancient history.'

'But is that the way you want it, girl?'

From the way Breda was looking at her, Dannie knew that her misery was showing in her face. 'Let's just say I made a mistake of monumental proportions,' she said. 'Hey! Genius!' Paloma had materialized with the groceries. 'Now. Can you think of anything else we need?'

'Ice-cream,' said Paloma.

'The machine's broken,' said Breda. 'But go on over to the cabinet and see what takes your fancy. And the ice-cream's on me.'

'Thank you, Breda!' Paloma was off again.

'What do I owe you?' Dannie took her purse out of her bag as Breda started ringing up the bill. 'And are you sure about the ice-cream?'

'Course I'm sure.'

'It's tragic, so it is,' came a Northern Irish accent as a couple of elderly tourists opened the shop door. 'It was completely written off.' Dannie's ears pricked up. 'I hope the ambulance managed to make it into Galway in time through all that traffic. That ring road was chock-a-block.'

'Sports cars like that shouldn't be allowed,' came the response. 'There's always the temptation to drive too fast in a car like that. I know somebody who — '

Dannie's brain was feeling so fizzy she almost couldn't speak. 'Excuse me?' she said, turning to the couple. 'Has there been a car accident somewhere?'

'Oh, yes, miss. There has. A car went off the road on a bend near Oughterard. It was a complete write-off, so it was.'

'What kind of a car was it?' asked Dannie. Her brain was feeling fizzier.

448

'It was one of them American cars — a convertible.'

'Not a Corvette?'

'Yes, that's exactly what it was. A wee red Corvette,' said the man.

19

Deirdre was getting ready for the wrap party, which was due to start at six o'clock in the village hall. She was wearing the dress she'd worn the evening Rory had gunned his hired motorcycle out of Kilrowan — the dress that had been intended for Jethro's birthday dinner — and she was sitting in front of the mirror trying to do something with her hair.

Rory came into the room with a glass of wine for her. 'It's crap,' she said. 'Bloody *Fluffy's* hair looked better than mine today. Cleo must have some hairdressery knack — maybe I should ask her to come round and do mine.'

'Who's Cleo?'

'Cleo,' said Deirdre, 'is the girl I told you about. The one who was *really* having an affair with Pablo.' She was delighted to see that the meaningful emphasis she put on the word 'really' made Rory flinch.

'Don't remind me,' said Rory, coming up behind her. 'Anyway, I think you look gorgeous. And even more gorgeous since that Botox has started to wear off.' He set the glass down on her dressing table, kissed the nape of her neck, then slid a hand down her décolletage and cupped her breast.

'What are you doing, Dad?' came a reedy voice from the doorway.

'I'm just checking to make sure that your

mom's dress is on right,' he said, withdrawing his hand and smoothing the silk over her shoulders. 'Doesn't she look pretty!'

'Is Bruno coming to the party tonight?'

'No. He wouldn't enjoy it.'

'Yay!' And Grace ran back into the sitting room and chanted: 'You're no-ot coming! You're no-ot coming!'

'Stop it, Grace!' called Deirdre. 'It's not fair on Emma if you wind him up. She's the one who's going to have to cope with him once we're gone.' She hooked on a pair of dangly earrings, took a sip of wine, and then said: 'I'm ready. How about you?'

'Yeah. Let's go.'

They said goodbye to Emma and Bruno, who was doing finger painting with yoghurt on a tray, and left the flat.

Out on the street, Aoife and Grace took off in the direction of the village hall, where bunting was festooned around windows and doors. Tubs of flowers had been strategically placed at the front of the building in an attempt to cheer up its air of breeze-block functionality, and waltz music was floating from speakers.

The village looked particularly pretty today with its bobbing boats and its canopy of benign blue sky: the atmosphere was one of relaxed festivity. A tour bus went past, and all the passengers craned their necks as they passed Mimi's polka-dotted front door. The fact that a major movie had just been filmed here had put Kilrowan even more firmly on the tourist map.

Deirdre and Rory strolled hand in hand past

the bookshop (where Colleen's book was still prominently displayed in the window) and the harbour and Breda's store. They strolled past O'Toole's pub and the post office and the lane that led down to Dannie's cottage. Smoke was coming from the chimney, Deirdre noticed: Dannie must have found a tenant. They strolled on past 1, 2, 3 and 4, the Blackthorns — where a gleaming camper van was parked — and came to a halt at number 5, where Aoife and Grace were staring at the burnt-out ruin of Cleo's house.

'Jesus! What happened there?' asked Rory.

'That's Cleo's house — you know, the Cleo who was *really* having an affair with Pablo?' She gave him her best disingenuous look, and Rory raised his eyes to heaven.

'Yeah yeah yeah — but what happened to her house?' he asked.

'She left a candle burning. It's bloody tragic — she'd only just moved in after winning the lottery.'

Just then the door of the camper van opened, and Fluffy emerged, followed by a barefoot Cleo, who was looking rather tousled, as if she'd just fallen out of bed.

'That's Cleo,' Deirdre told Rory. 'The one who's *really* — '

'I get the picture.'

'Hey, Cleo!' she called. 'What's with the camper van?'

'Deirdre, hi!' Cleo beckoned excitedly. 'Come and have a look around our new home!'

'*Our* new home?'

'Yes! We're going travelling. Come in, come in! Isn't it gorgeous!'

Aoife, who had lost interest in the burnt-out building, had hunkered down to pet Fluffy. 'Can Grace and me play with your dog?' she asked Cleo. 'We love her hair accessories.'

'Of course! Of course! Play away!'

On the step of the camper van, Deirdre introduced Rory to Cleo, who said: '*Another* film star? This calls for champagne — even though I'm getting quite blasé about film stars now. Welcome to my humble abode!'

They stepped into the camper van, and Cleo moved to the fridge and took out a bottle of Veuve Clicquot. 'Will you get glasses, Deirdre? They're in that cupboard. I've spent the past hour unpacking all my new purchases and making the place homey.' She stripped off the foil and the wire, popped the cork, and poured. 'Cheers!' she said, handing flutes to Deirdre and Rory. 'Here's to our travels!'

'Are you actually living here?' asked Deirdre, looking round. There was a jug of flowers on the table beside a half-empty cafetière and two mugs. There was a stack of carrier bags on a banquette. Fluffy's lead hung from a hook and there, resplendent on the wall, was the nude portrait of Cleo, with her own face on.

'Yes.'

'And Pablo's finished your portrait.'

'Yes!'

'It's really very lovely,' said Rory, looking at the portrait. 'You don't — um — *mind* me scrutinizing it, do you?'

'Not at all,' said Cleo complacently. 'I've decided I'm completely shameless.'

'What's the significance of the cockatoo?'

In the portrait, a white cockatoo was nibbling at Cleo's rosy toes.

'A cockatoo symbolizes devotion,' said Cleo. 'They're the original lovebirds, don'tchaknow.'

'This masterly portrait,' said Deirdre, giving Rory a look of hauteur, 'is the one I was telling you about. The one that Pablo painted of Cleo, who is, as you may have realized by now, the broad who is *really* having an affair with — oops!' She stopped short and sent Cleo a guilty look. 'Don't worry, Cleo, I promise I haven't told anybody else.'

'I don't mind who you tell,' said Cleo happily. 'It's all out in the open now.'

'What? Your dangerous liaison with Pablo?'

'Yes. Isn't it brilliant? It's not dangerous any more. Colleen's gone off with Margot, so she can hardly rant and rave about Pablo getting it on with me.'

'*Margot?*' Deirdre sat down on the banquette and shook her head in disbelief. '*What* have you just said, Cleo? Colleen and *Margot*? Are you having me on?'

'No. God's honest truth. Margot's decided she's a lesbian, and she's become Colleen's new muse.'

'When did you find out?'

'Just before my Blackthorn burnt down. At first I thought that Colleen must have burnt it down out of vengeance, but even she's not that doolally. Anyway, she's kicked Pablo out of *his*

454

Blackthorn, so we decided to buy a camper van. We went into Galway today to pick it up, and of course I had to buy a whole load of new clothes because all my threads got ruined in the fire.' Cleo moved to the stack of Brown Thomas bags that had been dumped on the banquette. 'Look at this!' she said, taking a little filigreed confection from the glossy carrier and displaying it to Deirdre. 'Isn't it delicious! I'm going to wear it tonight, to the party. It's a Lainey Keogh,' she added, 'but I *did* get it in the sale, and the insurance money'll pay for it.'

Rory gave her an amused look. 'It never ceases to amaze me,' he said, 'the way women have to justify expensive purchases — even a lottery winner like you, Cleo.'

'It's just habit. I was quite poor, once, you see. But now I can afford to celebrate the purchase of a camper van with vintage Veuve Clicquot and Louise Kennedy crystal. Pablo's started calling me trailer trash.'

'When did he move out of his Blackthorn?' asked Deirdre.

'He hasn't yet — he doesn't have to pack his bags for a couple of weeks because Colleen gave him a month's notice. But we've decided that it's much more fun living here. We're going to try out the power sofa later.'

'What's a power sofa?'

'Apparently it makes bedmaking easier.'

'Sounds like my kind of sofa.'

'That's exactly what I said!'

'Where's Pablo now?' asked Deirdre.

'Gone off to sort things out with Colleen.'

455

'Will there be sparks?'

'Oh, no — I don't mean sort out their relationship. I mean sort things out financially. She's an incredibly shrewd businesswoman, you know.'

'Really?'

'Mm hm. She knows how much she's owed down to every last red cent of rent. She won't let him off by so much as a penny.'

'What about Colleen and Margot?' Deirdre felt very strange referring to Colleen and Margot as an item. 'What are they going to do? Has Margot — um — come out yet?'

'Oh yeah — she's moved into Colleen's spooky house. But I heard a rumour in Breda's shop today that Colleen's bought an island on Clew Bay, and that they're going there to live in splendid Sapphic isolation.'

'Jesus!' said Rory, his voice full of admiration. 'I'd *love* to be a girl. I'd *love* to be able to speak girl-talk the way you two do. Can I be your girlfriend, Cleo, like in the Prince song, and watch you get into your party frock?'

Cleo's smile was wider than Kate Hudson's. 'I don't think my lov*air* would allow that.'

'And I don't think *I* would, either,' said Deirdre, sending Rory a glance of mock-reproval. She looked back at Cleo, who was sitting on the banquette opposite, hugging her knees to her chest. Her chin was resting on her knees, and she looked like the cat who'd got the full-fat double cream. Deirdre had to hand it to her. 'You're really, really happy, Cleo, aren't you?'

'Yes,' she said, sounding categorical. 'And I'm not ashamed of it. It's something I learned from Eva. You don't have to be embarrassed about being happy. There's no point in me being all apologetic just because I won the lottery. What's the use of having that kind of money if it's only going to make me feel guilty and miserable?'

'You're absolutely right,' said Deirdre.

But the mention of Eva had made her go empty inside. It would be very tough indeed having to act happy and sociable at this shindig tonight. 'We'd better get a move on, Rory,' she said, knocking back the remains of her champagne. 'I promised Eva we'd get to the party early because Dorcas is dying to meet up with the girls again.'

'Oops! The party!' said Cleo. 'I'd better get my act together and shimmy into my little Lainey.'

Deirdre set her glass down and moved to the door of the camper van. When she saw Rory direct another appreciative look at Cleo's portrait, she gave him a dig with her elbow.

'Sorry,' he said, not sounding sorry at all.

Outside, Fluffy was being taught tricks by Aoife and Grace. 'Fetch! Fetch! Fetch!' Aoife was saying, pointing to where Grace was standing several yards away, holding out a stick. But Fluffy just sat there and smilingly refused to oblige.

'Bad dog!' Grace told her. 'Bad, bad, bad dog!'

'Come on, girls,' said Rory. 'It's time to party.'

'If I don't see you later,' said Deirdre over her shoulder to Cleo, who was standing in the doorway of the camper van, watching them go, 'enjoy your power sofa!'

'I will,' said Cleo, just as the Angelus started to ring six o'clock. She looked anxious suddenly. 'Oh! Six o'clock. I must watch the news. I don't mean to rain on your parade, but I've just remembered something awful — we passed a dreadful accident near Oughterard on our way back this afternoon. Ironic that you should have mentioned a Prince song, Rory.'

Deirdre turned, curious. 'What on earth has an accident to do with a Prince song, Cleo?'

'The car involved was a Corvette,' she said. 'A little red Corvette.'

*   *   *

Deirdre and Rory ran to the village hall, dragging the girls with them. There weren't many people there yet — just the catering staff and a handful of people putting finishing touches to the décor. There were bunches of bright helium balloons everywhere, and tables covered in polka-dotted tablecloths, and tangles of tickertape. There were plates piled high with iced buns and sandwiches and there were jars of multicoloured sweets on each table. 'The Blue Danube' was playing. The idea had been to give the party an old-fashioned vibe because *Mimi's Remedies* was such an old-fashioned kind of film.

Deirdre approached one of the sparks who was rigging fairy lights. 'Have you heard anything?' she asked him breathlessly, 'about an accident?'

'What kind of accident?'

'A car accident on the Galway road?'

The electrician looked bemused. 'No,' he said.

Deirdre and Rory looked at each other. 'Maybe we should just hot-tail it back to Cleo,' said Rory. 'See if there's anything about it on the news.'

'No,' said Deirdre. 'I've a better idea.' She reached into her bag, produced her mobile and speed-dialled first Jethro's number, then Eva's. 'They've both gone to voice mail,' she said, looking at Rory with desperate eyes. She remembered how someone had described the aftermath of a rail disaster — how the most unendurable thing had been hearing mobile phones going off in the wreckage — and she put her face in her hands. 'Oh Christ,' she said, swaying a little. 'What can we do?'

'We'll go back to Cleo's,' said Rory with authority.

They headed back up the road, the girls protesting. As they drew near the Blackthorns they saw Dannie Moore on the village street, looking distraught and carrying Paloma on her hip.

'Dannie!' called Deirdre, waving to attract her attention.

The two parties converged outside Pablo's house. The faces of both women were strained.

'Have you heard?' asked Dannie.

'The Corvette?'

'Yes.'

'*The news!*' said Dannie. 'It's bound to be on the six o'clock news. I'll — '

'Cleo's watching it.'

The door to the camper van was still open. Cleo was standing framed in the window, her hands pressed against her mouth. Deirdre and Dannie stepped over the threshold.

On the television, Ann Doyle was wearing her grave expression as she wound up her report: ' . . . taken to Galway University Hospital. The car went off the road at a notorious blackspot not far from Oughterard. This is the third fatality on the roads in Galway since the beginning of the month.'

Displayed on the television screen was a familiar image of carnage. Red metal lay twisted by the side of a picturesque country road. Shards of glass glittered diamantine on asphalt. A hubcap gleamed on a grassy verge. A rainbow-coloured chiffon scarf hung from a thorn bush, lifting a little in the breeze.

'The driver was killed instantly,' said Cleo in a whisper.

'Jethro!' Deirdre heard Dannie's pitiful cry from behind her.

'No,' said Cleo. 'It wasn't a man's body they took from the wreckage. It was the body of a woman.'

★ ★ ★

It was almost as bad as the time Rory had left her. She reached for him in Cleo's camper van and he wrapped her in his arms, and Deirdre knew for definite that all her tears had been cried away for ever that time they'd clung together outside Eva's suite in Ballynahinch Castle, because no tears came now, no tears at all, even though she was back in hell.

Eva was gone. Golden, gorgeous, witchy Eva was gone out of her life! Her friend, her support, her mentor, her confidante was gone for ever. She would never hear her laugh again, never share her secrets, never clink a champagne glass with her ever, ever again. She would never pick up the phone to her again, never say hello, never say goodbye. She would never say 'Sweet dreams.' She would never say 'See you tomorrow!' She would never embrace her again, never kiss her on the cheek, never whisper in her ear. She would never laugh again.

Rory was disengaging himself. Several minutes of comforting and hair-stroking and murmuring had gone on, during which Deirdre remained dry-eyed and silent. But Rory clearly had a plan. 'I know it's unendurable, darling,' he said in a hoarse voice. 'But we've things to do.'

'*Things*? What *things*? What *can* we do?'

'I'm taking the girls back to the flat and leaving them with Emma, and then I'm going down to the hall.'

'You're going to the *hall*? To the party?'

'There will be no party now,' said Rory. 'But there will be a valediction.'

'Oh!' Deirdre couldn't relinquish Eva. She couldn't let go of her friend just yet — she wasn't ready to say goodbye.

The three women stood motionless, and then Rory took action. 'Good girls,' he said to the gaggle of confused children standing on the step of the camper van, regarding parents who were behaving in a way which was quite alien to them. 'Let's go get popcorn and a DVD.'

'Can Paloma go with them?' asked Dannie. 'I've no-one to mind her.'

'Of course.' Rory stepped down from the camper van, reached down and swept Paloma up.

'Me too!' demanded Grace, reaching up her arms to her father. Rory settled Paloma on one hip and scooped Grace up to balance her on the other, and then he started to move away, tailed by Aoife. Deirdre could hear the sound of the little girls' laughter as they bounced on Rory's hip, and then came Aoife's voice saying: 'Dad? What's a valley-diction?'

'It's when you say goodbye to someone,' said Rory, and the chirrup of reedy voices receded into the distance as he made off down the road.

Deirdre and Dannie and Cleo stood looking at each other, and then Cleo moved to the table, where the half-full bottle of Veuve Clicquot still stood. She grabbed it, poured fizz into three flutes and handed them round. 'You propose the toast, Deirdre,' she said.

Deirdre nodded and adopted the stance she knew so well, the stance favoured by Eva every time *she* cracked open a bottle of champagne. She lifted her chin, tilted her head at an autocratic angle, set her shoulders back and raised her glass, holding the stem between middle finger and thumb.

'To Eva Lavery,' she said. 'The brightest star in the firmament.'

And as crystal clinked against crystal, the

462

three of them looked up through the skylight of Cleo's camper van, up towards the blue heaven that hung over Kilrowan, and said: 'To Eva.'

★ ★ ★

The village hall had taken on the air of a place of pilgrimage. It was as if people were drawn there by some supernatural force. The inhabitants of Kilrowan joined cast, crew and caterers for what Rory had described as a 'valediction' to Eva. Gradually the hall filled up until it was crowded; but the assembly was subdued — almost silent — and the fairy lights and the balloons, the jars crammed with bright sweeties and the polka-dotted tablecloths lent the event a surreal atmosphere. No music played, no champagne corks popped.

Jethro was nursing a bourbon and talking on his phone when Deirdre and Dannie found him. He looked very rough. He turned off his phone and gathered Deirdre to him, and then he reached out and took Dannie's hand. She leaned against him, and he slid his arm about her.

'Why did I allow her to take the car?' he said to Deirdre. 'Why didn't I discourage her? She looked knackered yesterday after filming — I should have *known* that it wasn't a good idea for her to drive herself anywhere.'

'How could you have known what was going to happen? You're not to start blaming yourself, Jethro, for Christ's sake,' said Deirdre.

'It's one of those fucking 'if only' situations, isn't it? 'If only' the bookshop in Kilrowan

463

hadn't been closed. 'If only' we hadn't happened to meet up in the pub. 'If only' I hadn't hired a flash car. Oh, fuck! What was I thinking of?'

'Don't, Jethro.'

Deirdre was thinking of another 'if only'. 'If only' Eva hadn't taken a painkiller shortly before driving. Had that been a contributory factor to the accident? That and the Guinness? Had it even *been* an accident? she wondered now. Had Eva decided perhaps to go for it and take her life — or rather, the ending of it — into her own hands? To end it all fast, in a sexy car with the soft top down and the wind in her hair and 'Little Red Corvette' playing on the sound system? A rock 'n' roll death for a rock 'n' roll chick . . . And then Deirdre remembered the rainbow-coloured chiffon scarf on the thorn bush, and her heart turned over. It was a sign, she felt sure. A sign from Eva to say: 'Don't worry! Be happy!'

'Have you spoken to David?' she asked now, not knowing that she could bear to hear the answer.

'Yes. He's gone into Galway to identify the body.'

'Oh, God!'

'The press are on to it already. That's how the camera crew got to the scene in time for the six o'clock news. When word got out that a $25,000 classic car had totalled, people put two and two together and realized that a celebrity had to be involved.'

'They know it's Eva?'

'Yeah. I guess. Oh, sweet Jesus!' Jethro turned

464

away and put his head in his hands. Deirdre saw Dannie reach out and touch his shoulder, and she knew it was time to leave them alone.

Every other person she saw as she walked through the village hall was talking on their mobile phone in hushed tones. Rory was no exception. 'I'm going into Galway,' he said, when he ended the call. 'David's going to need help. Will you come with me? It's cool with Emma — she said she'd stay with the kids overnight if necessary.'

'Of course I'll come.'

They left the hall to find the car park outside crowded with photographers and camera crews. The jackals had arrived already. 'There's Rory McDonagh!' rose a shout, and suddenly there were cameras in their faces and mics under their noses and they were barraged with questions.

Rory and Deirdre moved through the crowd without breaking step. They were used to this kind of attention, but that didn't make it any less unpleasant. 'How are you feeling, Rory?' 'Deirdre! I understand you're writing a biography of Eva! Are you likely to sell the movie rights?' 'How *are* you feeling, Rory?'

'How the fuck do you think I'm feeling?' said Rory directly to camera.

'Have you spoken to David Lawless?' 'Who would you see starring as Eva in a biopic?' 'There's a rumour circulating that Prince's 'Little Red Corvette' was playing in the car at the time of the accident. Could either of you corroborate that?' 'When will the funeral be?'

It was this last question that did for Rory.

'Some time after yours,' he said, grabbing the hack by the collar and jabbing a fist in his belly.

Deirdre grabbed his arm. 'No, no, Rory! No! Eva wouldn't have wanted it this way.'

Amidst outraged expletives and muttered threats of legal action, Deirdre and Rory finally made it through the crowd and walked fast to where their car was parked in the lane next to the flat. The polka dots on the front door of Mimi's shop that had used to make her smile made Deirdre feel even more gutted. She got into the car wondering if she would ever smile at anything, ever again.

It stupidly hadn't occurred to her that the drive to Galway would take them past the scene of the accident. In the distance, Deirdre saw the mangled remains of the red Corvette on the verge of the road. She turned away and covered her eyes immediately, but when Rory said, 'The scarf you gave her is still there,' Deirdre removed her hands and said: 'Stop the car.'

They pulled over and got out. A uniformed guard was on duty at the scene. Deirdre recognized him as the local Kilrowan guard, the one who'd been roped in for traffic management any time filming had taken place on the main street of the village. He looked utterly miserable.

'Padraig,' said Deirdre, and the guard took her hand and shook it and said: 'I'm sorry for your trouble. I know she was a good friend of yours.'

'She was,' said Deirdre. 'That's why I stopped. The scarf — ' she indicated the silk chiffon that glimmered in the dusk like a wraith ' — belongs to me. I lent it to Eva, and I want it back.'

The guard looked dubiously at the scarf suspended on the thorn bush. 'Ah. I'm sorry. I don't know if I can let you have it,' he said. 'That's why I'm here, you see. To stop people from helping themselves to souvenirs.'

'What do you mean?' asked Deirdre.

The guard looked stiff with embarrassment. 'Well, word is out that it was a celebrity car crash,' he said. 'Some people — um — *take* things, you know?'

'*No!*' Deirdre howled the word, and then the tears came. Rory held her until the shuddering set in, and then he looked at the guard who had gone red with mortification, and said: 'Please do this for her.'

The guard looked to his right and left as if afraid that some authority figure might be observing him, and then he moved to the thorn bush, plucked the wisp of rainbow silk from the branch and handed it to Deirdre.

'Thank you, Padraig,' she said, holding the scarf to her face. She closed her eyes and breathed in, and then she passed it to Rory. 'It smells of Chanel 19,' she said. 'It smells of Eva.'

★ ★ ★

It was three o'clock in the morning, and the hordes of journalists that had descended on Kilrowan were camping out at the gates of Ballynahinch Castle. Flashbulbs went off as Rory turned into the long driveway, and in the passenger seat David Lawless put his head in his hands.

The night porter greeted them when they came through the front door, and said, with manifest sincerity: 'I'm sorry for your trouble, Mr Lawless.'

David nodded. 'Thanks. I'd like a bottle of brandy brought to my room,' he told him, 'and after that I don't want to be disturbed.' He turned to Rory and Deirdre. 'Thank you both for everything. I'll be in touch.' And then David turned away and made for the stairs.

'Fuck. Fuck. Fuck.' Rory slumped against the wall, wilting at last. He'd been the proverbial tower of strength for the past six hours. 'That was the most difficult fucking thing I've ever had to do in my life. I need a drink. We're booking in,' he told the night porter, 'and can you please bring brandy for us, too?'

'Certainly, sir.'

The night porter showed them to the room they'd stayed in last time — the one with the amazing view of the river where Deirdre had taken that Garbo-esque picture of Eva. Rory tipped him, then sloshed reckless levels of brandy into glasses.

'To Eva,' he said, and Deirdre toasted the actress for the second time that evening. She slung her bag on the coffee table and lay back on the couch. She had wound the silk scarf around her head and neck because she found that inhaling Eva's scent was so comforting. Copious amounts of brandy and residual traces of Chanel 19 might keep reality at bay for a while.

'I'm completely wrecked,' said Rory. 'I'm not

going to be able to sleep. I just want to drink myself senseless.'

'Me too. But we'll be no help to David tomorrow if we do that. You've been fantastic, Rory. You've got to carry on being fantastic.' She held out a hand to him, then pulled him onto the couch beside her and wrapped her arms around him. 'Don't ever dare leave me,' she said. 'Don't ever dare die on me. I'm useless without you.'

'David's useless without Eva, that's for sure. I've never seen a man look so hollow.' Rory took a swig from his glass, then turned to her and fixed her with point-blank seriousness. 'I'm going to tell him, Deirdre,' he said.

'Tell him what?'

'Tell him about Eva's diagnosis.'

There was a silence, and then Deirdre said: 'Are you sure that's wise?'

'Yes. I am. Think about it. If I died in a car wreck tomorrow in the full of my health it would be tragic. But if you knew I had terminal cancer that could cause me incremental pain and discomfort for the remaining six months of my life, wouldn't you rather know that I'd got out fast instead of prolonging the agony and staggering on like someone in a Beckett novel? Eva died in style, the way she would have wanted. Jesus! What a way to go! I'd rather die at 100 m.p.h. on my Norton than in a hospital bed.'

'I've thought about that too. Eva couldn't have chosen a more glamorous exit.'

Rory gave her an oblique look. 'D'you think she did? Choose it?'

'The thought had struck me. I wonder, if Jethro had been with her, would the accident have happened, Rory?'

'Don't go there, baby. That kind of thinking does your head in.'

Another silence, then: 'When will you tell David?' asked Deirdre.

'After the funeral. No timing is perfect for something like this, but the knowledge may help in the aftermath.'

'How will you do it?'

'I'll show him the letter.'

'Oh, God. Will I have to be there? I don't think I could bear it.'

'No, sweetheart. You won't have to be there.' He ran a finger down her cheek, then dropped a kiss on her shoulder, and the tenderness of the gesture made Deirdre feel snuffly again. She reached for her bag and rooted for a tissue, but the first thing her hand encountered was the envelope that Eva had given her. 'Oh!' she said. 'Eva's tape.'

'What tape?' asked Rory.

'She gave me a tape earlier today — no, yesterday — in O'Toole's.'

Yesterday? It *had* been only yesterday, she realized. It felt like a lifetime ago. Dear God! The events of the past twelve hours felt like a bad dream.

She opened the envelope and took out the cassette.

'What does it say?' asked Rory. 'On the spine.'

Deirdre turned the little box over. There, on the spine, in purple ink was written one word:

'Requiescat'. They looked at each other without speaking. Each of them knew that a requiescat was a wish for the repose of a dead person's soul. Several moments passed before Deirdre could summon the resolve to take out her little tape recorder. She inserted the cassette, and white noise played. Then came the ghost of a sigh, and Eva's voice was in the room.

'Hi, Deirdre!' they heard, and Deirdre immediately pressed 'stop'.

'Can't you bear it?' asked Rory. 'Don't listen if you can't.'

Deirdre was fiddling with the ends of her scarf. She raised the silk chiffon to her face and inhaled Eva's perfume, and then she said: 'No. Go for it.'

Rory took the recorder from her, and again came that intake of breath before Eva spoke.

'Hi, Deirdre! Forgive me — I'm a bit pissed! I'm recording this in the early hours of the morning — David and Dorcas are sleeping, but I can't, so I'm running a little high on pills and champagne and adrenalin. My plan is to bamboozle you by telling you that this recording is an anecdote about the remake of *All About Eve* and Sophie's involvement, but — ha! It ain't. Although I will say that Sophie was quite sick-makingly nice to me on that shoot. I truly believe she was 'inhabiting' the character. Talk about typecasting!

'Anyway, I'll be brief. It struck me that I should outline my plans for my funeral. I haven't a clue when it will be, but if anything should happen to me between now and my projected death from you-know-what, I should like to think that someone will be clued in about the kind of send-off I want. I know David will go to pieces and won't get it right. So I thought I'd put the onus on you, as my biographer. Sorry, darling! You must rue the day I roped you in on this.

'I told you that 'Mimi' has been the happiest shoot of my life. I've kinda fallen in love with Kilrowan, so I'd like my ashes to be scattered on Lissnakeelagh strand, at the little inlet where I go skinny-dipping. I want to be cremated wearing a sarong, please, no (obvious!) make-up, but with red toenails and nude fingernails. And could you persuade somebody to do my roots, d'you think?

'Music? Something from Bono, please. And a reading of a Kate Clanchy poem I love would be splendid. Perhaps Rory would do the honours? I couldn't trust you not to blub, O'Dare! I can't remember the name of the collection it's in, but I have it by heart. It goes like this:

'I leave myself about, slatternly,
bits of me, and times I liked:
I let them go on lying where
they fall, crumple, if they will.
I know fine how to make them walk
and breathe again. Sometimes at night,
or on the train, I dream I'm dancing,
or lying in someone's arms who says
he loves my eyes in French, and again
and again I am walking up your road,
that first time, bidden and wanted,
the blossom on the trees, light,

472

light and buoyant. *Pull yourself together*, they say, quite rightly, but she is stubborn, that girl, that hopeful one, still walking . . .

'Um. What else? Oh, yes. I know it's not really the done thing any more, but I'd really like flowers. And it goes without saying that *it must be private*. If people like Ann Fitzroy or Sophie Burke show up I'll be turning in the proverbial.

'Get it right and I'll send you a sign. Please drink loads of champagne, please don't cry too much. I want a party, not a dirge. And don't worry. Be happy! *I* was! I've had a fantastic life!'

There was a click on the recording, white noise came over the speaker, and Eva's voice was silenced.

Deirdre and Rory looked at each other. And smiled.

20

At three o'clock in the morning, Jethro and Dannie were sitting on Lissnakeelagh strand. The moon was reflected in the water, silver on pewter. The rhythm of the waves was comforting, consoling — like a mother going 'hushhh! hushhh!'

Jethro was talking about Eva. He was quite drunk. His stories oscillated between the maudlin and the amusing, the sensational and the sorrowful. When he cried, Dannie held his hand. When he recalled something funny, she laughed. When he ran out of steam, he turned to her and said: 'You were always a terrific listener, Dannie.'

She shook her head. 'I've never listened hard enough. If I'd listened a bit harder to what my brother Joe had to say to me — for example — I mightn't have fouled up so spectacularly.'

'Elarobate,' said Jethro. 'I mean, *elaborate*.'

It was time to eat crow. Dannie could barely meet his eyes. 'Joe warned me years ago about getting involved with Oliver. He told me that I'd regret it. He was right.'

'Yeah?' said Jethro.

'I didn't love Oliver, Jethro. Feck it, I didn't even really know him. I wanted to marry him for all the wrong reasons, and I got my comeuppance bigtime. I deserve all the opprobrium you can heap on me, so I do.'

'Why would I want to heap opp-ro-brium?' He articulated the word very carefully.

'Because I hurt you. And I hurt Paloma, too, by messing around with our lives.'

'You were doing what you thought was for the best.' Jethro picked up a handful of sand and let it trickle through his fingers. 'And if things hadn't gone so wrong with Oliver, you could have been right to do what you did, Dannie. I've been a crap father to Paloma.'

'That doesn't mean you don't love her. It doesn't mean she doesn't love you.'

'I guess.' He looked up at the stars, as if trying to see his future in them, or hers. 'What are you going to do now?' he asked.

'I'm getting out of Kilrowan. I can't stay here, and there's nothing to keep me here any more.'

'Where will you go?'

'I don't know yet.'

Jethro took her left hand and ran his fingertips over the palm, then traced the slight indentation at the base of her ring finger where her engagement ring had been. Sand dislodged from under his nails, and she felt it rough against her skin. She wanted him to touch more of her. 'Will you come and live with me?' he asked.

'Oh, Jethro, you big gombeen! You know I can't live in LA. And you know I can't live on an island in the middle of the Mediterranean. We've discussed this to death.'

'I'm not asking you to do either of those things. I'm going to sell that house on Gozo. And I don't want to live in fucking LA any more. I need more in my life.'

'More? More what?'

'More important things. I had a long talk with Eva recently. Some broadsheet had been sniffy about her making a film as commercial as *Mimi's Remedies* — described her as having 'sold out'. I asked her was she upset about it, and she laughed. She said: 'Why should I be upset? I'm making a feel-good movie. What's so *wrong* about making people feel good?' '

'There's no answer to that,' said Dannie.

'No, there isn't!' said Jethro, in the impassioned tones of someone who's fairly well oiled. 'There's nothing fucking wrong with making people feel good! But I will confess that that's not the reason *I* decided to do the film. Why did *I* do it? I did it because the money men made me an offer I couldn't refuse. And what am I going to do with all this loot, Dannie? Buy a yacht? Keep an expensive mistress? Buy a penthouse where I can look down at the little people below and feel like an emperor? Is that what life's about? I looked at Eva that day, and I saw her with David and Dorcas, and I *saw* — I actually *saw* — the aura of love that surrounded them, and I thought: 'That — *that* — is what it's all about.' It's not about power and it's not about money. It's about *love*, and fuck it, Dannie Moore, I love you and Paloma so much!' And then Jethro put his head in his big hands and started to cry.

Dannie put her arms around him and held him, and when his sobs had subsided she said: 'And we love you too. You know that.'

'So what are we going to do about it?'

'Make it manifest,' said Dannie. She stood up and moved to the dunes, and when she got to a place where the sheep had cropped the grass smooth as a carpet, she turned to Jethro and beckoned to him. She lay back on the grass and opened her arms, and then Jethro was there, looking down at her, and she remembered how once in a previous life she had lain on a beach watching his face and feeling a wrench in her gut when she realized how dear and familiar it had become to her, and knowing that he would soon be gone. And she knew now that she could never, ever let him go again.

And then Jethro's weight was on top of her. He started to make love to her without preamble, with a kind of desperate need, and Dannie accommodated him, shucking off her jeans and panties. And as he came inside her with a shudder and a groan, she heard his voice in her ear saying: 'Oh, God, Dannie. Oh, God. Thank you. Thank you for allowing me to come home at last.'

★　★　★

Eva's funeral service was held in Dublin because the only crematorium in the country was there, in Glasnevin, on the north side of the capital. Dannie drove up with Jethro.

Deirdre had specified in the 'Deaths' column in the *Irish Times* that the funeral was to be private, but Dannie had been invited in her capacity as Jethro's soulmate and support, and she was glad to be there because after all the

477

days she'd spent hiding in Eva's suite, she felt that Eva had become a real friend.

But while Deirdre had been able to arrange a private service in the chapel, she couldn't prevent people from turning up at the cemetery. And turn up they did, in droves. There were posers, there were politicians, there were pretenders to the throne in the form of myriad wannabes looking to be discovered. There was press. There were pushy photographers and weeping fans and curious tourists, there was an ex-Taoiseach, there were art-istocrats, there were camera crews, there was a supermodel. *Le tout* Dublin had rolled up for this nonpareil photo opportunity. Glitterati and flowers proliferated. Delivery van after delivery van pulled into Glasnevin cemetery, and Dannie marvelled at the crassness of some of the floral tributes.

Inside the chapel Eva's friend Bono sang 'Grace', and Rory read the Kate Clanchy piece that Eva had asked for. It was profoundly moving, but it was all over very fast, and within ten minutes they were outside the chapel again, amidst mayhem.

Dannie felt deeply uncomfortable when Jethro left her side to go and commiserate with David Lawless. She didn't want to go with him — she'd never met David, and she didn't want to intrude upon his grief. Other people didn't seem to have a problem with that, though. There were rather a lot of histrionics going on, with some luvvie types weeping ostentatiously and comforting each other for the cameras, and chattering knots of people swapping 'Eva' stories, each clearly trying to outdo the other by showing off just how well they'd known her. '*I* remember when she — ' 'She told *me* — ' '*I* sat next to her — ' '*We* had such a blast at that party — ' 'David and Eva came to *our* — '

What a grotesque way to go, thought Dannie, looking round to see a thunder-faced Deirdre surveying the circus with something close to disgust. Dannie elbowed her way through the crowd until she came abreast of her.

'This is fucking *awful*,' said Deirdre. 'Eva would have *hated* this. Look!' A woman all in black, wearing an outrageous hat with a veil, walked past, sobbing into a lace-trimmed handkerchief, her progress monitored by a television camera. 'We've got to get David away from here.'

Dannie looked over to where David was standing beside Jethro on the chapel steps, looking confused as people filed past him, pressing his flesh and reminding him of their connection to Eva. Some of them were genuinely grief-stricken, but it was clear that a percentage were there to see and be seen. Dorcas was standing by her father's side, her face rigid with shock and incomprehension. She was holding the hand of a striking-looking dark-haired man.

'Who is he?' Dannie asked Deirdre. 'He looks familiar, somehow.'

'That's Sebastian, Dorcas's brother.'

'I didn't know Dorcas had a brother.'

'He lives in England. He's an actor. You'd know him from the telly.'

'Oh, *now* I have you.'

'There's an amazing story about how he found out who his real parents were. It was all over the papers when it came out. Did you read about it?'

'Remind me.'

'Well, Sebastian was adopted as a baby and — oh, *shit*! Here comes Finbar de Rossa. I gotta get out of here, Dannie.'

'Hey, Deirdre!' said an ageing guy in an actor-y voice. He was sporting designer shades and cutting-edge threads that were far too young for him. 'Long time no see! We're all heading over to the Ice Bar at the Four Seasons — d'you fancy joining us?'

'No, Finbar, I don't.' Deirdre's voice was tight. 'Come on, Dannie. Let's go.'

As they moved towards the chapel, Dannie heard snatches of conversation. 'Oh, yeah. My part in that series paid for my new Mercedes convertible.'

'Did you know that they're seeing people for the new Jim Sheridan film next week?'

'I thought Calypso O'Kelly would be here. Bummer!'

'That last session was a cattle market. I've told my agent not to put me up for anything she's casting again.'

'Oh, God,' said Deirdre. 'This is Eva's worst nightmare come true.'

They reached the chapel, and Dannie watched as Deirdre put a hand on David's arm and leaned in to whisper something in his ear. Then she turned to Dannie and Jethro, and said: 'Fallon's. The Coombe. D'you know it?'

'I do,' said Dannie. 'I used to live just across

480

the road from there.'

'It was Eva's local when she had the house off the South Circular,' said Deirdre. 'That's where we're going.'

David and Dorcas followed Deirdre across to the car park where Rory was leaning against his hire car, talking to Astrid. 'Come, little princess!' said Astrid to Dorcas when she saw her. 'Sebastian and I are taking you to the zoo!'

And then Dorcas and Astrid and Sebastian were ensconced in the transport Merc, and David was sat in the passenger seat of Rory's hire car with Deirdre in the back, and Jethro had taken Dannie by the hand and was leading her to where she'd parked her car earlier.

And half an hour later, in the privacy of the snug in Fallon's unpretentious little pub just across the road from St Patrick's Cathedral, David Lawless was able to do what most Irish men need to do when they've been bereaved. He wept into his pint for his beloved dead wife, away at last from the eyes of curious observers, away from the lenses of the press photographers, away from the scrutiny of journalists avid for an exclusive: far from the madding crowd.

★　★　★

Dannie and Jethro drove back to their hotel later, ordered wine and food to be sent to their room, and sat out on their roof terrace. The atmosphere was close and humid, and muddy-looking clouds hung in the sky. Below them the

River Liffey wound its turgid way through the heart of Dublin.

There was nothing remotely romantic about the view. It was a dull cityscape of rooftops and chimneys and satellite dishes, an ugly grey vista of concrete edifices and dirty red-brick buildings and the ubiquitous giant skeletons of cranes. Traffic noise rose from the streets below as juggernauts roared their way along the quays, and the shrill unpleasant screams of scavenging seagulls came from overhead. That pointless monument, the Dublin Spire, stuck out from O'Connell Street like a giant, blunt needle.

But for Dannie, anywhere on the face of the planet was romantic now, as long as Jethro was there with her.

'What made you decide to sell the house on Gozo?' she asked him.

'It wasn't a home.'

'What about the place in LA? Are you going to sell that, too?'

'No. I'll use it as a turn-key base. I'm not giving up on LA entirely, but I'm going to cut my workload right back. I'm gonna be a homeboy, Dannie. Gotta make up for all that time spent apart from the wife and kid.'

She smiled. 'Wife?'

'How about it?'

'So this is a proposal of marriage?'

'Yeah. Why not think about it? Paloma could be our bridesmaid. It would give me an excuse to buy her a gorgeous new outfit.'

Dannie felt a flutter of excitement. A wedding! She could design a fabulous bouquet for herself, and wear a fairytale dress and *fantastic* underwear! 'I'd love for us to be married, Jethro,' she said.

'And so would I. It might minimize the chances of you bolting again.'

She hit him a dig. 'Where'll we do it?' she asked.

'Depends on where you want to live.'

She gave him a hopeful look. 'I've thought about France. I couldn't live in a city ever again, Jethro, I honestly couldn't. I mean, look at this!' She indicated the urban sprawl with a sweep of her arm. 'I can't believe I lived not half a mile from here in a former life. Living in Connemara has me spoiled.'

'France it is, then, ma'am.' Jethro went back into the room and emerged with his laptop and cell phone.

'What are you doing?' asked Dannie.

'Finding our home.'

'But theez eez all 'appening so fast!' she said in a bogus French accent. 'You 'ave swept me off my feet, Monsieur!'

'You forget, Dannie, that I am a mover and shaker *par excellence*.'

He logged on, and Dannie moved her chair next to his so that she could look over his shoulder. 'Houses for sale in the South of France,' he typed into Google, then: 'Any particular region?' he asked.

'The Languedoc's meant to be lovely.'

' 'Languedoc region',' typed Jethro, and within seconds a list of properties for sale appeared on the screen.

'No, no, no, no, no,' he said, scrolling down the list until he came to the last — and by far the most expensive — house on offer. '*Maison de maître*,' he read. 'Hey! I like the sound of that. That means I could be he who must be obeyed.'

'OK, lord and *maître*,' said Dannie. 'Click on it.'

He clicked, and this is what they read:

Situated in a picturesque village a short drive from the River Hérault, a magnificent *maison de maître* in classic style and in impeccable condition. Spacious, well-proportioned accommodation on three floors comprises:

Ground floor — two living rooms, dining room, study, cloakroom with WC, fitted kitchen, laundry room, shower room, cellar and enclosed patio.

First floor — four double bedrooms (bath-rooms en suite), separate bathroom.

Second floor — (for conversion). Space for four further rooms. Extensive grounds, pool, summer kitchen and numerous out-buildings.

'Summer kitchen!' exclaimed Dannie, 'Janey! I *love* it!'

'What in hell's name's a summer kitchen?'

'I haven't a feckin' clue, but I know now that I've always hankered after one. Let's look at the pics.'

It was a virtual château. It had balustraded balconies and stuccoed walls. Bougainvillaea trailed along trellises and embraced a sapphire-blue swimming pool. There were palm trees and pots of bright flowers. There were terracotta tiles — the kind you knew would be warm under bare feet.

'Go to 'Interior detail'!' urged Dannie.

Inside, tall windows boasted wooden shutters. There was intricate plasterwork on walls and fireplaces, and there were — to Dannie's delight — original ceiling roses. The long table in the dining room could accommodate ten settings; the kitchen was a work of art in jewel-coloured mosaic.

'You could convert the second floor into an edit suite, Jethro!'

'The thought had occurred to me. Shall we buy it?'

'Just like that?'

'Just like that.'

'But I don't deserve it,' said Dannie in a small voice.

'I do. I've earned it. Are we buying it?'

Dannie gave Jethro a spaniel look, and then she wound her arms round his neck and deposited kisses all over his face. 'Yes, please,' she said. She smiled as she felt his hands move to her waist and slide up under her shirt, and her smile became more provocative as he started to caress the silk over her breasts.

'Let's go test the mattress, Ms Moore,' he said.

'I'll be Ms Palmer,' she said, 'if you have your wicked way and marry me.'

'Ha! Just imagine if you'd married Oliver. You'd be Dannie *Dunne*, Dannie! What a name!'

Jethro started undoing buttons.

'Yes,' she said. 'It's a daft feckin' name. And I had a very lucky escape. Daniella Palmer sounds *posh.*'

'You're not posh. You're — what's the word you use again?'

'I'm a bogger from Connemara.'

'A very *soignée* bogger.' He peeled off her shirt and held it aloft. 'Just look at what you have on under your shirt! Transparent ivory silk.'

'Jethro!' she protested. 'What if anyone's spying on us?'

'I don't care. My baby's gonna marry me and I feel like announcing it from the rooftops.'

Just then came the sound of a loud wolf whistle from the balcony of an adjacent apartment block.

'Give me that!' Dannie snatched the shirt from him and shrugged into it.

'Hey, dude!' called Jethro, getting to his feet and raising his glass at a man who was leaning over a railing, observing them. 'My girl's just agreed to marry me!'

'Congratulations!' came the response. 'She's a classy chick!'

'No, I'm not,' called Dannie. 'I'm a bogger from Connemara. And feckin' proud of it, too!'

She executed an elaborate bow and sent the man a big smile before giving him one final flash of her bra. Then, laughing, she turned away, took Jethro by the hand and led him to bed.

★ ★ ★

486

It was time to tell David Eva's secret.

Deirdre and Rory were sitting in their hotel room the morning after the funeral service, looking at each other helplessly. 'You're going to have to do it on your own, Rory,' said Deirdre. 'I'm sorry, but I'd cry and make things worse.'

'I know, sweetheart. You'd be completely crap. This is one of those awful moments in life when a man's gotta do what a man's gotta do.'

He took a deep breath, then reached for the phone. 'David. How are you?' he said into the receiver. 'Yeah. Yeah. Listen, man. There's something I think you ought to know. Yeah. I'll come up to your room now, if that's OK? See you shortly.'

He put the phone down and turned to Deirdre, who was holding Eva's letter — the letter that had saved their marriage. She'd reread it earlier, and wept. 'Give it to me,' he said, sounding wretched. 'Let's get this over with. Will you have the car waiting? I'd like to hit the road as soon as I've done the needful.'

'Sure. Text me and I'll get the valet to bring it round.'

'Wish me luck.' Rory took the letter from Deirdre, and kissed her before moving to the door.

'Good luck, darling,' she said. 'Be brave.'

While she waited for his text message, she busied herself with packing the overnight things they'd brought with them from Kilrowan. There weren't many — they'd travelled so light that Rory didn't even have a clean shirt to wear today. The two of them planned to head back to

Kilrowan this afternoon, but David had decided against going back to the place where he'd last seen his wife alive. He'd asked a PA to pack up all the stuff Eva had brought with her to Ireland, and have it shipped to him.

The bags were packed and ready to go when Rory's message arrived half an hour later. 'Da deed is dun,' she read. 'C u in da lobby.' Deirdre picked up the phone to the concierge, then took the lift to the lobby to settle their bill while she waited for the car to be sent round.

Rory looked even more wrecked when he emerged from the lift. His threads were well creased, and his golden stubble was too pronounced to be designer. His eyes were hidden behind sunglasses, but there was no disguising the fact that he'd just been through hell.

'I'll drive,' said Deirdre, taking the car keys from him and tipping the valet.

They didn't talk for ages. Rory kept his face turned away from her, concentrating on the cityscape scrolling past beyond the passenger window. The traffic was unspeakable. She negotiated roadworks and road rage and kamikaze motorcycle couriers, and finally, finally they turned onto the N4, heading west.

'How was it?' she asked.

'It was fucking awful, Deirdre. It was nearly as bad as the time we went to Galway after he'd identified her body.' Rory took off his shades and rubbed his eyes with a thumb. 'But I think — I *hope* — it was the right thing to do. I told him that whatever medication she was on meant that her pain was manageable, but that to have kept up the act for another six months might have been too tough on her.'

'That's mentioned in the letter — about the pain management.'

'I know, but it was absolutely crucial that he took it in.'

'Did he?'

'Yeah. He thanked me for being straight with him. And he sent thanks to you. Wished you all the luck in the world with the biography, and said he couldn't imagine a better person to write it.'

Deirdre bit her lip. 'It's a big responsibility now,' she said.

'You can do it, Deirdre,' he said. 'Hey! Just picture it. In a year's time the bookshops will all have displays of your book in the window, and Dorcas will have a trust fund worth thousands. What are you going to do with *your* percentage, by the way?'

'It's going to cancer research.'

Rory gave her an approving look. 'That's my girl,' he said.

⋆   ⋆   ⋆

Several hours later they were sitting at a table by the window in O'Toole's pub in Kilrowan, eating crab claws and drinking Guinness — which had the effect on Deirdre of making her a little maudlin. Bruno was slumbering on an adjacent banquette, watched over by Aoife who was reading Grace a story.

'Eva did so *much* for everybody,' Deirdre was

saying. 'She went out in a blaze of glory, really. I mean — just think of the legacy she left. She got *us* back together again, she taught Cleo not to feel guilty about winning the lottery, and I'm pretty certain that she was responsible for getting Jethro and Dannie back together, too. She's raised a shitload of money for Cancer Research by proxy. And she's made sure that Dorcas will be well cared for for the rest of her life.'

'At least she died knowing that the world was a better place for her having been in it.'

'Just like Mimi. What a swan song!' She took a swig of Guinness, then set her glass down and turned, distressed, to Rory. 'Oh, God. I've just thought of something I don't think I can bear.'

'What?'

'Remember that day in Ballynahinch when we compared each other to birds, and you compared David to some kind of falcon?'

'A gerfalcon?'

'Yes. But he's not now, is he? He's a swan.'

'Why?'

'Because swans only have one mate for life. I know Eva said that she'd love for him to marry again, but can you really imagine David with anyone else? It's unthinkable.'

Rory put his hand over hers. 'Then don't think about it, Deirdre. Let's stop beating ourselves up. It's not what Eva would have wanted. Remember the last thing she said to us that night in her suite, when she chased us away because David was due?'

'Yes.'

'What did she say?'

'She said: 'Don't worry. Be happy.''

'So *that's* her swan song. 'Don't worry. Be happy.' Life goes on, and we can't live it in a vale of tears. Say it again, Deirdre.'

'Don't worry,' repeated Deirdre. 'Be happy.'

And Deirdre and Rory smiled at each other just as the door opened and Colleen swirled into the pub, followed by Margot. They looked as if they hadn't a worry in the world. In fact, they looked positively, unhiply *happy*!

'Deirdre,' purred Colleen, adopting an expression of sympathy. 'And Rory. You are welcome back to Kilrowan after your sore trial. May I buy you a drink?'

'Um . . . '

But they had no choice in the matter. Colleen raised an arm to indicate to the barman to bring drinks, then descended upon them.

'I know it has been a sad time for you,' she said, 'but life goes on. Ah! Life goes on.' She bestowed an enigmatic smile upon her lov*air*. 'We — Margot and I — shall be repairing to our island soon, to work on our respective novels.'

Deirdre smiled inwardly as she pictured Colleen and Margot rowing off to their remote island, like the Owl and the Pussycat. Rory must have thought something similar, because she saw a muscle in his jaw move — that muscle you use when you're trying not to smile. *Don't worry! Be happy!*

'What's your new novel about, Colleen?' asked Rory, adopting the kind of grave expression one felt necessary to adopt when talking to Colleen about her *magna opera*.

491

'It is about a woman whose quest for love takes her from the strong arms of a Spanish artist to the compliant embrace of a woman with the spirit of a poet,' announced Colleen, in tones loud enough to be overheard by every punter in the pub. 'The artist dies of grief,' added Colleen happily.

Just then a spanking-new camper van pulled up outside the pub. An extremely handsome Spanish-looking artist was in the driver's seat talking on his mobile phone, and Cleo was waving from the passenger seat.

'There's Cleo,' said Margot. 'Honestly! Can you credit the irresponsibility! She's off round the world with — ' here she shot a glance at Colleen's closed expression ' — with that awful dog, and she's simply left her house boarded up. I shall have to organize a contractor to fix it up for her — and I've enough on my plate as it is.'

Cleo was beckoning to Deirdre now, looking animated. 'Oh, excuse me,' Deirdre said, getting to her feet. 'I'd better go and see what she wants.' Rory sent her a black look as she escaped out through the door.

'Hi, darling. What's up?' said Deirdre through Cleo's rolled-down window.

'I just wanted to say goodbye,' said Cleo, 'and get your e-mail address. We're off to see the Wizard! The wonderful Wizard of Oz!'

'Australia in a camper van?'

'Well, we might not get that far. We're driving all round the Irish coast first, and then we hit the Continent once Fluffy's got her passport. Imagine! Fluffy with her very own passport! I won't come in to the pub,' she added, glancing at the window where the resplendent silhouette of Colleen sat centre stage. 'Colleen's still a bit frosty round me, and I've already said goodbye to Margot. Did you know that — ' Cleo broke off and clamped a hand over her mouth. 'Oh, God, I'm so sorry. Here I am rabbiting on about myself when you must be in the absolute bloody pits. How did the funeral go, Deirdre?'

'Fine.' She didn't want to talk about the event that had probably been one of the better-attended in the Dublin social calendar in recent years.

'What's happening . . . to the ashes?'

'David's keeping them until he feels ready to scatter them. He's going to let her out on Lissnakeelagh.'

'Oh, what a lovely idea! Remember the day . . . '

'Yeah,' said Deirdre. 'I remember.'

'She gave me a photograph not long ago, of you and me running along the strand.' Cleo pushed back her hair and managed a smile. 'I'll make a copy and send it to you.'

'Thanks. I'd love that.' Deirdre noticed the tears that were starting to pool in Cleo's eyes. *Life goes on* . . . she thought. 'Here. Give me a pen and something to write our e-mail contacts on.'

Cleo obliged, handing Deirdre a marabou-feather trimmed pen.

'So. What happens to you when you come back from your travels?' Deirdre asked, scribbling down details. 'Will you move back into your Blackthorn? Or will your flat in Dublin be ready by then?'

Cleo made a face. 'Phooey. I don't think that flat in Dublin will ever be ready. Margot was right when she warned me against buying it off the plans. I'll be drawing my pension and walking with the aid of a Zimmer frame before it's finished.'

'You hardly *need* a pension, Cleo,' Deirdre pointed out.

A big smile. 'That's true!'

'How long are you going for?'

'For as long as we like! Aren't we, Pablo?'

Don't worry! Be happy!

Pablo had slung his phone into the glove compartment. 'Too right,' he said. 'Hi, girls!' This to Aoife and Grace who had come out to admire Fluffy. Fluff was sitting on the rear shelf of the camper van, holding court and smiling and nodding like a toy dog. Pablo looked at his watch. 'We'd better hit the road, sweetheart,' he said to Cleo, releasing the handbrake and sliding the van into gear. 'We've a long drive to Castle Leslie.'

'Castle Leslie! You lucky things — I've always wanted to stay in that hotel! Off you go,' said Deirdre, standing on tiptoe to kiss Cleo on the cheek. 'Good luck, and have a blast! I hope we meet again some day.'

'So do I,' said Cleo. 'It's been fun. Bye!'

And as the camper van rolled down the main street, Aoife and Grace and Deirdre were left standing on the footpath, waving good-bye to a beaming, beribboned Fluffy as she headed off in

494

style to live *her* dream.

Deirdre watched as the van rounded the corner. There was something very final about it all. The movie was finished; the friendships she'd made here were finished. A good time was finished; a bad time was finished. But then she remembered something Eva had once said to her about there being no endings, only beginnings. It was time to start over. It was time to tell Eva's story.

Deirdre turned and walked back into the pub, where Rory was draining his pint. 'Come on,' she said, picking a dozy Bruno up from his comatose position on the banquette. 'I know it's a bore, but it's time for us to pack up as well.'

★ ★ ★

A day and a bit later, Deirdre and Rory had shut Mimi's rainbow-hued polka-dotted door behind them for the last time and were on the plane back to LA. Deirdre was drafting an e-mail to her agent instructing him that he was to get the best deal possible for Eva's biography or he was out of a job. *Plus* she wanted it on the shelves the same week as the movie of *Mimi's Remedies* premièred. Deirdre O'Dare was going to help *Mimi* open in a blaze of glory. She was going to coin it good for Dorcas. She was going to bolster the coffers of cancer research. And she was going to pay it forward bigtime for her friend Eva Lavery.

21

Dannie was watching Jethro on Euronews as he walked up the red carpet at the première of *Mimi's Remedies* in Dublin. There, too, were Deirdre O'Dare and Rory McDonagh. And Colin Farrell and Ben Tarrant and the Taoiseach and loads and loads of other luminaries. There was no sign of David Lawless. Jethro had told her that he'd attended a preview, but that he didn't feel up to the kind of public scrutiny a première would expose him to.

Dannie didn't blame him. Jethro had asked her if she'd wanted to accompany him to the stellar event, but she was perfectly happy here in her house in France. No glitz or glamour could beat the warm, comfortable sensation of being in her own home at last. And she certainly didn't want any stress or hustle-bustle in her life. She was pregnant — only three months, but she knew the first three months were critical. She didn't want *anything* going wrong.

The première coverage had finished, and a politician appeared on the screen. Dannie zapped off the television and went upstairs to her bedroom for her afternoon siesta. She was knackered. The first three months had been the most knackering with Paloma, too.

On her bedside table was the new biography of Eva Lavery that Deirdre O'Dare had sent her, but Dannie was too tired to read this afternoon.

She lay down on the bed, feeling sublimely content despite her tiredness, and cast her mind back to the day she'd first seen her new home — her *maison de maître* — in the flesh. It had taken a fair few months for Jethro to untangle the red, white and blue tickertape that was French bureaucracy, but one day Dannie had finally received a significant phone call from him.

'Guess where I am!' he'd said.

'Oh — at some shit-hot Hollywood power breakfast, knowing the same Mister Palmer.'

'Wrong. I'm where the heart is.'

'What?'

'Where the heart is. In other words — honey, I'm home!'

'In the *maison de maître*? Our brand-new gaff? Are you really?'

'Sure am, ma'am. The *tapis rouge* has all been unravelled. Get your ass on the next flight to Montpellier, baby, and bring my other baby with you.'

'Oh, God!' Dannie had been breathless with excitement. 'I'm coming! I'm coming right now!'

'Those words are music to my ears,' he said.

When Dannie put the phone down, she ran to where Paloma was pulling the heads off daisies in the garden. 'Come on, acushla — let's pack our bags! We're going to the airport!'

'To go flying on a plane?'

'Yes!'

'Where to?'

'To our new house in France, sweetheart. We're going home at last.'

'Really home, Mammy?'

And Dannie had smiled at her daughter through her tears. '*Really* home, Paloma Palmer,' she'd said.

★ ★ ★

From Montpellier they'd taken a taxi to the village and their *maison de maître*. Dannie called Jethro to say they'd arrived, and to get directions.

'Where are you now?' he asked.

'We're just passing the *boulangerie*. And the *tabac*. And there's a *caveaux* sign! Yay! Local Languedoc wine practically on tap! Oh and look — there's a dotey wee café!'

'OK, *chérie*! I get where you're coming from. Now, take the next turn *à gauche*, then *à droite*, then *encore à gauche*.'

Dannie laughed at his woeful French. His Southern drawl mangled the accent. The taxi negotiated the turns in the narrow streets, and there, suddenly, was Jethro, standing in front of a pair of high wrought-iron gates. Paloma tumbled out of the taxi, shouting 'Daddy!'

'No,' he said with a laugh. 'You must call me 'Papa' now.'

Dannie paid off the driver, then stood in front of her new home, regarding it with an expression that verged on the worshipful.

'Let me give you the guided tour. How does it feel to be here in real life rather than virtuality?'

'It still feels like virtuality,' she said. 'I feel as if I'm in a dream.'

'Come on.' He took her by the hand, and

Paloma by the other, and led them up the drive and through the door of the house into the front hall. From there he led them through a succession of empty rooms, the sound of their footsteps ringing out against the stone flags of the floors. Finally, they mounted the cantilevered staircase that led to the first floor. '*Le premier étage!*' Dannie told Paloma. 'Let's start you on your French lessons, *petit chou!*'

'*Non, merci!*' said Paloma. It was the only French phrase she'd picked up.

'This,' said Jethro, throwing open the first door they came to, 'is going to be the *maître* bedroom, Daniella Palmer.'

Dannie walked into the bare room and smiled. Sunlight was cascading in through three windows that stretched from floor to white-washed ceiling. She moved straight to the middle window and looked down at the swimming pool, and at the bright bougainvillaea and the warm terracotta tiles on the *terrasse*, and as she did so, she remembered how she'd lain on a beach once, years ago, before she'd even known she was pregnant with Paloma. It had been a blue-sky day — what her grandmother would have called a 'pet' day — and she and Jethro and a friend's child called Lottie had taken a picnic to Brittas Bay in Wicklow and gone swimming. Dozing on the beach afterwards she had pictured herself in some faraway time and place, lying in the sun after a swim and a picnic with Jethro and their own little girl, listening to father and daughter chatting like equals. She'd thought even then that he would make a fantastic father — that he'd spoil their girl rotten. Where would they be? she had wondered. And she'd visualized herself from a great height, stretched out against terracotta earth, while beside her Jethro and . . . and . . . *Paloma!* — she'd always loved the name Paloma — played Cat's Cradle or Paper, Stone, Scissors and laughed: the child's high reedy tones in *contrapunto* to Jethro's drawly Southern growl . . .

And she thought as she looked down at the garden of her new home that that dream had been made real.

Dannie turned to Jethro to tell him what she'd just been thinking, but the words never made it out of her mouth. She'd thought the room was empty when she walked in. It wasn't. There was a single painting on the wall opposite the window, and the sight of it struck her stone dumb. It was the painting that Jethro had bought from her brothers. It was the Daniel Lennox portrait of her mother.

'It's your wedding present,' said Jethro.

* * *

On that very first day in their new home, Dannie had thought it would be wildly romantic to have a picnic of crusty French bread and runny Brie on the *terrasse*, but practicalities had put paid to that. There was nothing in the house to eat off — no plates, no knives, no forks. No glasses for the wine she'd love to buy at the local *caveaux*, no cup for Paloma's juice. There were, of course, no beds to sleep on either — Jethro had booked

500

them all into a hotel in Montpellier for the night. But Paloma had wanted to explore the village, and it was decided that they'd mosey down to the café that Dannie and Paloma had passed earlier in the taxi.

They sat outside at an enamel table, and ordered a *pichet* of local red wine, and omelettes. Paloma had *frites* and Coke. Six o'clock chimed from a little church nearby.

Dannie felt a bit self-conscious. There were locals on a square opposite playing *boules*, and she wondered if they realized that these were the new owners of the *maison de maître*. She had always looked slightly askance at the wealthy foreigners who bought second homes in Kilrowan: now *she* knew what it was like to be looked at askance!

Families started to converge on the café for their evening meals or pre-prandial *pastis*. A small girl of around Paloma's age had just arrived on the *terrasse* of the café with her mother and was loitering nearby, clearly keen to strike up a conversation with the *petite étrangère*. Her mother sat down at an adjacent table, and summoned the waiter. 'Maurice! *Deux pastis, s'il vous plaît. Et un Orangina pour Rosa.*' She turned to Dannie and smiled. '*Bonsoir,*' she said pleasantly.

'*Bonsoir, Madame,*' replied Dannie, wondering how far her schoolgirl French would take her.

'*Vous êtes touristes?*'

'*Non. Nous sommes ici parce que nous avons —* '

'Oh! You're English!'

There could be no clearer indication of how crap her French accent was. She'd been rumbled instantly! 'Well, no, actually,' said Dannie, 'Jethro's from the States and I'm — '

'You're Irish!' said the woman. 'From somewhere near Galway, judging by your accent.'

'Oh! How did you guess?'

'I'm from Dublin myself.' The woman leaned towards Dannie and stretched out her hand. 'My name's Madeleine. Madeleine Lennox. Welcome to Saint-Geyroux.'

'Nice to meet you, Madeleine,' said Dannie, taking the proffered hand. 'I'm Dannie Moore, and this is Jethro Palmer — '

'Jethro *Palmer*? The film director Jethro Palmer?'

'The very same.' Jethro rose to his feet, took the hand of the woman called Madeleine, and raised it to his lips. 'Delighted to meet you, ma'am.'

Smooth bastard! thought Dannie. Those Southern gent manners of his never failed to impress.

'Delighted, likewise,' said Madeleine. 'And is this your daughter?'

'Yes,' said Dannie. 'This is Paloma.'

'Beautiful name,' observed Madeleine Lennox, then: 'This — ' she indicated her own child, who had retreated to the sanctuary of her mother's arms and was squirming in her lap ' — is Rosa.'

'*Salut*, Rosa!' said Dannie, and Rosa buried her face in the folds of her mother's skirt.

'What brings you here to Saint-Geyroux?' asked Madeleine. 'It's not the buzziest *ville* in the world.'

'Peace and quiet is what we're after. We've just bought the *maison de maître*,' explained Dannie.

'No! Then we're practically neighbours. We're in number 1, rue des Artistes. It's just round the corner from you.'

Neighbours! The name had such a welcoming ring to it. What was it in French? *Voisins. Nos nouveaux voisins!* How funny! How *lovely!*

'Have you been living in Saint-Geyroux long?' asked Dannie.

'I've been here for about five years. Daniel's been here for yonks.'

'Daniel?'

'My husband.'

'Hold your horses!' interjected Jethro. '*Daniel?* You're married to Daniel Lennox? The painter?'

'That's right. You know his work?'

And Dannie and Jethro had looked at each other in astonishment before they started to laugh.

'What's the joke?' asked Madeleine.

'Well,' said Jethro. 'We don't have a stick of furniture in our new home yet, but we do have a painting — and it just happens to be a Daniel Lennox!'

'*No!*' said Madeleine, looking gobsmacked. 'Serendipity! Tell me all about it!'

And as Dannie and Jethro filled Madeleine Lennox in on the story behind the portrait that was hanging on the wall of their new bedroom, Rosa unsquirmed herself from her mother's

503

arms and tentatively approached Paloma.

'Do you like Orangina?' she said.

'I don't know what it is.'

'It's a drink.'

'Is it like Coke?'

'No. It's orange. I'm Rosa Lennox,' said Rosa. 'What's your name?'

'I'm Paloma Palmer. And that's my ma and my pa.'

'Well, that's *my* mama,' said Rosa. 'And here comes my papa. And my dog.'

'What's its name?'

'Pilot Lennox. Don't be scared of him. He's like my papa, so Mama always says.'

'How is he like your papa?'

'His bark is worse than his bite.'

Then Rosa had taken Paloma by the hand and led her over to the big purple-grey dog, and Daniel Lennox had sat down at the table opposite his wife and allowed her to fill him in on the great story she'd just heard. A couple more *pichets* of wine and a *pastis* or four later, the adults continued to sit as dusk fell on the village, listening to each other's life stories and laughing. And the two little girls just worked away, trying hard to teach an old dog new tricks.

* * *

Dannie breathed in deep — savouring the scent of lavender in the air — happy in the knowledge that the beautiful, loving portrait of her mother watched over her. From a couple of gardens away she could hear the sound of children laughing, and she knew that Paloma and Rosa were at play in Daniel Lennox's long back garden, probably teasing poor Pilot the dog.

She hadn't told Jethro about her pregnancy yet, but she had told her new friend, Madeleine, who had said that once the bloom came upon her and she started to show, Daniel would want to paint her. She thought about the young journeyman painter who'd painted her mother all those years before when Daniella had been pregnant with her, Dannie, and she thought: *If only you knew, Mammy!*

And when Dannie opened her eyes after her siesta, something told her that her mother *did* know what had become of her only daughter, because the message was there on her serene, painted face. *Carpe diem, Daniella mia. Live your dream . . .*

★ ★ ★

Cleo and Pablo were sitting in a cinema in Siena, watching *Mimi's Remedies* on the screen of a multiplex. It had been a shock to see Eva up there, radiant and beautiful and larger than life, and Cleo had blinked back tears. But the movie was so feel-good and so upbeat and so incredibly *vibrant* that by the end Cleo had banished all mournful thoughts from her head — which was, she suspected, exactly the effect Eva would have wanted her swan song to have on people.

The only time she hated the film was when *she* made an appearance as a Minx. She looked like a half-wit. She was completely mortified, and even more mortified when she realized that all her old friends who were no longer friends in Dublin would see her up on the screen making an eejit of herself. Well, fuck them, she thought. Fuck those begrudgers! Here she was in a cinema in Siena sitting beside a *ride* of a painter, and their camper van was in the car park with a good bottle of wine in the fridge just asking to be drunk, and her faithful hound was waiting to be walked, and her destination was . . . wherever she wanted it to be! *And* the *Erotic Review* had expressed an interest in publishing her favourite Ricardo story. She was steeped!

As the credits rolled, Pablo turned to her and said: 'Wow! Your tits looked great all pushed up like that in that bodice yoke. Maybe we should try and buy you one of those minxy outfits somewhere, Cleo. And as for hearing you dubbed into Italian . . . '

She gave him an 'as if' look. 'I only said 'rhubarb'!' she said.

'Yeah, but you sounded so *hot*. I'm going to buy that film as soon as it comes out on DVD and replay that scene again and again and again.'

'Sad git. Get a life.'

They left the cinema hand in hand, and Pablo turned to Cleo and said: 'Where are we off to now?'

'Somewhere dreamy,' said Cleo. 'Florence? Venice? Capri? You decide. I had an idea, incidentally, for a new story.'

'Yeah?'

'Mm. Ricardo is sunbathing naked in a private cove somewhere on Capri. He's feeling mighty horny. And then a girl wearing a minxy outfit strolls past speaking in an Italian accent and — '

'Capri it is,' said Pablo.

★　★　★

Deirdre and Rory were in Dublin for the première of *Mimi's Remedies* when the phone call from David Lawless came through.

'Will you come west with me, Deirdre?' he asked. 'And help me and Dorcas scatter Eva's ashes? I feel badly that I've kept her to myself for so long. But I *couldn't* let go until I saw the film. It was only then I realized that it was an act of pure selfishness to have held her captive for so long.' His voice on the phone sounded embarrassed. 'Oh, God. Does that sound deranged? As if I've treated her like some kind of a genie?'

'No, David, it doesn't sound deranged at all,' Deirdre said categorically. 'She *was* a kind of a genie. She granted people's wishes. But you're right. That free spirit of hers has to be *set* free at last. Will Sebastian make it over?'

'No. He's working with the RSC. But he's given us the go-ahead to perform the ceremony without him. And he made a fantastic suggestion for her valediction.'

'Oh? Tell.'

'Dorcas is going to give us Prospero's speech. From *The Tempest*. She spent all last week learning it.'

' 'Our revels now are ended'?'

'That's the one.'

'How perfect.'

'A perfect ending,' said David, 'to a perfect life.'

So the day after the première, Rory and Deirdre drove to Kilrowan to meet up with David and Dorcas on Lissnakeelagh strand on the coast of Connemara.

It felt strange to drive down the street of the village that they had last seen on screen in *Mimi's Remedies*. The corner shop above which she'd had her flat a year ago was an expensive-looking boutique now, and the polka dots on the door had been painted over in a tasteful shade of eau-de-Nil.

The film last night had opened on a shot of Eva as Mimi, painting on the polka dots. She'd had smudges of paint on her face and streaks of it in her hair, and she'd made some arch remark to Colin Farrell when he'd teased her about it; then laughed, relented and kissed him. The final shot of the film had featured Mimi standing on the road looking back at the village (above which a CGI rainbow had been superimposed), then turning and walking away with a rucksack full of her remedies on her back. And when the words 'In Loving Memory of Eva Lavery' appeared on the screen, the audience had, as one, risen to their feet and applauded so long and so hard that Deirdre suspected it would feature in the next *Guinness Book of Records* as the lengthiest standing ovation ever.

Tears flowed along with the champagne at the post-première party in Dublin Castle, and Rory and Deirdre had been papped to pieces with

— unusually — Deirdre taking the lion's share of the attention. Her biography of Eva had shot straight to number one in the non-fiction bestseller list. Colleen's *To the Island* was number one in fiction hardbacks, Lily Wright was at number two in the mass-market list with the film tie-in of *Mimi's Remedies*, and Pixie Pirelli was at number one with her new bestseller, *An Angel in Manolos*.

There were all those titles, now, prominently displayed in the window of the village bookshop, where the cardboard cut-out of Colleen had been dusted down. It stood magisterially in the place it had stood just over a year ago, against a background of posters advertising — Deirdre was glad to see — Eva's biography. The publishers had gone with the photograph that Deirdre had taken of Eva on the bridge at Ballynahinch for the jacket, and Deirdre felt a flash of pride every time she saw it. It had been all over the airport in Dublin.

Apart from the display of brand-new bestsellers, there was something else different about the shop. A FOR SALE sign had been put up above the door. 'Oh!' said Deirdre. 'I do hope Cleo buys it!'

'Why?' asked Rory.

'She told me it was her dream to own her own bookshop.'

'Would it do business? The village hibernates for half the year, doesn't it?'

'That hardly matters to Cleo, since she's a millionaire. Anyway, she'd probably love it if it didn't do business. That would mean she could sit around all day long and read books to her heart's content.'

On the opposite side of the road to the bookshop, Breda Shanley was standing outside her store talking to the barman from O'Toole's. Deirdre waved at them from the passenger window of their hire car, but they both looked blank, and Deirdre realized that they hadn't recognized her.

A very posh Saab was parked outside Pablo's old Blackthorn, and Deirdre wondered about who might be living there now. Number 5 was looking smart again — the builders had clearly been and gone. But there was no camper van outside, and no sign of Fluffy, and the blinds were drawn. Deirdre supposed that Cleo and Pablo were still off on their travels. She'd e-mail her — let her know that the bookshop in Kilrowan was up for grabs and that maybe it was time for her to come home . . .

On the coast road they passed another FOR SALE sign. It was up outside the old Glebe House, where Dannie had lived for such a short time when she'd been engaged to Oliver Dunne. Business mustn't have taken off for Dannie's ex if the joint had closed after just a year, Deirdre thought. Jethro had told her last night that Dannie was supremely happy living in their *maison de maître* in the South of France, and that he, too, was enjoying his new laid-back lifestyle, and had even taken up that most laid-back of hobbies — *boules*.

'Life is weird, Rory, isn't it?' she said suddenly. He turned to her with that smile that contrived to make her go all mushy inside — even after all these years of marriage — and she sent a little song of praise to Eva, who had worked such wonders for them. 'Life,' he said, 'is *spooky*.'

They swung into the car park that abutted Lissnakeelagh. Below them the beach gleamed rose gold in the evening sunlight. It was deserted apart from two figures. One of them was familiar. David Lawless cut as elegant a dash as ever. But Dorcas had grown taller, and as Deirdre drew nearer she saw that the child was looking more like her mother than ever. Barefoot, golden, smiling.

They all greeted each other with hugs and kisses, and then David said: 'Let's get her show on the road.' By 'her', Deirdre knew he meant Eva. He reached into a box that he'd set at his feet, and took out the urn. Then he broke the seal, bowed his head, and took a deep breath before holding it out to Dorcas. 'Are you sure you've got your speech off by heart, baby? I'll prompt you if you need me to.'

'No, Daddy. You won't need to. I know it. Mummy's been helping me.'

'Of course she has,' he said with a smile. 'And remember what I told you? This is a happy occasion, sweetpea.'

Dorcas nodded and smiled back at her father, then she raised her chin and cleared her throat.

'Our revels now are ended. These our actors,
As I foretold you, were all spirits and

511

Are melted into air, into thin air:
And, like the baseless fabric of this vision,
The cloud-capp'd towers, the gorgeous
   palaces,
The solemn temples, the great globe itself,
Yea, all which it inherit, shall dissolve
And, like this insubstantial pageant faded,
Leave not a rack behind. We are such stuff
As dreams are made on, and our little life
Is rounded with a sleep.'

And then Dorcas stepped into the sea. She took a handful of ashes from the container and threw them with all her might into the waves that foamed in little crests around her thighs. 'Go, Mummy!' she cried.

'You, now, Rory,' said David, and Rory laughed out loud as a gust of wind took the ashes from him and sent them scattering towards where the sun glimmered on the aquamarine horizon.

'Deirdre.' David proffered her the urn.

She took it — surprised at its weight — and said a silent prayer, hoping it would reach the ears of whichever deity had watched over Eva during her life. Eva's ashes were grainy between her fingers. Funny — she'd always expected ashes to be soft and powdery. She took a handful and flung them out to sea as far as she could, and as she did so, a flock of small birds swooshed past, white underbellies gleaming in the low-slung sun. They performed a kind of synchronized aerial ballet against the darkening blue of the sky, moving as one in a complex series of twists and turns before scudding away across the water, and when Deirdre looked down at her hand she saw that a tiny white feather had landed on her palm. A sign! Eva had said that she'd send a sign if they got things right!

And then Eva's voice sounded in her ears as clear as on the day they'd gone walking by the river at Ballynahinch. *I know it's a terrible cliché, but this really is one of those days that makes you feel glad to be alive, isn't it . . .*

Deirdre handed the urn to David, with a big smile. He was just about to delve his hand into the vessel, when something made him stop. 'Look,' he said. 'Over there to the east.' A star had appeared in the sky above Kilrowan. 'It's the evening star.'

'The evening star?' said Rory. 'Isn't Venus the evening star?'

'Damn right,' said David, and for a brief, awful moment Deirdre thought he was going to cry. Then: 'Godspeed, Eva!' he called, raising his hand high above his head.

And there on Lissnakeelagh strand the four of them watched as the wind snatched the last of Eva Lavery's ashes from her devoted husband's hand and sent them hurtling towards deep blue heaven.

We do hope that you have enjoyed reading
this large print book.

Did you know that all of our titles
are available for purchase?

We publish a wide range of high quality
large print books including:
Romances, Mysteries, Classics
General Fiction
Non Fiction and Westerns

Special interest titles available in
large print are:
The Little Oxford Dictionary
Music Book
Song Book
Hymn Book
Service Book

Also available from us courtesy of Oxford
University Press:
Young Readers' Dictionary
(large print edition)
Young Readers' Thesaurus
(large print edition)

For further information or a free
brochure, please contact us at:
Ulverscroft Large Print Books Ltd.,
The Green, Bradgate Road, Anstey,
Leicester, LE7 7FU, England.
Tel: (00 44) 0116 236 4325
Fax: (00 44) 0116 234 0205

Other titles published by
The House of Ulverscroft:

AFTER MIDNIGHT

Robert Ryan

In 1944, a Liberator bomber pilot writes a letter to his daughter on the occasion of her first birthday. He posts it moments before embarking on a mission in Northern Italy. Tragically, he never returns. In 1964, Linda Carr resolves to find out what happened to her father on that terrible night. It is a mystery that has haunted her all her life. She employs the help of motorcycle TT racer Jack Kirby, a man who has his own inner demons to combat. He was a Mosquito fighter pilot during the War and experienced at first hand the astonishing courage of the Italian partisans. Jack is keen to find one of the partisans, a woman he fell passionately in love with all those years ago . . .

LOVE AND DEVOTION

Erica James

At the age of thirty-two, Harriet Swift thinks she has the perfect life — a satisfying career, her own flat and a new boyfriend. But when her only sister is killed in a car crash, Harriet is forced to move back to her childhood home, Maple Drive, to help her parents look after her orphaned niece and nephew. Meanwhile, the shabbiest house in Maple Drive has a new occupant. In his mid-forties, Will Hart also thinks he has the perfect life. Having swapped his successful career as a lawyer for that of an antiques dealer, Will believes in living for the moment. Then, from nowhere, tragedy strikes. Both Harriet and Will have no choice but to piece together a new future for themselves, but can they see it through?